Jonny Nexus is a Brighton based IT gu
his spare time. When not doing that,
daughter, and dog; reads; watches TV, films, and the occasional
theatre; and plays the occasional board game.

Jonny began his writing career by launching the cult gaming webzine
Critical Miss (criticalmiss.com), before moving on to write regular
columns for the roleplaying magazines *Valkyrie* and *Signs & Portents*, as
well as penning the *Slayer's Guide to Games Masters* for Mongoose
Publishing.

If Pigs Could Fly is his second novel. His first novel, *Game Night*, was
shortlisted for an ENnie award in 2008.

If Pigs Could Fly

WKPDA Book 1

By Jonny Nexus

First published in the United States and the United Kingdom in 2015 by Wild Jester Press.

ISBN 978-1512059083

10 9 8 7 6 5 4 3 2 1

Web: www.jonnynexus.com
Email: jonny@jonnynexus.com
Twitter: @jonnynexus

Wild Jester Press
Brighton
East Sussex
United Kingdom

www.wildjesterpress.com

Cover design and art by Jon Hodgson.

www.jonhodgson.net

Thanks to Jules, for the love, encouragement and support that she gave me throughout the writing of this book;

to Chris and Kris (Vicky), for the support and encouragement;

to Warren and Bairbre, for the advice;

to Amanda and Ro for their help shepherding this book into the world;

to Costa at Farringdon, and Caffè Nero at London Bridge, for the rocket fuel;

and finally to First Capital Connect and Southern Railways, for providing me with my office. My seat was always comfortable and the views were frequently superb.

Chapter One

The mist clung to the moorland like a blanket staple-gunned to a bed. Ravinder Shah shuddered. By day, the landscape they were driving through was no doubt foreboding, but with nightfall fast approaching it was becoming positively grim.

"Well, Prof," he said to the man who sat beside him. "I guess this is Yorkshire."

His older companion was clad in a tweed suit of the sort you'd wear if you were about to head out for a day's shooting and the year was 1927. He peered through the car's windscreen. "It is a tad rugged, isn't it? You half expect to see a wild young Heathcliffe running across the moors screaming for his lost love Cathy."

"What's Kate Bush got to do with any of this?"

The older man gave him a pained look. "Very droll, Ravinder. I am, of course, referring to Emily Brontë's classic work of literature Wuthering Heights, as well you know."

Rav nodded. "I read it at school. If he was anyplace like this, you can see why the poor bastard went off his nuts."

Ahead of them, the state of the road, already bad, worsened, its surface now so appalling that it really needed to confess to being a mere track, and a not particularly good one at that. Rav changed down to second and aimed the car – a Honda Civic he'd borrowed from his cousin Mindy – along the route's right-hand side, on the grounds that the potholes scattered across that portion appeared slightly less vicious.

Thus far, he'd avoided discussing the reason for their excursion with the Professor. One of the many problems the older man suffered from was a tendency to become quite confused and anxious over events that merited, at most, mild concern and a measured amount of grumbling. In this current instance, as with many such things, timing would likely be vital. Rav waited while the car clambered across a particularly unacceptable stretch of rubble-strewn mud, before attempting to broach the subject.

"There's something I should probably mention, Prof."

"And what exactly would that be?"

"We didn't come out here just for a drive."

"I see. I confess I have been somewhat curious as to why you've driven me more than two hundred miles up the M1, beyond your stated reason of taking me for a drive."

"I've got a job."

"I know you've got a job, Ravinder. You're my social worker."

"I mean an investigation job."

The Professor smiled. "Oh, that sort of job. Like the one we had in Epping Forest? The middle-aged woman who'd heard the howls and screams of demonic beasts whilst walking her dog late at night?"

"Yes, well-"

"Noises which turned out to come from what might, in my day, have been described as courting couples? Although I'm not sure they were necessarily courting, nor am I sure that they were all arranged in pairs."

"Well, yeah, that one turned out to be a bit of a bust."

"Or the other assignment? The elderly lady whose home was haunted by a poltergeist?"

"Look-"

"An elderly lady who found that things were habitually not where she remembered leaving them?"

Rav interrupted him with a waved hand. "Yeah, yeah, I know. So far it's all been a waste of time. But not this one, this one's different."

"Will we be staying out for the night?"

"Probably."

The Professor shook his head. "You know I'm not supposed to leave the hospital for overnight stays."

"You're fine. I signed you out. It's all legal and above board."

"Really?" The Professor sighed, then waved a languid hand. "Well, I suppose it might prove an interesting diversion. So what exactly is this job?"

"I got a phone call this morning from a farmer who runs a small-holding somewhere-" Rav pointed at the mist, "-out there."

"And his problem is?"

Rav paused, wanting to savour the moment, wanting to enjoy the feeling of excitement simmering within him. It was six months since he'd set up the West Kensington Paranormal Detective Agency. He'd been in search of a life less ordinary than the one fate, destiny and personal laziness had granted him. He'd hoped that the truth was indeed out there. But if it was, a half year of searching had singularly failed to find it. When he'd woken up that morning he'd been just about ready to give it up, jack it in, and walk away, accepting the mediocre existence that was apparently all he was worth.

And then his mobile had rung with a Yorkshire farmer on the other end who'd told him a story so incredible it might actually be true. This could be it. This might be the one. Rav knew he was grinning a big cheesy grin but he didn't care. He took a deep breath, and then delivered to the Professor the stunning line that Jonathan Partridge had, that very morning, delivered to him.

"He's being stalked by flying pigs."

Partridge's smallholding turned out to be located on a small shelf of mostly flat land jutting out from the side of a rock-strewn hill, with a stone cottage set upon it in a manner that seemed not so much built as deposited. In front was a small area of dirt and gravel, upon which Rav dumped the Civic before climbing out and taking in his surroundings.

The whole place smelt of cow shit, damp, and diesel. The Professor had also exited the car, the look on his face revealing that, having carried out the same initial sensory survey as Rav, he'd come to the same conclusion: this place smelt of the countryside, but not in any kind of good way.

Rav opened the driver's-side rear door and looked in. Two mournful eyes stared unhappily back at him. The eyes belonged to the third member of what Rav liked to call his "Lead Investigation Unit". It was a balanced team, Rav felt. He supplied leadership. The Professor supplied insight and deduction. And this third member of the team bought an array of skills and expertise in information gathering and clue detection. "Come on, Jess," Rav told his unhappy subordinate. "We're here."

Jess clambered out of the car, sniffed suspiciously at the muddy gravel with her black and white snout, scratched at a spot of dirt with a paw, and then crouched down to take a wee. Like the Civic, she was borrowed; unlike the Civic, her loan had been accompanied by an exchange of cold, hard cash overlain by solemn promises bound by threats. The dog wandered off, tail conspicuously refusing to wag. Rav nodded at the Professor. "C'mon. Let's see if we can find our client."

After a fruitless sixty seconds spent ringing the doorbell, they ventured around the side of the cottage. There, they found a burly man wearing a cloth cap and dirty overalls busily engaged in forking something that looked bad and smelt worse into a rusty wheelbarrow. A white cable ran to headphone earbuds from which some kind of tinny beat was emerging. After a few seconds he noticed them, and looked up with a start. He pulled out the earbuds and peered suspiciously at them. "Can I help you, lads?"

Rav held out his hand. "Mr Partridge? Dr Ravinder Shah. West Kensington Paranormal Detective Agency. We spoke this morning."

A relieved expression appeared on Partridge's face. "Aye, of course. I weren't sure you'd come, Dr Shah. But it's right good to see you." He paused, and his brow furrowed slightly. "I thought you said there'd be three of you?"

"There are three of us," Rav told him.

Partridge looked from Rav, to the Professor, and then down to Jess. The Border Collie stared back at him. "Right. Okay. Let me show you round." The farmer jabbed his fork into the mound of crap with enough force that it stayed standing when he let it go, then headed off towards the back of the cottage, a friendly wave telling them to follow. They did, Rav and the Professor placing their feet carefully, Jess placing her nose with equal thoroughness.

Behind the cottage was a huge, unkempt vegetable patch, across which were scattered old tyres, poles, tarpaulins, pots (small, large, broken and upturned), a couple of ramshackle sheds, a hen-house and run, and an ancient, wheel-less tractor standing on piles of bricks. As agricultural scenes went, this certainly wasn't one that was in danger of appearing on any tea-towels or jigsaw puzzles.

At the end of the garden, guarded only by a low, rusting three-wire fence, the ground dropped precipitously in a manner that, if not quite a cliff, was certainly too steep to be termed a slope. Beyond lay a wide, U-shaped valley, with a mist-shrouded village sprawled along its bottom some way below.

"The pigs, they come this way," Partridge explained, pointing into the void, the words tumbling out in a rush. "Each night, after dark, they come, landing just around 'ere. They root around – they've right trashed most of my crops. They break into sheds. I try to stop 'em, but they ain't normal, not right. There's summat of the beast about 'em. And then they go. They run, jump over fence, and they're gone."

If there was anything about this situation that was making Rav just a tad nervous, it was seeing this big, bluff Yorkshire farmer so scared he was shaking. He slapped Partridge gently on the shoulder. "We're on it. We'll find out what it is and sort it. You wait in the house tonight and leave it to us." He took a look out across the valley. "We're professionals."

"Fine by me, Dr Shah. I'll stay in t'house with shotgun and leave it to you folks."

"Shotgun?"

"Aye. It'll not be any use no how. I've tried shooting 'em with it but it just seems to make 'em angrier." Partridge tapped his cap. "I'll see you after they come."

Some time had passed since they'd arrived at this place of smells, and night was coming. Jess wasn't quite sure what was going on, but her

4

canine brain was very good at sensing human emotions, and right now Rav's body language, tone of voice, and scent were in unanimous agreement on one point – that he was scared shitless.

Rav was sat beside her, on the dirt patch at the end of the garden, stroking her just a little too firmly. She hoped it was making him feel better. Beside them, the Professor was talking about something or other. He seemed calmer than Rav, or Jess herself, come to that. Something wasn't right. She didn't know what it was, but this place of many and strange odours was clearly one of danger. Jess stayed focussed, lying down on her belly, her front paws stretched in front of her, her back paws poised to launch her into motion. Meanwhile, her snout gently rocked to and fro as she sniffed the air.

Somewhere out beyond the mist, the sun slowly dipped below the horizon, leaving behind a blurred crimson sky that gradually faded to black. Still they waited. Still Rav stroked her. Still the Professor burbled happily on. Then – something. Not a smell, but a sound. Quiet, faint, audible only because of the total silence of their surroundings. A flapping. Then a sight of something, a not quite grey smudge in the blackness.

Jess growled, once, warning.

And then.

Chaos.

A later, post-attack, forensic analysis of the Professor's now-broken wristwatch would establish that the attack had begun at 9.37pm, plus or minus however many minutes said wristwatch was accurate to. Opinions of how long the attack had lasted varied, from a low of five minutes (Rav) to a high of twenty minutes (the Professor), with Partridge weighing in with a middling ten minutes and Jess expressing no opinion beyond continued and extreme unhappiness.

What was more certain was that the WKPDA's Lead Investigation Unit had suffered a total breakdown of both unit cohesion and operational capability some five to ten seconds after the onset of the assault. Rav's memories of the events beyond that point were fragmentary and blurred, resisting any attempts he might have made to fit them into a chronological narrative.

Now, two hours later, he was sitting in Partridge's kitchen with a blank pad lying on the table in front of him. Words, fragments and recollections drifted slowly around his brain, like an old-style computer screen-saver endlessly twisting and tumbling a three-dimensional phrase across its screen.

Jess growling.

Oinking, screaming, snarling. Pink and black fur, moving faster than anything had a right to move. Grabbing something (a rake?), swinging, hitting something that turned out to be so hard and unyielding that he'd feared his wrists had shattered. Watching the something's shaft break in turn, smashed like matchwood.

Running. Hiding. Running. Screaming. (Both himself, and the pigs). Hiding. Then finally, eventually, the pigs retreating, blurs vaulting over the wire fence and disappearing into the darkness. He'd found the Professor sheltering behind the old tractor, and they'd eventually found Jess wedged underneath one of the sheds, a position from which extracting her took a good deal of gentle persuasion.

Still the memories played. Rav gave up on the task of trying to make notes, and looked around the room, at first Partridge and then the Professor. From beneath the table Jess gave another protesting sigh.

"So. We've seen what they do. Any thoughts?" He hoped to God they had something, because all he had right now was a screaming desire to get back into Mindy's car, start driving, and not stop until he was inside the M25.

Beside him, the Professor appeared contemplative. "They didn't look like normal, regular pigs."

Rav coughed. "No shit."

"I fear you miss my point, Ravinder, which is that they didn't look like the breed of pigs one might see on a standard farm." The older man leaned forward and looked at Partridge. "Mr Partridge, do you recognise which breed the pigs belong to?"

"I do, Professor Richardson. They's Old Spots. I know that because I sometimes breed them myself. Sold some about six months ago, in fact."

"Could these have been the ones you sold?"

"I dunno. I mean, they're pigs, ain't they? It ain't like I give 'em names."

"Of course." The Professor steepled his fingers in thought. "Pigs are highly intelligent. It could well be that these are the pigs you bred, that they've escaped from their new home, and that they are now returning to a place they've previously known. Whilst a perhaps un-provable hypothesis, it seems to me, nonetheless, to be a compelling one."

"Fine," Rav told him. "Great. They're homing pigs, we get that. What we don't get is how they fly, and how come they're so psychotically strong and inhumanly fast."

"Patience, Ravinder, patience. We are in search of conclusions, not assumptions, and a conclusion should be an edifice built upon a foundation of facts." The older man settled back into his chair, apparently deep in thought. For long minutes he said nothing, brain ticking. Then he spoke.

"Mr Partridge?"

"Aye?"

"When they attack, they destroy your garden. But you've not said anything about your house. Do they attack the house?"

The farmer considered the question. "Why no, not really. They've scraped at t'door. But there's been times when I've been running from 'em and figured they'd follow me in, but they ain't."

"And you say that they've destroyed nearly all your crops. Are there any crops they haven't destroyed?"

"I don't rightly know, Professor Richardson."

"Do you grow any garlic?"

"Well, it's not something I'd normally grow, but I did try a bit recently."

"And were the pigs at all interested in that?"

"Now you come to mention it, no."

The Professor smiled. "Then the answer is obvious."

It might have been obvious to the Professor, but it certainly wasn't to Rav. "How exactly is it obvious?" he asked the Professor. The older man silenced him politely with a finger and continued talking to the farmer. "Mr Partridge, I notice you have a number of small mirrors scattered about the garden?"

"Aye, Professor Richardson. To try to scare birds, stop 'em from eating my crops."

"Ravinder, did you happen to take a glance into one of the mirrors during the incident?"

"No, I was kind of busy not being killed at the time."

"Well, I did happen to glance at one of them, and saw nothing in the mirror."

"So?"

"One of the pigs was standing in front of it."

Rav considered what the older man was saying. Garlic. No reflections in mirrors. Not entering a home. "Come on, you aren't seriously trying to tell me that–"

The Professor was still smiling. "That's exactly what I'm trying to tell you, Ravinder. These aren't any old pigs. These are vampire pigs."

Chapter Two

It wasn't until Rav was well into his second slice of toast at breakfast the next morning that he felt able to address the matter at hand. He took a sip of tea, smeared a splodge of marmalade over the remaining piece, and then jabbed the orange-brown mass pointedly at the Professor. "There's no such thing as vampires."

"That is indeed the received wisdom. But then received wisdom also holds flying pigs to be similarly non-existent."

"Good point," Rav conceded. It was indeed a good point, good enough to make him stop jabbing the toast and eat it instead, thinking as he chewed.

The Professor gave him a moment, and then continued. "As Sir Arthur Conan Doyle's opium-taking protagonist once said, once one has 'eliminated the impossible, whatever remains, however improbable, must be the truth'."

"I think you could have got Holmes out of his skull on heroin, crack and Evostick and still find him having problems putting vampire pigs in the merely improbable category. And that's before he had to run it past Dr Watson."

"Quite possibly. But Holmes and Watson aren't here. We are. We aren't cavemen sitting around a fire trying to understand why the sky turns. We are civilised men of the twentieth century–"

"Twenty-first."

"Is it really? Did I miss some of sort of millennial celebrations?"

"Yes."

"Oh well. The point is that we are civilised and educated men. We must start with the facts and work towards our explanation, and not vice versa. After all, we are attempting to investigate a case, not create a religion. In all of this, we have only two facts. There are pigs. And they can fly."

Partridge chose that moment to appear with three plates laden with sausages, eggs, beans, mushrooms, tomatoes, and fried bread, presented in a sauce of oil and grease. He slid a plate each in front of Rav and the Professor, and popped the third down on the floor in front of Jess. The dog sniffed suspiciously at the concoction before giving the canine equivalent of a shrug and shoving her snout in.

Partridge sat down at the end of the table. "My old ma always said problems seem smaller once you've 'ad yourself a good breakfast." He smiled, clearly unconcerned by the total lack of any connection between the weapons of culinary destruction he'd just delivered and the phrase "good breakfast". For a moment the farmer paused, seemingly lost in memories. Then he looked back at Rav. "So, Dr Shah, what's the plan?"

"Don't know." Rav turned to the Professor. "Prof?"

"The details of the plan depend upon the nature of our objective, Mr Partridge. Do you wish to eliminate the pigs entirely, or merely persuade them to depart forthwith, never to return?"

Partridge replied with a helpless shrug. "I just want 'em to leave me alone."

"Excellent! Non-violent persuasion it is. We shall require provisions. Mr Partridge?"

"Aye?"

"Is there some sort of greengrocer in the village yonder? And perhaps some sort of ironmongers?"

"There's a twenty-four hour Tesco's and a garden centre?"

The Professor sighed. "That will suffice, I suppose. Ravinder. To the chariot!"

Jess was dozing in front of the fireplace when Rav and the Professor returned to the smallholding, laden with supplies. Her ears and nose were twitching, and her legs slowly paddled at the air. Partridge indicated her with a nod. "She's probably off chasing rabbits." Rav nodded, although personally, given the breakfast she'd eaten, he figured it was just as likely that the rabbits were chasing her. The farmer turned his attention to the collection of bags Rav and the Professor were hauling in. "What have you got there?"

Rav dropped two of the carrier bags onto the table. "Garlic."

"As a general deterrent," the Professor added.

"That's a lot of garlic."

Rav shrugged. "That's what the woman at the checkout said."

"And what do we do with it?"

"Place it in the ground around the perimeter of the smallholding, apparently." He looked up at the Professor. "What do you think, Prof? One bulb, broken up, per metre?"

"I'd rather have one bulb per yard."

"That's pretty much the same thing."

"Is it really? I'm afraid I never did get to grip with that particular Napoleonic system."

"Whatever. One bulb per yard." Rav reached down and lifted up the next set of carrier bags. "This is a water pump," he told Partridge. "And a whole bunch of pond lining. You'll need to dig a trench, about six inches deep, right around the smallholding, just inside the garlic, with the trench getting deeper and deeper so that the bottom slopes downward. Just where the high point meets the low point, you bury this pump and pipes and connect it to your household electricity supply. Plug it in, fill the trench with water, and voila, running water, in a big circle."

"Right," said Partridge, nodding. "So you want me to dig a trench?"

"Yes."

"And what will you be doing?"

Rav looked at the farmer with the authority that came from having made sure to have already asked the Professor this question on the drive back to the smallholding. "We need to go talk to a priest."

The Professor was not a religious man. Spiritual perhaps, but organised religion had never held any appeal for him. He'd been blessed, or perhaps cursed, with a mind that chose questions over answers, pursuing an infinite universe of knowledge in preference to a closed world of "truth". He'd long ago accepted that his would be a life built not on certainty, but on doubt. The path of a religious man might perhaps have been an easier path to walk, but it was a path he'd left untaken, preferring instead to find his own route across existence.

The events of the previous night had, however, taken him to the place he now sat in: the cramped office of Grimethorpe's Anglican vicar. His and Rav's purpose in visiting was entirely practical, rather than spiritual. But from the moment they'd knocked on Father Adrian's door and he'd ushered them into his office, the enthusiastic priest had done nothing else but talk of matters religious, resisting every attempt the Professor and Rav had made to take charge of the conversation.

The fifteen minutes of continuous monologue had, however, established one, possibly worrying, fact, which was that the Father Adrian himself appeared to be following a similar, individualistic trail through creation, unaffiliated with any organised system of belief the Professor had yet come across.

"As I said, when you talk about God," the vicar was saying, his hands animated, "I think you really have to get rid of the notion of God as some kind of being, sitting above us, in Heaven. Surely God is all around us, in everything good? You could say that God is goodness, and if God is goodness and goodness is God, then an act of kindness, for example, is God. Would you not agree?"

The Professor was about to seize this rare chance to enter the conversation, but Rav beat him to it. "Well, to be honest, Father, I'm a Hindu. I'm not sure I have an opinion."

That wasn't strictly true. In reality, Rav was a Hindu in the same way that the average white Englishman is "Church of England". It was a label that implied how and where his birth, marriage, and death might be celebrated, as well as which days he would spend in feast and celebration with his family, without necessarily implying anything in the way of strong religious sentiment. A more accurate description might have been "geeky sort of lazy agnostic from a Hindu background, who doesn't let an absence of actual religious belief prevent him from enjoying the fireworks and food at Diwali". It did occur to him that he should perhaps give a more nuanced reply to Father Adrian, but the vicar was already replying, his hands animated.

"Nonsense. Only a fool would claim to have a monopoly on the truth. I'm certainly not going to argue that Christianity is any more valid than Hinduism. I might believe that Christ was the son of God who rose from the dead, or then again I might not. Frankly, it all seems a bit too much like a fairy story to me, but if it gives comfort to the scared, who am I to criticise? We all have to live on this world together. Why on Earth would I argue that my belief in Christ has any more validity than your belief in your Hindu gods?"

The Professor leaned forward. "Because you're an ordained minister in the Church of England?"

"Well, yes. Quite." Father Adrian paused for a moment. "Sorry, why did you come here again?"

Rav lifted a couple of heavily laden carrier bags onto the vicar's desk, each of which contained four two-litre bottles of Tesco's own-brand, mineral water.

"We need you to bless some water."

When they finally left the vicarage they found the car outside where they'd left it, which wasn't particularly surprising given that this was a quiet North Yorkshire village and not a crime-ridden sink estate in, say, inner London. Rav dumped the now blessed bottles into the boot, and slammed the tailgate down. He wasn't feeling at all good about this part of the plan. In day-to-day life, Rav was vaguely approving of the happy-clappy, hippy-dippy, wishy-washy ecumenical fringe of the Christian faith. But when faced with several hundred kilos of angry, undead porker, he'd rather have a bit of judgemental, Ian Paisley-style, Old Testament zealotry at his back. Less, "Perhaps we should have an inter-faith workshop to discuss the issues?" and more, "Get thee behind me, you thrice-damned spawn of Satan!" He looked hard at the Professor. "Is this holy water stuff actually going to work?"

The Professor gave a measured shrug in reply. "Do I know it's going to work? No. Do I think it's going to work? Perhaps. Do I hope it's going to work? Most definitely yes."

"But he doesn't even believe in God."

"I think that's perhaps an unfair characterisation of Father Adrian's theological position."

"Did you miss the bit where he pointed out of the window at his rockery and said that the big rock on the left was God?"

"Well, I think he was actually making a point about the Almighty's general omnipresence. But the key fact here is that he was ordained by a bishop, who was ordained by a bishop, who was ordained by a bishop, in an unbroken chain that stretches back all the way to Saint Peter himself."

"Who was, like, Jesus's best mate and sidekick, right?"

The Professor sighed. "Well, I'm not sure that those would be the words St Thomas Aquinas would have used to describe the Prince of the Apostles."

"But the point is that, believer or not, he's on God's payroll and he's got a license to bless?"

"That would be the theory, although I would have thought that as a Hindu, you might disagree?"

"Well, it's all the same in the end, isn't it?"

"I suppose that were one to take a more liberal, ecumenical point of view, one might come to that conclusion."

"So it'll work?"

"Ask me in twenty-four hours, Ravinder."

In the distance, the last visible portion of the sun's disk dipped below the horizon, and a deepening gloom settled upon the landscape. Rav tightened his grip on his Super Soaker and tried to stop his heart thumping. He had a half-litre magazine full of holy water locked and loaded with another three full magazines on the ground beside him, ready to go.

He waited.

The sky slowly deepened to something more slate grey than true black, dark fluffy clouds obscuring all but the occasional star. Waiting. Jess was lying beside him, alert, ears pricked, head gently moving from side to side. Her snout twitched; she inched forward. And growled.

"Think we've got incoming," Rav whispered to the Professor and Partridge, who were sheltering several feet back behind an improvised sandbag wall.

There was a glimpse of movement, of something small that flapped, and then a pig appeared – blinking into existence just above the fence that lay at the end of Partridge's garden. It hit the ground running and bounced forward, before coming to a screaming, skidding halt as it reached the line of garlic. It was not now small. In fact, it was big and ugly, with hairy blotchy skin and a build more reminiscent of a wild boar than anything you might find in a child's book of farmyard animals.

Behind it, others appeared, landed, followed.

The lead porker sniffed, snarled, then advanced grunting through the line of garlic and up to the shallow channel, along which gurgled the pump-driven water. Rav forced his lungs to take a breath. The garlic had deterred but not stopped it. How would it feel about six inches of running water?

The pig pawed at the dirt in apparent anguish, roared as though in pain, paused, then jumped over the channel. Its comrades surged forward, following in its wake. Only several unobstructed yards of empty soil now stood between the pigs and Rav.

This was it, Rav realised. Warrior stuff. Light against dark. Man against beast. Logical thought against primeval anger. Ten quid's worth of Chinese manufactured electric motor in a moulded plastic case against a two hundred pound vampiric porker having a bad night.

He dropped down into a kneeling position, jammed the Super Soaker's butt into his shoulder, aimed, and fired, sending a series of sharp bursts across the pig's snout, head, and back, the whine of the soaker's electric motor piercing in the still night air. The pig stopped, and gave him a look that was beyond anger, beyond fury, beyond anything that had any right to exist in this or any other existence–

And took a step forward.

This wasn't warrior stuff, Rav realised. This was out of your screaming depth, stuff. This was get in your car and drive like hell, to anywhere else but here, stuff. This was realise that of all the mistakes your life will ultimately contain, none of them will ever be worse than this mistake that you're currently making, stuff. The part of his brain still functioning knew that his arms were dropped limply at his sides, the Super Soaker hanging loosely from just one hand, its muzzle resting on the ground. But he was helpless, his inability to act paralysing.

Then Jess launched herself forward in a long leaping bound, barking furiously as she planted herself before the lead pig, tail swishing at the air. The pig paused briefly, a pause just long enough for something inside of Rav to snap him back into the present. He brought the Super Soaker up to his shoulder and fired a long burst along the pig's back and into the mass of pigs that had followed in its wake. He clicked the empty magazine free, reached down to grab a replacement, rammed it home, and fired again, sending out a series of long sweeping bursts.

The lead pig let out an enraged scream, but its eyes held a look of something new. Fear? Confusion? Doubt? Rav emptied the last of the magazine across its back, then turned his head to shout at the Professor and Partridge behind him.

"Now, guys! Now!"

The two men stepped out from behind their emplacement, each carrying a pink, wobbling spherical object, decorated with stars and wands and the words "Happy Birthday". Partridge hurled his, one-handed, goalkeeper style. The balloon arced up, seeming almost to hang in the air, before crashing down and exploding on the lead pig's back, showering holy water across the furry pink skin. Partridge grabbed the second balloon from the Professor and launched it after the first, into the mass of pigs bunched up behind their leader.

A ton or two's worth of pig screamed. A smell drifted across the battlefield; burning pork crossed with something evil, like barbecue night at Satan's gaff. Rav grabbed the third magazine and emptied it into the screaming, snarling, crying mass. And then the pigs ran, climbing over themselves in their eagerness to escape. They vaulted over the end fence, and disappeared.

For several long seconds no one spoke. Then Jess took a half step forward and gave a final, good-riddance, bark. Rav walked over to her, crouched down, and tickled her behind an ear. "Well done, girl. You did good."

Partridge was staring into the darkness through which the pigs had escaped. "Do you think that will be it, Dr Shah, Professor? Will they come back?"

The Professor shook his head. "I think not. Pigs are intelligent creatures. Whatever homing instinct might have compelled them to return here will be gone now. This is no longer a place they would ever wish to visit."

Rav smiled. "Well, I think we can call that job done. Let's get some sleep. We'll be having an early start tomorrow."

After a quick shower each and a couple of mugs of tea, they'd headed off, declining Partridge's offer of breakfast and making it onto the road by seven. It was now well past nine, and still the motorway's southbound carriageway stretched away in front of them.

They flashed past a line of cars that were apparently content to pootle along the middle lane at a mere five miles an hour over the speed limit. A sign approached, motorway blue, with white lettering. London, eighty-five miles.

Rav kept his foot hard down. It was a Monday, and he had a place to be, that being his actual workplace, Hounslow Council's Social Services department. He'd phoned in to say he was running late before they'd left, but, as someone who'd never been in any danger of winning the employee of the month award, he was bitterly aware that the later he arrived, the better the excuse he needed.

He did a quick bit of mental arithmetic and realised he really should have called in sick. Dammit. Too late now. He put his foot down another notch, causing the speedo to edge up from "just about socially acceptable speeding" to "completely taking the piss".

The Professor, who, after spending the first half hour of the journey talking about the influence of the Counter-Reformation on central European architecture, had then drifted off lost in thought, chose this moment to speak. "We might have solved Mr Partridge's problem, but we haven't actually solved the mystery, have we?"

This was not a point Rav had failed to realise. While much of his attention during the last two hours had been occupied with the task of driving from Yorkshire to London rather quickly without actually killing them all, the part of his attention not thus engaged had been mulling over this very question.

This was a real, honest-to-God Mulder and Scully job, just the sort of thing he'd secretly dreamed of when setting up the agency. But living a life straight out of a TV series was one thing; following a pack of vampire pigs back to whoever, or whatever, had spawned them, was something else. Having stumbled upon a bit of genuine paranormal strangeness, Rav wasn't sure he had the guts to poke it with a stick and wake it up. "We don't actually have a client," he pointed out.

The Professor smiled across at him, a twinkle in his eye. "My dear Ravinder. Since when did one need a client in order to search for hidden truths?"

"Yeah, but where would we start?"

"With the facts, Ravinder. We would start with the facts."

Chapter Three

It was a fair way past eleven when Rav arrived at the office, having had to first drop off Jess, the Professor, and finally the car. He tried to sneak in, but found himself being blocked by his boss, Fenella, who'd glided effortlessly in like some kind of power-dressed, public-sector ninja in heels.

"Rav. I'm so glad you could join us."

"Look, Fen–"

She cut him off with a viciously pointing finger. "No excuses, Rav. I'm not in the mood. So let's start again. Why exactly are you arriving for work more than two hours late?"

Rav raised his assessment of her mood from his previous estimate of "severely pissed off" to a significantly higher "absolutely fucking furious".

"I can explain."

"Really?" She folded her arms. "Go on then."

A cold metal ball of panic rolled across the pinball table of Rav's brain, bounced several times off the bumper marked "bugger", trundled across the lights marked "crap", "bollocks", and "dammit", and then dropped neatly between the helpless twin flippers of "action" and "thought". Rav had never hated anyone more than he hated his own self of an hour ago, who, in all of this, had totally forgotten to come up with an actual excuse. What to say? That he'd overslept? No, that'd be a confession rather than an explanation. Burst water pipe? Yes. Result!

"I had a burst water pipe."

"Where?"

"Where... what?"

"Where was the burst water pipe?"

"In my flat."

"Where in your flat?"

"Erm... In the kitchen?"

She sighed, which somehow managed to be more terrifying than the previous ranting had been. "You know what, Rav? I really can't be bothered with this. If you carry on bullshitting me I'm only going to lose my rag and kill you, which would leave an annoying stain on my management record and an even more annoying stain on the office carpet. So just sod off and do some work."

Rav backed carefully away, smiling the sort of smile one is advised to give to mad dogs and psychopaths. "Yeah, sure. On it."

"And take this as a final verbal warning. I know it's practically impossible to get anyone sacked round here, but piss me off again and I might actually have a go."

After escaping from Fen and retreating to the sanctuary of his folder-littered desk, Rav had been forced to deal with a series of difficult phone calls. Some of these calls had been angry: Jess's owner Brian – "What the fuck have you been feeding Jess on? She's shitting yellow gloop!" – and Mindy – "What the hell have you been doing to my car? Rallying? There's mud in places I didn't know existed!" Some of them had been confused: the Professor – "Why isn't Richard Whiteley hosting Countdown? Who's this new chap?" And some of them had just been plain awkward, coming as they did from the difficult and dysfunctional people his profession bought him into regular contact with. (Not his clients, who he'd been trained to deal with, but his fellow social workers, who – by and large – he hadn't).

It had been a relief to escape the office at the end of the day and head for home. Most nights, Rav ended up slumped in front of the telly, watching a bunch of blokes shooting the crap out of other bunches of blokes. On some nights, Rav would forgo the delights of a DVD and instead fire up the PS3, and, while he would still then spend the night watching a bunch of blokes shooting the crap out of another bunch of blokes, it would be with a somewhat straighter back and as an enthusiastic participant.

Tonight though, he did neither. He had a case to solve, and as the Professor had said, he needed to start with the facts. He rooted around in the box of stuff that stood in his lounge's corner and pulled out a pack of multi-coloured index cards he'd liberated from the office stationary cupboard. (Rav felt no guilt at this act of technical theft, given that the office didn't use multi-coloured index cards in any way whatsoever. In fact, it hadn't used them since about 1993, but local authority purchasing orders are notoriously hard to amend.)

He began to write the facts as he understood them upon each index card, one fact per card.

"There are pigs."
"The pigs can fly."
"The pigs seem attracted to Partridge's Farm."
"The pigs are Old Spots."
"Partridge sold some Old Spots six months ago."
"The pigs are affected by anti-vampiric defences."

He looked through the cards again one by one. Nothing. He shuffled them, then laid them down in a three-by-two grid. That still sparked no inspiration, so he reshuffled them into a two-by-three grid, feeling like a fraudulent clairvoyant with a fistful of mismatched tarot cards trying to assemble them into something resembling a story.

Still nothing. He grabbed his laptop and spent half an hour reading the various Wikipedia entries on vampires but found himself merely retreading the territory he'd covered as a twelve-year-old exploring the more exotic sections of the local library, albeit with more grammatical errors and the occasional random bit of vandalism. He tried searching for "flying pigs", but that unearthed only random anecdotes about unlikely happenings, jokes about police helicopters, and the upcoming concert schedule of a Flying Pickets tribute band.

He looked again at the cards. The fifth card he'd written, the one recording Partridge's sale of some Old Spots six months ago, caught his eye. It was a weak lead, but it was looking like the only one he had. He picked up his phone, found the farmer's number in his contacts, and hit dial. The farmer answered on the fourth ring. "Yes? What? Hullo?"

"Mr Partridge? It's Dr Shah here."

"Ah. Right. Dr Shah. There's nowt wrong, is there?"

"No, no. Everything's fine. I'm just pursuing some follow-up investigations. I believe you said that you sold some pigs of the same breed six months ago?"

"Aye. What of it?"

"Well, I was thinking that if those were the same pigs, I could track them down."

"Right."

"So do you have any records of who you sold them to? I understand that these sort of things are pretty regimented nowadays, since BSE and Foot and Mouth? All forms and livestock passports and tags and chips?"

The farmer took a moment to reply. "Aye, it is. But I don't do nowt of that crap. Start doing that and before you know it you'll have the taxman round with his hand out!"

"So you don't have any records of the sale?"

"The bloke offered cash. Notes with the Queen's Head on them were good enough for my father and his father, so they're good enough for me. I don't hold with cheques and the like."

"Bloke?"

"Aye. It were a bloke."

"Did he give you a name?"

"No."

"What did he look like?"

"Dunno."

"You don't know what he looked like?"

"It were dark, and it were raining, and he were wearing a raincoat with the hood up."

"How did he get in contact with you?"

"He phoned me. Said he'd heard I had pigs for sale. He'd seen the card what I put up in the newsagents."

"Have you got his number?"

"No. It were on my landline."

"Right. How did he take the pigs away?"

"He had a trailer thing, attached to a Range Rover."

"What colour was the Range Rover."

"Dunno. It were dark. Everything looks black when it's dark, doesn't it?"

Rav tried to imagine he was Inspector Morse, or failing that Lewis. Morse would have a cerebral question to ask, a shaft of inspiration that would unlock the case. A man. Buying pigs. Buying. Which meant talking. "What did he sound like?"

"What do you mean?"

"Did he sound like he was from Yorkshire?"

"Maybe. He didn't say much, best I recall."

A further five minutes of conversation failed to root out anything of any consequence, leaving Rav with the near-impossible task of searching for a bloke with a rain coat who might have been from Yorkshire, had a vaguely dark-coloured Range Rover, and who had a predilection for buying pigs for cash, no questions either asked or answered.

Maybe it was time to call it a night.

Rav had slumped into his bed sometime after eleven with a general intention of getting some sleep, in preparation for another fun and rewarding day's work as a social worker. The reality, however, turned out to involve much tossing and turning and the unwanted grinding of jammed mental cogs. After a couple of hours, he gave up, got out of bed, and opened up his laptop. If Mohammed couldn't come to the mountain, on account of having no sodding idea where the mountain might be or even what it might look like, then perhaps he ought to try asking for directions. He fired up his browser and hit the bookmark on the toolbar marked "The Zone".

The Zone was an online home for those individuals who'd like to believe that there are truths "out there" more interesting than those you might find in your everyday newspaper. It was a place to hang out at if you believed that the Apollo astronauts hadn't landed on the moon, but Hitler's flying saucers had. It provided sanctuary to those who believed that fluoride was added to the water not to build healthy teeth, but to create malleable minds. It was a haven for those who believed that the world was actually run by either Nazis, or lizards, or in the case of the Royal Family, both. And it was also pretty good for old X-Files fan-fiction – although Rav was still scarred from the accidental reading of a Mulder/Cigarette Smoking Man slash story.

He navigated through to the main forum and clicked on the "New Post" button. Subject. What to say? "Vampire Pigs," he typed. "In either legend, lore or real-life – any details or stories?" He spent a couple of minutes composing a vague query about vampire pigs, making sure to not mention anything specific, but instead merely asking if anyone had come across anything of that description. That done, he reread it, corrected a few typos, then hit post.

He closed the laptop's lid and settled back down into his bed. The lure was cast, the bait left. He'd check in tomorrow to see if he'd caught anything.

Some two hundred miles to the north of Rav, his message was not going unread.

Teenage girls who've read too much Twilight love the idea of a three hundred and twenty-year-old vampire who looks like a twenty-year-old boy. Alan was indeed a three hundred and twenty-year-old vampire. He did not, however, look like a twenty-year-old boy. Nor did he look like a three hundred and twenty-year-old man. Alan's problem was that he looked like the corpse of a twenty-year-old boy after it had spent three hundred years rotting six feet under.

Alan did not sparkle. He was not full of life. Had he been the protagonist of a young adult, paranormal romance, novel, his not sleeping with the novel's young female protagonist would not have seemed an awkward concession to puritanical interests. He was, quite literally, a dead man walking, or more accurately shambling. Decomposing. Decaying. Crumbling. A contraceptive in bipedal, locomotive form kept on this Earth not by life, but by a stubborn, biblical, cursed inability to actually depart for somewhere, anywhere, else. Once, some years ago, Alan had watched the Star Wars trilogy on a fuzzy and crackling set of pirated VHS tapes. At the end of the third and final film, Darth Vader's helmet had been removed, to reveal a white, bloated and scarred face. Alan would have killed for such a face.

He was employed as the night porter at a small and somewhat archaic hotel in York, manning the front desk through the unsociable hours between dusk and dawn. As jobs went, it quite suited him. Avoiding the sunlit portion of the day was useful not only in masking the hideousness of his features, but also in allowing him to walk to and from work without bursting into flames. The job didn't stretch him. The small hours are a forgiving time in the customer service industry. As long as the correct key is proffered with only a small delay, all else is overlooked, whether it be a dubious smell, a suspicious Eastern European accent, or a hideous and frankly supernatural visage.

It also allowed him to spend the long periods of time between returning guests browsing the Internet on his cheap Android tablet. The Internet was a wondrous thing, perhaps the most wondrous thing Alan had yet encountered on this Earth, which, given that Alan was a three hundred and twenty-year-old being who had – to quote Rutger Hauer – seen things people wouldn't believe, was quite some statement. So far tonight, he'd browsed Wikipedia, read a bit of Mail Online, and surfed some porn, all the while checking in at the Zone periodically to see if Tabitha had left him a message. He tried again now, but his inbox there was still empty. It was several days since her last message. He tried to tell himself that perhaps she was simply busy, that it meant nothing, but an icy fear still gripped him, as it always did whenever she failed to message him.

He clicked through to the main forum, more out of habit than anything else, and immediately found his eye caught by a post a few lines down from the top. "Vampire Pigs, in either legend, lore or real-life - any details or stories?" Alan did indeed have stories about vampire pigs. Stories of angry pigs. Clever pigs. Sneaky, crafty, ungrateful, duplicitous pigs. In the ranks of the conspiracy to which he belonged, Alan had been assigned two jobs. The first job had been to feed the pigs without allowing them to escape. The second was to monitor the various social networks out there on the Internet for anything that might be relevant to, or an issue for, the conspiracy's primary project.

Alan had failed utterly at his first job. He didn't intend to fail at his second. He clicked through to the post, hit the "Private Message" button, and began to type out a message to user "WKPDA", whoever that might be.

Chapter Four

It had been past three by the time Rav finally fell into a state approaching sleep, and when his phone's alarm woke him at seven, he not surprisingly felt like shit. He staggered into the shower, and staggered back out some indeterminable amount of minutes later, now awake if not quite sentient; shaved; brushed his teeth; and headed into the kitchen for some tea and toast, grabbing his laptop on the way.

If the shower hadn't quite woken him, what he found in his email inbox sure as hell did. It was a notification of a private message from a Zone user called "Alan57", who knew all about vampire pigs and was apparently willing to talk. "Would like to meet," the message concluded. "Can you come to York?"

London to York was quite a journey, especially when it was based on nothing more than a tenuous message regarding a case he wasn't even being paid to complete. But then again, it wasn't as though he had anything better to be doing. He quickly tapped out a reply and headed off to work, where he spent the morning alternating between making phone calls and studying case files, and hitting refresh on the web browser he'd pointed at his Zone inbox. It wasn't until just before lunch that the answer came, and that answer was that the meeting with Alan57 was on. As leads went, this was pretty loose. Hell, it had "wild goose chase" written all over it. But since, as options went, it was currently sitting at the top of a shortlist of one, Rav figured he might as well follow it up. He grabbed his phone and dialled the Professor's landline. The older man answered on the second ring. "Ravinder?"

"How'd you know it's me?"

"Who else would it be?"

"Good point. Anyhow, clear your diary for this weekend, because Saturday you, me and Jess are heading to York. We're going to talk to a guy about vampire pigs."

The week passed, slowly, as weeks are prone to do, but Saturday eventually arrived, albeit not without baggage. Some tasks in life are simple. Getting a dog and an elderly man through Kings Cross station is not one of them, especially when one of them has a tendency to wander off in random directions. (The Professor, who, unlike the dog, appeared to possess no concept of pack unity). But eventually, the three of them were seated on the 1pm Virgin East Coast service to York, and Rav felt he could relax just a little.

The Professor was scribbling away in his notebook. After a few minutes, he looked up. "So who is this person we're going to see?"

"Alan57."

"That's a strange kind of name."

"It's not a name. It's an Internet handle."

"Ah. So what's his actual name?"

"Alan something, I guess."

"Why might he call himself Alan57?"

"I don't know. Maybe he was born in 1957."

"So what else do we know about him?"

"Nothing. Just that he says he knows something about vampire pigs and would like to talk."

"And then what do we do?"

"Don't know. Talk to him. See what we can find out."

"Has it occurred to you that this might be a trap?"

"Yeah, it could be. But then again, it's York, not inner-city Manchester. What's the worst that could happen?"

The Professor thought for a moment, then nodded. The rest of the journey passed in relative peace, save for one unfortunate incident involving Jess's outstretched tail, a catering trolley, and an RMT union member who apparently took great exception to being barked and growled at on his own train, thank you very much.

A little under three hours after leaving Kings Cross they slid into York station, and headed for the dog friendly guesthouse that Rav had booked a few days earlier. There, as they made their final preparations, Rav could feel the anticipation rising within him.

This might just be it.

As he sat in the bar, waiting, Alan was nervous. Within the conspiracy's hierarchy, he was something of a mid-ranking junior officer. It could have been argued – and, if this went wrong, no doubt would be argued – that he should have informed his superiors of the action he was in the process of carrying out. But just for once, he wanted to prove himself. Wanted to show he could be trusted. Wanted to be a player, a big man.

He'd planned the meeting carefully, selecting a location – a tucked-away pub off Petergate in the shadow of the old walls – where he could wait, surrounded by trusted allies. He sat now, in the furthest, darkest corner alcove, taking nervous sips at the JD and coke in front of him. This was a very dangerous moment, one he couldn't afford to screw up.

The cards had been dealt. Now he just had to play them.

According to the maps app on Rav's phone, the bar in which Alan had agreed to meet them was just inside the city walls. Following the blinking blue dot on the phone's display, they crossed over a pedestrian crossing and found themselves in front of a huge stone gatehouse that would have been out of place in a Hollywood production only by virtue of being too authentic.

"Magnificent!" sighed the Professor.

"Yeah, t'riffic," Rav replied, not looking up from his phone.

They walked through the gate. A cast iron sign set high upon an adjacent wall proclaimed that they were now in High Petergate. They walked a little further, then stopped, while Rav waited for the blue dot on his phone to figure out where it was. Eventually, it settled, right where they needed to be. He looked up, and spotted an alley to their right. "Think it's down here. Bloke said he'd be sitting at the back, wearing some kind of mask."

"A mask?"

"Apparently, he needs to protect his identity." Rav set off down the alleyway. "You coming?"

"Wouldn't miss it for the world, Ravinder."

Alan's paper bag mask was scratchy upon his face.

The mask was actually his mark two attempt at a disguise, after the mark one version based upon a Tesco's plastic carrier bag had proved to be a miscalculation of such epic magnitude that only the technicality of his already being dead had saved him from an additional death by way of suffocation.

Alan put that memory aside. He had not come to the bar alone. He nodded now at his companions, who were discreetly scattered across a cluster of adjacent tables. Every cult or conspiracy needs its foot-soldiers and minions, and these were they. They nodded back, faces taut under their thick white makeup and black eye-shadow.

Then the door at the far end of the club opened, and two men walked in. The first of the two was a youngish Asian man. He had a neat close-cropped beard and wore a well-fitting suit. Alan recognised him from the picture he'd found on the WKPDA website. This was the Dr Ravinder Shah he'd come here to meet. The second man was older, and white, with slightly wild grey hair and a gentle smile.

Shah and his companion looked around, clearly unable to see much of anything in the club's dim interior. Alan waved, feeling vaguely self-conscious, and then waved again, until eventually they saw him, and headed over. He motioned to the two chairs in front of his table, which they pulled out and sat down upon.

Then a third head popped up between them, nestled between a pair of paws placed on the table's edge. The head was black, white and tufty, with a snout at the front behind which was set a pair of penetrating eyes. The eyes regarded Alan suspiciously; the snout began to curl, to reveal a set of teeth. Fear shot through Alan's unbeating heart. The hound knew he was the beast.

It knew.

Border Collies are often assumed to be friendly and non-aggressive. After all, people reason, they wouldn't be allowed around sheep if they were aggressive, would they? As with many things in life, this is a drastic oversimplification. While it is true that one never reads of a man being savaged to death by a Border Collie, an overly enthusiastic greeting made to a neurotic and nervous member of the breed (as with people, the drawback of possessing a high intelligence is often that it merely gives you more to worry about) is likely to result in a warning nip at any outstretched hands.

But the instincts now firing inside Jess were different. They went beyond aggression and beyond warning nips. This thing possessed the same scent of the beast that had been disturbing her sleep for the past week. Jess's forebears had trotted alongside men for tens of thousands of years and for thousands of generations, but this thing was not a man. This thing was not any kind of human.

Jess had upward of two hundred million scent receptors in her nose, and every single one of them was telling her that this thing was wrong on a level too fundamental to be accepted. The message hit her brain with such force that it not only bypassed two hundred years of sheepdog breeding, but the twenty thousand years of domestication that had come before that. Somewhere deep inside Jess, the Siberian steppe-wolf that lurks within every dog came alive, took charge, and leapt – for the beast's throat.

In theory, Alan was possessed of a supernatural speed and inhuman strength; in practice, he was as vulnerable as the next man to the twin opponents of surprise and shock. It was no doubt this that enabled the hound to get its teeth clamped tight around his neck, with its claws scrabbling hard all the while against his chest. He realised he could no longer see. Panic surged within him. The beast had blinded him. Was this how his centuries' long existence would end? Savaged to death by a dog in a basement club in this God-forsaken land?

Then he realised his paper bag mask had shifted. He reached up and ripped if off, and found himself looking into the enraged eyes of the black-and-white hound, eyes so furious they wouldn't have looked out of place had they been guarding the very gates of Hell. He reached down to hold the beast at either side of its ribcage, then pushed hard, feeling the skin of his neck tearing as the dog came loose. He threw it across the room, then vaulted over the table, landing next to the slim figure of Shah who was standing frozen, his hand still extended in greeting. This was a fiasco, a fiasco that was rapidly turning into a disaster of such magnitude that he didn't even want to consider the monster bollocking that would inevitably be heading his way. He had to get out of here. Now. He took a step, but found Shah somehow blocking his way. Instinct took over where his thoughts were still stalled. He swung his arm, hooking the man around the chest and launching him into the air. He didn't care where the investigator went. He cared only that there was now nothing between him and the exit.

Rav's encounter with Alan had thus far occupied so little time that it could scarcely be termed an encounter, let alone a meeting. But it already counted as a point along Rav's lifepath in which the mental framework by which he interpreted reality had changed forever. The ferocity with which Jess had attacked the masked man had been shocking; the ease with which he'd flung her away, incomprehensible. Given time, Rav might perhaps have been able to put his feelings into words. But he'd been given no such time. He'd had, instead, a mere instant to gaze upon Alan's unmasked, and frankly disgusting face, before joining his canine companion in a flight across the darkened room.

It has often been said of flight that flying is easy, it's the landing that's hard, and this was never more true than in Rav's case, because after effortlessly traversing the length of the room, clearing several tables-worth of goths on the way, he bounced hard off the counter and crashed into the bank of bottles set upon the wall behind it, eventually ending up in a glass-covered heap behind the bar – an unfortunate condition he shared with the barman who'd been unlucky enough to be standing behind the section of bar he'd hit.

For several long seconds Rav stared, stunned, at the ceiling, his brain attempting first to reboot itself, and then to re-establish communications with the rest of his body. Then some instinct took over, and he sat up. Something that sounded Australian moaned and squirmed beneath him: the barman, Rav realised. He scrambled to his feet, an action that triggered an aggrieved sounding "Streuth, mate!" and, having neither the energy nor the gymnastic skill to vault over the bar, settled instead for rolling over its counter top, falling off the other side into something vaguely crouch-like.

He was just in time to see Alan heading out the door. Rav looked around. The Professor was standing where he himself had stood only seconds previously, a stunned look upon his face, his hat slightly askew. Jess, meanwhile, was scrabbling to find her feet upon a beer covered table. She shook herself dry, launched herself forward, and landed at Rav's feet, a determined expression on her little face, snout set, ears back.

This Alan, whatever he was – and a large part of Rav's brain was currently actively engaged in consciously ignoring several large and obvious truths – was clearly the key to all this. They couldn't just let him get away. Rav stumbled towards the door, Jess at his heels. He burst through the opening and skidded into a sharp turn. Alan was at the end of the alleyway, heading into the street.

"Oi!" Rav shouted. "I want a word!"

Chapter Five

Rav skidded into the street, lungs already starting to burn from the potent fuel of stress, excitement, fear and exertion on which he was currently running them. Ahead of him, Alan was moving in what could only be described as a fast but inelegant shambling motion. It took him through the gatehouse's open maw, where he ducked to the right and disappeared.

Several long seconds later, Rav followed him through the gatehouse and found... nothing. He looked around, letting Jess sniff away on her own investigation. Beside the huge main opening of the gatehouse was a smaller, man-sized opening, behind which a flight of stone stairs led upwards. Beside this smaller opening, lying flat on the ground, was a wrought-iron gate. A padlock was attacked to the gate; two broken hinges were set into the stonework. Something had ripped this iron gate off its hinges and thrown it aside as though it were no more difficult a task than tearing open a packet of cornflakes.

Alan.

The fraternity of unwanted, unneeded truths swirling around Rav's brain shouting for attention gained an additional member. Jess advanced to the opening, sniffing, then looked up at him, a questioning expression on her face. Rav nodded a reply to her then launched himself through the opening and up the steep, narrow stairs, pushing hard, until he found himself standing at the start of a section of city wall, atop the narrow battlement that led along the wall's top, from where medieval archers could shoot through the crenulations at invading Scotsmen.

Somewhere ahead in the darkness, a murky figure was moving fast away from them. Rav set off after him. "Alan!" he shouted through burning lungs. "Alan! We just want to talk."

Alan had lived in York for several years now, having moved there along with the rest of his vampiric comrades when their homeland of Romania entered the European Union in 2007. In all that time, he'd never walked along any of the three stretches of surviving wall. Having lived, as he had, for more than three hundred years, Alan had already seen many ancient things - and besides, the city walls were locked up after dark for reasons of health and safety.

Having finally made it up here, he found a narrow walkway guarded on its inner edge by only a simple metal rail. Undeterred, he sprinted along it as best he could, hampered by a knee he'd first knackered in 1873 and which hadn't been quite the same since. After several seconds, he reached a ninety degree bend. He skidded round it, and set off once more. To his left, just inside the walls, lay a large and magnificent garden, beyond which stood a building that, if not a palace, certainly qualified as an impressively grand house. It was at around this point, when Alan was entirely failing to appreciate the history and culture past which he was currently sprinting, that his right foot slipped on a patch of well-worn stone smoothed by eight hundred years of footfall, sending him tumbling over the guardrail.

It could be said that allowing continued public access to a narrow stone walkway set above a twenty foot drop guarded only by a relatively low metal railing represented a rare triumph for common sense and history against the apparently unstoppable juggernaut that is the modern health, safety, and liability culture. On another occasion, one in which he wasn't diving face first towards a gravel path some twenty feet below him, Alan might have agreed with that proposition.

This wasn't that occasion.

Of all the rules that Alan was supposed to obey, one stood head and shoulders above the rest. Public use of vampiric powers was strictly prohibited. It was bad enough that Alan had twice used his inhuman strength in the last five minutes; to use further powers would risk the most serious censure. But this had to be balanced against another consideration, that consideration being that Alan was currently accelerating towards the aforementioned gravel path at a rate of nine point eight metres per second squared, with the part of his body first scheduled to make contact being a face that already looked like it had, at some point in the past, partaken of a gravel massage.

Alan transformed.

Rav was no athlete, but neither – it had become apparent – was Alan, and as the chase bore on he and Jess seemed to be gaining. The two of them skidded round a ninety degree bend in hot pursuit, the dog managing the task with considerably more grace than her human companion. Rav bounced off the wall, slipped, caught himself, overcompensated, drifted alarmingly towards the only semi-guarded edge, and then finally regained his equilibrium and set off after Jess – pushing himself forward in a fist-pumping, high-stepping sprint that had this been a scene in a film might well have been set in slow-motion to a strident orchestral soundtrack of the sort John Barry might have written had John Barry not now been dead.

A little way ahead, Alan managed to slip on nothing much in particular and launched himself forward off the walkway. For an instant he arced through the air, his body spread-eagled against a landscape of historic roofs beyond. And then he disappeared.

Rav reached the point where Alan had slipped, and skidded to a halt. The night was black, with just a crescent moon to cast its dim light upon proceedings. He looked across, and spotted something small and dark flapping away. It flew underneath a cast iron light set upon a wall in the garden below and for an instant its form was revealed. A bat. From beside Rav's feet, a confused and protesting whine emerged from Jess's closed mouth.

A little while later, the Professor came shambling up, his breathing hard enough to make it clear that he wouldn't be speaking for at least a few seconds. "Too late," Rav wheezed at the older man, still pretty out of breath himself. "He just turned into a bat and flew away. Chase's over."

"Chase?" managed the Professor between coughs.

"Yeah. We're not chasing anyone now."

"My dear Ravinder," said the Professor, pausing to take a long, deep breath. "I wasn't chasing anyone. I was being chased."

"What? Who by?"

The Professor pointed a finger back behind him. "By them."

Some yards away, a motley group of goths stumbled to a halt, amid a welter of coughs, splutters, and moans. Some collapsed down onto their haunches, others doubled over, using their walking canes for support. At least one tripped on his cloak and was only saved from tumbling over the edge by the quick intervention of a friend.

"Why were they chasing you?"

"They were in the bar. They appear to be associates of this Alan chap." The Professor looked deep into Rav's eyes, a haunted expression upon his face. "I think they're the ghosts of Victorian poets."

Rav pushed past the older man and took a few steps towards the assemblage of goths. "All right. Which of you pasty-faced wankers wants to tell me what the fuck's going on?"

White faces turned towards each other in terror, like a bunch of mimes trapped in an invisible box within which one of the occupants has farted. They let out a series of cries, groans, curses and shouts, scrambled to their feet, and set off back along the wall, heading away from Rav, the Professor, and Jess. Rav paused for a moment to express his displeasure to no one in particular, then headed back after them, ignoring the protesting aches and pains currently emerging from various portions of his legs and circulatory system. The goths sprinted along the wall with a degree of enthusiasm that in other circumstances he might have deemed admirable, tumbled down the gatehouse's inner staircase, and then split a dozen different ways when they reached street level.

Rav paused for a moment, trying to figure out which one to follow. It had to be another bloke, he realised; a man chasing a woman along a street at night is always going to look bad, and is practically asking for a have-a-go hero to, well, have a go. But which bloke? Pick one with a cloak, he realised. Much easier to follow through crowds. He spotted a bloke with a cloak running back down High Petergate and set off after him, Jess still keeping hard to his heels. Rav was getting seriously out of breath now, but he managed to point at the bloke and wheeze: "Go get him, Jess!"

The dog gave him a look that made it pretty clear that, while she might be happy to trot alongside him, this was very much a "you go, I follow" type situation. They chased the cloaked bloke past the Minister and along a meandering and vaguely medieval street and then – in the shadow of another gatehouse – they caught up with him.

Rav lunged forward, grabbed the cloak, and yanked hard. The goth's head snapped backwards, and he crashed down to the ground with somewhat more impact than Rav had intended. Having waited for Rav to do all the actual work, Jess then chose that moment to slip in and nip the goth's ankle. A passing couple on the opposite side of the street looked over, clearly concerned. Rav flashed them a reassuring smile, and shouted over. "It's okay, I'm a social worker. This guy's just escaped from a secure unit. And this is, erm, a specially trained mental healthcare dog."

The couple peered over, took in Rav's suit, and the goth's cloak, cane, and facepaint, and then nodded, relief clear upon their faces as they fully accepted Rav's explanation. Rav knelt down beside the goth. He looked to be in his late teens, slightly emaciated, and quite scared. Rav stared hard at the guy, giving him a few seconds to appreciate Rav's resolve, then spoke, aiming for a calm measured tone. "What's your name?"

"Lord Johann Cruz de Lacy," the goth said, in an exaggerated, upper-class drawl.

"What's your actual name?"

The boy's bravado disappeared, and when he spoke next it was in an accent more genuine, though still undeniably posh. "George. George Parker."

Rav nodded. He spotted the Professor approaching, so he waited a few seconds for the older man to come staggering up to them and then collapse in a wheezing heap, before speaking again. "Okay, George. Here's how it's going to be. We're going to go off somewhere where we can have a chat, and you're going to tell us all about how you came to be hanging around with a vampire."

Chapter Six

Rav blew a little on his latte, placed his notebook in front of him on the table, then turned his attention back to the already very nervous George. "Okay, let's get started."

"Who are you?" George asked. "Police?"

"Do we look like police?"

"Well, no–"

"And do police hunt vampires?"

"I suppose not."

"We're not police. That's all you need to know. You got any ID?"

George nodded tearfully, then reached into his coat and pulled out a leather wallet. Rav leafed quickly through its contents, not quite sure what he was looking for. Inside was a small amount of cash, some receipts and various forms of ID – credit card, student ID, driving licence – in the name of George Parker. The driving licence gave an address in Canterbury. He wrote it down in his notebook, underneath the doodle he'd drawn on the train. There was a different address on the student ID. He read it out. "Janet Baker Court?"

"That's the halls of residence where I live during term-time."

The Professor leaned forward. "I suspect it's named after Dame Janet Baker, the opera singer."

"Right. Thank you." Rav turned back to George. "How do you know Alan?"

"He came along to one of our sessions."

"Sessions?"

"Of the Coven. For the game."

"Game?"

George shifted awkwardly, and looked down at the table. "We're all members of a vampire LARP."

"What exactly is a LARP?"

"It's a Live Action Role Playing game."

"A roleplaying game?" A worrying thought began to occur to Rav.

"It's nothing sexual!" George blurted out, obviously aware of exactly which thought Rav was beginning to have. "We just hire a room above the bar where you met Alan tonight and get together, and..."

"And?"

"Well, we pretend to be vampires, basically." George's shoulders slumped so much that Rav would have felt sorry for him, were he not still highly upset about having been thrown the length of a room.

"You pretend to be vampires?"

"Yeah, it's like acting, except it's a game. It's a kind of freeform interactive storytelling. And it's not stupid, there are rules and everything." George sat up straight and crossed his arms across his chest. "Like, if I do this, it means I'm invisible."

Rav leaned forward, and spoke his next words quite carefully. "But I can still see you."

"Yeah. But you're supposed to pretend you can't see me."

"Really." Rav decided he needed to get this interrogation back on track. He took a sip of his latte, opened his packet of crisps, shoved a big handful of its contents into his mouth, munched, crunched and swallowed, and then leaned back in his chair. "Okay. So Alan came along to one of your sessions."

"Yeah, he said he wanted to join the game, so we created a character for him-"

"A character?"

"It's like a part in a play, or a role in the script, except there's no script, just a role. You know, a name, a description, and a list of abilities. Anyhow, after that, Alan came along every week."

"But... Didn't you wonder why he looked so, well, hideous?"

George shrugged. "We just thought he wanted to play an old-school vampire and was really good with makeup."

"And these were the only times you ever met him?"

"Yes."

"Did you ever meet anyone else, any friends of his?"

"No. We never did anything with him outside the game. He stayed in character the whole time."

"So you never went to his house? You never talked about his life outside the game?"

George was practically crying now, so much so that Rav was wondering if he perhaps should have bought the boy the hot chocolate he'd asked for. "No. I don't know anything about him, except that he calls himself Alan, he looks like that, and he used to come to our game. I didn't know anything about him being, well..."

"Different?"

"Yeah, different. I didn't know anything about that until tonight. I swear."

Rav thought for a moment. His gut feeling was that George was telling the truth when he said he knew nothing. He nodded, then reached into his wallet, pulled out one of his WKPDA business cards, and threw it onto the table in front of his erstwhile interviewee. "That's got my number on it. If you think of anything else, or if Alan tries to contact you, give me a ring. I think we're done here. You can go." George scuttled away, clearly not needing to be told twice.

"So what now, Ravinder?" the Professor asked.

"Don't know. Seems like Alan has the advantage over us."

"In what way?"

"I've been using my West Kensington PDA account on the Zone to contact him, and it links back to our website. So he knows my full name and what I look like, while all I know about him is that he goes by the name of Alan and looks like the back end of a crashed bus."

"I see." The older man thought for a moment, then smiled. "But, in return, we have learned one thing."

"Which is?"

The older man reached down to stroke Jess on the top of her head. "Jess can smell vampires."

"True. Now we just need to train her to make like a pointer when she smells one, rather than going for its throat." Rav stood up, his legs quite stiff. "Come on. Let's get back to the hotel. Isn't much else we're going to get done tonight."

When Rav had woken the next morning, it had been from a sleep made troubled by nightmares featuring goths and vampires, and broken by the Professor's frequent toilet visits. Personally, he'd have been more than happy to spend the day in bed before catching the evening train home. However, during the previous night's walk back to the hotel he'd promised the Professor a chance to do some sight-seeing; and, as the Professor had pointed out, he was legally required to accompany the older man at all times.

It was as a result of this rash promise that he now found himself sampling the delights of York's Jorvik Viking Experience. This was the third stop on the Professor's self-organised tour, and the limited supplies of enthusiasm Rav had begun the day with had long since run out. It wasn't that he had no interest in either history or culture, but he did rather prefer to enjoy such delights in bite-sized morsels, as a plate of hors d'oeuvres rather than the twelve inch long, culture filled baguette the Professor was currently force-feeding him. Tickets bought, and souvenir programmes politely, but firmly, declined, the two of them emerged into a large, slightly gloomy room. Beneath their feet was a glass floor, underneath which were displayed various excavations, complete with artefacts. Arrayed around them were the inevitable glass display cases flanked by tablet-like information slabs.

Rav quickly found himself drifting ahead of the Professor, largely because the Professor was insisting on reading every sign and examining every displayed object, and Rav, largely, wasn't. Periodically, a little voice inside him suggested he think about the case. But what, exactly, should he be thinking about? Alan was gone, and they'd got pretty much no leads on him save a bunch of goth gamers whose knowledge likely amounted to something between zilch and damn all. And what if the pasty-faced freaks did turn out to know something? What could Rav do about it? It wasn't like he had a warrant card, a dimly lit interrogation room, and the legal option of punching someone in the face and then charging them with assaulting his fist.

At some point during his slow, wandering daydream, Rav bounced into a slim figure wearing a grey hoodie. He muttered an embarrassed apology, but then felt a surprisingly firm hand gripping his arm. "Keep walking," the figure told him. The voice was female, calm, and possessed of an accent neutral to the point of blandness. The woman led him to the corridor at the far end of the room, where they joined a queue of people.

The woman released her grip on Rav's arm, but said nothing, instead simply staring straight ahead. It occurred to Rav that maybe he could say something, but that thought came unaccompanied by any suggestions of what he might actually talk about. Should he resist? He could walk away right now, call out to one of the staff, but say what? That a woman wearing a hoodie had taken him by the arm? And what if she was with Alan? What if she was a vampire herself? It was daylight, true, but perhaps the hoodie was to shield her from the sun's rays? On top of all this, he now realised he really needed to go for a piss, but he suspected that whatever her agenda was, it wouldn't include any toilet breaks. Then a genuinely panicky thought occurred to him – the Professor!

He turned his head, slowly so as not to alarm anyone who might be in the mood to become alarmed. The Professor was fine, oblivious in fact, still working his way along the first set of display cases. For want of anything better to do, Rav stayed in the queue. A couple of minutes later, each of which had passed in silence, Rav and the mystery woman reached the front of the line, where a uniformed attendant motioned them to wait a moment. A few seconds later, a sleek grey vehicle glided out of the opening to their left. It was like something from a fairground ride, or one of those 1970s science-fiction movies where the men all wore jumpsuits, the women all wore mini-dresses, and improbably sophisticated public transportation systems operated at even more improbable levels of efficiency and reliability.

The vehicle had a single bench seat and no wheels, hanging instead from an overhead rail, leaving a clear six inches of gap between it and the floor. The woman scooted on board, sliding up to the far end of the bench seat, her hooded head staring straight forward all the while. Rav clamped down a momentary bout of panic and slid in alongside her. The attendant pulled a tubular metal safety restraint over them, of the sort that Rav never recalled seeing in 1970s science-fiction movies, and the car slid smoothly forward, into the tunnel mouth, and round a bend. In front of the seat was an array of buttons, each with a national flag on it. The woman leaned forward and pressed the Union Jack button. "Just so we can't be overheard."

Rav gave her a confused nod. A voice, of the modulated posh sort employed by struggling actors trying a tad too hard on voiceover jobs, emerged from speakers to either side of them. It started saying something about a riverbank, but Rav didn't catch it, because the woman was speaking again.

"You've been busy." It was said as a statement rather than as a question but ended with a sharp silence that seemed intended to solicit a reply.

"Well, yeah, we did the Yorkshire Museum and then the Richard III and then-"

"I'm not talking about the museums."

"Right."

The car was passing a section of river diorama now, animatronic fisherman fishing while the voiceover, unsurprisingly, spoke about fish. The car rotated through ninety degrees to give them a better view. Rav was already finding events hard to follow; being in a vehicle that was currently facing in one direction while moving in another wasn't making things any easier. "Who are you?" he asked. He turned to look at her, but she was still staring straight ahead, her face completely hidden behind her fleece hood.

"You can call me Reece."

"Is that your name?"

"Well, it's a name. And one I'll answer to."

"Okay. Erm, why are we here?"

She paused for a moment before replying, allowing the car's speakers to inform Rav that they were currently passing an antler worker, and that antler was a versatile material often used to make combs. "We need to talk about Alan."

"What about him?"

"You have worked out that he's a vampire, yes?"

"Erm, yeah. You knew that?"

"Of course. Alan and his friends and Alan's little goth minions have been a concern of mine for some time now. But we're not here to talk about me. We're here to talk about Alan, and you."

The car again spun round on its axis, this time to display an animatronic woodworker carving a cup on a lathe. As such displays went, it did strike Rav as moderately impressive, in that while there was no possibility of an onlooker mistaking it for an actual human being, it did nonetheless give the impression of having been constructed by an army of workers in an expensive Hollywood workshop, rather than being something knocked up by a bloke called Barry in a lockup on the Old Kent Road, as he'd found was so often the case with British tourist attractions. "I spotted the question you asked on The Zone," she told Rav. "I've got an account there; although, unlike you, I took the precaution of using a false name. I suspected Alan might reply, and when I realised you were travelling to York, it was obvious that it was to meet him."

"How did you know I was travelling to York?"

"You tweeted that you'd just bought two tickets for the Saturday one o'clock train to York through Mega Cheap Tickets dot com."

"No, I didn't!"

She shook her head and sighed. "You really do need to uncheck all those already checked checkboxes when booking tickets through dubious third-party sites. And don't just click yes to everything."

"Thank you. I'll bear that in mind." This wasn't how this sort of thing went down in films. "Aren't you supposed to be smoking or something?"

"I'm trying to give up bad clichés."

The car slid slowly into the interior of a Viking house, flying smoothly over the rough dirt floor, but then stopped abruptly. After a few seconds, a different voice cut in over the car's speakers. "Sorry, folks. We seem to be having some kind of technical problem. Please stay in the cars while we restart the system."

"I thought we might need some extra time to chat," said the woman.

"You did this?"

She shrugged. "Not so much did, as arranged. But let's get back to Alan. I saw how your meeting went. It was somewhat brief."

"Yeah. Hang on – you were at the meeting?"

"Yes."

"How did you know where it was?"

"I suppose I could be all mysterious here, but the rather simpler truth is that I knew from your tweet which train you were on, and I knew from your website what you looked like, so I simply waited for you to arrive, followed you while you walked to your a hotel, and then followed you from there to the bar."

"But weren't you scared I might spot you following us?"

Her reply was crushing in its immediacy. "No." She paused for a moment, and then continued. "If you survive all this, you perhaps should make some attempt to gain a little expertise in the pursuit you claim as your profession. This is a dangerous world. It's true the truth is out there, but the truth does indeed often hurt, sometimes in a way that proves terminal."

"I'll make a note," said Rav, a reply that was neither witty nor incisive but was about the best his currently disintegrating ego could come up with.

"What were your plans regarding Alan? I presume you do have plans, beyond visiting museums?" It was quite freaky the way her voice never changed tone, always calm, always measured.

"I was kind of taking a step back to evaluate my options."

She sighed, the first sign of emotion she'd displayed in the five minutes Rav had known her. "And having taken a step back, what options do you see?"

This was starting to feel like being back at school, with her as the frosty teacher, whose knickers Rav didn't even dare dream of getting into, and him as the not quite rebellious schoolboy. "There was this goth kid, George, one of Alan's minions, who we caught last night. I could go back to him, get some details of some of the other goths, and, you know?"

"You know... what?"

"Well, like, lean on them."

She tutted. He suspected he wasn't currently up for a gold star. "Anything else?"

"Send another message to Alan, arranging another meeting?"

"You realise that there would be only one reason why he would say yes to such a thing, and that would be to kill you?"

"Yeah, that's a good point." They sat, saying nothing, the silence broken only by the car's now looping commentary system launching into its ninth attempt to tell them about the house they were parked inside. Finally, something within Rav snapped. "Look, if you're so sodding clever, what the fuck am I supposed to do?"

"What do you know about Whitby?"

As conversational changes of tack went, this was something of a boomerang job, but answering it seemed the best option. "Yorkshire seaside resort. Was the place Dracula arrived in Bram Stoker's novel." He stopped. "You're telling me I'm supposed to go to Whitby because it appeared in a work of fiction written a hundred and something years ago?"

"No, Mr Shah. You're supposed to go to Whitby because there's a Vampire convention being held there next weekend. I believe Alan and his friends are planning on attending it, in search of new minions."

"Oh, right."

She turned towards him, only slightly, but enough for him to see just a suggestion of face beneath the hood. "Good hunting, Mr Shah. I might contact you again, should I think you need it." She reached down to grab the metal safety bar, flipped it up, then vaulted out of the car in one smooth and very athletic move, landing like a cat on the house's dirt floor. She began to walk away.

"But what if I need to contact you?" Rav shouted at her departing back.

She didn't turn. "You can't." She ducked out of the house's front entrance and disappeared behind a display of leather goods. The car's electric motors whined abruptly into action, the car gliding smoothly out of the house and round a bend before swivelling to show an arguing animatronic couple.

All his life Rav had dreamed of appearing in a real-life movie, and now it seemed like he was. There was just one slight snag. He wasn't quite sure that it was a movie in which he was the star.

Chapter Seven

Again, the next week passed slowly, allowing doubts to emerge from the cracks in Rav's confidence and test his resolve. He was spending money he didn't really have, to follow a lead that wasn't really a lead, on a case that wasn't really a case. Logic, common sense, and apathy: all were telling him to leave it, give it up, walk away. But deep down, a stubborn compulsion endured. This might be a fool's errand, but when set against the boring, drab mediocrity that would be his life were he to walk away, it was a path he had to follow, fool's errand or not, doubts or no doubts. He'd made up his mind. The WKPDA's Lead Investigation Unit was going to Whitby.

A difficult journey might have tested that resolve. But thankfully, the journey to York via Kings Cross went smoothly, aided as it was by the lessons he'd learned the previous week. (Regular toilet breaks, watch out for outstretched tails, and have a good supply of newspapers and puzzle books to hand).

Which just left just the final leg of their journey.

Whitby's position in a post-Beeching world was such that the quickest, non-car method of reaching it culminated in a rather long journey by bus. This wasn't necessarily a bad thing. In Rav's experience, the Professor's love of buses was such that a journey on one would keep his erratically misfiring mind occupied for a good hour at least. Unfortunately, the bus on which they were travelling the forty-seven miles between York and Whitby had taken that good hour and entirely failed to get to Whitby before it ended. At about sixty-three minutes into the journey, Rav was aroused from the Yorkshire guidebook he'd been studying by the sound of the Professor thinking aloud.

"So we're going to Whitby for no reason other than said action being the expressed wish of this mysterious Miss Reece?"

This wasn't a conversation Rav particularly wanted to have, given that he had enough doubts of his own. "That's about it."

"But having expressed that wish, she failed to give you any particular idea of what we should do when we get there, beyond look for vampires?"

"Yep."

"Or vampire pigs?"

"Them too."

The Professor considered this for a little while before speaking. "Have you considered the possibility that you might be fulfilling the role of a tethered goat?"

Rav gave up on trying to read the guide-book. "Tethered what?"

"Goat, Ravinder. Tethered goat. As in a goat left tethered by a hunter to attract the hunter's prey."

"Like the one that got eaten by the T-Rex in Jurassic Park?"

"Well, that is perhaps the most celebrated example of the analogy in contemporary popular culture. But it's a concept that has its roots in antiquity. A hunter hunting a dangerous predator, a mountain lion perhaps, would leave a goat tethered in an inviting location and then retreat to a nearby hiding place. When the lion attacked the goat, the hunter would pounce."

Rav gave the Professor a very hard stare. "I'm not a tethered goat."

The Professor paused just long enough for Rav to go back to his book, and then resumed speaking. "I fear you may be failing to see the bigger picture. Consider this. There are three parties involved in this little affair. Yourself, Alan, and Miss Reece. One of you is the hunter, sheltering behind a rock with a rifle placed against your shoulder. One of you is the mountain lion, on the prowl for prey. And one of you is the goat, tethered to a stake and eating grass. If you are not the goat, then which of the hunter and the lion are you? And which of Alan and Miss Reece is the goat?"

"Why does anyone have to be the sodding goat? Why can't we all be bloody lions!" Rav realised that he'd been speaking just a tad too loudly, and so devoted a few seconds to giving reassuring smiles to the several shocked faces staring back at him.

The Professor shook his head. "If you say so, Ravinder. If you say so."

Given a choice, Alan wouldn't have chosen to spend the whole of Saturday cooped up in a shabby twin-bed room in a cheap hotel in Whitby. And again, if given a choice, he wouldn't have chosen to spend any amount of time cooped up with Nicolae. But he'd not been given a choice. He had orders; orders he was required to follow. That morning, in the early hours, Nicolae had picked him up in his prized second-hand 2009 Skoda Octavia and had driven them both to Whitby, arriving at the hotel safely before sunrise.

Once there, Alan would rather have taken the chance to catch up with his sleep, or perhaps get out his tablet and make yet another attempt – subject to being able to find someone else's insecure Wi-Fi connection – to contact Tabitha. It was getting on three weeks now since her last email, and what had been worry and concern was starting to turn to outright fear. But Nicolae had been too excited to sleep, and had instead insisted on them watching Die Hards I to IV – acknowledged classics, according to his fellow vampire – on the hotel room's cheap DVD player.

Now, after several hours of watching Bruce Willis carve his way through assorted European bad guys, it was nearly sunset. Nearly time for them to do that which they'd come here to do. Alan felt sick. Tabitha. Nicolae. This. Now.

Nicolae was packing a backpack. He put a last item in, adjusted the position of some of the contents, zipped it closed, and then looked up. "Are you still sulking, Alin?" he asked in their Rumanian tongue, using the native form of Alan's name. "Still pissed off that I wouldn't let you watch the Sound of Music?"

Once, a few hundred years ago, Nicolae had stood before Alan on a rocky Transylvanian hillside, lit only by a distant moon, and promised him immortality. It had been an empty and insincere promise, fuelled by a vampiric blood lust that Alan had not then understood and built upon a structure of half-truths braced with outright lies. But in the end, when push came to shove, as it so often did, Nicolae's words had contained more truths than lies. For while the life that Alan had valued had ended that night, the half-life that had replaced it endured still.

Later, much later, only several years ago in fact, Nicolae had stood on that same rocky hillside and made a further series of promises, not only to Alan, but to his other vampiric "children". He talked of something called the "European Union", which their land was apparently entering, and of the riches they could make by moving to the fabled realm of England. He spoke of glittering trains full of people who dripped wealth, where a man with a hand-written sign could make hundreds of dollars a day. He spoke of houses, empty, there for the taking. He spoke of a government that would hand out huge sums of money, week after week, to anyone who agreed to not work.

It hadn't taken Alan long to realise that Nicolae had been full of bullshit; as always, the "truths" he'd spouted that night had been the same old mixture of half-truths and lies. But by then it was too late. He was a migrant, a stranger in a strange land, marked now not only by the hideousness of his face, but by the foreignness of his accent and his inability to speak the native tongue. In Romania, he'd been hated for being a cursed, evil abomination, and had been forced to live his life in hiding, forever concealing his true form. In England, concealing his form was not enough. Its inhabitants didn't need to know he was a vampire in order for them to hate him. Simply being from Romania was enough.

Nicolae was still staring at him. "Come on, Alin. We need to go." He smiled. "The time for experiments is over. It's time to start the

Operational Phase."

Just what kind of establishment might host a convention for vampires had been a source of some worry for the Professor. But those concerns were, he now realised, misplaced. Far from being hosted in a seedy or sordid location, the convention's home turned out to be Whitby's Regal Hotel. This was a reassuringly handsome Victorian structure, which was currently bearing the large "Dracucon 5" banner that hung from its frontage with much the same resigned air that a middle-aged bride wears the "Bride" sash during the hen night her married and equally middle-aged friends have insisted upon.

Unlike more ostentatious purveyors of accommodation in wealthier localities, the Regal was not posh enough to merit a Dickensian-dressed doorman standing outside. It did, however, have an off-duty porter standing to one side of the doorway, enjoying an off-duty smoke, who appeared to be fulfilling much the same function, albeit with considerably less class.

The porter took a last drag on his cigarette, threw the butt away to one side, then took a long, hard look at Jess. "No dogs allowed," he said, pointing at the small sign attached to one side of the doorway.

The Professor didn't like confrontation at the best of times, certainly not with someone in possession of both a suit and a name badge, as this individual was. He took Rav aside and whispered in his ear. "Perhaps we'd better take Jess back to the guesthouse?"

Rav shook his head. "No. We need her in there to sniff out any vampires."

"But you heard what he said. Dogs aren't allowed in the hotel."

Rav gave him a tight smile. "It's okay. It's not a problem." The younger man turned back to the porter and motioned him to wait one moment, then took off his backpack and began to root around inside it. He pushed various items first this way and then that, clearly searching for something. Finally, he let out an exclamation and pulled something from its interior. When unfolded, the something proved to be a square of green fabric with white text printed upon it. Various buckle-equipped straps hung from its edges. Rav straightened out the straps, then started attaching it to Jess. It was, the Professor realised, a dog coat of some kind. Dog coat attached, Rav advanced up the steps towards the waiting doorman, Jess beside him on the lead.

"You deaf?" the porter asked him. "I said no dogs."

Rav pointed down at Jess. "She's an assistance dog."

The man looked closely at Rav. "But you ain't blind."

"I didn't say she was a guide dog. I said she was an assistance dog." Rav pointed down at the dog coat. "I've got anger management issues. She's trained to help me keep calm."

The porter bent down to examine the dog coat, as did the Professor. "PAWS 4 PAUSE ASSISTANCE DOG" said the main caption, written in large, blocky sans-serif capitals. Underneath that, in a smaller, flowing script font, were the words, "Helping those suffering from anger-management issues". Beside the text was a logo. Drawn in simple strokes of white upon green, it depicted a clenched human fist with a dog's paw lain, in a restraining fashion, upon the fist's wrist.

The porter considered this for a moment, then straightened up and pointed at the sign. "It says no dogs except guide dogs. Assistance dogs don't count."

"That's a pretty shitty attitude to take," Rav said, with just a hint of menace underlying his words. "Not very disabled friendly, is it?" He clenched his fists and began to count slowly upwards from one, leaving an uncomfortable pause between each number, each pause accompanied by a twitch.

The porter took a step back, eyes flickering nervously from side to side, clearly considering the wisdom of pissing off a bloke who was apparently such a hair-trigger psycho that he'd been given a dog specially trained to keep him from losing it. Eventually he sighed, and took a step to the side. "Fine, whatever. Go in."

Having got into the hotel's lobby, admission to the convention itself proved simple, requiring only the joining of a queue followed by the handing over of two crisp twenty pound notes – for which they received in return laminated badges to hang round their necks, a couple of convention programmes, and a pair of what the two women behind the desk termed "goodie bags", which turned out to be carrier bags containing several free books and a bunch of fliers.

Unlike the porter, the two women behind the registration desk appeared much more accepting of Jess's status as an assistance dog. Whether this was due to a more open and less judgemental attitude, or simply to being quicker on the uptake, Rav didn't know. But after a quick consultation with a guy who was apparently the convention director, a third laminated badge was produced and clipped onto her collar. Now, all badged up, they continued on past the registration desk and into the open lobby area beyond.

"This looks interesting," said the Professor.

Rav turned his attention away from his perusal of the lobby's inhabitants. "What looks interesting?"

The Professor was studying the programme. "At six o'clock there's a talk on the influence of local Yorkshire folklore upon the work of Bram Stoker." He looked at his watch. "That's in five minutes. Apparently, he stayed in this very hotel whilst writing the novel."

"Fascinating. But we're here to find vampires."

"Ah, yes. True." The older man thought for a moment. "And how do we do that?"

"I don't know. Wander around. Wait until Jess goes psycho. Then see if it's because of a cat, a skateboarder, or some bloke who looks like a monster."

"But could we not take in some talks while we're wandering around? We don't want to stand out, and the best way to blend in is to look like we've come to enjoy the convention, is it not?"

"Okay, fine. Lead on!"

Rav managed to get almost twenty minutes into the talk before the waves of ever-increasing boredom crashing over the breakwater of his soul triggered a decision to leave. To be fair, that probably said more about him than the talk, which appeared to be both well-written and well-presented, receiving from those in the audience revelatory nods and appreciative chuckles in equal measure.

The problem was quite simply that Rav didn't give a shit about either Bram Stoker, his novel, or local Whitby folklore, with the result that his intellect was at about the same level of arousal as a gay man's libido in a lap-dancing club. He whispered into the Professor's ear. "I'm just going to circulate. I'll see you around."

The Professor waved a vague hand, his attention never once leaving the speaker at the front of the room. Rav woke Jess with a gentle prod. "Come on girl," he whispered. "Let's go find some vampires."

Chapter Eight

Nicolae swept majestically up the Regal's stairs and into its lobby, striding like the prince he so frequently claimed to be. Alan followed in his wake. A girl looked up at them, and smiled. "Awesome makeup, guys. Must have taken you ages."

People. So many people. And all of them smiling at him, nodding approval. To a former human being as starved of human contact as Alan was, it was almost overwhelming. He'd always had Nicolae, of course. Visiting every few days, ostensibly there to check on his welfare, but in reality appearing only in order to bully, belittle, and boast. What Alan had wasn't a life, and hadn't been for a very long time. He knew that. Then Nicolae's touch pulled his mind out of its daydreaming. "Come on, Alin. The prey is here. We need to go hunting."

Rav was learning that finding vampires was easier said than done. This wasn't particularly surprising. A large number of the convention's attendees were dressed in some form of costume, and many of those who weren't were attired in a manner that could be deemed "eccentric". (It would have been easy for Rav to categorise the convention's inhabitants as "weird". But he didn't, partly because he wasn't a judgemental kind of guy, and partly because working as a front-line mental health social worker in a London borough gives one a deeper appreciation of what truly counts as weird.)

As a result, he'd been forced to build his vampire hunting strategy entirely around Jess, and while she'd thus far given some of the strangely costumed individuals some searching looks, she hadn't reacted in the way she'd reacted to Alan. His continuing wanderings around the hotel eventually took him into some sort of trade hall, whose cavernous interior was filled with a variety of stands selling books, DVDs, costumes, jewellery, and general assorted crap. A girl behind a jewellery stand smiled at him, saw Jess trotting at his heels, appeared to spend a moment thinking, and then abruptly stopped smiling.

Frankly, Rav found that a little strange.

He walked over to her desk and casually examined a few items of jewellery. "Hi!" he said, giving her his best come to bed smile. (In actual use, it hadn't ever smiled a woman into bed, but it equally hadn't smiled one out of it, either).

"Erm, hi," she replied. She picked nervously at the sleeve of her dress and stared off into the distance.

This was strange, spooky, and weird all wrapped up in one. "Are you okay?" he asked the girl.

"Yeah. Yeah. I'm fine."

"Only, you seem a little jumpy."

She paused for a moment, and then pointed at something behind him. He turned. Mounted on the wall was a large LCD monitor, upon which was displayed a screen of scrolling computer text. Rav scanned down, and realised that it was a filtered feed of Twitter posts about the convention.

@Joey37: Having gr8 time at #dracucon.

Nope.

@FangsAndFings: Wish I was at #dracucon.

Nope.

@Redblackdead: Awesome! RT @jonny17p: apparently the bloke with the green coat dogs a registered psycho. Dogs trained to stop him going nutso! #dracucon

Yeah. That would be it.

@SpawnOfLucifer: Wowzer! RT @jonny17p: apparently the bloke with the green coat dogs a registered psycho. Dogs trained to stop him going nutso! #dracucon

And that one.

@Lucy567: @jonny17p: He's not a psycho. He's a man facing very difficult issues and you should be more understanding! #dracucon

That one too.

@jonny17p: apparently the bloke with the green coat dogs a registered psycho. Dogs trained to stop him going nutso! #dracucon

And that one. Thank you jonny17p, Rav thought. Whoever the hell you are. As Rav stared at the screen, the data on it scrolled down to reveal a new tweet.

@PeteTheGeek: shit that psycho nutter dog guys just arrived in the trade hall! #dracucon #ohshitohshitohshit

Rav found himself feeling a strong urge to turn to the assembled inhabitants of the trade hall and scream at the top of his lungs, "Which one of you bastards is Pete the Geek?" Luckily, that lizard brain urge had riding alongside it the equally strong realisation that such a reaction might not be the best way to counter the tweets now shooting through the tweetosphere. And he couldn't even complain. He was the one who'd bought the coat off some psychopath on eBay who'd managed to end up with two of them. And it was him who'd put it on Jess to get her in here. He turned to the girl on the jewellery stall and dialled his smile's level down from the now clearly inappropriate "hi there, gorgeous!" to a hopefully more appropriate "good evening".

"Yes, now, erm. I think people have slightly misunderstood what Jess is." He threw in a bit of arm-waving in an effort to look sincere.

"Jess?"

"My dog." He pointed down, then realised that he was pointing at an empty space. He looked around. No dog. Dammit. Why'd he taken the lead off? And where the hell had she got to?

While Rav had been busy spraying pheromones at the female human behind the table, Jess had not been idle. She'd sniffed at each table leg in turn, had an experimental nibble at the sheet that hung between them, and then wandered off to have a sniff across the stretch of carpet the rows of tables flanked. And then she smelt it. That smell. The smell that had been keeping her awake at night. The smell that had caused her to try to rip out the throat of the thing that looked like a human being but wasn't.

Jess wasn't big on self-awareness, but that didn't make her stupid. She might not have been capable of explaining the relationship between cause and effect, nor even of identifying those two aspects of the universe, but she was fully capable of learning from her experiences. The last time she'd smelled that smell she'd ended up flying across the room and enduring a rather painful landing. Whatever that thing was, it was clearly a lot higher up the food chain than she was. This was something to stalk, not attack.

She sniffed again. Overlain among that scent of her nightmares was another smell, similar, and similarly wrong, but different. There were two of the beasts. And they'd been here just recently. She set off, slowly and warily, snout down to follow the trail upon the carpet, eyes hard upward to scan for danger ahead.

It seemed to Alan that they were walking round in circles; probably because they were, he realised. Nicolae was pointing, at something ahead of them. "Let's double back into the trade hall. I've just seen a girl go in there. She looks–" He paused, and then smiled. "Weak. And ready."

Fresh meat. Alan had long ago realised that this was all human beings were to Nicolae. Fresh human meat to provide fresh human blood. And, if he were honest, that was largely what they were to Alan himself, also. It's said of a human being that they can typically survive three minutes without air, three days without water and three weeks without food. A vampire is not of this world and thus needs none of those three substances. Oxygen, water and food are for those beings still alive, and a vampire is very much dead. A vampire wants for only one thing. Blood. It is more than lust; more than a compulsion. When Alan first became a vampire, he and Nicolae had feasted regularly on human blood. Alan would always stop himself, go so far and no further, halting at the point where his victims, weak and traumatised as they were, could still recover. But Nicolae had never possessed such a conscience. He would drink deep, until his victim was nothing more than a bloodless husk to be casually tossed aside.

As times changed, Nicolae had adapted, taking an often unhappy and unwilling Alan with him. With the coming of communism, they'd found their way into the feared Securitate, communist Romania's secret police, the Pretorian Guard of the dictator Ceausescu. Once again, they'd feasted upon the dregs of society, the weak and the powerless. But then in 1989, a revolution came, and from then on it was Alan and Nicolae who found themselves on the margins of society, scavenging and hiding.

Since then, they'd been forced to subsist almost entirely on animal blood. Sometimes they got by on pig, cow, or sheep blood purchased from slaughterhouse cleaners on the take. Sometimes, crazed with blood-hunger, they were forced to hunt rats in empty houses, or dodge perverts in the park while in pursuit of squirrels. But whichever animal the blood came from, and from whatever the source, it was never the same. Where human blood slipped down the throat like freshly harvested honey and fired up the soul like the finest of wines, animal blood merely nourished the flesh without ever quite sating the hunger.

Now though, here, this Saturday night in Whitby, they would feast once more on human blood, taking a risk Alan had not dared take in more than seven years. Because now it was about more than hunger. Now it was about the plan. The project. Their glittering, glorious, sparkling future. Nicolae was already striding away, through a set of double-doors. Alan hurried after him, his doubts following.

Of all the forces that drive a human being, none is more powerful than embarrassment. Fear, greed, anger, love; both vices and virtues kneel in tribute before the absolute, inconceivable awfulness of a truly embarrassing moment. It's not courage that drives men to climb out of a trench and into a hail of machine-gun fire; it's the shame caused by even the mere thought of saying, "Actually, I think I'll stay here in the trench, if it's all okay with you chaps?"

Airline co-pilots have watched silently as their commanding officers flew both they and their hundreds of passengers to certain death, rendered mute by the social awkwardness of correcting a superior. Whenever a bridge collapses, a spaceship explodes, an invasion fails, or a government IT system on which thirty billion pounds has been spent proves to be only marginally more useful than two chimpanzees and an abacus, the failure will inevitably be revealed to have become apparent long before, but with everyone involved feeling unable to point it out.

And it was embarrassment that was hindering Rav's attempts to find his wandering dog. Under normal circumstances – such as when in the middle of a large and empty field – getting your dog to return to you is simple. You simply shout its name very loudly, and it returns. Of course, things are not so simple when the location in which you've mislaid your hound is a crowded room, full of strangers, a significant number of whom already think you're a lunatic. In such circumstances, just raising one's voice, let alone shouting, would require self-assurance and confidence at levels typically found only in full-blown narcissists. With shouting Jess's name at the top of his lungs being an option unavailable to him, Rav was forced instead to make his way slowly round the room hissing her name, whilst bending down to look under each table. Of course, this in itself was an activity that made him look somewhat strange, resulting in further whispering and shaking of heads.

No Jess. He straightened up, looked back around the room, and saw yet another tweet appear on the large screen.

> @PeteTheGeek: oh shit now hes lost his dog! If he starts turning green, run! #dracucon

He took a further look around the room, looking at the people this time, wondering which one was Pete the Geek. Him, holding the phone over there, perhaps? Or the guy sitting behind a book-filled table conspicuously failing to make eye-contact with him? Or–

Alan.

Alan followed Nicolae through the open double doors that led to the trade hall, nodding at the convention staffer who sat on a chair beside the door. The large room was pretty much the same as it had been when they'd first walked through there, ten minutes previously.

People. Things. People masquerading as things. In contrast to himself and Nicolae, who were – he realised – things masquerading as people. Stalls. Slightly shabby carpet. Dusty chandelier. All was as it had been those ten minutes earlier, save for one addition, one new feature that the room had not then boasted: one Dr Ravinder Shah of the West

Kensington Paranormal Detective Agency.

Shah was standing on the other side of the room from them, framed by two racks of books, a look of dumb surprise hanging slack upon his face. Alan stared back at him, horribly aware that he too most likely wore a similar look. Why was Shah here? How much did he know? Out of the half-watched corner of his eye he saw Nicolae pause, then turn, swaggering as always. "Alin, she's over– what is it?"

Alan said nothing, which only forced Nicolae to follow his gaze, and spot the man, Shah, who was staring back. "Who is he?" Nicolae hissed. "Why is he staring at us?"

Thought-deficient words bounced around Alan's brain, random, disconnected, useless. What should he say? What could he say? Nicolae was very close now, close enough that Alan could see the saliva glistening on his fangs. He spoke with the calm voice he'd always used when torturing dissidents. "Alin. What have you done?"

"I haven't done anything?" Alan stuttered out. "He's, erm–"

"Yes?"

"He's a vampire hunter." Truth upon guess upon desperate bullshit. The words tumbled out, almost unbidden by any conscious thought of Alan's.

"A vampire hunter?"

"I've read about him. On the net. He's a doctor, Dr Ravinder Shah. I was supposed to monitor that sort of thing, remember?"

Nicolae nodded. "You've done well, Alin."

"But what do we do now?"

"I shall carry on with the plan. The Operational Phase cannot be stopped. Meanwhile, I will entrust to you the task of dealing with this vampire hunter."

"What do you want me to do?"

Nicolae smiled. "Kill him. Feast upon his blood, then dump his carcass where only the fishes will find it."

Chapter Nine

All men, be they full of bravery or bravado, have their limits. There comes a point in a man's life when he reaches into his backpack of courage and finds that its tank is empty, its battery flat. To his horror and surprise – and frankly disappointment given that he had but recently begun to reach into his backpack of courage – Rav now found himself at just that point.

He watched transfixed as Alan talked to his clearly vampiric friend. Whatever language it was they might be speaking in, he couldn't lip-read it. But he didn't need to. Sometimes the way a person looks at another tells a story all of its own, and this long stare was telling a story so clear a man would have had to be both blind and stupid not to see it.

They were going to kill him. Not scare him. Not beat him up a bit. Not even maim him. Dead. Proper dead. Norwegian Blue parrot nailed to its perch dead. Funeral performed, body cremated, ashes scattered, will executed dead.

Dead-dead.

As Alan began to advance upon him, an unwanted thought appeared in his mind. It was a squatter of a thought. A trespasser. As welcome as dog shit on a shag pile carpet, or sunshine on the wedding day of your ex-girlfriend and the bloke she dumped you for. But unwanted as it was, the thought sat there regardless, written so bright upon his consciousness that he could think of nothing else.

I'm the goat, Rav thought.

Jess had followed the trail of the two beasts out of the big room's far door, along a corridor and through a bar, where she paused momentarily to munch up a whole set of dropped crisp fragments someone had deposited under a table. Then she returned to the path, which took her along another corridor and through another set of doors, where she found herself back where she'd started, in the big room.

And there they were. Two of them, their bestial nature so vile she could smell their scent in the air itself, flowing straight off them. She dived beneath a cloth-covered table, commando-crawled under a couple of chairs, and eventually found herself secreted in a convenient spot from which she could survey the room. Directly in front of her were two sets of legs, sets of legs that she knew belonged to the beasts. Part of her, the part of her whose ancestors had roamed the endless Siberian steppe, wanted to burst out now, to rip and tear at that vile, tainted flesh. But there was another part of her, the part that some tens of thousands of years ago had seen a bunch of bipedal, hairless apes walking around and thought, "These guys look like they know what they're doing". And that part of her knew that sometimes the predator has to guard against becoming the prey, and that this was one such moment.

She scanned around the room, and found herself looking at an apparently terrified Rav. One of the sets of legs started to move now, walking in a slow but inexorable path towards him. Rav didn't move, but merely stood, watching, like a rabbit being stalked by a Doberman. Somewhere in Jess's little brain, what passed for her doggy conscience began to have a debate with a few million years of evolved instinct.

As the vampire walked towards him, it seemed to Rav as though time was slowing to a crawl. It wasn't, of course. Time was still advancing at its usual leisurely rate of one second per second, as it habitually does, and any appearance to the contrary was entirely caused by the fact that Rav's brain was racing like the engine of a 950cc Fiat at the hands of the fourteen-year-old scroat who's just stolen it.

Idea upon idea occurred to him, every one of which he realised to be crap the instant he'd thought it. Then he found himself shouting at the top of his lungs, having discovered that there is actually an emotion more powerful than embarrassment and that's the awful realisation of imminent and horrible death. "You can't kill me. Not here. These people are watching. They're witnesses!" He'd thought that a pretty good point. But good point or not, it didn't cause Alan to in any way break stride. Rav turned to the stallholders whose stalls he was standing in front of. "He's a vampire!"

The nearest stallholder, a fifty-something women with hair dyed jet-black, thick white makeup caking her face, and a set of fake fangs in her mouth, smiled back. "We're all vampires here, love. It's a vampire convention."

Rav pointed desperately at Alan. "No, he's a real vampire!"

A younger man stood beside the woman. He looked puzzled for a moment, then nodded, smiling, in a clear "oh, I see" type way. He crossed his arms across his chest and stood back to watch the action.

"We're not playing one of your fucking games," Rav screamed at him. "He's a real fucking vampire and he's going to fucking kill me." Blank, dispassionate faces stared back at him. Several more people crossed their arms across their chests, again with knowing smiles. "It's not a game!" Rav shouted at them. "Jesus Christ, don't you freaks have some kind of fucking safe word?" He looked back at Alan just in time to see a new message appear on the screen mounted upon the far wall.

@PeteTheGeek: nutters gone psycho! i say we nuke the
trade hall from orbit. only way to be sure #dracucon

So this was how his life was going to end. Ripped to pieces by a vampire in Whitby at a convention full of weirdos, with the whole pitiful process being tweeted live on the Internet by some wanker called Pete the Geek.

@PeteTheGeek: and nathans filming it on his phone. well
upload it later #dracucon

Correction. Tweeted live on the Internet... And uploaded to YouTube. And then Alan was in front of him, speaking. "You're going to come with me. Now."

And Rav found himself going with him.

The beasts had split, one heading towards Rav, the other heading down another aisle, its attention apparently fixed elsewhere. For the moment, Jess stayed where she was, considering her options. She could follow the first beast, the one who she'd so spectacularly failed to deal with several days ago, and who now looked to be advancing on Rav with what she could smell to be furious intent even from a fair distance away. If that encounter broke out into the slashing fight to the death her instincts told her was about to erupt, Rav might have need of an extra pair of teeth.

But on the other hand, it seemed like he was up for a fight – or at least, he was making a lot of noise. And while Jess wasn't exactly scared, she wasn't stupid either, and she wasn't particularly eager to take on something that had so clearly demonstrated its superiority in strength over her. Then there was the other beast, the one who was clearly the pack leader of the first beast. If her pack was threatened by its pack, then it was surely the one she needed to be stopping? Her doggy thought processes snapped to a conclusion. Follow the alpha beast, and leave her pack leader to deal with its pack follower.

She slithered out from her cover and dashed across the aisle, diving beneath the far table and scrabbling along its length before popping a careful snout through a gap in the hanging cloth. There the beast was, staring at a youngish woman who seemed oblivious to his presence.

Jess watched.

Of the many things the Professor missed from his previous, pre-breakdown life, the foremost was the lack of opportunities to exercise his mind. There are only so many games of afternoon bingo a man can play, and only so many episodes of Countdown he can watch, before he reaches

54

the point where he would be driven insane, had he not already arrived at that destination.

The talk on Bram Stoker had been something of a revelation. It was shot through with wit underpinned by a deep and appreciative knowledge delivered to a standard the Professor would have expected from a lecturer at one of the better universities. Of course, when he took the chance to grab a few words with the speaker after the conclusion of the talk, he found out that in his day job, the speaker was, in fact, a lecturer at one of the better universities.

Sometimes in life a man is forced to first admit and then reject his prejudices, and the Professor realised that this was just such an occasion. He'd assumed that a "vampire convention" would consist of only the strange and the alienated, driven to a cultural extreme by the poverty of both their imagination and their education. But he'd been wrong. This was a fascinating place, full of good people, united only by their interest in a subset of literature that drew deep from ancient cultural folklore. There was nothing to fear here.

He concluded his pleasantries with the moonlighting lecturer and grabbed his programme. It was clear that Dracucon 5 contained much that was of interest, and he intended to take in as much of it as he could.

Alan led Shah gently out of the trade hall and into the maze of corridors that lay beyond. His captive made no attempt to resist or to alert others to his plight. He was enraptured and enslaved by what Nicolae called in their native tongue "*Fascinaţia*" – the Fascination – a vampiric power that could bind a human to a vampire's will, controlling their thoughts and actions as surely as a puppet is controlled by its strings.

It didn't always work; it was often not worth even attempting. For a creature to become bound by the Fascination, an emotional link must already exist between the creature and its vampiric captor; a link that will open the victim's mind to commands and suggestion. Sometimes it could be lust, or envy, or curiosity; that was why they were here now, for the Operational Phase, looking for fans already in love with vampires, or at least the idea of them. But sometimes a more basic emotion would do: fear. Fear could narrow a creature's focus, put it into a state where every thought it had was of the vampire who wished to control it. Get a man so terrified of you that you've become his entire universe and you're already halfway to enslaving him.

And this Dr Ravinder Shah was now well and truly enslaved. Alan led him down the corridor, their feet padding softly on the plush carpet. He ignored the various laser printed signs directing convention goers to the different parts of the convention. He ignored the glances – some admiring, others scared – of fellow attendees: he would have smiled, but in his experience that often made things worse. He ignored, tempting as it was, the pick 'n' mix sweet selection at the little hotel shop. (Vampires don't need to eat, but they still like to, and under other circumstances Alan would have been all over that pick 'n' mix like a crack-addicted ferret in a crack-house). He did, though, make a mental note to return to the pick 'n' mix once he'd finished with Shah.

A little further down the corridor Alan found what he'd been looking for: a door marked "Staff Only", with that little extra wear on the carpet before it that indicated the entrance to a thoroughfare, rather than to a mere cupboard or office. He opened it and found a staircase, its steps concrete, its walls unpainted breezeblock. He pulled Rav through and closed the door behind him.

All he needed was somewhere quiet and out of the way. Somewhere where they would not be disturbed.

As a dog, Jess was unaware of her position as one of the West Kensington Paranormal Detective Agency's three-man Lead Investigation Team. She was, similarly, utterly unaware that of that three-man team, one had been captured, and one was currently hopelessly distracted, leaving her as the only operative still, for want of a better word, operational. Of course, that she was unaware of this fact did not prevent it from being true.

Right now she knew only two things. Firstly, that the beast she was following was the leader of a pack that threatened the pack she currently, albeit temporarily, belonged to. And secondly, that he was an abomination, something that – like cats – simply could not be allowed to continue to walk upon the Earth.

The beast had trailed the young woman through the big room and into a smaller room beyond. Jess had been born of a lineage of hunters; she knew predator from prey and knew that the beast was a predator and this female his prey. She expected him to pounce, but he didn't, at least not in the way Jess had expected. He had approached the woman, true, but his approach was made with open arms and a friendly smile and led to the two of them sitting down at a table with two drinks placed between them.

Not for the first time in her life, Jess found herself in a situation beyond the comprehension of her limited intellect. Usually when faced with such a circumstance, she would simply accept it as just one more aspect of the conundrum that humans so often were, and settle instead for a vigorous chew of her bone or a snooze on her blanket. But this was a beast, and deep in her somewhat simplified soul Jess knew it had to be stopped. She dived beneath the nearest table, and began to work a careful path through, between and around the various legs – both wooden and human – that lay between her and her quarry.

Rav didn't awake, for he hadn't been asleep. He didn't open his eyes, as they hadn't been closed. There was no sensation of his consciousness transitioning from a dream world to reality, for his consciousness had not been dreaming. He simply went from nothing to something, from a nothing where the mind of Ravinder Shah had ceased to exist to a something where he was very much back. In his frozen, suspended mind he heard a click, impossibly loud and yet distant-sounding, also; clear as a chime yet muffled, too. And like a DVD when the play button is pressed, he was alive once more.

Directly in front of him was the horrific sight of Alan's face, horrific not only in its appearance, but in the realisation it triggered. He struggled, but found himself bound; he tried to scream, but found himself gagged as well. He felt himself going dizzy from the exertion and lack of oxygen; if he'd known someone was going to gag him he'd have made sure to pick his nose first. He looked around, as much as his bindings would allow him. He appeared to be in some kind of store room, its walls lined with metal shelves upon which sat cardboard boxes, metal tins, and shrink-wrapped supplies of various kinds. His arms and legs were bound with white linen sheets to the cheap plastic chair upon which he sat.

The vampire leaned in close to him and stared hard. "I let you speak. If you scream, I kill you. If you shout, I kill you. If you make noise, I kill you. If you try escape, I kill you. You understand?"

Rav nodded.

"Good."

Rav felt the vampire's hands reaching behind his neck, roughly untying the gag. The cloth was pulled free, allowing him to draw in a long shuddering breath. Alan sat back in his own chair. "I want to know who you is, and why you follow us."

Chapter Ten

Time passed.

Hidden in her lair beneath a nest of tables and chairs, Jess lay, observing the beast. Patient watching came easy to her; she was a Border Collie, and patient watching is what they do. Time continued to pass, and still Jess watched. Then the beast stood, motioning to the girl to join him. As the beast moved away, his prey followed, trailing in his wake, a blank expression upon her face. Something about her had changed. That spark of free will that distinguishes humans from sheep was gone. This was wrong. This was very, very wrong.

Jess quickly slithered back through the maze of tables, taking up a position beside the doorway that the beast and the girl were walking toward. Jess was a sheep dog, not a shepherd dog, bred to herd sheep rather than protect them from wolves. But something of that shepherd dog instinct still flowed within her, that inner belief that she must protect sheep from wolves. She came to a decision.

The beast had to be stopped.

If this had been Star Wars, and Grand Master Yoda had been present, he might have observed that, while the Force did not run strong in Rav, the bullshit most certainly did. From damn near the moment Alan had removed his gag, the words had started flowing: desperate, only barely coherent, lies and truth all jumbled together, tumbling forth like a mountain stream down a rocky slope. Rav was horribly aware that he was bullshitting for his very existence now, with the prize for success being a continued life, and the penalty for failure being death.

"I'm not a private detective," he told Alan. "That's just a cover. I'm with MI5."

"MI5?"

"Well more MI5 and a bit. We're running a joint operation with Special Branch, MI6, the SAS, the CIA, the FBI and the RAC – I mean the RUC – you know that lot from Northern Ireland, 'cept they're the PSNI now – I mean, God knows they're a bit weird, you know, bowler hats and sashes and drums and all that – not that there's anything wrong with drums, I like drums, drums are good – do you like drums?"

The vampire said nothing, which somehow induced Rav, almost against his will, to resume the verbal vomiting that currently appeared to be his conversational limit. "We've had tip-offs and information and stuff from satellites – the satellites know everything – we can detect DNA from orbit – you want to know who Prince Harry's real dad is – we know that!"

Alan leaned forward. "So, who is he?"

"Who's... what?"

"Prince Harry real dad. I read your magazines. Hello, OK, Heat. They talk about this but they always vague. Always like telling joke where punchline never comes. Is Hewitt, no? The one who went on Big Brother and all other reality shit?"

"Yeah, yeah, it's him. We had a camera in the room and microphones in the bed and everything."

"I thought you read DNA from orbit?"

"Well, that too. Now, not then. That was, like, thirty years ago."

The vampire considered this for a moment, then waved his hands. "Enough. Is stupid. You is bullshitter. I work forty years for Securitate. I know bullshitters. I see men die, see truth then. What you know that make me not kill you?"

"I know about the pigs."

"The pigs?"

"The vampire pigs!"

"What about them?"

"They're vampires."

"And?"

"They can fly."

The vampire shrugged. "Of course they fly. They vampires. What you know I not know?"

"They're on the loose?"

His captor sighed. "You know nothing. I kill you now."

Rav got as far as, "Please don't kill me–" before the gag was jammed firmly back into his mouth. He kicked and wriggled, trying desperately to break his bonds, but succeeded only in painfully pulling something in the area of his groin.

Alan looked around the room, apparently weighing up the various options and methods by which he might kill Rav. The mundane way in which he was going about it, as though the biggest question he faced was how to minimise the cleaning up, made it all the more terrifying. The vampire got to his feet, spent some minutes gathering items – a sheet, a blanket, some cleaning fluid, a largish screwdriver – and then returned to where Rav lay trapped. "I merciful man. I make this quick."

He hefted the screwdriver, spinning it around his hand as though checking it for balance, then snapped it back into place. This was it, Rav realised. Game over. No extra lives. No replay option. Then a ringtone broke the silence. The vampire reached into his pocket and pulled out a cheap looking phone. He glanced at the screen, blinked, then hit the answer button.

"Da?"

It was Nicolae calling, on his latest model iPhone. Alan would have loved to have had an iPhone, but the cheapest deal he could find was thirty-five pounds a month for twenty-four months and his hotel wages didn't quite stretch to that. Which is why he only had a cheap Android handset that Nicolae always laughed at.

"Have you killed the vampire hunter yet?"

Nicolae sounded very, very angry; angrier than Alan had heard him for several years. Fear pushed Alan into an instinctive lie. "Yes. It's done. I just need to dispose of his body."

"Do it. Then get back here. I need you."

"Is something wrong?"

There was a very long pause. "I had the girl. I had her. I'd drawn her in and charmed her and then laid the Fascination upon her. We were leaving."

"And?"

There was an even longer pause. "I was attacked by a medium-sized black-and-white dog."

The hair follicles on the back of Alan's neck were dead, as was the skin within which they sat, but they nonetheless managed to tighten. "A dog?"

"Yes. A dog. The infernal beast grabbed hold of my leg and by the time I'd shaken it free the Fascination had broken. The girl realised something had happened and started screaming and saying I'd put something in her drink and the whole bar was looking at me, and – I was asked to leave the convention."

"What happened to the dog?"

There was another long pause. "It ran off."

From a part of his soul Alan had long thought dead, a small flame of happiness flared. He shouldn't have felt this; what had just happened was a setback to a project that meant as much to him as it did to Nicolae – perhaps more, for his reasons were deep where Nicolae's were base and selfish. But such was his dislike of Nicolae that feel it he did. These thoughts of the project's success or failure conjured forth images of Tabitha. That part of his soul he'd long thought dead sparked again, but this time it burned with a mixture of regret and worry. Why had she stopped responding to him? Had she discovered his true nature? He looked again at the man he held captive before him, and for a moment considered: could this man help him?

He looked again.

No.

"I will finish here and then meet you at our room," he told Nicolae, then hung up. He picked up the screwdriver, feeling its weight, knowing its killing potential. Before him, his captive danced in the chair as much as his bonds would allow, desperately trying to talk past the gag. Was he trying to say something? Alan reached forward and tugged the gag free. "What is it?"

"Are you sure you want to do this?"

The vampire considered Rav's question for a disappointingly short moment.

"Yes."

"Why?"

"You are danger to our project."

"You've got a project?"

The vampire's eyes flicked nervously from left to right, as though concerned that someone besides he and Rav might have overheard. "That not your business."

Now that he was here, on the edge of a gruesome death, Rav felt strangely liberated. The fog of fear was gone, leaving nothing save a clear realisation that only his intellect could save him. He drilled deep into his memories, drawing upon his university years and even reaching back to the grade C GCSE in Psychology, the selection of which at age fourteen had so disappointed his mother. ("You need proper subjects if you want to become a doctor or a lawyer. You do want to become a doctor or a lawyer, don't you?")

He took a deep breath. "It's just that you don't look happy, and if this here, now, isn't making you happy, then I think you owe it to yourself to consider what would make you happy. That makes sense, right?"

The vampire sat back down and considered Rav's suggestion, idly twirling the screwdriver through his fingers as he did so. "I guess so."

"Good, good. This is really good. I think we're really making progress here."

"We is?"

"Of course we are. Admitting that we have needs and desires is the first step towards identifying what those needs and desires are, and then working out how we might achieve them. There's nothing wrong with having dreams."

"Yes. Is true. I have dreams." The vampire's ruined face crinkled for a moment in thought, then snapped back into the present, accompanied by a decisive click of the fingers. "That is why we have project. That is why I must kill you." The handle of the screwdriver slapped back into the palm of his hand.

"Wait, wait. Are you sure this project will achieve those dreams? We often fixate on short-term, stop-gap solutions in order to avoid thinking on the actual barriers that block the path to our dreams."

"You think?"

"I know." This was it, Rav realised. Shit or bust. Time to throw in his final reserves of logic, emotion, and argument. "I can help you. Whatever it is that troubles you, whatever it is you want but think you can't have, I can help you get it. Trust me. I'm a professional."

"I not know. How I know you speak truth?"

"You can at least tell me what your problem is, surely? That might help, and if after that you don't think I can help you, then you can still kill me, and things will be just as they were. You've got nothing to lose, right?"

"I guess."

Rav threw in a smile. "So what's your problem, mate?"

"I have girl. Sort of. Her name is Tabitha."

The Professor was in a larger room now, a room that was host to not merely one speaker, but four, three men and a woman. The third speaker, a white-haired and white-bearded gentleman, leaned forward and tapped his microphone. "Hello and welcome to this talk on Dracula in the twenty-first century: Is the Count still relevant to the post-Twilight generation?" He turned to the woman who sat beside him. "Mary. Is the Count still relevant?"

She smiled, paused, went to speak, and then stopped. Some kind of disturbance was occurring, a rising hubbub of erupting conversations rippling through the audience. At the far end of the row of seats in which the Professor now sat a black-and-white face appeared, sniffing the air. Jess looked up, saw the Professor, and then began to make her way down the row with some haste, climbing over bags, feet, and – on at least one occasion – a lap to reach him. Her green dog-coat was askew, her jaws were flecked with saliva, and deep in her eyes was a look of terror. She whined once, then wriggled under the Professor's chair and disappeared, silent save for her laboured breathing.

The multiple conversations slowly died.

Eventually, the white-haired and white-bearded man coughed. "If we're quite ready to continue? So, Mary. As we were saying. Is the Count still relevant?"

The woman smiled. "Well, David..."

Rav had never realised how much he liked to use his arms while talking until this, the moment when he'd found himself attempting to conduct an introductory interview with a "client" whilst tied and bound to a chair. It was very distracting, but he was trying his best to put all such distractions aside and keep his focus on the story Alan had just told him.

"Okay," he said to Alan. "So to summarise, you–" He paused to stress the next word. "Met–" (his inability to do air-quotes at this point was killing him) "–Tabitha online, via the Zone website."

"Yes. I have account there. She does too."

"And this was about six months ago?"

"Yes."

"You've only communicated via online chat and email?"

"Yes. She suggest phone once, but I scared. I not speak English good."

Rav gave him an encouraging smile. "Well, it's better than my Romanian."

"I not what she think. I tell her I twenty-year-old goth philosophy student from Leeds. I send her picture of boy I find in Google Images."

"Yeah, I can see a phone call would have been a bit of an issue."

"I vampire!" Alan wailed. "I Rumanian! I work in hotel!"

"You're employed in the hospitality services sector. You're the holder of a valid EU passport. And... you're a supernatural being with extraordinary abilities. Look, we can work on the vampire angle. Vampires are quite hot now, and you said yourself she's into that whole goth thing."

"But I not sparkle like vampires in movies. I look like corpse."

"Well, it's all about expectation management." Rav thought for a moment, still horribly aware that while he had at least got Alan communicating, death was still a strong and distinct possibility. "What do you want out of this situation? If you look at yourself in six months' time, a year, and five years, where do you want to be?"

"I want you find Tabitha. Want you tell her who I am – but in way so she still want me."

"You want me to, like, big you up? My mate Ace is really cool and all that?"

"Big me up? Ace?"

"Sorry, pop culture reference. I mean, make you sound like a cool sort of dude, once she gets past the, you know, vampire thing."

"Yes. Tell her I cool. So I can see her and go out with her and be with her."

"Okay. Well, I can try."

"No try. Do. Like puppet say in Star Wars, there is no try there is only do. You only try, I find you, I kill you. Or maybe I just tell Nicolae about you. I nice man. I kill you quickly. He not. He cruel man, enjoy killing you."

"Okay. Right. So the deal is that I take you on as a client for my detective agency. You want me to track down Tabitha and arrange a meeting between you and her, after explaining to her what you are, but stressing all your good points?"

"Yes. If she still want me then, you live. If she not want me, or you not find her, you die."

"No pressure there then," Rav muttered to himself. He gave Alan a big beaming smile. "Sounds like a deal. Perhaps you could untie me and we could shake on it?"

Chapter Eleven

Rav, Jess, and the Professor had left Whitby on the first bus of the morning, and by Sunday afternoon were back in Hounslow, safe, if not quite sound. But all the while, Alan's final parting words were playing through Rav's head.

"I give you two weeks. Then I find you and kill you. You understand, it not personal, no?"

If he were to be honest, Rav was finding it difficult to not take it very much personally, and had thus spent the journey south assembling a to-do list that he now proceeded to start working his way through. Within two hours of arriving home, a cheery locksmith was beavering away replacing Rav's motley collection of Chubbs and Yales with an array of hi-tech locks, bolts, catches, chains, and beefed-up, shielded hinges. Within three hours, the equally cheery Sikh owner of a local security firm was delivering an eye-wateringly large quote for a top of the range security system. "We're talking dual motion sensors in every room, separate upstairs and downstairs circuits, sensor-switches on the front and back doors, all controlled from a central console," he told Rav. "I ain't saying it'd keep Tom Cruise out, but it'll be good for your run-of-the-mill street-scum."

With physical matters in hand, Rav felt it was time to turn to matters more spiritual. He needed holy water, in quantity, and this time he wanted it blessed by a kosher priest – none of this wishy-washy, happy-clappy, Anglican shit. He wanted fire and brimstone and a belief in actual evil – together with a medieval attitude to dealing with said evil. Semi-blessed water that could just about scare a pig wasn't going to cut the mustard when you were facing two three hundred-year-old vampires who'd spent time working for Ceausescu's secret police. He needed full-fat holy water.

His initial Google search returned a shitload of entries. He grabbed a scrap of paper and started hunting for a pen, of which none were – of course – to be seen. Luckily, Rav still had his "James Bond pen" in the inside pocket of his suit jacket, where it habitually lived. He'd bought it from a spies-and-security type shop in Tottenham Court Road during the initial fit of enthusiasm he'd had when first setting up the agency. It looked just like a normal writing pen, if a little fat, with a big obvious slider thing at the top to extend the pen nib out. Except that to extend the pen nib out you actually needed to twist the bottom of the pen – sliding the slider thing actually fired a burst of pepper spray out of the top.

Unfortunately, Rav's mind being as distracted as it currently was, by the time he got back to his laptop he'd forgotten that this was his special spy pen, with the result that he then proceeded to fire a full dose of pepper spray into his face from point blank range. He staggered, crying, to the kitchen, bouncing off various pieces of furniture and at least one doorway on the way, and then proceeded to spend the next ten minutes splashing water into his eyes. Then he made himself a cup of coffee and made a mental note to never, ever, pepper spray himself in the face again, before resuming his search.

An hour later, having made a variety of fraudulent commitments to adopt Jesus Christ as his personal saviour, his hired mini-cab was heading for Toys "R" Us, its boot filled with freshly-blessed water. ("Can you imagine the agony of an eternity burning in Hell?" the Nigerian Reverend he'd eventually opted for had asked him, a question that's actually quite easy to answer when it is but sixty minutes since one had pepper sprayed oneself in the face).

By ten that night, he was locked up in his flat behind an array of locks and bolts and protected by the loaded, electrically-powered, water pistol he'd purchased from Toys "R" Us. He figured he was safe. Mostly. For now. He'd have felt happier if he'd had Jess with him to serve as a biological, vampire detecting alarm system, but when he'd raised that suggestion with Brian, he'd received a response that was blunt to the point of obscenity-laden rudeness in the manner in which it said "no". Then a guilty thought occurred to him. The Professor. He grabbed his phone and hit the entry in his favourites. The phone rang. And rang. Finally, on the seventh ring, the older man answered. "Yes?"

"It's me, Rav. You okay?"

"Why would I not be okay, Ravinder? I thought it was you whom Alan had promised to kill? And besides, don't you have two weeks?"

"Yeah, well, that's if Nicolae doesn't find out about us first. Then all bets are off."

"Very true. So what is the plan now?"

"Don't know. I've spent every hour since we got home getting in new locks, water pistols, and a metric shitload of holy water."

"What exactly is a metric shitload?"

"About two point two imperial shitloads. Listen, look out for anything weird, yeah?"

"Of course."

"Okay, I'll call you tomorrow."

There was a click, as the Professor hung up his old fashioned, NHS issue phone. Rav looked around. Might as well go to bed and attempt sleep. He grabbed the water pistol and headed up to his bedroom, shoving it under his pillow. This was serious shit.

This was very, very serious shit.

Rav spent that night dreaming many dreams: being soaked by a tropical thunderstorm, suffering the trauma of wetting himself in public, and then finally finding himself kidnapped by a man in a fluffy bunny suit who proceeded to try to drown him in a variety of muddy puddles. When he did finally awake, the cause of these dreams was revealed – his extended-magazine water pistol, which had leaked during the night, soaking his pillow and a large part of the mattress.

He got up, shaved, showered and dressed. Then, having first stuck a small square of sticky tape over the end of the barrel to stop it leaking again, he refilled his water-pistol and dropped it into the nifty concealed shoulder holster he'd bought for it, before heading off for the office.

He managed to avoid all contact with Fen until early in the afternoon, when she pounced on him while he was using the photocopier. "Rav!" She was smiling. That couldn't be good. "How are things going?"

"Good, good."

"Busy? No. Great, I've got a new client for you. Just been phoned in. Elderly man in Feltham, neighbours are worried about him. Haven't seen him for a while, that sort of thing." She handed over a printout. "Details are on here. Pop on over, take a shufty, check he's okay, yeah?"

"Well, I'm quite busy–"

"Now, Rav. Now."

Rav took the sheet and quickly skimmed through the contents, finding it remarkably light on details, such as the name of the old man concerned, or any mention of who exactly had phoned in the report. "It doesn't say the name of the bloke. Or the name of the neighbours."

"They didn't leave their name because they didn't want to get involved, and they don't know his name because this isn't the 1950s. Look, they haven't seen him for a while, they thought there might be a problem, so they called us. I want you to go out and find out if there is a problem. You can take one of the pool cars."

"Okay, I'll just–"

"You seem to be operating under a fundamental misunderstanding of how this whole thing works, Rav. I speak, you do. Comprende?"

Rav was already backing away towards the door. "I'm going, I'm going."

Some inner London housing estates find themselves described as no-go areas, in possession of a reputation so hostile that many years have passed since they've experienced any kind of police presence. Being a relatively richer borough on Greater London's outskirts, Hounslow didn't have any such areas, but it did have areas of deprivation, and Feltham's Watermead estate was one of them. While it wasn't an actual no-go area, it was often said that when it did receive a police visit, it was usually by ten officers in a Ford Transit rather than two officers in a Ford Fiesta.

But no-go area or not, Rav was still pretty scared as he parked the pool car in front of the old man's block of flats. After all, when a man's promised to kill you, making an anonymous phone call that will require you to visit one of the dodgier parts of town is a damn good way to initiate that process. Sure, Alan had given him two weeks, but what if he'd changed his mind? Or told Nicolae? Unfortunately, Rav was between a rock and a hard place, with the rock being Alan and the hard place his boss. So after giving himself a few moments to panic, he got out of the car, locked it, and headed over to the stained concrete building.

The alleged old man supposedly lived in flat number 37. A quick perusal of the sign by the entrance revealed this to be on the upper floor of the two story block. Rav made his way carefully up the concrete outside staircase, stepping over the urine stains and keeping to the outside, giving him the best possible view. Nothing. He made it onto the outside landing and edged slowly along to number 37.

The door was slightly ajar, a gap of a centimetre or so between it and the wooden door frame. Rav carefully pushed it open to reveal a short hallway, beyond which was a lounge. Both were filthy, with stubbed out cigarettes upon the dirty cream carpet and cobwebs hanging from the ceiling.

He stood there for several seconds, staring. No Romanian vampires leapt out to kill him, which didn't mean anything of course – if Alan or Nicolae were here they'd wait until he'd entered the flat.

He pulled the pistol out of the shoulder holster and peeled the sticky tape off its barrel. Taking a last look left and right, he stepped carefully over the threshold and into the flat. It stank, of damp and decay and death. To his left was a doorway, which led into a kitchen. He took a deep breath then spun round the door-frame, snapping down into a crouch, pistol held two-handed in the way he'd seen in a thousand US cop dramas.

The kitchen was empty, except for the flies buzzing around a sinkful of unwashed plates and mugs. He returned to the hallway, and looked forward into the lounge. The portion of it he could observe from his current vantage point was empty, save for one old and sagging easy chair. Of course, what he couldn't see might contain anything – or anyone. Rav mentally counted to three then hurled himself forward, launching himself into a combat roll that carried him behind the easy chair and into cover. He scrambled up onto his knees and snapped up, pistol ready to spray anyone who might be there.

A youngish woman, good-looking in a sort of tomboyish way, was sitting cross-legged, yoga style, on the floor across from him. She smiled. "Do you normally make your house visits this way?"

It took Rav a few seconds to work out who the young woman was, which was fair enough given that he'd previously met her only briefly, and then without actually seeing her face. "Reece."

"Well, you could sound at least a little glad to see me." She carefully unfolded her legs, then looked around the room. "This is a bit grim. Perhaps we should retire to your car?"

That was fine with Rav. He put the sticky tape back over the barrel of his pistol, returned it to the shoulder holster, and followed Reece out into the hallway. They walked out of the flat, along the landing, and down the stairs, in silence the whole way. A few local youths were eying the car up. Rav told them to piss off, clicked on the key fob to unlock the doors, and got in, figuring that Reece was the sort of girl who liked to open her own doors – and if she wasn't, well, frankly, she was shit out of luck.

It was at times like this he wished he'd taken up smoking. Not because of any desire to reduce stress, or look cool. No, it was just that right now, the traditional ritual for these types of meetings of gratuitously failing to ask her if she minded him smoking, taking out a cigarette, lighting it up, and then blowing smoke in her face, would have been deeply satisfying – albeit in a deeply misogynistic, black-and-white movie, kind of way.

In the end, it was she who broke the silence. "So how did it go in Whitby?"

"Fine. Look, Reece – actually, do you have a proper name?"

"A proper name?"

"A first name. I'm figuring Reece for a surname. You don't sound like the sort of girl who would have it for a first name. What with you not being American or from Essex."

"Why would you care what I call myself, Mr Shah?"

"I'm just thinking that if we're working together–"

"Who said we're working together?"

"Well, I ain't working for you. Don't seem to recall you offering to pay me anything."

"True, Mr Shah, very true. If you like, you can call me Emma."

"Is that your real name?"

"No. But then neither's Reece." She nodded at one of the youths who'd been congregating around the car and who now – having failed to actually piss off as Rav had instructed him – appeared to be talking about them, if his gesticulation was anything to go by. "I think the natives might be getting a bit restless. Perhaps you should put the key in the ignition and drive?"

Chapter Twelve

Mo's Place wasn't the most scenic of eateries, consisting as it did of a tatty mobile catering unit parked beside a busy roundabout. Nor was it the quietest, given its location underneath one of Heathrow Airport's two incoming flight paths. It did, however, serve the best kebabs in West London, with a garlic sauce of such quality that had kebab stands qualified for Michelin stars, Mo's would have had at least two stuck above one wheel. Having purchased a couple of the establishment's finest, complete with trimmings, Rav carried them back to the car and handed one to Reece. She examined the kebab, then looked back at Rav. "Do you bring all the girls here?"

"Only the posh ones who fancy slumming it with us proles."

She thought on that for a moment, then shrugged and tucked into the kebab. A few chews and one swallow later, she smiled. "That's not actually bad, Mr Shah. So, Whitby. What happened?"

"Like you don't know. You were probably there all the time, watching."

She shrugged. "I might have been."

"I'm not a tethered goat."

"Heaven forbid anyone might suggest you are!"

"Are you taking the piss?"

"Just a bit."

They finished the kebabs in a silence broken only by the descending planes roaring overhead every ninety seconds. When they'd finished, Reece turned to face him. "I was there, I was watching, but I didn't see everything. I want to know what happened. I might be able to help."

"Are you going to tell me everything you know?"

She shook her head. "No. I'm afraid I can't. This world we live in is far stranger, far darker, and much more mysterious than its people dare to believe. There are limits to what I'm able to tell you."

Her words crystallised a chain of thoughts that Rav had been thinking ever since that Saturday night in York. He'd previously only half believed that the truth was out there. He'd believed it because it was fun to believe it, and because he liked the idea of knowing things that others didn't know, even if it was knowledge based upon desire rather than fact. Now he'd found out that the truth, at least one particular aspect of it, was actually out there, was real, and was dangerous – suddenly it wasn't much fun anymore. "Vampires. They're real." He looked across at her for confirmation.

"Yes."

"Like real-real, kill you real."

"Yes."

"But how?"

"How are they real? If I were a xenobiologist I could perhaps give you an explanation, and if you were a xenobiologist you'd perhaps understand it, but since neither of us are xenobiologists perhaps we should just acknowledge their existence and leave it at that."

"But how can they just be walking around? In York? Alan works in a hotel, for Christ's sake."

"Well, it's not a very nice hotel."

"Yeah, but if vampires exist, why doesn't everyone know about it? Why does everyone think they're just a myth?"

"People believe the things they want to believe, the things that are easiest and most convenient to believe, and the things they've been told to believe. That was always the way. Add modern technology and you can make people believe that black is white and white is black." She paused for a moment, thinking. "Surely you've heard of Watford for example?"

"Watford?"

"Yes, Watford."

"Medium-sized town in Hertfordshire, about twenty miles out of London?"

"I'm not talking about the town, I'm talking about the event. I thought you were into all this conspiracy stuff?"

"Well, you know. Bits."

Reece gave Rav a look of disappointment, and shook her head. "The Watford Event was the result of a joint CIA/MI5 experiment conducted in the early spring of 1961 in the Northamptonshire town of Watford." One word in that sentence had been spoken with particular emphasis, that word being "Northamptonshire". She paused for a moment, as though daring Rav to interrupt, then continued. "As is almost always the case with these things, it was totally unauthorised by their supposed civilian masters. The plan was to put small quantities of hallucinogens into the water system in the early hours of the morning to test the effects on the population's susceptibility and compliance. A weird cocktail of stuff. LSD, mutant mushroom extract, and God alone knows what else."

"What happened?"

"There was a mix-up over units. Fluid ounces versus gallons or something. With the result that more than one hundred and twenty-eight times the intended amount was added. Instead of ending up with a population susceptible to manipulation, they ended up with a population totally off their heads. First anyone outside knew of it was when the milk-floats started crashing. The government was forced to activate a plan called Operation Eyam, which had originally been developed to handle potential zombie outbreaks."

"But there's no such – sorry. Carry on."

"They thought it would be enough to simply contain the situation, prevent news breaking out, do a bit of mind-wiping here and there, and just wait until the inhabitants of the town came back down. But then they found out that the water table had been permanently polluted, rendering the whole area uninhabitable for decades."

"Which is..."

"Which is why Watford's now in Hertfordshire, instead of Northamptonshire."

"They moved the whole town?"

"Yes. Aided by the fact that the entire population were off their heads enough not to notice."

"But wouldn't everyone else have known it used to be somewhere else?"

"As I said, Mr Shah, people believe what they want to believe and what they're told to believe. The government threw in a short-term foot and mouth epidemic, some rumours, took advantage of the older generation's trust in authority and belief that loose tongues cost lives, and backed it up by a massive programme of subliminal reprogramming via the BBC. Memories were simply rewritten."

"What about the people who only watch ITV?"

"They never knew where Watford was in the first place."

"And this worked?"

"Mostly. The Ministry of Transport cocked up their part of the plan, which is why you still have a Watford Gap service station fifty miles north of actual Watford. And there's still a stubborn belief in Londoners that the north begins at Watford. Some prejudices are just too low-level to be shifted."

"Wouldn't there have been long term effects on the people who actually lived in Watford?"

"Have you ever met anyone from Watford?"

Rav was trying to take this all in, but was frankly finding it hard. "No. This is bollocks. People know stuff. You can't just change it."

She gave Rav an almost reassuring smile. "Memory is fragile. We forget most of what we see and hear, and then re-remember it, when we need it. In the 2008 Beijing Olympics, the British team came fourth in the medals table out of two hundred and four countries. But four years later, a majority of British people expected their team to do poorly at the 2012

Olympics because, quote, 'we're useless at sport'. People remember events according to the story they've been told, by governments, or by newspapers, or by their fellow citizens. That's how people can meet a vampire, and then forget it. Because they've been told vampires don't exist their whole lives, and when faced with a conflict between what they've been told and what they see with their own eyes, they'll believe what they've been told every time." She gave Rav a couple of minutes to absorb that, the two of them sitting in silence, watching the cars stream by on the adjacent roundabout. Then, finally, she spoke again. "So Whitby. What did Alan say after he took you away?"

Rav gave Reece a full account of everything that had happened in Whitby, and she in return told him absolutely nothing. That wasn't, she reminded him when he protested, the way it worked. Back at the office, Rav entered in a description of a false alarm, put in a few fake details, then marked the case as closed. Reece had made it clear he was on his own when it came to tracking down the object of Alan's desire, so when he'd finished with the paperwork he grabbed his phone and called the Professor. "It's me. You okay?"

"Well, I haven't been killed by undead Romanians, if that was your concern."

"Cool. You fancy a Chinese tonight?"

"I've never been a man to turn down the offer of a free meal – I presume you are paying?"

"Yeah. Remember that place I took you to in Isleworth? The Great Wall of China? I'll meet you there at seven, yeah?"

There was the sound of a pencil scribbling. "Seven o'clock at the Great Wall in Isleworth. I will see you there."

It's often said that the Great Wall of China is the only man-made structure visible from space. Of course, whether that's true or not, when people repeat this factoid they're referring to the three thousand mile long defensive wall built across northern China in the third century BC, and not the thirty seat Chinese restaurant opened by Sammy Chan in Isleworth in the late 1990s. Far from being visible from orbit, the Great Wall of China was barely visible from its own postcode, hidden as it was behind a narrow frontage in a drab side street. Rav was only running ten minutes late when he arrived, which for him wasn't bad, and was good enough in this case that the Professor hadn't managed to leap to any deranged conclusions as to what might have happened to him. The older man was in fact sitting quietly at a window table, perusing the menu with some solemnity. Rav slid in opposite him.

"Ah, Ravinder. How goes the investigation?"

Rav waved at Sammy to come over, then answered the Professor. "It doesn't. I've tried all the standard missing persons databases and haven't found anything. Then again, all I've got to go on is a first name and a rough age, which isn't much."

Sammy arrived, in as much as slouching slowly over and introducing yourself with a depressed shrug can be described as an arrival. "You want to order?"

Rav quickly glanced over the menu. "I'll have a Carlsberg, sweet-and-sour pork with some egg fried rice, and can we have a bunch of spring rolls?"

"Sure."

Sammy turned his attention to the Professor, who appeared to be having some difficulty getting to grips with the menu, flipping through the laminated pages with a confused look on his face. "Do you have a wine list?"

"No wine list. No wine. You want a beer?"

Rav laid a gentle hand on Sammy's arm. "Just give him the same as me."

"No problem."

Sammy shuffled away.

The Professor steepled his hands in the way he often did when thinking. "So we're looking for a girl called Tabitha, who is apparently aged nineteen?"

"Yep."

"And all we know about her other than that is that she has an account on this Zone website thing?"

"Yep. According to Alan, she goes by the handle of TabbyCat27."

"That would be her Internet name?"

"Yeah. Except when I Google it, I get nothing, so she doesn't use it anywhere else other than the Zone."

"I see. Well, could you not contact the people who run this Zone and ask them what details they have on her?"

Rav shook his head. "No. The servers are somewhere in the Russian Far East. The company that owns the domain is registered in Panama. And it's run by a Texan called Travis who's so paranoid he pulled all his teeth out with pliers on account of the fact he'd become convinced the CIA had planted bugs in them."

"Could he not have gone to a dentist?"

"He thought the dentists were the ones putting the bugs in for them."

"I see. So it's an underground website run by a paranoid and delusional believer of conspiracy theories who is therefore unlikely to tell anyone anything about any subject whatsoever?"

"That's pretty much it."

They spent the ten minutes until their food arrived alternately making and then rejecting suggestions, without any success, after which they switched to munching in silence. Finally, the Professor waved a chopstick at Rav. "Perhaps we are, as our trans-Atlantic cousins would say, working the problem from the wrong end. Rather than dancing to Alan's tune, perhaps we should be stalking him. Perhaps the goat should become the predator, and the predator the prey?"

"How? I could track him down, maybe. Hell, I could go to York and spend my nights visiting every hotel in turn until I find the one he's working at, but then what do I say? I've been looking for you instead of Tabitha, please don't kill me?"

The Professor shook his head. "I'm not suggesting we investigate him directly. I'm thinking more of getting in behind him. Digging at his and Nicolae's history."

"And how do we do that?"

"Did Alan not tell you that he once worked for the Securitate secret police?"

"Yeah. Are you saying I should fly to Bucharest and start poking around their archives?"

"No. I'm suggesting this as a second plan of attack. We ourselves need to be here, looking for Tabitha. And besides, what we need to know isn't likely to be in public archives." The Professor paused, then looked first left and then right, in a manner so exaggerated that had anyone else been in the restaurant they would have immediately turned their heads to listen. He leaned forward, and whispered. "When I was an undergraduate at Cambridge, in the early 1970s, my tutor attempted to recruit me as a spy. Espionage, that sort of thing."

"Your tutor attempted to recruit you for MI6?"

The Professor rolled his eyes. "Don't be absurd. After the debacle with Burgess, Philby, and McClaine, the Secret Intelligence Service wanted nothing to do with Cambridge. They chose to concentrate their efforts on the newer, redbrick universities. I'm told the University of East Anglia was a particular favourite of theirs." He paused, as though allowing a particularly unpleasant smell to pass, then continued. "No. Roger was attempting to recruit me for the KGB."

"Your tutor was a Soviet spy?"

"Yes. Part-time, obviously. He had to fit it around his university work and his other interests. He was on the board of the BBC and used to do a lot of consultancy work for the Foreign Office."

"So what did you do when he asked you?"

"Well I said no, obviously, given that I entirely failed to share his beliefs in either the inevitability or the desirability of a proletarian revolution."

"I mean, did you tell anyone?"

The Professor looked shocked. "Of course not. Roger told me in confidence."

"Okay, fine. So what's the point of this?"

"Well, Roger – Sir Roger now of course – is getting on a bit in years, but the last time I spoke to him his mental facilities were still all in order. I could ask him if he could perhaps contact some of his old Soviet contacts and see if any of them can dig anything up on Alan and this Nicolae. If the Securitate really did have a vampire working for them, then his contacts might have acquired some knowledge of this."

"Worth a try."

"Good. I'll phone him this evening."

Rav finished the last of his sweet-and-sour pork and waved at Sammy, miming the universal sign for the bill. A few minutes later Sammy wandered over and deposited a chipped china plate onto the table, upon which sat a scrappily hand-written bill and two cellophane-wrapped fortune cookies. This was new. Rav ate at the Great Wall of China quite regularly, but it was for the food, not the trimmings, of which there were normally none. He picked up one of the cookie packages and shouted over to Sammy. "Hey, Sammy. Since when did you start giving out fortune cookies?"

Sammy turned, a grin on his face. "I got ten boxes cheap."

Rav ripped the cellophane packet open, and peered suspiciously at the cookie contained within. "Why? What's wrong with them?"

"Nothing. They're fine. Only some hackers got into the database and changed all the fortune messages. The company made two hundred thousand before they realised."

Rav snapped the cookie open and pulled the message slip out.

"What does it say?" asked the Professor.

Rav read out the message. "You will be murdered, horribly. What does yours say?"

The Professor broke open his own cookie. "You will get cancer of the bowel and die."

"Nice." Rav threw a twenty and a ten down on top of the bill and got up. "Okay, you phone this Sir Roger bloke and I'll keep looking for Tabitha."

"I will. And Ravinder?"

"Yes?"

"Try not to get murdered."

Chapter Thirteen

Having spent what remained of Monday evening followed by a fair chunk of Tuesday's early hours watching DVDs and drinking heavily, Rav slept straight through his phone's alarm, which for once was okay, given that he was staying in late to let the burglar alarm installers in. He eventually awoke a little before nine, roused from sleep by said installers ringing his entry phone. Having let them in, apologised for the delay, and made them tea and coffee, before taking a very quick shower and throwing on a random suit, he made it into the office just after ten, and proceeded to spend most of the rest of the day dodging Fen before finally sneaking off around fourish. He was bitterly aware that having started at T-minus fourteen days, the countdown was now down to T-minus eleven, and his progress thus far amounted to a gold-plated and diamond-encrusted fuck all.

He got home just in time to get a quick primer on how to use his new burglar alarm from the chief installer. The primer was enjoyable; the distressingly large cheque he was then required to write out, less so. After taking a few minutes to recover, he made himself a coffee (three sugars, which he knew was unhealthy, but he figured the odds on the sugar killing him before Alan slaughtered him Sunday week were pretty low), then grabbed his laptop, fired up its browser, and typed in the Zone's web address. He'd already checked out Tabitha's Zone profile on Sunday night via his phone and found nothing, and a Google of her handle on the wider web had drawn only a big fat blank. But now he was going to retrace his steps, slowly and calmly, like the blokes in all those cold-case, dead-people detective shows on the box. First step, her profile page on the Zone.

Profile name: TabbyCat27. He grabbed an index card and wrote that down at the top, in the heading section. Underneath that he wrote:

Tabby -> From Tabitha.

Cat -> Likes cats?

27 -> Significant number?

He turned his attention back to the profile. Its picture showed a youngish girl, heavily made up in a goth style with jet black hair cut in a pixie-style. Was that her? Or some cult film star or musician she admired? Interests? Vampires, ghosts, and horror, apparently. Which did at least suggest that when, or if, Rav eventually found her, Alan was looking good on two counts out of three. And that was that. The Zone's founder,

Travis, being what he was, which was both mad and paranoid, the forum's profiles were free of any of the Facebook links, email addresses, Twitter handles, joining dates, locations, or post counts you might find on sites run by saner individuals.

Rav's next port of call would have been the Zone's search engine, which on a conventional forum site would have allowed you to search for all posts by a specific individual. Except that on the Zone, it was intentionally disabled, something Rav already knew from his time spent there. And Rav also knew that using Google to search the site was a non-starter too, because not content with disabling his own site's search engine, Travis had configured the Zone to tell Google's searchbots to sod off also, rendering any and all posts made on the Zone pretty much unsearchable.

Which left only the old-fashioned way: fingers, eyeballs, and a kilo and a half of human grey matter. Rav clicked through to the "General" forum, and sighed. He was looking at a long night.

A very long time later, Rav hit select and copy on the last of Tabitha's posts on the last of the Zone's many sub-forums and pasted it into the Word document he'd been building up. He wasn't quite sure how many separate posts it contained, but it had to be in the several hundreds, if not thousands. The oldest of the posts had been made nearly two years ago, while the most recent was from three weeks ago – the same three weeks ago that she'd last contacted Alan, Rav realised. What he could say was that the document, containing, as it did, not just Tabitha's words, but the words of the people she was quoting in her replies, was – according to Word's status bar – two hundred and seventy-six pages long. The glowing clock on the cable box beneath the TV showed a time of 2:06 in the morning.

After eight hours solid spent copying and pasting text and URLs, Rav's eyes were having difficulty focussing, his wrists were practically on fire, and his brain was so mashed that, right then, getting killed by Alan would have been preferable to actually sitting down to read the document he'd so laboriously created. So he instead contented himself with switching his printer on, making sure it had a stack of paper in its tray, setting the document printing, and then heading on upstairs, pausing only to carefully set the burglar alarm, just as the Sikh installer had shown him.

Then he crawled into bed and fell into a restless sleep, broken by dreams of glowing text, and endlessly tapped keyboards.

Having spent the previous two days largely avoiding actual social work, he spent most of Wednesday working though his backlog, phoning his various clients, working his way through the stack of emails in his inbox, and studying the two new case files that had magically appeared on his desk. If nothing else, it took his mind off the ticking bomb of Damocles currently suspended over him. He did take a moment to shove the Zone printouts into an envelope addressed to the Professor and ask a colleague who was visiting one of the Professor's neighbours to drop the package off. He wasn't sure if the older man would be able to spot anything in there, but he figured it was worth a try.

Thursday passed similarly. Having struggled through the day largely pretending to work, Rav headed home via a takeaway fried chicken joint and spent a second evening rereading through Tabitha's posts and re-examining the case. But all he drew was still a big fat blank. He went to bed contemplating alternatives, wondering if he could cut some sort of deal with Alan, one which didn't require him to find Tabitha. Insomnia supplied the answer: no. Eventually, depression and exhaustion managed to overcome fear and adrenaline and he fell into something that was close enough to actual sleep to take him through to his alarm, which he then proceeded to ignore.

When he finally crawled out of bed a little after nine, it was only to call in sick, which wasn't exactly a lie. He realised now that he'd begun to react in the way everyone and anyone does when they've just been informed they've got a terminal condition; his terminal condition being, of course, that in just over a week a Romanian vampire with secret police training was going to hunt him down and kill him. Having been force-fed all this crap on a four-year social work degree, he even knew what it was called: the Kubler-Ross model.

He'd spent most of the week in denial, convinced that the solution bus would sooner or later arrive if he just waited patiently at the stop. The next stage in the classical model would have been anger, except that, as an ex-girlfriend had once observed, Rav didn't really do anger, as such. Not properly, as a real man would have done it. (She could have coped with a bit of genuine rage, she'd told him, but the ersatz blend of whining, sulking, and self-pity he'd offered instead apparently got right on her tits). No, it was now clear to Rav that having wasted most of the week on denial he'd jumped straight past anger to bargaining, and had now arrived at depression. Of course, understanding what was happening to him didn't help, especially given that such understanding came with the knowledge that the next stage was acceptance, and he wasn't yet ready to accept that it was his fate to be murdered by a Romanian vampire at the age of twenty-seven.

He made himself some toast and turned on the box. Might as well watch a bit of Jeremy Kyle while he waited to get topped.

By mid-morning Saturday, after yet another troubled night of sleep, Rav had departed completely from the classical Kubler-Ross model and was now very much "off-piste", oscillating between depression, panic, anger, denial, sulking acceptance, and the occasional animal urge to have sex, or failing that, a quick wank. At some point he realised he was hungry. He rooted around in the kitchen and found a not-too-past-its-sell-by-date Pot Noodle hiding at the back of a cupboard. He poured on boiling water, waited thirty seconds, then started to eat. Then, somehow, something changed. Maybe it was the nourishment. Or perhaps it was just a realisation that, if it was his fate to die soon, he really didn't want to spend what time he had left on this Earth watching Football Focus. Either way, some defiant instinct within Rav chose that moment to stir.

He flicked through the two hundred and seventy-six pages of Tabitha's posts, but it was still the same mash of self-indulgent teenaged twaddle it had been on Thursday night. He switched back to the Web and went to the Zone. The site sat there, on the screen, mocking him. He clicked round its forums and at some point found himself back on Tabitha's profile page. At the bottom was a Send Message button, which would allow him to send a private message to Tabitha, via the site, just as Alan had messaged him.

He could message Tabitha right now.

Such a move would be risky, perhaps even stupid. He'd always known this was an option, but he'd wanted to keep it as a last ditch alternative, to be used only when all other avenues had failed. And in sending the message, he would be admitting to himself the desperation of his situation. There was no control in this approach; either she voluntarily agreed to meet with him, or she didn't. And if she didn't, he'd have achieved nothing more than alert her that someone was looking for her, and if there was more to this story than Alan was telling him, which was entirely possible, that might be a very bad thing.

But not contacting her might ultimately end up with him failing to find her, and Alan as a result killing him, which would most definitely be a very bad thing. After a moment's thought he hit the button.

Hi Tabitha,
My name's Dr Ravinder Shah, and I work as an investigator. You don't know me, but I have something very important I need to discuss with you.

Is there any chance we could chat, either by phone, or perhaps face to face?

I do understand that this is a slightly strange request, so I'm very happy for any meeting to take place at a venue of your choice and at a time chosen by you, and for you to bring anyone else with you, if you would like.

I look forward to hearing from you.

Rav

He quickly read through it and corrected a couple of typos, then hit send before he changed his mind. Then his phone rang. When he saw who the caller was he strongly considered ignoring it. But depressed as he was, and as low as he was, there are some challenges a man must always face. "Hi Mum."

"Don't you 'hi' me. Where are you?"

"At home. Why? Where should I be?"

"At your cousin Sunita's wedding. You've already missed the temple. Try not to miss the reception too."

Rav muttered a silent curse. Bugger. What with worrying about his imminent death, he'd completely forgotten about Sunita's wedding, despite the ornate invitation box sitting on top of his XBox. Dammit. Dammit. Dammit. If Rav had been asked to list the activities he might have wanted to spend what could very well be the last weekend of his life engaged in, attending a wedding would not have been one of them. He wasn't being asked, of course. His was not a life in which his weekends were entirely his own. Not when that life included an Asian mother and an inconveniently large family. "Yeah, fine. I'll just finish off some things and then get ready and head on over."

"You'll get ready now and head on over straight away. And get a minicab. I don't want you blaming buses for turning up after everyone's gone. You know what people are like, what they'll say."

"Yeah, fine, Mum," Rav told her. "I'll be a half hour." Laptop reluctantly closed, he headed to the bedroom to find a suit and a clean shirt. Having quickly dressed he pulled on his shoulder holster, checked that he was still packing a full magazine of holy water, and set out in search of a cab. At least if Alan did decide to come after him a week early, he'd have some means of defending himself. That was if the vampire found him, of course, which would not be a trivially easy undertaking, given that the attendance at this wedding would likely measure in the high hundreds.

Some might have considered the presence on this weekend of a large wedding to which Rav was invited to be a fortunate stroke of luck, giving him, as it did, the chance to hide in a crowd. The truth, however, was that this coinciding of events had less to do with fate than it did with cold, hard maths. That Asian weddings are large affairs is a generally known truth. What is less appreciated is the logical outcome of this truth, which is that if you will be obligated to invite every single person you are even distantly related to or merely vaguely know to your wedding, then every single person you might vaguely know or be even distantly related to will at some point invite you to theirs. Which is a lot of weddings. It sometimes felt to Rav that to be born into the Asian community is to be fated to spend every weekend of your life attending weddings – so much so that if he were ever to appear on Mastermind, his choice of specialist subject would have been obvious.

"Your name is?"

"Ravinder Shah."

"Your occupation?"

"Mental health social worker."

"And your specialist subject?"

"Hotels and conference centres in the West London area, 1995 to the present day."

"Two minutes on West London hotels and conference centres, starting now. What was the name of the Victorian hotel and banqueting centre behind Uxbridge bus station that was later demolished to make way for an Asda superstore?"

Chapter Fourteen

The hotel where Sunita and her new husband were celebrating their wedding was in Southall, a couple of miles away as the crow flies. Of course, crows don't have to contend with Saturday afternoon traffic, deserted road-works, diversions, and cab drivers in possession of opinions so extreme and obnoxious that only a strong desire to get to one's location and a mild case of Stockholm Syndrome prevents one from simply asking them to drop one off mid-route.

If Rav hadn't have been in need of a drink before setting out, and frankly he had, he was certainly in need of several when he eventually arrived. If there was one plus point to attending a wedding right now, it would be the presence of a free bar, a slice of hospitality he intended to abuse mercilessly. He snuck in through a side door he habitually used when arriving late at this hotel and managed to navigate to the bar without encountering his mother, his aunts, or any other close female relatives who might feel the need to exchange something more than a grunt and a vague nod. "Vodka and diet coke, ice, no slice," he told the first barman to become free, shouting just enough to be heard over the background Indian music the DJ was pumping out. He grabbed his drink, turned, and found himself face to face with the Professor.

"I thought it was you," the Professor said. "So I thought I'd come on over and say hello." The older man looked around. "I must say, I am enjoying myself immensely. It's such a wonderful cultural experience. And such delicious food. You really must try - but of course, you'd be used to it."

He laughed. Rav didn't. "Why are you here?"

"I was invited."

"You were invited? Why?"

"Because I'm a client of yours."

Rav took a very large swig of his drink. "They invited you because you're a client of mine?"

"Maybe they didn't want you to be lonely?"

Rav was having to work very hard to contain his inner pout. Asian weddings might indeed have a large guest list, but this still smacked of one of his various relatives playing a very specific practical joke on him. Still, it could have been worse. They could have invited–

"Hello, Rav!"

"Fen! Hi. Good to see you. I wasn't, erm–"

"-expecting me? No, I don't suppose you were." She gave him the sort of smile a shark gives its lunch. "I'm actually a friend of the groom's family, just in case you were going to come up with some sort of narcissistically paranoid explanation involving yourself."

"No, no. Not at all."

The Professor tapped him on the arm. "Actually Ravinder, I have been meaning to talk to you about a couple of rather important things." The older man gave Rav a meaningful look.

"Really?" Rav replied, realising that this wasn't likely to be anything he'd want his boss overhearing. He gave Fen a resigned "Can't get out of work anywhere" shrug, grabbed the Professor by the arm, and led him out of the bar and into the function room. "So what's it you need to talk about?"

"Well, firstly, I think something might have happened to Richard Whiteley. He hasn't been on Countdown all week."

"Right." Rav took a slightly smaller swig of his drink and tried to look at least this side of happy. "I think maybe he might have, you know, moved on." He glanced around, just in time to catch his cousin Mindy advancing on them. She was dressed in a sari, and looked undeniably good, with the garment arranged to show a degree of flesh that cultural mores would have required her to cover up had she been wearing something Western. Sadly, though, the effect was somewhat spoiled by the angry scowl she wore upon her face.

"That's the last time I let you get your paws on anything of mine," she shouted, in a tone that seemed only partly mock anger.

"Yeah, the car. Sorry. I would have taken it through a car wash, but I knew I was already running late."

"I had to get the bus to work."

The Professor leaned in, interested. "Which bus?"

"Sorry?" Mindy replied, confused.

Rav took the opportunity to grab the steering wheel of the conversation and steer it sharply away from himself. He took an exaggerated look to either side of Mindy. "Here on your own?"

She replied through gritted teeth. "Yes."

"Oh, it's just that I was wondering if you were still going out with that Rocco bloke? And if he was still a total dickhead?"

"He's still a total dickhead, which is why I'm not still going out with him."

"Could have told you. Actually, I seem to recall I did."

She shrugged. "Yeah well, you know what it's like. The more people tell you, the more you want to prove them wrong. Way my love life's going right now I might be calling in our arrangement in three years' time."

The "arrangement" was an old joke that went back to their teens, back to when their families had first started trying to arrange a marriage between them. There'd been nothing heavy, of course. Their families weren't like that. No, this was just the standard stuff: hints, suggestions, more suggestions, sighs, tears, emotional blackmail, self-pity at having produced such a wayward son/daughter, and then more suggestions. Eventually, on a mutual cousin's birthday celebration that had turned into an epic drunken night out, they'd agreed over tequila shots that if they were still both single when they hit age thirty, they'd "let" their families marry them off. That had once seemed a long way off; at a mutual age of twenty-seven years and counting, not so much. Rav mock pouted at her. "Who's to say I'll still be single when we hit the big three-oh?"

"You bought an old white guy as your date to a wedding. Let's just say you're one option I figure I can rely on." She gave the Professor a dazzling smile. "No offence intended, love."

He tipped his head and smiled. "None taken, my dear. Actually, I don't believe we've been introduced." He stuck out his hand. "Quentin Richardson. And you are?"

She took his hand. "I'm Mindy. I'm the poor cow who loaned Rav her car the other weekend. I'm also his cousin."

"She's my Uncle Tony's daughter," Rav added.

"Ah. Is he your uncle on your mother or father's side?"

"Both," Rav told him. "Actually, neither. Well. My mother's aunt's, husband's first wife, who was also my father's uncle's – you know what? It's complicated."

Mindy disappeared into the bar and eventually returned with something long, thin, and in possession of a miniature paper umbrella. "So how are things?" she asked.

"Worse than you could possibly imagine, and then some more. Bad to an extent you wouldn't possibly believe."

She shrugged, sympathetically. "Shame. Have you seen your mother yet?"

"No. Why?"

"Because she's coming this way." She smiled over his shoulder. "Aunty Meera!"

"Mindy, my dear. You're such a good girl. Unlike some I could mention." His mother bustled round and gave Rav a disappointed stare. "When did you last have this suit dry-cleaned?"

"Hi Mum."

"Don't change the subject. Have you wished your cousin yet?"

"I was just about to." Rav reached into his inside pocket, pulled out his wallet, opened it, and extracted a twenty pound note.

"Last of the big spenders, eh?" giggled Mindy. His mother tutted.

He pulled out another twenty and – after a bit of rooting around – a torn and tattered tenner. "Fifty do?"

His mother gave him a full five seconds of disappointed staring before pulling a crisp, new, pink fifty pound note out of somewhere in her sari. She handed it over to him, grabbing the three old notes in return. "Luckily, your father remembered to go to the bank this morning."

Rav took a last swig of his drink, dropped it onto someone else's nearby table, and headed off into the hall, finding Sunita and her new husband somewhere in the centre of the room, surrounded by friends and family. Sunita had changed out of her heavy gold-encrusted wedding outfit into a more comfortable number, while her husband was still togged up in the full ceremonial regalia – Indian suit, turban, the works. Each wore a purple sash, upon which was pinned money. Rav eased his way through the throng and nodded at his cousin. "Sunita, hi. Good day?"

"Hi, Rav. Yeah, it has been. Didn't see you at the temple?"

"I was at the back."

"Liar." She nodded at her husband. "Have you met Sunil?"

Rav hadn't. He gave Sunil a respectful nod and manly handshake. "Having a good time?"

Sunil shrugged, then pulled at his collar. "Be better if I wasn't stuffed into this."

Sunita gave him a mock punch, then turned back to Rav. "Anyway, cuz, it's good to see you here. Any chance of a return invite some day?"

"Not real soon, no. Anyhow..." He grabbed a safety pin from a collection lying on a nearby table and neatly pinned the fifty pound note onto her sash – just in time to be damn near elbowed out of the way by a new arrival.

"Yo, Sunita, Sunil... Rav," the new arrival announced. "Vijay is in da house!"

"Hi Vijay," said Sunita, with slightly less warmth than she'd displayed towards Rav. "How's things?"

"I got a promotion. With a car. New BMW, full spec, init."

Vijay looked sneeringly at Rav's fifty pound note for a moment, then pulled out an already safety-pinned and assembled fan of five pink fifties, which he proceeded to pin onto Sunita's sash. He looked back at Rav and smiled the sort of smile that nine times out of ten will get you punched in the face. "So, Rav? You got new wheels yet? Man, I, like, pissed myself laughing when I heard you'd written off your old set."

"Glad to be of entertainment," Rav told him, nodding goodbye at

Sunita and attempting to step away, only to find Vijay following him.

"So, what you got planned for tonight?" Vijay asked him, leering in a manner so sleazy, that were it possible to bottle expressions, this one could have earned billions as a contraceptive.

Rav looked desperately around for an escape, only to immediately wish he'd both closed his eyes and plugged his ears instead. Across the room, Fenella was chatting with one of his many aunts. A little way behind her, his mother appeared to be engaged in the sort of hand-waving conversation that no doubt involved listing the many disappointments her wayward son had inflicted upon her. And the DJ sounded like he was just about to transition from the oldie's traditional stuff into the more modern bhangra that would have his many female cousins attempting to drag him onto the dance floor. "Sorry, mate, I've got stuff on, you know. Only stepping in for a moment to show my face."

He headed off before Vijay could reply and found the Professor describing to Mindy the negative repercussions of Carthage's defeat by Rome in 146 BC. The older man looked up as he arrived. "Ah Ravinder. There was that one other matter I wished to talk to you about, if you have a moment?"

Mindy used that as her excuse to whisper her apologies and slide gracefully away.

"Okay. What was this other thing?"

"Well, I think I've found a clue in Tabitha's postings."

"What?" Rav said, a little sharply, although in truth, it had taken huge self-control to not grab the Professor by the collar and scream the question into his face from a distance of an inch.

"I said, I think I've found a clue in Tabitha's postings."

"Yeah, yeah, I heard. What's the clue?"

"Ah, yes. Well, around eighteen months ago, in a rather long and rambling post discussing the merits of various musical acts within what appears to be termed the goth subculture, she made mention of a bisected hamster. It was used as part of a simile, but in such a manner as to suggest that she'd recently seen such a thing."

"And that's a clue, how?"

"Well, it would seem to be a reference to a somewhat controversial piece of art by the artist Richard Wright, entitled Hammy Bisected."

"Okay. So she's into dodgy modern art. That helps us how?"

The Professor smiled, in the manner of a man about to deliver a winning line. "Because Hammy Bisected was first shown to the public at an exhibition in January last year, two months after Tabitha made her post. Which suggests that she'd seen it while it was still in Mr Wright's workshop."

A cold bolt of hope was creeping down Rav's spine. "Where is this Richard Wright bloke?"

"Well this is where it gets interesting. One of the care workers at the hospital let me have a go on their Internet thingie, and I found this." He held out a printout. "His workshop is in Leeds, and as fate and coincidence would have it, he's throwing some sort of gathering there tonight, at eight o'clock. It did occur to me to call you earlier, but I didn't want to disturb you before the wedding."

Rav grabbed the printout and quickly read the details. Wright was launching his latest collection in Leeds, that night. It was a long shot, but if someone there might know Tabitha, it was a long shot worth taking. "I think we need to visit this gathering."

"But I'm due back at the hospital by eight."

Rav was already folding the printout up and shoving it into his pocket. "Don't worry. I'll give them a ring and get them to sign you out to me." He looked around for Mindy, and found her a few tables away, chatting to a couple of their many cousins.

"Hey, erm, Mind?"

"What?" She raised an eyebrow. "You only call me Mind when you're looking for a favour."

"I need to borrow your car for tonight. I'll have it back tomorrow. It's really important."

"No."

"It's a matter of life and death. As in, my current life, and my possible death."

"How?"

"Because I need to find a missing girl, and if I don't, a three hundred-year-old Romanian vampire's going to kill me, and I've just found out that someone who might know this girl is in Leeds, tonight."

"Fine! Don't tell me then." She reached into her handbag, pulling out a set of keys which she then proceeded to hurl straight at Rav's face in a manner impressive both in its accuracy and its venom. "But I'm warning you, cousin. If you bring my car back in anything less than pristine condition, it won't be three hundred-year-old Bulgarian vampires you'll have to worry about!"

"Romanian," Rav pointed out. He noticed the narrowing of her eyes, and decided withdrawal might be the best move. "Is it in the car park?"

"No, it's at home." She pointed at the glass of something alcoholic she was holding in her hand.

"Got it. I'll get a cab."

He grabbed the Professor and they headed to the hotel's entrance, where they proceeded to steal someone else's waiting mini-cab and head over to Mindy's parents' place in Hounslow. Her Honda Civic was parked on the paved front garden of the house, alongside her brother's Beamer and her Dad's Merc. They dived in and moved on to Rav's place, where he loaded the boot with the entire contents of his holy-water-based arsenal, plus several packets of crisps and a multi-pack of diet cokes.

That done, Rav plugged the sat nav in, tapped in the postcode from the flier, then stuck the unit onto the windscreen. After several seconds spent calculating, a route appeared on the sat nav's display. "Turn around when possible," it announced. Rav studied the display. "Okay, it says it's one hundred and ninety-nine miles, and that it will take us three hours and twenty-four minutes to get there, arriving at 7.45pm." He studied the flier. "Which is forty-five minutes after this thing starts." He looked down at the dash display. "Least we've got a full tank."

The Professor pulled a pair of sunglasses from somewhere inside his tweed suit, put them on, and turned to face Rav. "Well then, Ravinder. If it really is one hundred and ninety-nine miles to Leeds, and we are in possession of a full tank of fuel and are wearing sunglasses, then, in the immortal words of Jake Blues to his brother Elwood, I suggest that you hit it."

Chapter Fifteen

If Rav had ever in the past thought about the North – and, being a Londoner, he generally hadn't – the most likely adjectives to have come to his mind would have been "grim" and "gritty". Richard Wright's gallery was neither grim nor gritty. It was instead a swanky joint in the smart part of a modern, bustling city, with a glass frontage through which was revealed a spacious interior. Assembled on the other side of the plate glass were men in expensive suits and women in cocktail dresses, all chattering in the superficial manner that rich and posh people do, grazing all the while on the champagne and nibbles that an army of waiters and waitresses were distributing. Rav was wearing his best suit, but the people on view inside the gallery were managing to make him feel seriously underdressed. He nodded at the Professor and indicated the entrance, which lay a little way along the street, guarded by a tuxedo-wearing bouncer. Rav approached the goon in as casual a manner as he could manage. "We're here for the Richard Wright event."

The bouncer looked first at Rav, and then at the Professor, at no point failing to give an impression of anything other than casual disdain. He paused for a moment, sighed, then reached across to grab a clipboard that was hanging from a rail. "Name?" he asked, his Yorkshire accent adding just a touch of grit to the utterance.

"Well, we were added a bit late. Shah, Dr Ravinder Shah. And my colleague is Professor Quentin Richardson."

The goon studied the clipboard for a moment, his lips entirely failing to move in the manner a prejudiced Rav had been expecting, then looked back up. "You're not on the list."

"Well, as I said, we were added a little late."

"Looks like you weren't added at all, lads. Sorry. No name, no entry." The bouncer shifted slightly, his muscles moving under the tuxedo in a manner that clearly indicated that, however classy a doorman he might be, he was still very much capable of delivering a bout of savagely applied violence should circumstances so dictate.

"Is there someone else we could perhaps–"

"No."

"Okay. Well, sorry to trouble you." Rav grabbed the Professor's arm, and hauled him off down the pavement. "Let's see if we can get in the back."

The Professor had long possessed a romantic view of art and of artists, whether they be one-eared painters in damp Parisian garrets, or tubercolic writers in smoke-filled bars discussing politics with prostitutes long after both the sun and regular citizenry have bid the day farewell. But he could find nothing romantic about the event they were now attempting to gate-crash; neither in the opulent and modernistic luxury of the building's frontage and the gathering it was framing, nor in the rubbish–strewn back alley they were now attempting to traverse.

A little way ahead – past two puddles, several used syringes, and an overflowing industrial-sized bin – was a wooden door, remarkable only in the degree to which it managed to be both plain and ugly. It was also ajar. "Think it's some sort of back door," Rav announced, somewhat redundantly, given its status as an undeniable entrance at the undisputed rear of the building.

Sitting across from the door was a sleeping-bag clad down-and-out busily engaged in constructing a roll-up from several discarded cigarette butts. He looked up at Rav and the Professor. "Aye," he said, in an accent that hailed from somewhere a fair way north of Hadrian's Wall and a good bit west of Edinburgh. "It's a back door."

"Do you know whose back door it is?" the Professor asked him.

"Have you heard of an artist called Richard Wright?"

"Yes. I have."

"Well, that's his back door."

Rav took a cautious step towards the door, then looked back at the Professor. "Shall we go in?"

The Professor considered the question, and found a reckless urge he'd not known he possessed delivering an impulsive answer. "Why not? After all, for fortune to favour the brave, the brave do generally need to be foolhardy."

Rav nodded, then carefully pushed the door open to reveal a plain, functional corridor. The two of them began to creep forward along the grey tiled floor, Rav first, the Professor following close behind him. From an open door ahead came the sound of an angry Northerner, shouting. "Fuck's sake! I've got a room full of Leeds's fucking elite, all waiting to see my latest piece, a latest piece that isn't shitting finished because some twat can't manage to do a job so sodding simple my bloody dog could do it!"

"Calm down, Richard!" said a second voice, still northern, but with clear overtones of class and privilege together with a complete lack of incandescent anger. "Art's doing his best."

"I'm pushing, Mr Wright, I honestly am," said a third northern voice, presumably that of the aforementioned Art. "But there's nothing there."

Just ahead of the Professor, Rav halted, having reached the open door.

The younger man held up a warning hand, then crouched down and looked around the doorframe. For several seconds the Professor waited, increasingly impatient, until finally, with no information apparently forthcoming, he leaned over the younger man so that he too could peer through the open doorway. The resulting change in viewpoint revealed a scene so bizarre that Rav's failure to communicate it was instantly understandable.

It was not that the Professor had never seen a man naked from the waist down, squatting on top of a glass coffee table. He had. After all, he'd been an undergraduate at Cambridge during a period where sexual experimentation was not so much accepted as required. But of all the sights he'd been expecting to see upon entering Richard Wright's workshop – and given the man's reputation as a purveyor of "shock art" he hadn't been so naïve as to expect oil paintings and watercolours of landscapes and flowers – a half-naked man squatting on a coffee table had not been one of them.

Standing beside the glass coffee table, wearing a paint-stained apron over an expensive suit, was an angry man of an angular appearance. The face was familiar, the Professor having seen it in both newspapers and on the Internet. This was Richard Wright himself. Wright chose that moment to look across at the two intruders. "Who the fuck are you twats?"

In the last three weeks, Rav had been attacked by vampire pigs, kidnapped by a vampire, and metaphorically emasculated by some kind of female spook. It was therefore a tribute to the force of Richard Wright's personality, that even after having his baseline definition of threat so extensively re-calibrated, Wright's glare was still scary enough to set Rav's bowels quivering. He desperately searched for the excuse they really should have come up with before entering the building, but was saved by the man standing beside Wright. "For God's sake, Richard, they'll be the insurance adjusters I told you about."

Wright offered them an apologetic smile. "Sorry. Thought you might be some of those wankers from the party."

"Do they look like they're from the party, Richard? Look at their suits, for God's sake!"

Wright nodded, then removed the smile from his face with a swiftness that suggested a mercurial temperament in which moments of pleasantness were limited offers only. "Well, stay over there and don't get in the way. I'm an artist, and I allow nowt to get between me and my art." He turned back to the individual still squatting half-naked on the glass coffee table. The man looked to be in his mid-twenties, skinny rather than slim, with slightly shaggy ginger hair. Wright stared hard at him, regarding him in much the same way as a jogger might regard the dog whose dog shit he'd just trodden in.

"Let me try again," said the squatting man. "I'm sure there's something there." He breathed deeply, once, twice, then let out a long grunt of exertion. The pale skin stretched across his exposed buttocks rippled as the muscles lying beneath squeezed and contracted. A vein throbbed in his forehead, pulsing like a blinking LED on a machine about to explode. Finally, after long seconds in which literally nothing had managed to occur, the grunt turned to a groan, the groan turned to a moan, and the man settled back down onto his haunches. Despair, fear and exhaustion battled for control of his sweat-covered face. "I'm really sorry, Mr Wright," he said.

"It's okay, Art," said the second man.

"It's not bloody okay!" screamed Wright. "Eat some beans, I told him. Have a curry. On me, I told him. I delegate one, simple task to him, and he manages to fuck it up. This piece is supposed to be the centrepiece of the whole sodding exhibition. The entire show's built around it. Without this piece, none of it works. You know those bastards out there are just looking for a chance to take me down, just looking for an opportunity to stick the fucking stiletto in." He looked across at Rav and the Professor. "It's because I'm a Northerner. Northerners are supposed to stick to matchstick men, cloth caps and pictures of coal mines. Grit, you know?"

Rav gave him a vaguely affirmative nod.

"They bloody fawn over Damien sodding Hirst. Fucking southern bastard. He cuts a sheep in half and the whole establishment practically get down on their knees to give him a blowjob. I cut a hamster in half and they say it's a derivative copy." He gesticulated at the coffee table and it's unfortunate occupant. "This could have been my big chance, and now it's ruined. Ruined!"

"Well," said the second man. "You could perhaps try taking over from Art and perform the final creation of the piece yourself?"

Wright looked up. "What?"

"Well, you could climb up and–"

"And?"

"Take a shit yourself."

"You want me, Richard Wright, member of the Royal Academy, to climb up onto a glass coffee table and take a shit on it?"

"Well, it is what you were asking Art to do–"

"I am the artist! I am the creator! I am the visionary! Do you think Damien Hirst spent a half dozen hours sawing through that sheep by hand? Do you think he poured in the formaldehyde? Do you think he sticks on all those fucking diamonds or paints all those little sodding blobs?"

An uncomfortable silence settled upon the workshop, which Rav consciously avoided breaking for fear that someone might suggest that he climb up on the coffee table and attempt a dump. The guy on the coffee table, Art, cleared his throat. "How about Coco, Mr Wright?"

"What?"

Art pointed across the room, to where a Great Dane lay sleeping on a large, cushion-like dog bed. "It's been quite a few hours since we took her out for her to, well, do her business. Perhaps she could do something?"

Somehow, Wright's level of anger, which had already been set to a pretty much nova-heat ten, managed to find a level of eleven to notch up to. He advanced across the floor towards his minion, each slow step punctuated by a screamed-out monologue. "You what? I knew you were stupid, Art. I knew you had no sense of what counts as fucking art, Art. But even in my worse nightmares I never dreamed you might be as thick as sodding pig shit. This piece is intended to symbolise the duality of man, as both angel and beast. Possessing a mind brilliant enough to craft steel and glass into a glass and steel coffee table, but still, at the heart of it, an animal, with animal functions. You might not fucking get it, but those bastards out there will. Do you not think they might notice if I walk out there and try to persuade them that a piece of dog shit counts as art?"

"Well no, but–"

"Get out!" Wright roared. "Just fucking get out now!" He gave Art about half a second to react before dragging him off the table, still naked from the waist down, and then hauling him out of the room. There was the sound of scrabbling feet from the corridor outside, a last round of shouted protest, and then the thump of a heavy door slamming closed.

Wright returned to the room. "If he tries to come back," he told the second man. "Tell him he's sacked."

"There's are rules, Richard. Employment laws."

Wright drew himself up into what he presumably intended to be a noble pose. "My art cannot be constrained by rules. Art has no rules, no boundaries, no constraints." For a moment he held the pose, then reality came crashing back down upon him, and he collapsed into a chair, moaning softly. "What the fuck am I going to do? They're all here. All just waiting to laugh at me. This was supposed to be the centrepiece of the whole sodding exhibition, and now it's ruined. Utterly, fucking ruined."

Beside Rav, the Professor stirred. "Could you not just send out the table?"

"What?"

"Just send out the table."

The second man bounced forward. "Of course! The insurance guy's right, Richard. Just send out the table."

Wright's head lifted slowly up out of his cradling hands. "Are you two twats mad? You want me to send out the table, and just the table?"

"Yes," the second man told him.

"But it's just a sodding glass coffee table from IKEA that I put together. That's not art. It's not even fucking craft."

"Well strictly speaking Art and I put it together–"

"They will laugh at me!" Wright shouted, pointing at the wall, but presumably indicating the party beyond. "They will fucking piss themselves laughing."

"They won't, Richard. They really won't. It's your vision that makes it art. Your vision that takes mere glass and metal and gives it meaning."

Wright got up out of the chair, walked slowly past Rav and the Professor to a metal filing cabinet, opened it, took something out, and then returned, waving the object he'd retrieved as he did so. "This is the brochure for this exhibition. And what does it say is the main exhibit? The central pillar upon which the entire artistic vision for the collection rests? A work entitled 'Steaming Pile of Shit on a Glass Coffee Table'." He made little air-quotes as he ground out the final words. "Now, and I know this is a hard one, but do you think that if we just put a sodding coffee table out in front of them, those fuckers might, perhaps, maybe, half-pissed out of their fucking minds on my free bloody champagne as they might be, notice the total, complete, and utter absence of anything that could possibly be described as a steaming pile of shit?"

The Professor chose that moment to interject, answering a question that Rav had assumed to be hypothetical. "But isn't that the point?"

Wright looked hard at the Professor. "How exactly is that the fucking point?"

"Well, surely the steaming pile of shit is a metaphorical statement? When we look around we see the gleaming, modern world we wish to see, and studiously avoid seeing the dirt, destruction and suffering that lays beneath. That table looks sleek, perfect. But what of the CO_2 that was consumed in its production and transport? What of the third-world labour that went into its manufacture? As a piece of art, its very untarnished perfection invites the viewer to consider its true nature, and from that, the true nature of the world."

Rav nodded, not out of an agreement, but out of a desire to calm Wright down before he decided to do some performance art on someone's face with his fists. The second man jumped in.

"Exactly, Richard, that's it entirely. Hurst would go for the actual shit and miss the metaphor completely – just as he always does. But you're better than that. And your art is better than that."

For several long seconds Wright considered what they were saying. Then his craggy face split into a broad smile. "You're all right, of course you are. And I'm sorry about the shouting. Passions can run a little high here when we're in the business of creating art. Now, how can I help you, Mr–?"

"Shah," Rav told him. "Ravinder Shah."

He was about to elaborate further when a large shadow passed in front of him. It was the tuxedo-clad bouncer from the door. "I think they're getting a bit restless out there, Mr Wright. Is the final piece ready to be moved in?" He shifted on his feet whilst waiting for an answer, and then appeared to notice Rav and the Professor. He examined them for a moment, then turned back to Wright. "These two were trying to gate-crash the front door without tickets, sir. I turned them away. Are they friends of yours?"

"No, they're insurance people, I think. Isn't that right, Mr Shah?"

"Well, actually, no."

"You're not the insurance people?"

"No. We're actually doing an investigation."

Wright's earlier, momentary bonhomie, was gone now, replaced with a blunt suspicion. "You fuckers police?"

"No, no. Nothing like that."

"Good. Means I don't have to put up with you." He nodded at the bouncer. "Throw them out the back."

"Do you want me give them a good beating, Mr Wright?"

Wright at least had the common decency to spend a second or two thinking on his answer. "No. Just slap them about a bit."

Chapter Sixteen

The bouncer stood and examined his work for a moment, then stomped back into the building, slamming the heavy wooden door shut behind him as he did so. Rav felt like he'd just been punched several times in the face, which wasn't particularly surprising given that he had in fact just been punched several times in the face. After giving himself a few moments to lie on the cold tarmac moaning, he hauled himself up into a sitting position. He looked over at the Professor, who was in no apparent hurry to get up. "Well, that went well."

The older man sat up and brushed several large clumps of dirt from his jacket. "Yes. Exceedingly so." He nodded at the now closed, and probably locked, door. "Should we attempt to re-enter the building?"

Rav shook his head. If that was "a bit of a slapping about", he wasn't particularly keen to undergo the full "good beating" experience. He looked over at the down-and-out, who was by now putting the finishing touches to his recycled roll-up. "Hey mate? Did you see a bloke go past here with nothing on from the waist down?"

The down-and-out nodded. "Aye." He pointed down the alleyway. "I think you'll find the poor wee bastard hiding behind your bin there."

"Thanks," Rav told him. He pushed himself to his feet, helped the Professor up, then walked over to the bin and peered round its edge. Art was huddled against it, legs drawn up in a sort of seated foetal position. He was shivering, and his eyes were flicking from side to side. When he recognised Rav he instinctively lifted his hands.

"Please help me! I don't know what to do. My phone, my wallet, my bus pass... my trousers – they're all in there."

Rav took off his jacket and held it out to the crying man. "Wrap that around yourself, mate. How about we have a little chat, and then we can drive you home?"

Art was holding his coffee with both hands, like a toddler holding onto a much-loved stuffed toy. A haunted expression lurked behind his eyes. Rav gave him a reassuring smile, then showed him the copy of Tabitha's profile picture he'd saved on his phone. "Have you ever seen this girl? We think she might have come to the workshop for a private viewing of a previous work."

Art took the phone and examined the picture carefully. "Well, it's not a very good picture, and I only saw her a few times, but it looks a bit like Judith's daughter, Tabitha. Judith's Mr Wright's secretary."

This revelation didn't so much ease the tension within Rav as cause a large chunk of it to burst free – like a centuries-stuck Pacific Rim fault line suddenly slipping several dozen feet. As releases of tension go, it admittedly wasn't quite up there with taking a last drag on your final cigarette, only to find your hood being removed and the captain of the execution squad handing you a letter of reprieve from El Presidente. But this dramatic break in the case certainly qualified as a metaphorical dance-around-a-late-night-coffee-shop-kissing-random-strangers-of-both-genders level of release.

Rav didn't actually dance around the coffee shop. Common sense told him that he needed to avoid any and all sudden behaviours that might scare an already jumpy Art. Instead, he drew upon every single Zen technique he'd learned from Hong Kong martial arts movies to channel the release of tension inward, away, and down, into his inner core. The tension flowed down his spine and into his right leg, which then jerked violently upward into the table, his knee cap colliding with the solid underside with enough force to bring tears to his eyes. He gulped, took a moment to compose himself, took a sip of his latte, then looked back to Art. "So, Art. Tell me about Judith."

Forty-five minutes later – having found out what else Art knew about Judith, which wasn't much, and dropped him off at his place – they were driving into the outskirts of a small town that claimed to be named "Ecktonshaw" and in all likelihood probably was, this not being the sort of thing council signage departments lie about.

Art had told them that Judith lived in Ecktonshaw. Unfortunately, this was pretty much the point where his knowledge of Judith's life outside the office ended. If this had been a clichéd private eye movie, and Rav had been a clichéd private eye, the most obvious course of action for him to have then taken would have been to break back into Wright's place, find his office, rifle through a few random filing cabinets or hack into a few random PCs, and find Judith's employee file, electronic or otherwise. Truth be told, Rav had actually considered this, but had been dissuaded from this course of action by a sudden and terrifying image of Wright presenting a surprise political piece to his assembled guests, in which he would comment critically upon the War on Terror, extraordinary rendition, and Guantanamo's Camp X-Ray using only an orange jumpsuit and an Asian guy he'd just had his bouncer beat the living shit out of.

By now, it was well into the evening, and Ecktonshaw's high street was deserted, its shops shuttered, its pavements empty. Midway down its length was a 1960s concrete box of a pub with a car park just beyond. "Might as well ask around here," he told the Professor.

100

"Do you think they'll know anything?"

"Don't know. But I could murder something and chips if they're still serving."

As someone who'd been schooled in the finer points of gritty, 1960s kitchen-sink dramas written by angry, northern playwrights, the Professor found the pub to be something of a disappointment, entirely lacking as it did whippets, flat caps, and matronly battleaxes dispensing unwanted advice from behind the shield of a milk stout. Upon entering, he found instead only the standard polished wood interior decorated with brightly coloured signs and menus that now causes local public houses to be almost indistinguishable at first glance from low end Italian pizza joints. He followed Rav to the bar, where they climbed onto a couple of stools and ordered a Diet Coke, a white wine, and steak and ale pie with chips twice from a barman whose accent was most definitely not from anywhere nearby. Apparently undeterred by this, Rav got out his phone and held it up. "Hey mate, have you ever seen this girl around here?"

The barman peered carefully at the picture, then shrugged apologetically. "No, but I have only been here few weeks."

"Right," Rav said. "Where were you before, then?"

"Lithuania."

"Okay. Is there someone else who's been here longer?"

The barman thought for a moment. "Agnieszka's been here while. I ask." He went away, and then returned a few moments later with a good-looking blonde girl.

"You have question?" she asked.

"We're looking for a friend of ours," Rav told her. "We think she might have been round here." He held out the phone.

She too studied it for several seconds, before shaking her head. "I not recognise her. Sorry." She gestured around the room. "Maybe some of the customers might know her?"

"Yeah. Thanks anyway."

They retreated to an adjacent table and waited for their meals, which arrived after twenty minutes or so. The Professor ate his as his mother had taught him, slowly and precisely, each mouthful carefully chewed and then deliberately swallowed. Rav had either never had such training, or else was very, very hungry, because within a few minutes of his meal's arrival, all that was left on his plate was a pile of unwanted salad and a smear of ketchup. The younger man deposited his knife and fork on the plate and slid off his seat. "You stay here," he told the Professor. "And look after the drinks. I'll see if I can get anything out of the natives."

Rav liked to think of himself as a cosmopolitan chameleon, able to effortlessly and seamlessly adjust the way he presented himself in order to fit smoothly into any social context. In a kebab joint, one of the geezers; at work, a (mostly) professional social worker; on a date, a caring and thoughtful progressive. But there was something about this entirely white, semi-rural, slightly decaying Northern town that was managing to make him feel like the proverbial turd on a billiard table, the apparently sore thumb that was very much standing out. It wasn't what was said so much as what he could sense not being said; and not so much the looks he was receiving as the looks he could sense he wasn't receiving.

It wasn't a very nice feeling.

On another occasion, Rav might have been put off by this. Might have found himself making an excuse to leave. He generally operated very much from the position that ignorance is bliss, and that what one doesn't know can't piss one off. But that modus operandi was from an earlier time, from before he'd acquired as a client a lovelorn Romanian vampire for whom failure was not an option but a revenge killing most definitely was.

He paused for a moment, metaphorically adjusted his bollocks, and marched over to the nearest occupied table, around which sat an assortment of hoodie-clad youth of such desperate appearance that even the most fanatical patriot would, upon encountering them, feel compelled to immediately investigate the emigration options available to him. They looked up at him as he approached, their slack-jawed expressions not quite having the energy to manage dislike. "Hi!" he said, giving them a wave.

"What's he's doing here?" said one of the hoodies to his neighbour, totally ignoring Rav. "His lot normally stay up in Bradford."

"Probably trying to flog something," replied the second hoodie. "You know what them bloody Pakis are like." There was a chorus of mutters and nods around the table. The second hoodie looked back up. "Oi, pal. Piss off."

Rav spent a few seconds working very hard to not lose his rag at such a blatant display of racism, then decided that cold, calculating politeness and a refusal to be offended was actually the best revenge. "I was wondering if you guys could help me?"

The hoodie performed a double take at the sound of his accent. "You from London or something?"

"Yes." Rav gave him a cold smile. "We've got Pakis too."

"What d'ya want then? We ain't buying anything. We've only got our giros. We don't get to claim all them extra benefits like you Pakis do."

As generally easy-going as he was, this was not a level of abuse that Rav would normally tolerate. On any other occasion, in any other situation, he'd have liked nothing better than to surgically dissect the racist bullshit the hoodies were sprouting and fling the resulting pieces back into their faces. But this wasn't such an occasion. Instead, he held out his phone, making damn sure to keep hold of it rather than handing it over. "I'm looking for a girl. I think she's from round here."

The hoodie glanced at the image. "I ain't helping you get a white girl. You should stick to your own women. Ain't our fault they all dress like ninjas."

Rav shook his head. "I'm not looking to sleep with her." He pulled out his wallet, and extracted a ten pound note. "I'm a private detective. I've been hired to find her."

The hoodie looked suspiciously at the note, then looked back at the phone. He examined it for a few seconds, blinked, looked closer, and then spoke. "She looks like that bird who shagged Danny round the back of Asda."

He motioned to one of the other hoodies, a pimply teenager with greasy ginger hair. The carrot-top leaned in and studied the picture for several moments, but then shook his head. "No, it weren't Asda. It were Morrisons."

The address Rav had managed to bribe out of the hoodie teens turned out to be that of a modest house, set beside a road on the edge of town alongside several similarly modest houses. Its garden was neat, if not grand, with a small lawn surrounded by flowerbeds. A gravel path led up to a green door, set into which was a small, frosted glass window. Rav gave the doorbell a few sharp buzzes. After several seconds, a light was turned on in the hallway beyond. There was the sound of a chain being put on a latch, and then the door opened a few inches. A middle-aged woman wearing a dressing gown looked through the gap at them. "Yes?"

"Mrs Landon?" Rav asked. "Mrs Judith Landon?"

"Yes. Can I help you?"

"My name's Ravinder Shah. I'm a private detective. This is my colleague Quentin Richardson. We're very sorry to bother you so late at night, but we were wondering if we could talk to you about your daughter?"

The woman blinked. "Why? Is there a problem?"

Rav gave her a smile pitched as friendly, but serious, with a dose of concerned compassion mixed in. "It's nothing bad, but we think she might have got involved with something over the Internet. We'd just like to ask you some questions."

She nodded. "You'd better come in."

"It all started about six months ago," Judith told them, her hands wrapped around the mug of tea she'd made after inviting them in. "I'm not quite sure why. I think maybe she might have met a boy. She's had some trouble with boys, I'm afraid."

Rav took a sip of the coffee she'd made him, then glanced at the plate of biscuits that sat on the small table in front of him. These were serious biscuits, quality shit; the sort of posh assortment of Belgian pastry and confectionary a mid-ranking ambassador would serve at a diplomatic bash. He'd snaffled two early on and was working on convincing himself that to make a move on a third wouldn't look greedy. He tried to put the biscuits out of his mind and turned his attention back to Judith. "In what way?"

"Well, there was some nasty gossip in town not long after we moved here. She-" Judith choked on the next word, tears forming in her eyes.

The Professor was sitting on the sofa beside Rav. He smiled encouragingly at the clearly upset woman. "Go on, my dear."

The woman took a gulp, and then the words tumbled out of her. "She'd apparently been letting boys do things to her round the back of the Asda."

Rav leaned forward. "Actually, our investigations suggest it was more likely to have been Morrisons."

A half hour later they were crunching back down the pathway and getting into the car. Rav didn't start the engine, wanting first to get his head round the story Judith had just told them. "So let me get this straight. Six months ago she had a row with Tabitha, and Tabitha moved out. Judith doesn't know where she is now, because Tabitha won't tell her, but she occasionally calls, so she knows she's okay. She thinks she might have met some boy on the Internet, but doesn't know anything more than that. And that's pretty much all she can tell us. So other than the fact that we now have a surname, we're pretty much no better off."

For once, the Professor wasn't consulting his notebook. "That is indeed an accurate summary of what she's told us."

"It would all fit, wouldn't it? Alan said that he'd met Tabitha online about six months ago." He looked across at the Professor, who merely looked back, a half smile upon his lips. "What?"

"It might, as you put it, all fit. But I think this is one of those occasions where, while two pieces of a puzzle might fit, it is an incorrect join, for they do not come from adjacent parts of the picture."

"I have no idea what you're talking about."

"I think we should reverse the car a little way down the road, and then wait. Here. And watch." The older man settled back down into his seat, apparently not inclined to volunteer additional information. Rav did as he suggested and reversed a few houses down, twiddled around a bit on the radio until he found a local station and then sat back to listen.

They waited.

And waited.

Time passed, slowly and painfully, like a lazy, bad-tempered and unionised mule currently engaged in a work-to-rule labour dispute. Rav had already been pretty depressed at the apparent termination of what had but hours ago seemed such a promising lead. Now, as the minutes ticked slowly and pointlessly by, he started to develop cravings. Not necessarily for anything in particular – although crisps, chocolate, and some kind of caffeine-containing carbonated drink were coming to mind. He really just wanted to get out of the car for a few minutes. He remembered spotting a small corner-shop-stroke-off-license at the top of the street of the open most hours sort. "I'm just going to the shop at the end of the road to get some stuff," he told the Professor. "You want anything?"

"Perhaps some cream cakes and a small pot of Earl Grey?"

"I don't think it's that sort of place."

The older man looked disappointed.

Rav patted him on the shoulder. "I'll see what I can do." He got out of the car and headed down the street to the shop. It proved to be claustrophobically small, made more so by the huge array of goods that had been shoehorned into its non-spacious interior. Within its tiny space it offered snack foods, cigarettes, pills for headaches and indigestion, condoms, soft drinks, beer, wine, spirits and pornography, thus covering ninety-five per cent of the typical man's daily needs. Rav grabbed a flapjack and a tin of some beverage that claimed to be tea-related for the Professor, and a Diet Coke and a tube of Pringles for himself.

The middle-aged Asian guy behind the till managed to ring up the purchase without once moving his eyes away from the small TV set mounted beneath his counter, an impressive feat of manual dexterity, if not of customer service. Rav grabbed his change, shoved his purchases into the gossamer thin carrier bag the bloke had thrown at him – after spending the requisite thirty seconds trying to perform the feat of advanced conjuring required to get such a bag to open – and then headed for the doorway.

A young woman arrived on the way in, as he was headed out. They did the classic no, you; no, sorry, me; no, sorry, you, dance for a few seconds. Rav eventually smiled, stepped back, waved her in, and looked at her properly for the first time.

It was Tabitha.

Chapter Seventeen

Tabitha's hair was blonde, now, not dark, and her eyes were made up a delicate shade of pink, rather than panda style, and the coat she was wearing was coloured the hue that a Dulux chart will tell you is cobalt blue. Rav didn't know it was cobalt blue, but he knew it sure as hell wasn't black, even though this was sure as hell her. She gave him a smile that was friendly, but only to the point of politeness, then headed past him into the shop.

Rav stood stunned for a few seconds, then quickly scuttled out of the shop and found a hiding place in an adjacent doorway, where he loitered, attempting to not look overly suspicious. It was, he realised, yet another of those occasions where smoking is a distinct advantage. A smoker can always loiter, either in or out of doorways; it's what they do. And when they want to stop loitering, they can simply discard the cigarette and move on; that, again, being simply what they do. Rav made a mental note to buy some cigarettes. Some of those herbal ones, maybe. No point adding lung cancer to the list of things that might kill him.

A couple of minutes later, Tabitha emerged from the shop with a carrier bag bulging with purchases and set off down the street, away from Rav's hiding place, but towards her mother's house. He followed, as discreetly and casually as he could, watching as she turned at the house, walked down the path and let herself in with a key. He slid in beside the Professor, and handed over the can of the tea-related beverage and the flapjack. "That's all they had. Sorry."

The Professor regarded the can with an expression that hovered somewhere between curiosity and distaste. "How curious." He carefully opened the ring pull, then took a dubious sip, the resulting raised eyebrow perhaps indicating that it was not as bad as he'd feared. "Interesting. Anyway, I presume you saw the young lady entering the house."

"It was Tabitha."

"Well, obviously. Who else would it have been?"

"You knew she was coming home, didn't you?"

The older man considered Rav's accusation for a moment. "Strictly speaking, I knew only that she was still living in that house. I was merely hoping that she would be returning home tonight."

"How did you know?"

"My dear Ravinder. You really do need to be more observant. The information you needed to know was all there in plain sight." The Professor took another sip of the tea-related beverage, then began to examine the flapjack.

"Such as?"

"Let's start with what we saw when we went in. We have a somewhat cultured woman, living in an area that we might charitably describe as being of a lower class than her. She was wearing clothing that looked to my admittedly amateur eye to be of a high quality, but perhaps slightly worn, and more importantly based on fashion trends of perhaps two or three years ago."

"What do you know about fashion?"

"More than you, it appears. Can I continue?"

"Yes. Sorry."

"Thank you. The furniture was again of a slightly too high quality, but, more importantly, there was too much of it. You might have noticed that the interior of the house was cluttered. In other contexts, one might assume this was simply due to a clutter-disposed personality. But such a person hoards not only furniture but all possessions in general, and when selecting those items displays neither taste nor discrimination. Put simply, when someone has too much furniture, they usually also have too many ornaments, too many photos, and too many rugs, most of which will be cheap, and many of which will be nasty."

This was starting to sound horribly like an analysis of Rav's mother's taste in interior decoration. He put that thought aside. "And that wasn't the case here?"

"No. This was quality furniture, carefully chosen to form an overall coherent pattern. There was just too much of it for the house. The obvious conclusion is that we have someone downsizing, from a larger and more prestigious home, to a smaller and more humble home."

"Well, she did say that they'd moved there a couple of years ago after her marriage broke up, so we're only really confirming what we already knew, right?"

"We are. But confirming things is what we want to be doing, and in addition, it is giving us insights into who Mrs Landon is."

"Good point. So what else?"

"As you know, before we left I requested her permission to use the toilet, something which you no doubt wrote off to simply my being an elderly man with an equally elderly prostate."

"Well, yeah."

"To be fair, I do have an elderly prostate, and I did need to go. But I also wanted to have a look at her bathroom. Bathrooms are terribly useful things. Not only can you learn more about someone from their bathroom than their bedroom, gaining access to it is far easier."

"So what did you learn?"

"Well, firstly, that Mrs Landon is apparently taking both hormone replacement therapy and the contraceptive pill."

"Ah."

"Ah indeed."

"But couldn't the contraceptive pills have been an old set that Tabitha left behind?"

The Professor gave Rav a disappointed look. "If there's one thing a young lady will take with her when she goes somewhere, it is her contraceptive pills. Avoiding unwanted pregnancy is of considerable importance to them, unlike, it appears, young men such as yourself. Besides, the box was placed in front of the HRT pills, implying that it was the one most recently used."

"Okay. Fair point. Was there more?"

The Professor started to tick points off on his fingers. "Two separate and incompatible ranges of toiletries. I know that to our male eyes, it usually just looks like an explosion of bottles, jars, brushes and combs, but there is actually method in their madness, and in this case there were two separate and distinct methods."

"Right."

"On the coffee table were two magazines, Woman's Realm and Heat. Both of which were the current editions. I can believe that in her depressed and somewhat fallen state, Judith might find herself watching cheap talent shows and tacky reality television, but I find it hard to believe that she'd go to a shop to buy a magazine about it."

"True."

"Then we have shoes, coats, the way the cushions were arranged on the sofa, and a set of car keys carelessly discarded on the shelf by the door, even though Judith doesn't drive."

"How do you know she doesn't drive?"

"There were three separate cards for minicab firms on the small table in the hallway where the phone sits."

"Well that only proves that one of them doesn't drive. The cards might have been for Tabitha."

"A teenaged girl wouldn't even use a landline in a hallway, let alone keep business cards next to it. She'd call on her mobile phone having used an app of some kind to find the number."

"Right." Quite frankly, Rav was feeling a bit stupid now. "Is there any more?"

"Considerably. Would you like to hear it?"

"Not really. So now what? Go back in and talk to Tabitha and find out how she feels about Alan, I guess?"

The Professor looked at Rav with the expression one might use when encountering a small child who's just taken a dump on your sofa and is now grinning at you as though awaiting applause – that expression being one that mixes shock with profound disappointment. "Why on Earth would we want to talk to Tabitha about Alan when she isn't even aware of his existence?"

"How can she not be aware of his existence? Alan's been talking to her for the last – oh."

"Oh indeed."

"You think he's been talking to–" Synapses fired randomly in Rav's brain, like spark plugs connected to a wonky camshaft, "–Judith?"

"Why else would Judith tell us that Tabitha had left home six months ago after a row between the two of them?"

"But what's that got to do with who's talking to Alan?"

"Everything."

"I'm not following you. She's clearly been lying about Tabitha leaving home. What I don't get is why that lie suggests she's the one who's been talking to Alan?"

"Because lies are not constructed in a vacuum, Ravinder. Sociopaths aside, lies are birthed amid guilt and shame. People will weave as much truth in as they can, even when those truths are so far out of context that they are effectively yet more lies. Judith wouldn't have invented the figure of six months, but would have stolen it from an entirely different truth."

"So you're saying that something else happened six months ago?"

"Yes. Consider the other facts. It was six months ago that Alan began his online relationship with someone he believed to be Tabitha. And when looking through the text of Tabitha's posts, I did notice a change in both frequency and language at around that point. At the time, I put it down to the relationship, to trying to impress a suitor. I now realise it was the opposite, someone attempting to match another's style."

"Sorry, let me get this straight. Six months ago, Tabitha started to sound a bit more grown up. You thought she was trying to appear grown up to impress Alan, but it was actually Judith trying to dumb herself down to her daughter's level, and not quite making it?"

"Exactly. Then we have the final piece in the jigsaw puzzle, which is that Tabitha is no longer a member of the gothic subculture she so frequently mentioned in her posts. I had suspected this might be the case, but it was only when I saw her changed appearance that I could be certain that it was Judith with whom Alan has been having his online relationship."

"How do you know she's not a goth anymore? Maybe she was coming back from work or something."

"That would explain the non-goth clothing, and the non-goth makeup. It wouldn't explain her hair now being blonde rather than black."

Rav realised that everything the Professor was saying was undeniably true. The urge to swear loudly while pounding the car's steering wheel was almost overwhelming, but after taking several deep breaths he managed somehow to get his emotions under control. "Okay. Right. So your theory is that, six months ago, Tabitha had some kind of Road to Damascus conversion and decided to suddenly become normal. And as part of that, she stopped doing all her online goth things. Which left an account at the Zone, in her name, with her picture, and a full posting history, that her mother, well, stole?"

"That is indeed my hypothesis."

"It's a bit sketchy."

The older man shrugged. "Hypotheses often are. When Judith answered the door, she appeared stressed and worried, which is to be expected, given her status as a lonely divorcee with money troubles who works for a narcissistic brute with delusions of grandeur. But when you revealed us to be private detectives, something most people would find either intriguing or disturbing or both, there was almost no reaction whatsoever."

"Because she'd got a mail from me this morning via the Zone, and knew who I was the moment I introduced myself."

"Exactly. And when you explained that you were looking for Tabitha, in a way that clearly indicated you to have no idea of her, Judith's, role in this whole affair, she relaxed."

The last shred of hope that Rav had been holding onto melted away. "So I'm screwed. Alan's going to kill me if I don't set him up with his girl, and now it turns out that the girl he thinks he's in love with is a fictional construct created by some lying, dried up old cow who stole her own daughter's identity in order to mess with some poor bastard's head on the Internet."

"Well, our friend Alan isn't entirely innocent in this matter, is he?" the Professor pointed out. "I seem to recall he's told Judith that he's a good-looking twenty-one-year-old student from Leeds."

"Of course! You're absolutely right. I'll just point that out to him, and he'll realise that it would be hypocritical to be angry at her." This time Rav did give the steering wheel a thump. "Maybe we should go in and have it out with Judith?"

"And what precisely will that achieve?"

"Well, it's something to do before Alan kills me."

"Things aren't perhaps quite as bleak as you fear."

Rav gave the Professor a very hard stare. "How do you make that out? Because from where I'm sitting, things are looking pretty damn bleak."

"Because while the principle that knowledge is power is a phrase repeated so oft as to be cliché, it is nonetheless true. We know things that others do not. We know where the woman with whom Alan is communicating lives, her true name, her true identity. These are all things Alan does not know. And we know Alan's true identity, something that Judith does not know. And, in addition, there are things they themselves know but are unaware that we know."

"Such as?"

"We know that Judith has been pretending to be Tabitha, but she doesn't know that we know that. She thinks her deception has gone unnoticed. That gives us an edge. Not much of an edge, admittedly. But an edge worth preserving. The last thing we should do now is tell Judith what we know. We must wait, and see how events unfold."

It was around then that Rav became aware of a vibration near his groin. It was his phone, set to silent. He reached into his trouser pocket and pulled it out. There was a landline number on the screen he didn't recognise. He wasn't particularly in the mood for conversation, but since it wasn't as though he had anything better to be doing he answered, giving his standard reply. "West Kensington Paranormal Detective Agency. Dr Ravinder Shah speaking. No case too weird, no problem too bizarre. Strangeness a speciality. How can I help you?"

"Ah, Mr Shah. My name is Sir Roger Trent. I apologise for calling at such a late hour, but I'm afraid I've become something of a night owl in my twilight years. You don't know me, but my former student, Quentin Richardson, recently contacted me regarding a somewhat delicate matter and gave me your number."

"You've found something?"

"I think I might have. Perhaps we could meet for lunch tomorrow? There's a rather nice restaurant just round the corner from my home."

"Yeah, course. Where are you?"

"A little town called Hebdon Bridge. It's in West Yorkshire, just past Halifax."

Chapter Eighteen

The Professor had always loved Hebdon Bridge; after a hiatus of more than twenty years, it was good to be visiting it again. And having resumed his relationship with it, he found it much as it had been then: a small, bohemian town nestled improbably high in the Pennine Hills, through which a canal even more improbably passed (a legacy of early nineteenth century engineers who'd been tasked with connecting Manchester to Leeds and weren't prepared to let an inconvenience such as gravity defeat them).

They found Sir Roger waiting for them at the restaurant, happily ensconced behind a window table with a large glass of something white in front of him. The Sir Roger that the Professor had known – first as his tutor, then as a mentor, and finally as a friend – had always been a vigorous man, always passionate, whether the matter at hand was a discussion of the merits of the pre-Raphaelite movement or the historical inevitability of proletarian revolution and the intrinsic superiority of the Soviet system.

More than twenty years had passed since last they'd met, but though age had somewhat withered the older man, whiskers and wrinkled skin aside, he was much as the Professor remembered him. His blue eyes still sparkled, and the handshake he offered after climbing unsteadily to his feet was firm, but friendly. "Quentin, it's good to see you, my friend. It really has been too long."

"It has Roger, it has." The Professor indicated Rav. "May I present my colleague Ravinder Shah?"

Sir Roger took Rav's hand and gave him a warm, two-handed shake. "Mr Shah. It is always good to meet one of Quentin's friends." He sat back down again. "Now, may I recommend the escabeche of mackerel fillet to start followed by the paillard of chicken breast. And perhaps some more of the Touraine sauvignon to drink?"

As restaurant food went, the fare produced by the Stuffed Pheasant wasn't bad. It wasn't the best Rav had ever eaten, and certainly couldn't have competed with one of Mo's kebabs, but then any dish not in possession of a wickedly strong garlic sauce would be onto a loser there. Sir Roger waited until they'd got onto the cheese and biscuits before turning to the matter at hand, having spent the intervening couple of hours engaged in an incomprehensible discussion of classical literature. (Incomprehensible, at least, to Rav – the Professor had seemed perfectly able to follow it). "So, you'll be wanting to hear what I've learned of your friend Alan, and his friend Nicolae."

"Well, yes," Rav stuttered, caught by surprise while engaged in an attempt to manoeuvre a freshly-sliced chunk of brie onto a cracker.

"Now, you'll understand that much of what I'm about to tell you is second-hand, perhaps even third-hand, based largely on Nicolae's communications with former colleagues from the Securitate?"

"Yeah, yeah. Understood."

Sir Roger acknowledged Rav's reply with a nod, then began to speak in a smooth modulated tone that had a highly professorial air. "Nicolae was a colonel in the Securitate from the late 1950s through to the revolution in 1989, with Alan as his deputy. Nicolae was not a nice man, even by the standards of the organisation to which he belonged. He was a personal confident of both Ceausescu senior and his son, Nico, and frequently worked as their personal enforcer." Sir Roger paused to spear a slice of cheese, then looked back up at Rav. "You're aware that they're both vampires, I presume?"

"Yes."

"Well, after the revolution, the trail goes somewhat cold. Having spent thirty years adding enemies to a list that was already rather full, they apparently went into hiding. I suspect this would have been something of a shocking change in lifestyle for them, accustomed as they were to being able to arbitrarily appropriate anything, or anyone, at either whim or wish. In fact, there's no firm record of them until just a few years ago, when they resurfaced here in Yorkshire of all places. But I understand you already knew that they were here?"

Rav quickly gulped down a lump of cheese and cracker. "We know that they're here and we know that they're working on some kind of project that has to do with vampire pigs. But that's it."

The old man chuckled. "Vampire pigs, eh? Well I never." He took a sip of wine. "But that would fit with what I've learned."

"Which is?"

"It appears that, following their arrival, Nicolae started putting out feelers to various organisations, both in the UK and abroad. Initially, it seems he was merely offering his services for hire, without much in the way of success. Despite what you might read in some of the more downmarket tabloids, the market for sadistic killers who can only operate during the hours of darkness is actually somewhat small. But then it seems that he found himself being offered something of a joint venture with an organisation of considerable power, so considerable that frankly when I realised they were involved I spent some time contemplating the option of forgetting that my former student here had ever contacted me."

"What organisation is this?"

"I'm not sure you wish to know, Mr Shah. They have a global reach and an influence that extends to every government and corporation on this planet." The old man paused, clearly troubled, but after a sip of his wine he continued. "Not a decision is taken, anywhere, without it having been approved by one of their people. They have no ideology, no higher purpose, no long-term aim. Influence and power itself is their sole raison d'être. Trust me on this, Mr Shah. Nicolae and Alan are the least of your problems. Don't fear the vampires. Fear these people, and whatever it is they want to do with your vampires."

"And what's that?"

"That I can't tell you, save to let you know that Nicolae was using his contacts in Romania to recruit certain specialists. Biologists. Geneticists. Doctors. People who, earlier in their lives, before the fall of communism, had followed certain state-sponsored lines of research, if you get my meaning. Something very bad is happening here, Mr Shah, and you appear to have wandered straight into the middle of it. If I were you, I'd be tempted to find a new life somewhere very, very far away."

"But who are these people? CIA? Ex-KGB? No, wait. It's the Illuminati, isn't it?"

The old man shook his head, sadly. "The Illuminati are a fictional organisation, Mr Shah, which exists only in the minds of madmen and fools. This is the real world, in which real people do real things."

"So who is it?"

Sir Roger looked first to his left, and then to his right, in an exaggerated manner that would have been funny were he not so obviously on the verge of soiling himself. Finally, he gulped, looked Rav straight in the eye, and then spoke in a whisper.

"The Rotarians."

"What?"

"The Rotarians." The old man sighed, exasperated. "You know, Rotary Clubs."

"The Rotary Club!"

The old man took another panicky look left and right, frantically waving at Rav to keep his voice down as he did so. "You must be quiet." he hissed. "Don't you understand? They have clubs in every city and every town. There might be some of them here, now."

"But that's just stupid."

The Professor laid a hand on Rav's arm. "Three weeks ago you would have described a suggestion that vampires exist as stupid, let alone vampire pigs. But they do. Is this really any less improbable?"

"Well yeah, but..."

Sir Roger stared hard at Rav. "Do you really think that hundreds of thousands of men and women, from countries all across the globe, would come together in one global organisation for no reason other than fellowship, benevolence, and the chance to engage in a bit of low-level networking? Like some sort of golf club for people who don't like golf?"

Thoughts ran backwards and forwards across Rav's mind, like the colliding, clashing ripples caused when a rather large rock is hurled into a correspondingly small pond. Three weeks previously he'd have dismissed Sir Roger as a deluded madman, peddling a conspiracy theory absurd enough to qualify as satire. But now, after what he'd seen, this was not a dismissal he could easily make. Something here was clearly absurd to the point where one could only laugh and point at it in horrified hysteria, but that something might not be Sir Roger. It might be the world itself. Rav managed a confused shrug, and a desperate, "Well, perhaps. Maybe. I don't know."

The old man stood, abruptly. "You're a naïve man, Mr Shah. A very naïve man. I would wish you luck, as I fear you will shortly need it." He took a step towards the nearby coat stand, upon which his coat and hat were standing, but then jerked to an abrupt halt, clutching his chest. "Quentin, I... I–"

He crashed to the ground.

Rav slid out of his chair and knelt down beside the old man. He'd done a fair few first aid courses as part of his training, so he knew the symptoms of a cardiac arrest. Two waiters and a half dozen diners were staring slack-jawed at him. "Call 999!" he shouted. "Tell them someone's having a heart attack." He locked his hands and started giving the old man chest compressions, interspersed with kiss-of-life breaths into his mouth. Pump, pump, pump, pump, thirty times, then breathe, twice.

"Hold on, Roger," he could hear the Professor shouting. "The ambulance is on its way."

Still Rav continued, robotically, fatigue kept at bay by the knowledge that a man's life was teetering on the very cusp of death and that only his efforts were preventing it from slipping away. Finally, a hand appeared on his shoulder.

"It's okay, mate. Well done. We'll take it from here."

The hand belonged to a sandy-haired, green-clad paramedic, who proceeded to take over Sir Roger's treatment with a calm and professional efficiency. Within minutes, a stretcher containing the old man was being loaded into the ambulance. Rav stood beside the

Professor at the restaurant's front entrance and watched as it drove smoothly down the street and disappeared around the corner.

The manager of the restaurant appeared beside them. "Given the circumstances, there won't be a charge for lunch," he told them, in a tone that somehow managed to combine a degree of compassion with a clear note of displeasure at people who embarrassed his establishment by attempting to die in it. He left them outside.

Rav touched the Professor on the arm. "I know he's your friend. I hope he'll be okay."

The Professor found a bench and sat down, clearly shaken. "Well, he's in the best possible place now, and you gave him the best chance. What happens now is in the hands of fate and destiny. He's had a good innings, and if this is his time, then it's his time."

Rav sat down beside him, trying to work out the best way to broach the subject he actually wanted to talk about. "That stuff he was saying. It seemed pretty far out. Is he for real?"

"Well, the Russians seemed to think so. I have it on very good authority that they secretly decorated him with the Hero of the Soviet Union, and I understand that he still receives a pension from the FSB, the KGB's successor organisation."

Rav could feel himself starting to panic. "Well, if he is for real, and if there really is some giant world spanning conspiracy out to get me, what the sodding hell am I supposed to do now?"

"We could investigate further. Dig deeper into what he's found out."

"How? In case you hadn't noticed, he ain't exactly in a position to speak right now."

"No. But he might have left some notes." Grim-faced, the Professor reached into the inside pocket of his tweed jacket and pulled out a set of keys. "While you were treating him I took the liberty of removing these from his pocket."

"You picked his pocket while he was lying there?"

"It might seem a tad callous, I know. But given that I might be about to lose one friend, Sir Roger, to the Grim Reaper, I see no reason to let his scythe take you, also."

"But we don't know where he lives."

The Professor reached into his other inside pocket and pulled out his slim, leather bound address book. "Yes, we do."

Chapter Nineteen

When the Professor had last visited Sir Roger, his mentor had lived in a palatial pile a few miles outside of Cambridge, set behind a well-mown lawn that stretched down to the gently flowing waters of the Great Ouse. His current home, by contrast, was much less grand, being a small, three room flat in a retirement complex on the edge of Hebdon Bridge. But everything about it still bore Sir Roger's touch, from the elegant Regency wallpaper that served as a backdrop to framed Soviet propaganda prints, to the plush, patterned carpet upon which sat furniture of the sort one inherited rather than bought.

After a brief discussion, he and Rav spilt up: he to search the bedroom, Rav to search the somewhat larger room that served as a combined lounge, dining room and kitchen. It took the Professor barely ten minutes to exhaust his search of the bedroom. Some men fill their homes with such clutter that merely finding the TV remote control can become a labour worthy of Hercules himself. Sir Roger had not been such a man; his home was neat, tidy, Spartan, and apparently not home to any secrets – at least not in that portion of it the Professor had examined. Having drawn, as the Americans would say, a blank, the Professor returned to the main room, where he found Rav perched on the arm of an easy chair, scanning the room, a troubled expression on his face.

"Any luck, Ravinder?"

"Nope. Few bank statements. Some old letters. Everything all neatly filed away. You?"

"The same, I'm afraid."

A silence settled, and it was several seconds before the Professor realised that the younger man was staring hard at the antique writing desk that stood in front of the window. Without saying a word, Rav slid off his perch, walked over to it and began to slide its various drawers in and out.

"What is it?" the Professor asked.

"These drawers. They're not deep enough." The younger man marked out a gap with his hands. "They're this deep, but the unit itself–" he moved his hands apart slightly, "–is this deep."

"You think there's a secret compartment?"

Rav was already tapping away at the side of the unit. "Yeah." The Professor watched as he tapped and twiddled and pushed and pressed. Finally, he let out a happy "Ah ha!" as something slid, twisted and turned to reveal a narrow, but deep void built into the upper portion of the desk. The younger man bent down to peer into it, slid in his hand, and pulled out a single sheet of cream-coloured writing paper. The Professor stepped across to peer over his shoulder.

The sheet was covered with the familiar loops of Sir Roger's elegant penmanship. Most of the information contained on the sheet appeared to merely duplicate what Sir Roger had told them over lunch, but at the bottom was something else. Two words. Planet Vision. The Professor jabbed a finger at it. "Planet Vision?"

Rav already had his phone out and was tapping away. After a few seconds he started reading the resulting finds aloud. "Okay. It's an opticians in Bradford. Only one branch." He read a bit more. "Owned and run by a Peter Everidge."

"So we have an independent, locally owned business with a proprietor who would appear to fit the classic profile of a Rotary Club member, of whose existence Sir Roger's ex-Soviet contacts apparently thought worthy of informing him."

"Exactly."

"So what are we going to do now?"

"I think I might go get my eyes tested."

"Is that wise? Perhaps we should take some precautions."

"Yeah. We should."

Alan was not having a good day, which wasn't surprising. Frankly, his life sucked harder than a new Dyson with a fresh filter, and had done for some time, with Tabitha the only bright spot. And even that was a bright spot that came in a wrapping of fears, lies, and uncertainty. Today, though, was a particularly bad day. Any day in which Nicolae made an appearance was fated to be an unpleasant one, and today was a day in which Nicolae had appeared.

Alan hadn't been rostered to work this particular Sunday, and so had planned on having a quiet day, rising late at around 7pm and then watching the Sunday night television. American Idol on ITV2, perhaps. Maybe a film, if there was something on. It wasn't much of a plan, but it had been enough to get him through his previous night's shift. The plan lasted right up until the moment he was awakened by Nicolae phoning to demand that he come over as soon as it fell dark. "Get the bus," Nicolae had hissed down the phone. "We watch a film. Or sport."

The front door of Nicolae's flat was already ajar when Alan arrived. He knocked, and received in reply a shout of "Come on in." Alan entered. Nicolae's place wasn't bad. It was council, illegally sub-let from a girl who'd moved in with her boyfriend but kept her tenancy, but still far superior to Alan's grotty one-room bedsit. Nicolae had two bedrooms (one of which held a velvet lined, mahogany coffin far superior to the cheap, used model Alan had purchased from a corrupt crematorium worker), a bathroom, and a reasonably sized lounge off which was a small galley kitchen. Nicolae was in the kitchen now, holding up a clear plastic bag that contained something red and slushy.

"Frozen pigs' blood," he called out. "Good shit. Organic, you know? You want some?" Alan gave him a shrugged "yes" in reply. He didn't particularly like accepting Nicolae's hospitality; they say that hospitality is never free, and with Nicolae that was certainly true. But it had been some days since he'd fed, and his withered organs were calling for sustenance. "We watch Sky Sports, yeah?" Nicolae continued. "Or maybe something on Sky Movies?"

Nicolae had the complete Sky package, something he rarely failed to mention. Alan could only afford a basic Freeview box. On those occasions when Nicolae visited Alan, he would flick through Alan's limited selection of TV channels, mocking. "Look," he would say. "I've only pressed the channel up button ten times and I'm already in the shopping shit." Alan liked the shopping shit. He liked to watch the bright-eyed presenters, endlessly enthusiastic about everything they had to sell, be it a plate, jewellery, or a cordless power drill, complete with bits. Alan had bought the power drill. On dark days he fantasised about using it on Nicolae.

A few minutes later, his sire appeared with two mugs of freshly defrosted blood. He handed one to Alan. There was a look on his face that suggested he was about to say something that might almost be sincere. It took him a while, sincerity not being something with which he was familiar, but finally, he spoke. "You did good the other weekend, Alin. I know we weren't able to start the Operational Phase, but we'll try again, soon. And if you hadn't spotted that vampire hunter, it could have been bad, very bad." He sat down in the easy chair opposite Alan. "I know you don't like killing, but the vampire hunter needed to be killed."

Alan found himself looking away.

Nicolae's eyes narrowed in suspicion. "You did kill the vampire hunter, didn't you?"

Brian Fletcher was a powerfully built East Londoner in his mid-forties who both looked and sounded like the sort of bloke John Thaw had spent the 1970s arresting. Work aside, he was a man of few words, with many of those not only unprintable, but frequently unrepeatable. Some men pride themselves on calling a spade a spade; Brian was the sort of man who will call a spade a shovel and then dare you to tell him otherwise. Rav was still some distance away from him, but his booming voice was clearly audible, even above the noise of the jets gliding in to land at the nearby Heathrow airport.

"You are all weak. Feeble. Degenerate. A disgrace to both yourselves and your families." Given that it was a Monday, and early enough in the morning that the grass was still flecked with frost, Hounslow's Lampton Park was mostly empty, something that was probably for the best. "But now you've met me. Your pampered twenty-first century existence ends here and it ends now. It's goodbye to flab and hello to fitness because for the next half hour you are mine!"

The shouts and abuse continued as Rav approached, stopping only when Rav drew up beside their source. "Brian."

"Rav."

Rav nodded at the objects of Brian's wrath. "What you got?"

Brian sniffed. He considered Rav's question for a moment, then shrugged. "Usual bunch. Couple of German Shepherds. Great Dane. King Charles Cavalier. Few crosses, a Staffie, and a Jack Russell. The Jack Russell looks like trouble but the rest should be fine."

Brian's canine charges were lined up in front of him, some sitting, some standing, wearing an assortment of red and green dog coats with numbers on them. (Red and green bibs with numbers on them was the way the army had taught him to do it, Brian had once told Rav, and he saw no reason to change now). To one side, lying crouched, alert, and ready, was Jess. She gave Rav a wary look, then turned her attention back to the waiting line. Brian paused for a moment, staring hard at each dog in turn. In return, the dogs stared back, at his green-brown camouflage trousers and blue sweatshirt upon which was printed, "Happy Dog Fitness Training". Brian nodded to himself, then pointed at the far end of the park. "Okay. Five laps. Now!"

The dogs turned as one to follow his pointing finger, but remained collectively rooted to their spot.

"Going to be like that, is it? Fine. You want confrontation, we can have confrontation. Easy way or hard way, it's all the same to me." He looked to the side "Jess? Laps."

The Border Collie shot up and away into a looping run that took her behind the assembled dogs. She dropped into a lain posture, then began edging forward, snarling gently. For a couple of moments pack solidarity kept the dogs together, but then individual fear took over and they broke. All except for the Jack Russell, who turned to face Jess, attitude showing in every movement, defiance written in his very stance. He was either totally oblivious to the fact that she was quite literally twice his size, or just plain didn't care. Jess paused, growled, and then lunged, nipping at his neck. He yelped, turned, and set off after the rest of his pack-mates, with Jess hard on his heels in a determined but controlled pursuit.

Rav stood behind Brian, watching as Jess chased the dogs round and round the park, the collie occasionally stopping to foil any attempts to hide behind bushes or benches. "Business good?"

"Not bad."

"People still up for this, then?"

"Knackered dog's a happy dog, Rav. Been that way since we was all in caves. Aren't you supposed to be working?"

"Phoned in sick. Told them I had man-flu."

Ten minutes later it was all over. Exhausted canines were scattered across the grass, jaws flecked with saliva, ribcages heaving. Jess trotted over to Brian and sat down. He bent down and rubbed her behind the ears. "Good girl." Then he turned his attention back to Rav. "If you're going to say you want Jess the answer's no. I don't mind you having her at weekends, but during the week she's already got a job."

"I just need her for the next few days."

"No way."

"I'll pay you extra."

"How much extra?"

Chapter Twenty

If Leeds had challenged Rav's prejudices, then Bradford, its poorer, dowdier sibling, had restored them. It wasn't particularly shabby, and it wasn't particularly bleak, but it had the air of a place trying to be something it wasn't, and knowing deep down that it wasn't quite succeeding.

Rav parked the car on a mostly empty level of a crumbling multi-storey car park that was located a convenient, but not too convenient, distance away from the street in which Planet Vision was located. His bag of hardware was still in the boot of the car. He was already packing a pistol in his shoulder holster, but now he grabbed a second pistol from the bag and shoved it down the waistband at the back of his trousers, gangster style, pulling his suit jacket over the top of it to hide it. There was a sick feeling in the pit of his stomach, which the added weaponry seemed to only irritate rather than soothe. "You ready?" he asked the Professor.

"As I ever will be," the older man replied. "Do we have a plan?"

Rav shrugged. "Head on over to the place, let Jess sniff around the entrance. If she's happy you can stay outside with her and I'll go in and book myself an eye test. According to the shop's website, Everidge is the senior optician as well as the owner, so let's just hope he's in today."

"Let's indeed hope so."

Rav wasn't in the habit of judging men by the frontage of their shops, but if he had been, he'd have scored Everidge a solid eight out of ten, and perhaps even a nine if he was feeling generous. Their suspect's establishment was bright and clean, with a wide, plate-glass frontage set beneath a colourful, but authoritative sign that proclaimed the property to be "Planet Vision", adding in a smaller font its claim to be "Bradford's Best Range of Spectacles and Contact Lenses".

Rav and the Professor wandered past, letting Jess sniff her way along the base of the glass. When they got to the shop on the other side, they paused. The dog looked back up at them. She seemed perfectly calm, bored even. Rav looked up at the older man. "I'd say that's a negative on any vampires in the immediate vicinity."

"It would seem so."

Rav handed him the lead, then pointed at a small cafe across the pedestrianized street, outside of which were located a number of tables and chairs. "I'd get yourself a coffee or tea, and then sit down there where you can see the front of the shop. If you hear screaming, come running in."

"Will do." The Professor began to walk away, then stopped, and turned. "Ravinder?"

"Yeah?"

"Be careful."

The shop assistant who greeted him at the counter was dressed in a vaguely nurse-like uniform, the effect presumably intended to imply a quasi-medical edge to proceedings. After taking down his details she led Rav through a door at the back of the shop, down a corridor, and into an examining room. "Take a seat," she told him. "Mr Everidge will be with you shortly." Then she left, closing the door behind her.

Rav waited until the door clicked shut, then bounced up out of the chair and began to prowl around the small room, trying to take in every detail. Posters advertising the potentially tragic consequences of not having regular eye-tests. Racks of equipment and things on casters, all of it coloured that precise shade of cream that medical devices had started being when they stopped being gun-metal grey. A small sink. A bin. A man standing in the open doorway, silently watching Rav examine the room.

Rav managed to both straighten up with a start and jump flinchingly backwards in one, not-quite fluid moment. "Oh, hi. Erm. Mr Everidge?"

Facing him was a man in his mid-fifties, with neat but thinning grey hair that framed a kind and pleasant face, upon which sat a slightly old-fashioned moustache and a pair of rather plain spectacles that, given the range presumably available to him, spoke of a somewhat limited taste. He stuck out a hand, and smiled. "The very man. And you must be Mr Shah? Or can I call you Ravinder?"

This wasn't the kind of bloke Rav had expected to be meeting, and frankly he was somewhat taken aback. He took the man's hand, and gave it a confused shake. "Rav's fine."

"Good, good. And just call me Peter. Now, have you had an eye test before?"

Rav tried to push his fears, his doubts, and his many confused thoughts to one side. Bullshit is dangerous stuff, and needs to be delivered by a clear mind, a moist tongue, and steady hands. And of course, bullshit's best delivered as a metaphorical sandwich, with the corned beef of lies neatly topped and tailed by the sliced bread of truth. "No, this is my first time."

Start with the truth. Always start with the truth, and keep with the truth right up until the point when you start lying through your teeth.

"Have you been having any trouble in particular?"

"Not really. But I've felt myself getting tired sometimes, and I am getting older, and I just thought better safe than sorry."

Everidge nodded vigorously. "Very sensible. Well, you'll find it's a simple and painless process. We've got all the latest equipment here. I pride myself on giving the best possible service and if it means shipping a load of tech over from California then that's what I'll do."

"Well, that's good," Rav told him.

Everidge motioned him to sit back down on the swivel chair then disappeared through a second doorway into an adjacent room, returning with a sleek, high-tech trolley that was topped with a weird frame of metal and glass. He slid the trolley in front of Rav.

"This is our combined examination and scanning unit. Not only can we check your vision optically, we can also scan the inside of your eyes and your optic nerve. A few years ago you'd have needed a million pound scanner in a major hospital, just to do what we can do here."

"That's good." Rav was so wired with exhaustion, stress, and terror that he'd have thought it impossible for any new worries to raise their heads above the parapet. But he was wrong, for a new fear occurred to him now. What if Everidge's hi-tech Californian scanner found something wrong with his eyes? Things were already bleak enough without potential blindness being added to the problem list.

"Okay. Rest your chin on the bar here."

Rav leaned forward and lowered his chin onto the U-shaped rest Everidge had indicated, bringing his eyes in line with a vaguely binocular shaped object. Everidge popped a dome shaped device down on top of the metal framework, and dropped it down into place; it fitted neatly just over Rav's skull. Everidge gave him a reassuring smile.

"Now the scanner requires you to be absolutely still, so I just need to secure you in." He reached round behind Rav and looped something around him. Rav felt his chin being forced down into the bar, firmly enough so as to be almost painful. "Don't worry," said Everidge brightly. "Won't be long. It only takes thirty seconds to get a complete three-sixty scan."

"It's a bit painful."

"Good," said Everidge as he snapped something silver down over Rav's left arm, almost immediately followed by something else on Rav's right arm.

"What?"

"I said good. I'm glad it's a bit painful."

Rav tried to get out of the machine, but his head was now firmly locked into the device. He pulled with his arms, but both were tightly shackled to the arm-rests. He managed to look down out of the corner of his eye, and saw something glinting silver. Hand-cuffs. He pushed backwards with his feet, but the office chair appeared to be locked in some way.

Everidge appeared back in front of him, an evil grin upon his face as he shook his head from side to side in wonderment. "I can't believe you fell for that scanning bullshit. You really never have had an eye-test before, have you?"

One of Rav's many interests was old movies, and in such movies the etiquette to be followed by a hero imprisoned by the villain is for the hero to respond in a manner that is eloquent, defiant and courageous. Given a choice, this would have been the manner in which Rav would have liked to respond now to Everidge, but he was somewhat hampered in this desire by firstly the fact that his jaw was clamped so tightly he could only talk through gritted teeth, and secondly, by the fact that he was currently feeling like the world's biggest twat. "What – do – you – want?" he instead slurred, in the manner of a very bad ventriloquist.

"It's very simple, Mr Shah. You're going to tell me everything you know. And then I'm going to kill you. If you talk without me having to get nasty, I'll kill you nicely. If you force me to start doing things to your eyes with scalpels, you'll end up telling me anyway, and then I'll kill you in a very horrible way. Either way, you'll tell me what you know and then you'll end up dead."

"You – can't."

"Yes I can, Mr Shah." Everidge indicated the room with a wave of his hand. "I had this entire building kitted out according to my precise plans. This room is extensively sound-proofed. We have a private waste disposal contract. All the staff are hand-picked by myself. For you, escape is simply not a possibility, and when it comes to options you have none. But I will give you one piece of advice for free, not that you have much of a life left in which to act upon it." He dropped to one knee beside Rav. "Never, ever fuck with people like me."

"I've – got – people – outside."

"An old man and a dog. The old man's currently doing a crossword. The dog's sleeping beneath a table. I looked before I came in. I'm not sure what religion you follow Mr Shah, if any, but I suggest now might be a good time to start making peace with your maker."

Chapter Twenty One

The Professor had initially made good progress, working his way down the grid from the top-left corner. But then he'd met his nemesis, in the shape of six across. Tap-dancing pooch causes offence at dinner. Something N, something P, something something.

He took a quick glance at the opticians. It all seemed quiet. He continued looking for a moment more, then turned his attention back to the crossword. Maybe he might have better luck with seven down. He examined the clue. Skydiving priest over Alpine slopes. Something something D.

Time for the dictionary, perhaps.

If his actions were anything to go by, Everidge had been extensively trained in the ways of interrogation; if not, he was a natural born torturer. He hadn't led with questions. He presumably knew that basic pride would lead Rav to initially either refuse to answer or to lie, so Everidge had begun by talking. Not about his plans, of course; only in bad films and even worse novels does the antagonist capture the protagonist and then proceed to reveal his entire evil scheme. Everidge might have been many things (optician, Rotarian, an utter shit of the sort that decent people scrape off their shoes), but he was not a cliché.

No, Everidge spent the first five minutes talking about the things he was going to do to Rav, and of just how much he was going to enjoy doing them. He spoke of scalpels and of cigarette burns and of the exquisite agony that could be produced by inserting cut chillies into the urethra, the last being such a clearly specific and yet deeply strange threat that the likelihood of its use seemed extremely high. Finally, the Rotarian pulled up a seat beside Rav and leaned in close. "So, Mr Shah, are you going to talk?"

In the movies, this is the moment when the captured protagonist makes a desperate attempt to rip himself loose, reasoning that if he can just free some part of himself – a limb, or a head, even – it will be enough to at least partially assault his captor. This wasn't a movie, but Rav had a go anyway, smashing and pulling his body in several directions while simultaneously pulling at the handcuffs and trying to rip his head free from its restraint. Unfortunately, his violent thrashings succeeded only in snapping the plastic water pistol stuffed down the back of his trousers. The cold water flowed around his groin, turning the light grey material of his suit trousers a far darker grey.

Everidge looked down at the spreading wet stain and chuckled. "Good. I see you're ready to talk. Now I'm going to ask you some questions and you're going to answer them, fully and honestly. Whole truth, nothing but the truth, you know the sort of thing."

He reached over to his desk and grabbed a pad, then hunted around for something else, presumably a pen. "Dammit," he muttered. "Where the hell do they get to?" He looked back at Rav, and smiled a cold and evil smile. "I don't suppose you've got a pen I could borrow, Mr Shah?" Before Rav had a chance to answer, Everidge reached inside his jacket, missing the shoulder holster, but finding the pen Rav had in his inside pocket. "Thought so."

He gave Rav a very superior smirk, then pulled the slider down and pepper sprayed himself full in the face. He let out a long scream of agony and then proceeded to stagger around the small room, clawing at his eyes while bouncing off various items, all the while emitting a chorus of cries, screams, and whimpers, interspersed with assorted outbursts of swearing and blasphemy. Rav didn't waste time trying to come up with a plan. He wasn't really in a planning sort of space right now. Planning requires logic and analysis, but right now, the captain's seat of the USS Ravinder Shah was occupied by Lieutenant-Commander Epic Fear, backed up by Lieutenant Total Panic on helm. Meanwhile, the engines were dialled up to a hundred and fifty per cent and every single photon torpedo was either still being loaded or already fired.

Planning was for other people right now, people who weren't currently strapped into a torture device. Instead, Rav just thrashed about in the chair, pulling and pushing with everything he had. For several seconds he achieved nothing save to viciously cut himself across his wrists and face.

Then, with Everidge still screaming "Jesus Fucking Christ!" in the background, something in the apparatus holding his head came loose.

His upper body popped free. He looked around, and saw Everidge at the sink, attempting to turn the taps on. Rav's forearms were still firmly handcuffed to the arms of the chair, but his legs were free. He hooked them down underneath the chair, pushed, and found himself waddling across the floor holding the chair against his arse.

Everidge heard him coming and turned, but the action was too late, succeeding only in presenting his face to Rav's oncoming shoulder, a shoulder backed up not only by Rav's weight but also by several dozen pounds of metal and leather chair. The two of them smashed into the sink, with Everidge's head producing a very satisfying clunk as it collided with the ceramic. As assaults go, it was neither elegant nor necessarily effective, but it did have the result of producing a heap upon the floor which consisted of Everidge, Rav, and the chair, and from which Rav was able to deliver a vicious head-butt to the Rotarian's face.

Everidge's eyes were tightly closed, and he was still screaming and swearing. Rav hauled himself to his feet, fighting to keep the chair balanced on his back, stamped a few times on Everidge's chest, stomach and groin, gave the groin another stamp for luck, then launched himself at the door. It looked quite cheap and rather nasty, but looks can often be deceiving, and this was the case here, for while it gave slightly, it not only held, but rebounded back. Rav smashed his shoulder into it again and again, ignoring the waves of pain coming from his battered and bruised body, knowing only that he had to escape, smashing, shoving, pushing – and then he remembered that Everidge hadn't actually locked it.

He shifted the chair around until his hand could reach the knob. It twisted easily, allowing the door to swing open towards him. Rav grabbed hold of the chair again and waddled out into the corridor, retracing the route the receptionist had led him along. Through another door; past the tiny kitchen; through a third door; out into the main shop area.

Horrified faces greeted him as he waddled past the counter and towards the open doors. Somewhere deep within his brain, the conscious part of Rav that was merely an observer right now noted that when you're waiting to see the optician, you just don't expect to see a badly beaten and bleeding man who's got a huge wet patch on his crotch come waddling out, handcuffed to a chair.

Once more, Rav found reality failing to match the expectations set by a lifetime of watching feature films, as he yet again failed to come out with a witty and ironic killer of a line. (In his defence, had this been a movie he'd have been a six foot four, Austrian body-builder or Belgian kick-boxer with a team of kick-ass screenwriters on tap). He instead blurted out the best his brain could currently manage – "I'd go to SpecSavers, these guys are shit." – and staggered out into the shopping centre's main thoroughfare.

The Professor was sitting at a table in front of the cafe, engrossed in his newspaper, a pen in his hand. Beneath the table, a sleeping Jess slept. The dog awoke, blinked at Rav, and then began to paw at the older man's leg. The Professor looked up, let out a cry of alarm, and came rushing over. "What happened?"

"Well, he said I'm okay to drive but I might need glasses for reading – what the hell do you think happened? He knew who I was. He waited until I was strapped into the machine for the eye test and then announced he was going to torture me."

The Professor looked confused. "But you don't need to get strapped into a machine for an eye test."

"Well, I know that now." Rav looked back at the shop. The assistant who'd taken him to the examination-room-cum-torture-chamber was conversing urgently with another member of staff, all the while pointing at Rav. "We need to get out of here." He tried to walk away, but hunched over and supporting the weight of the chair as he was, he could only manage a moderately fast waddle. He sat back down on the chair. "You'll have to wheel me." He felt a shove behind him, but it merely sent the chair tipping forward.

"It won't move," the Professor shouted.

"There must be some sort of brake."

He sensed rather than saw the Professor fiddling around underneath the chair. Then there was a muttered, "Ah ha!" and he found himself gliding at some pace along the street with Jess running cover at his side. They careered into the car park, skidded into a lift that smelt of piss, hammered frantically on the buttons, and then burst out onto their level to find the car exactly where they'd left it, one flickering candle of success in a night-black sea of failure. "The keys are in my right jacket pocket," Rav shouted to the Professor. The older man reached in and retrieved them, then regarded them with some confusion.

"There's some clicky thing you have to do, isn't there?"

"Just give them here."

The Professor dropped the keys into Rav's hand, which was as outstretched as a hand can be when its handcuffed to a chair. He juggled them around one-handed until he had the fob gripped between thumb and forefinger, then pressed the unlock stud. The car beeped and flashed its lights.

"Now what?" asked the Professor, indicating the chair.

Rav thought for a moment. There was no way he was going to be able to get in with a chair attached to his back, but there was no quick and easy way of separating him from it, and they didn't have time to mess around. Everidge might be arriving at any moment, tooled up with scalpels and accompanied by a bunch of his Rotarian mates. Rav didn't have a shortlist of desired ways to die, but had he had such a list it wouldn't have included being stabbed to death in a multi-storey car park by a bunch of middle-aged small business owners. "Open the tailgate, take out the parcel shelf and fold the seats down. Quickly!"

The Professor managed to open the tailgate after just a few seconds of fumbling, and it took only a few seconds more for him to remove the parcel shelf, throw it inside, and then fold down the seats. Rav waddled up to the open rear and threw himself in as best as he could, aided by some helpful shoves from the Professor. There was the sound of claws as Jess scrabbled in beside him. "Okay!" he shouted. "I'm in." He felt the chair judder, as something presumably collided with it.

"The door won't shut," the Professor shouted.

"Leave it! Just drive."

"I haven't driven for more than twenty years."

"It's like riding a bike."

"But I haven't ridden one of those for nearer forty."

"They haven't changed. Key in ignition, turn. Clutch down, gear stick into first, accelerator down, release clutch."

"Understood."

There was the sound of the driver's door opening and then closing, followed by the sound of the engine starting. It revved hard for a few seconds before the car lurched forward, only to stop abruptly.

"Sorry. The clutch appears to be somewhat sensitive."

The engine started again and the car rolled away, this time without stalling. From his vantage position on the carpeted back of a folded down car seat with an office chair stuck on top of him, Rav couldn't see a damn thing. But he felt the car go through first one turn, down a ramp, and then into another turn. Several more turns and descents followed, the chair careering about the rear of the car with each change of direction and orientation, something that made Rav rather unhappy, strapped, as he was, to the piece of furniture concerned.

A final squealing turn and a crunching gear change up to second indicated that the car had now exited the car park. "We are now on the open road," the Professor announced, a statement that he followed up with another crunching gear change.

Rav started breathing again. "Okay. I guess we need to find some kind of locksmiths. Someone who'll be able to cut me out of this."

Getting Rav freed from the chair proved surprisingly easy. As a rule, locksmiths are not generally inclined to cut handcuffs off people, fearing – with good reason – that the person to whom the handcuffs are attached will be a violent criminal on the run from the police. But hard-left conspiracy theories aside, the British police are not in the habit of handcuffing people to a bog-standard office chair and then beating the crap out of them, making Rav's cover story of a homosexual BDSM session gone tragically wrong ("First I forgot the safe word and then he got flustered and dropped the key through a crack in our dungeon's floorboards") highly believable. In fact, it seemed like the locksmith couldn't get them out of his premises fast enough, so freaked out and disturbed was he by their story. ("It's okay mate, no charge, really. Erm, just, in future, you know...")

Once back in the car and rolling they began to discuss their options, which didn't take very long. In metaphorical terms, they were currently attempting to traverse Excrement Creek with the metaphorically appropriate number of paddles, that number being – of course – zero. Which by a not particularly cosmic coincidence, exactly equalled the number of apparently viable options available to them. "Could we go to the police?" suggested the Professor.

"And tell them what? That I'm being hunted by the Rotary Club? You know, the other ones, the ones who aren't the Round Table. Oh, and there's a Romanian vampire who's going to kill me as well if I don't convince a girl who doesn't actually exist to go out with him."

"Yes, quite. As reports of crimes go, it does all lack a certain plausibility. Would it help if we went to your local police in Hounslow?"

"Not particularly, no." In fact, Rav knew exactly how that particular conversation would go. "A vampire?" they'd say, while searching for the number of the duty mental-health social worker. "Working with the Rotary Club?" Then they'd shove him in an interview room while they waited for one of his workmates to show up – assuming it wasn't Rav himself whose name was on the rota for that night. Rav wasn't quite sure how one of his work colleagues would react to a fellow social worker with paranoid delusions about vampires and Rotarian conspiracies, but he'd personally had people sectioned for far less.

"Could your manager help? Ms Macmillan? She's always struck me as a formidable woman."

Rav nodded. "True. If it was her versus Everidge down a dark alleyway she'd have him singing feminist theory castrato within about thirty seconds, but I'm not sure she'd be buying the whole Rotary Club plus vampires thing, either."

"Yes. I can see that. It would appear, therefore, that we must proceed on the basis of our own resources." They continued driving on in silence, heading nowhere in particular at a speed of thirty-eight miles per hour. The Professor waved a thoughtful finger. "Perhaps we should find somewhere to hole up? Somewhere where we can regroup, and plan our next move?"

"That's a perfectly reasonable plan, limited only by the fact that we don't have anywhere to hole up."

The car, perhaps aided by the combined forces of fate, chance, and plain dumb luck, chose that precise moment to pass a road sign upon

132

which was written a list of destinations, a list that included among their number a locality by the name of "Grimethorpe" that was apparently a mere seventeen miles away. The Professor was the first to utter the thought that Rav was already thinking. "Was Grimethorpe not the village that Mr Partridge's smallholding overlooked?"

Rav smiled at the older man. "It was, and seeing as how we never actually charged him anything I figure he owes us a favour."

Chapter Twenty Two

It wasn't the noise that woke Jess up from her night-time sleep, nor the smell. Millions of years of evolution on what might be termed the "mid-list" portion of the food chain has granted dogs an almost intuitive sixth sense that remains alert even while sleep has shut down their five primary senses. Burglars fumbling at the lock of a conservatory door, chavs scratching at the lock of a parked car, an opened packet of biscuits carelessly left downstairs on the lounge coffee table: all are capable of rousing a dog from an apparently deep slumber.

But once her sixth sense had roused her, there was plenty for Jess to hear and smell, even tucked away as she was in the small attic bedroom at the top of Partridge's cottage. Muttered curses. Whispers so sharp and piercing that they carried further than if they'd been shouted. Strange smells, over and above the strange smells of this place of beasts to which they'd returned. Urban smells. Sweat. Fear. Anger. Jess instincts were speaking to her, talking of fight or flight. She padded over to the bed where Rav lay sleeping and prodded his face with her snout. Independent minded as she often was, there were times when she was happy to defer to a notional pack leader and this seemed like one of those times.

Prod. Prod. Growl.

Rav was awakened by a wet nose repeatedly prodding his cheek and a low growling in his ear. Jess.

"What is it?" he asked her, realising as he did so the stupidity of his question. This wasn't a low-budget, sentimental children's film, and this conversation was not going to move onto, "What's that, girl? The Professor went into town to try and buy a copy of the Times, but fell down an old abandoned mine shaft?"

He sat up, an action that bought his head up alongside the window the Professor had insisted on leaving open a crack, "For ventilation", and which was, as a result, letting in a wicked draft. Fragments of whispered speech drifted in on the cold night air.

"Fuck!" "...up?" "I've... stepped... cow shit!" "Shut the... up!"

Rav didn't need a talking dog to tell him what was going on. Christ knows how they'd tracked them down, but this could only be some sort of Rotarian hit-squad. He slid out of bed, trying to let his feet glide across the rug-strewn floor, and gently shook the Professor awake. "Prof! Wake up. The Rotarians are here." The older man blinked a couple of times, nodded, then slipped out of bed himself and began to pull his clothes on.

About seventeen seconds later they were crouched in front of the door, carefully opening it a crack.

Rav peered through, his holy water-filled water pistol clutched firmly in his hand. Partridge was sat in a chair on the landing, apparently asleep, lit only by the dim moonlight that filtered through the narrow window, a mobile phone perched upon his gut. A small glass of something yellow sat beside him on a small table beside a mostly full bottle of scotch and an unopened pack of cigarettes.

Rav shoved his gun into his waistband, pushed open the door, and advanced upon the farmer. Partridge woke up with a stir, just in time for Rav to put his hand around his throat and press him hard into the back of the chair. "You grassed us up, didn't you?"

The reply was coughed past Rav's claw-like grip. "Bloke came yesterday. Bloke who bought pigs. Asked me if anyone 'ad asked after 'em. Gave me card. Said there was a reward."

"You sold us?" said the Professor. "For money?"

Partridge shrugged as best as he could, given that Rav was still pinning him into the chair. "My old ma, she always said a farmer can't let sentiment get between him and money."

There was a crash from somewhere down below, inside the house, now, followed by more muttered curses and recriminations and a shout of, "Look, I'm a bouncer not a fucking copper!" Then came the sound that in pulp novels is always described as "unmistakable", that sound being some kind of firearm being readied for a spot of unpleasantness. Rav let go of Partridge, looked over the bannister and saw a shadow at the base of the stairs. The shadow reacted, lifting its arm. Something that sounded awfully like a gunshot cracked up the stairwell. Something that felt awfully like a bullet whined an inch past Rav's head. And something that looked awfully like a bullet hole appeared in the plastered wall just beyond. Somewhere within Rav's genitals, the tightened muscle that was all that stood between his full bladder and a socially embarrassing accident began to twitch in fear. He ducked back. There was the sound of a dull thud below, and a cry of, "Shit. I've dropped my fucking shooter."

Rav's heart began to thump, his body's autonomous systems preparing for a course of either fight or flight even while the mind in control of that body examined both alternatives and came up with precious few options for either of them. What to do? Attack? Throw himself down a narrow staircase armed only with a water-pistol against men armed with the real thing? Run? Where? This was a situation for an action hero, but right now Rav felt very much like a mental-health social worker who was both shit-scared and shit out of luck.

The muttering and strangled shouts that had been emerging from below since the firing of the gun abruptly halted, as though acts were in the process of being got together. A cautious creak sounded on the staircase. Rav felt a presence at his feet and looked down, but found only a waiting Jess staring back. He looked around the narrow landing. Partridge. Professor. Jess. Chair. Table. Scotch. Cigarettes. Matchbook. Matches.

He quickly turned back to the Professor. "Give me your hankie."

The Professor reached into his tweed suit's breast pocket and pulled out a neatly folded linen handkerchief, adding as he did so, "I'm afraid I have used it."

That the handkerchief was used was not something that Rav was in any way concerned about. He splashed a liberal quantity of scotch onto it, stuffed it into the open neck of the bottle of scotch, ripped a match out of the matchbook, and scraped it along the book's brown scraping surface. It lit first time, sparking into a flame that burned a beautiful yellow-orange in the dim light. He touched it to the scotch-socked handkerchief, paused a beat for the fabric to catch, then tossed the Highland-flavoured Molotov cocktail over the banister.

From down below came, in short order, the sound of smashing glass, a bright flash of white light, and an extended chorus of screams coming from people who were either on fire, very angry, or quite possibly both. Rav wasn't naïve enough to believe that a lit bottle of Scotch would turn back their Rotarian pursuers. All he'd bought them was a few seconds, seconds which it was vital they use wisely. He spent a couple of those seconds punching Partridge in the face, then barged his way through the door that led to the farmer's bedroom, the other upstairs room in the small cottage. He vaulted over the bed and slammed into the window that was set in the wall at the far end of the room. A shuffling of feet and scrabbling of claws from behind told him that his two colleagues were close on his heels.

The window's catch opened with a flick of Rav's wrist letting the glass swing open to reveal the sloped, slate roof of one of the outbuildings that adjoined the cottage. Rav squeezed through the opening and then lowered himself carefully down until he felt his feet touching slate. The Professor was already pushing a not obviously happy Jess through the gap. Rav grabbed her and set off along the roof, one foot either side of the ridge, moving at a sort of fast shuffle that balanced his desire to not fall off the roof with his equally strong desire to not still be on it when a pistol wielding Rotarian who'd recently suffered some first-degree burns reached the window. At the far end of the outbuilding was a shed, set against the wall in a sort of lean-to arrangement. Rav dropped Jess onto its asphalt roof, then followed her down, turning back to help the Professor. One bit of scrabbling later and the three of them were in the dirt beside the shed.

"What now?" the Professor asked. "The car?"

Rav shook his head. The car was parked on the opposite side of the cottage, and besides, the keys they needed to start it were currently sitting on the bedside cabinet next to the bed Rav had recently been sleeping in. He pointed away from the cottage, at the night-shrouded moorland that flanked the smallholding. The Professor nodded. The three of them crept around the back of the henhouse, Jess leading the way, climbed carefully between the wires of Partridge's three-wire fence, then headed out into the blackness.

No shots came.

Every generation has the crime that marks its loss of innocence. For those born during the 1950s, as the Professor had been, that crime was the Moors murders. It had seemed then, to a young boy listening to the horrified conversations of adults or to the sombre tones of a TV reporter, that these Yorkshire moors were strange and unearthly places, supernatural even. Places where a soul might wonder lost for an eternity, disappear without trace, be gone for ever.

Being lost on a bitterly cold night on just such a windswept moor, as the Professor now was, wasn't going any way towards dispelling that childhood belief, and the fact that one of his shoes had been sucked off by some kind of quicksand-like bog more than half an hour ago wasn't much helping either. But eventually, Rav called a halt. "Think we must have lost them," he announced, his face dimly illuminated by the glow from his phone's screen. "Dammit," he muttered. "No signal."

"Well, we've certainly lost ourselves," the Professor replied. He'd stopped shivering some time ago and his foot felt like a block of ice attached to a leg filled with pain; both bad signs he knew. "Perhaps we should find somewhere sheltered. I could do with warming up."

A look of genuine concern and contrition settled upon the younger man's face. "You okay?"

The Professor forced out a smile. "Nothing that a dry, wind-free cave and a roaring fire won't solve, although I suspect the latter might be beyond our capabilities."

Rav nodded. "Yeah, even if we could find something to burn we've got nothing to light it–" He stopped talking and reached into his pocket, his hand emerging with the matchbook with which he'd lit his improvised

Molotov cocktail. He smiled. "Must have put it back in my pocket without realising." He looked around and then pointed to their right. "Looks like a craggy bit over there. Might be somewhere we can get a fire going that can't be seen. Come on."

Lighting a fire carried an obvious risk of detection, but Rav was more concerned about the Professor's health right now, so it was a risk he was more than willing to take. They found a nook at the base of the rocky outcrop that as best as Rav could figure was on the far side of the crag from Partridge's place, and thus invisible save to anyone who'd followed them all this way and then circled round. What he found on a five minute forage wasn't so much firewood as twigs and brush, but when combined with a kindling of torn up receipts from his wallet, which he'd left, somewhat fortuitously, in one of his trouser pockets, it managed to burn with enough intensity to produce something approaching warmth. Sat beside the fire, and with a Border Collie cuddled up to him, it didn't take long for the colour to come back to the older man's face, and when it did, their discussion turned to their wider predicament.

"One doesn't wish to appear defeatist," the Professor said, holding his hands out to the fire. "But where exactly do we go from here?"

"I think if we head west for a couple of miles we'll get to a main road. We might be able to hitch a lift there."

"I was meaning in the more general sense."

"Right."

The Professor steepled his hands for a moment. "Perhaps we should consider the resources available to us?"

"Well, that's basically you, me, Jess, a debit card I'm not sure is safe to use, about thirty quid in cash, a water pistol, the clothes we currently have on our backs, and a book of matches." Rav looked at the matchbook, which was currently lying on a flat bit of rock a foot or so from the fire. What kind of place would still give out matchbooks in the twenty-first century, anyhow? He grabbed it and examined it in the light of the fire. The card was stiff and glossy and coloured an elegant shade of cream, and the name written across it was in a smooth and flowing hand-script font. He read the text out loud. "The Charleston Club."

"Sounds somewhat old-fashioned."

"Yeah. But if it's some kind of retro place it might explain why they're still giving out matchbooks." Rav flipped the matchbook over to discover an address written on the back. "It's somewhere in Manchester."

"Why would a somewhat unsophisticated Yorkshire farmer, like Partridge, be in possession of a matchbook from some sort of nightclub in

Manchester?"

"No idea."

There was a thought forming in Rav's brain, a memory shouting for attention, almost tangible but frustratingly out of reach. Then the Professor produced the connection that Rav had been failing to grasp. "Last night, one of the men who came for us said something along the lines of being a bouncer and not a policeman."

Rav clicked his fingers. "Yes! That's it. And if they were bouncers, then the guy who bought the pigs and visited Partridge yesterday might have been a bouncer too, or maybe their boss or something."

"And when he visited Partridge he might have accidentally left the matchbook behind."

"Exactly." Rav thought for a moment more. As leads went, it wasn't much. But weak as it might be, right now, it was the only game in town. "The question is, how can we check this place out?"

The Professor smiled, his face lit by the flickering fire. "Well, this time I'd advise against simply walking in through the front door."

Chapter Twenty Three

When daylight returned, the moors seemed somewhat less foreboding. After all, the Professor reflected, as he stared out across the landscape, this was West Yorkshire, not the American West or the Australian Outback. A man might be able to wander for days here, but only if he persisted in both walking in circles and hiding from ramblers. Some way away in the distance, tiny dots zoomed along a winding road; commuters no doubt, heading for work. He indicated the faraway cars to Rav with a nod. "Perhaps we should try hitching a lift?"

"We've got a dog, and we're all covered in mud, crap, and bits of vegetation. Who's going to stop for us?"

"You'd be surprised by what people do, Ravinder. When I was eighteen a friend and I hitch-hiked from Canterbury to India via Yugoslavia, Iran, and Afghanistan. Not everyone in this world's an axe-murderer."

"No, just the people I seem to be meeting." The younger man threw up his hands in defeat. "Fine. Let's head to the road and see if anyone stops. A random driver's probably safer than a mini-cab firm, anyway."

It took them a couple of hours to reach the road, during which the Professor lost his remaining shoe, but finally they were there, able to stick out their thumbs and put hopeful grins upon their faces. Car after car sped by. After several minutes, Rav snapped. "Look, this is pointless. No one's going to stop for us. I sure as hell wouldn't."

Then, as though on cue, a battered old Ford Escort slid to a halt beside them, and its passenger side window slid down with a whine. The Professor bent forward to look inside and found the almost unnaturally happy face of Father Adrian looking back at him.

"I thought it was you two," the priest said. "And you looked in need of assistance, so I thought I'd better stop. You know, Good Samaritan and all that?"

"It is most appreciated," the Professor replied.

"Well, climb in. Don't worry about the seats. Where can I take you to?"

Rav shoved his way into the conversation. "Manchester."

Reasonable request or not, Father Adrian did drive them all the way to Manchester. And rather than simply dumping them in the city's centre he instead took Rav and the Professor to a homeless shelter run by a Jesuit acquaintance of his. The two priests provided them with a twin bed room, treated their various cuts and bruises, and provided them with replacement sets of warm, if slightly shabby, clothing from the shelter's stockpile of donated supplies. Then, having already far exceeded all of Christ's exhortations to treat one's neighbours as you would hope to be treated yourself, the two priests then treated their guests to a slap up breakfast, Father Adrian wielding the frying pan for Rav and the Professor, his friend, Father Thomas, breaking out the emergency dog-food supplies for Jess.

It was almost enough to restore Rav's faith in humanity. Father Adrian's beliefs might politely have been described as "highly ecumenical", but they were clearly sincerely held and the man himself seemed positively overflowing with goodness, with the same going for Father Thomas. But, tempting as Rav might have found it to open up his heart to the love of Jesus Christ and invite him into his life, he knew that would do bugger all good given that an unholy alliance of conspirators and vampires had committed themselves to his death, and were planning on opening up his heart via his ribcage.

After waving Father Adrian off, back to whatever it was he'd been doing before they'd flagged him down, they'd left Jess snoozing in their room and headed off into the surrounding Manchester streets. The Professor waited until they'd put a few paces between themselves and the shelter and then turned to Rav. "So have you thought of a means by which we might investigate this club?"

Rav nodded. Following a quick perusal of the Charleston's website on his phone over breakfast he did indeed have a plan. "I might have. But I need to arrange something first." He pulled his phone out and dialled an entry from its contacts list. The phone rang twice and then was answered.

"Yo, Rav, what's up?"

"I need a favour, Charlie."

"No problems blud, what's you wanting?" Charlie spoke with the classic thick, fake, and horribly exaggerated Jafrican accent of a nicely bought up middle-class white boy from Uxbridge.

"I need a flash mob organised for tonight. A really big one, and not traceable back to a source."

The voice on the other end laughed. "Dat's it? No sweat man. I'll call da boys. Hit Facebook, Twitter, all dem usual places. Where, when, an' what?"

"10pm tonight, at a club called the Charleston. It's some kind of retro 1920s style place, sort of dance music fused with jazz. So the flash mob should be for a 1920s themed fancy dress party. You know, a masked ball type thing."

"Safe blud. It's gonna be sick."

The phone clicked dead. Rav slapped the Professor on the shoulders and smiled. "Well, that's part one of the plan up and running."

"And what would be part two?"

"Now we need to find some kind of fancy dress shop." Rav thought a bit more. "And I guess I ought to call the office. Upgrade my man-flu to something more contagious." He fished out his phone and hit a number from his favourites. "Sandra... It's Rav... Yeah, I'm still bad... I'm having some sort of discharge..."

The Charleston Club turned out to be a handsome, Edwardian edifice. Having apparently survived the best efforts of the Luftwaffe, 1960s architects, and the Provisional IRA to reduce it to rubble, it appeared to have then suffered a failed attempt at remodelling, with the designers overshooting their intended landing point of "classic retro" and crash-landing instead on "frankly, quite seriously tacky".

But Rav wasn't here to judge architecture. By the time he and the Professor arrived the flash mob was already going strong, with a throng of costumed individuals attempting to file past a team of slightly bewildered doormen. It was a motley assortment, united only by a common failure to in any way adhere to the supposed 1920s theme. A "jockey" riding an ostrich. Rubber-faced American ex-Presidents (Nixon, Reagan, two George W Bushes and three Bill Clintons). A permanently grinning Tony Blair. A frowning Barack Obama. A space-suited astronaut. The back half of a Pantomime horse, apparently engaged in a search for his missing front half. Two individuals who may or may not have been policeman. One individual dressed as a PCSO who probably was a PCSO (that not being the sort of thing one dresses up as). Grown-up women dressed as schoolgirls. Schoolgirls dressed as grown-up women. Fat men in nappies. Spitfire pilots.

Jesus of Nazareth.

Twice.

And two men clad in costumes they'd hired that afternoon from a fancy dress shop, shortly after the making of the phone call that had set this whole event up. Rav, who was wearing a Harlequin gimp suit, turned to the Professor, who was dressed as a masked highwayman. "Okay, let's try and slip through behind those guys dressed as porn actresses." Getting past the doormen, in the pocket created by six rugby forwards in dresses, proved surprisingly easy. Once inside the club's cavernous interior, Rav left the Professor in a side booth with a G & T and headed off to work his way around the dancing, drinking masses. Towards the back, beside the bar, he found a door marked "staff only", and, after taking a short moment to consider the fact that this was probably a really stupid idea, he ducked through it.

When he was eight years old, one of Rav's many uncles had gifted him an entire set of Fighting Fantasy "choose your own adventure" game-books. Rav had devoured the entire collection within months. He'd loved the feeling of finding his own path, loved the way that mere words could fire the imagination. From there it was just one step to the online world of 80s style, retro, text adventure games – the rat-infested crack house to Fighting Fantasy's middle-class cannabis joint. The situation that Rav now found himself in reminded him of nothing so much as one of those old-style computer games.

> You are in a long, rectangular room. At the far end is a table, upon which sits a clock. A tapestry hangs from the west wall. Exits are to the north, east, and south.

> Examine clock.

> It's a clock.

> Examine tapestry.

> Behind the tapestry is an empty alcove.

> Go east.

> You are in a small office. There is a desk, upon which sits a computer and a pocket calculator. There is a single exit to the west.

> Get calculator.

> You get the calculator. You are now holding a calculator, a wallet, a phone and a book of matches.

> Use computer.

> You don't appear to know how to use the computer.

> Go west.

> You are in a long, rectangular room. At the far end is a table, upon which sits a clock. A man is standing in front of the clock with his back to you. He does not appear to have noticed you. A tapestry hangs from the west wall. Exits are to the north, east and south.

> Go west.

> You are hiding behind the tapestry.

Rav's plan, such as it was, had been to remain in hiding behind the tapestry until he heard the mysterious clock-examiner leave. It was a reasonable enough plan with just one flaw, that being that it depended on the clock-examiner at some point leaving, an action that he was apparently in no particular hurry to carry out. After several minutes spent standing in the narrow void behind the hanging tapestry, his nose an inch away from its rough underside, Rav's legs were starting to stiffen. He shifted slightly, trying to get the blood flowing, but as he did so, his elbow brushed the dado rail that ran along the length of the wall, alcove included.

It shifted underneath him.

Very, very carefully, he shuffled round, then risked using the light from his phone's screen to see what was going on. Sure enough, there was a six inch long section of dado rail that rotated down, like a door handle, and when it did a vertical crack appeared in the wall above and below it. Rav twisted and pushed, and found a section of wall rotating in and away from him. Despite the stress and tension he was currently under, Rav found himself smiling. He'd just found a real, honest-to-God secret door. Beyond was a dark void, which the dim light from his phone's screen entirely failed to illuminate. He shuffled carefully forward, let the door close behind him, then fired up the phone's torch app.

The phone torch revealed a narrow passageway lined with rough, unfinished plaster and with a floor of bare concrete. It ran for several feet in front of him before turning through ninety degrees. It appeared that the Charleston Club did indeed have secrets beneath its tacky exterior.

Rav began to edge forward.

Chapter Twenty Four

The passageway was narrow, barely wider than Rav's shoulders. It would have been built so, he realised, because it was squeezed between two rooms that anyone visiting would assume to be adjacent, with the discrepancy in dimensions being small enough that only an estate agent's survey or an attempt to install a connecting door would reveal the passageway that secretly separated them. Heart thumping, muscles twitching, Rav carefully edged along the passage and then around the corner, his phone-torch's light revealing that the secret route ran for a few feet more before terminating in a very dead end. He spent a few minutes conducting a finger-tip examination of the plastered wall, but found nothing.

Why would someone build a secret passage that ran from somewhere to nowhere? Confused, Rav shone the phone's beam of light around the narrow dead-end space. There was nothing – no, wait! To one side was a flat, letterbox-sized panel, painted to be the same off-brown colour as the plaster, but smooth where the plaster was rough. Rav felt around it and felt it lifting up – it was hinged at the top somehow. Two dim points of light were revealed where the flap had been, each around the size of a ten pence piece, and set apart by about the width of the gap between a man's eyes. Rav shut down the torch app, then edged forward to peer through the eye holes. The scene beyond was both dark and strange; dark enough that it took his vision some time to adjust, strange enough that it took him a while to comprehend just what it was he was viewing.

He was looking into a square room lit by twin flaming torches that stood in holders at either side of the room. Between them was a round table, around which a dozen figures dressed in hooded robes sat. A skull was placed at the centre of the table, blood rhythmically pulsing from its mouth into the bowl in which it stood. The figure who was sitting at the far end of the table, facing Rav, lifted his head. There was something wrong with his face. It was smooth, shiny, false – a white mask, Rav realised.

The figure paused for a moment, then raised his arms wide and began to chant words and phrases in what might have been Latin. (Or might not have, given that Latin was a language the London Borough of Hounslow's education system had not felt the need to teach Rav). Rav felt the excitement building within him. This was it, the occult conspiracy the tinfoil hat brigade had long talked of. True, they'd generally pointed their

145

fingers at the Illuminati or the Masons rather than the Rotary Club, but that was just details.

This was the truth.

And then a hand clamped onto his forearm like a hydraulic claw. "I think you've seen enough," said a voice that sounded like hob-nailed boots crunching on a gravelled path.

Rav found himself being thrust face-first into the wall, fast enough that he had no time to react; a hand pressed firmly into his back ensured that he stayed there. He sensed, rather than saw, his unseen captor fiddling with something to the side, and then he felt the wall moving away from him. Another sharp push to his back sent him falling forward into the room he'd just recently been observing. The robed figures looked up sharply, and the chanting stopped.

"I found this man in the passageway, Master," Rav's unseen captor said from behind him. "Watching."

The figure at the head of the table looked hard at Rav, his white mask disturbingly alien. "Watching?"

"Yes, Master."

"What did he see?"

"Everything."

The robed figure considered this for a moment. "That is regrettable. The secrets of this room are for this room only. They cannot be allowed to leave. We must hand this matter to our infernal Lord, and the payment he shall demand will be this intruder's blood and his eternal soul."

From somewhere inside Rav's stomach, a cold ball of terror began to pulse; a shiver began to work its way up his spine, towards his terror-frozen brain.

For long seconds, the twelve masked and hooded figures stared at Rav until, almost as one, they began to laugh, uncontrollably, shoulders heaving, some doubled over as though in agony, others lifting their masks to wipe away tears. Finally, one by one, they regained their composure, save for one slim, female figure who carried on laughing, letting out an annoying snuffly, snorting laugh of the sort that would make one consider divorce, were one to find oneself married to it. Rav had heard that annoying snuffly, snorting laugh before. That afternoon, at the fancy dress shop where they'd rented their costumes. It had belonged to Bev, the proprietor of the shop.

Bev, the small-business woman.

Bev the Rotarian.

The Rotarians had been onto them the whole time, he realised. Had known they'd hired costumes. Had undoubtedly found out about the flash

146

mob at the Charleston and had added a not particularly difficult two to an equally obvious two to come up with an easy four.

Which meant—

The regular, non-secret door at the side of the room opened, and the Professor was rudely shoved through, another goon following close behind him. The hooded figure at the head of the table, the apparent leader, waved a hand towards the doorway. "Okay, ladies and gentlemen," he said in a gruff Northern accent. "We've had our fun. I think it's best if you leave me to talk to our two guests."

The other hooded figures filed out, the last one shutting the door behind them, leaving just the robed leader, the two goons, Rav and the Professor. The robed leader flicked his hood down and removed his mask, to reveal an elderly, but still imposing face. He smiled a not particularly kindly smile, and indicated to Rav and the Professor that they should each take a chair. "I hope you'll forgive us our little joke. We're actually more a wine, cheese, and crackers crowd, but we thought we'd jazz it up and give you a show." He nodded over at the skull. "Novelty item. Red food colouring, apparently." He turned back to Rav and smiled. "I am going to kill you, mind."

The faint feeling of relief and optimism that Rav had been about to feel evaporated. "You can't!"

"Don't tell me what I can and can't do, son. I learned from the master. Back in the 50s, me and Jimmy ran all the dancehalls between here and Scarborough, before he went down south to be on the TV. No one crossed him and no one crosses me."

Then the side door crashed open, so hard that it rebounded off the wall. One of the club's bouncers tumbled into the room. "Mr J! We've got trouble out there."

Rav realised that for the first time since his capture no one's attention was focussed upon him. He didn't waste time thinking, but instead leapt up and kicked the elderly Rotarian in the face. It wasn't a particularly elegant kick, but it was enough to send the old man's chair tumbling backwards, with the old man tumbling backwards with it. The three goons jumped instinctively towards their master, giving Rav just enough time to grab the Professor and drag him through the doorway and into the corridor beyond.

A couple of hastily guessed turns later they emerged into the Charleston's main bar to find a scene of utter, raw, chaos. It appeared that Charlie and the boys had perhaps been too efficient, for the flash mob they'd created had now spawned a social-media fuelled firestorm of positively Dresdenesque proportions. It had already engulfed the

Charleston and was now spreading to the surrounding neighbourhood, remorselessly sucking new participants into an ever-expanding zone of chaos and confusion. Somewhere along the way, a new generation of party-goers had joined the flash mob: men whose idea of a 1920s themed fancy dress outfit was a faded hoodie, decorated with blood or vomit, and accessorised by a beer can in one hand and some sort of improvised weapon in the other, and whose idea of fun typically involved activities proscribed by law, and punishable by a custodial sentence. From the street outside came the gentle whumph of a petrol bomb being thrown into the newly smashed window of a parked car.

This was clearly no place for men wearing rented costumes, even if they did have no intention of returning said garments. Rav grabbed the Professor's shoulder. "Come on. Let's get the hell out of here."

It was shortly after this, while attempting to follow a man dressed as a bondage bear between a looted phone shop and an upturned G-Wiz, that Rav and the Professor were arrested on suspicion of belonging to an illegal flash mob.

Chapter Twenty Five

It is a truth near universally acknowledged that a man in possession of a BNP membership card is in need of a good kicking. Rav didn't know if the man who'd been loaded into the police van in front of him was the possessor of such a card, but he was clad in a replica SS uniform, and he did appear to have taken a reasonably enthusiastic beating in his recent past. Rav would never have suggested that the Greater Manchester police officers who'd loaded the man into the van might have been the perpetrators of this beating; however, the casual manner in which they'd thrown him into the back of the van didn't necessarily inspire confidence.

Rav's entry into the van was slightly gentler, but not significantly so. He skidded onto the bench seat, and then quickly shifted along in time to avoid the Professor thudding down next to him. The older man took a moment to adjust his highwayman's costume, then turned his attention back to the policeman who'd just tossed him into the van's interior. "Excuse me, officer? Might I enquire as to precisely which piece of legislation we have been arrested under?"

It was Rav's experience that such a question was unlikely to achieve any good result, given that the typical police modus operandi in these sorts of occasions typically consists of arresting everyone present and then working out what they may or may not be guilty of at a later date. He desperately patted the Professor's arm in an attempt to get him to shut up, but it was too late, because the policeman was already staring at the two of them with suspiciously narrow eyes. "Why? If you've done nothing wrong then it shouldn't matter, should it?"

Rav gave the policeman a smile he hoped was dialled to the unthreatening but respectful sweet spot one needs on such occasions. "It's okay. He's just a bit confused."

Now it was Rav's turn to get the stare of suspicion. "What's it to you?"

The Professor leaned in, helpfully. "He's my social worker."

"Your social worker?"

Rav sighed an inward sigh. There were a number of ways things could go from here, and none of them were particularly good.

It took some hours for the police to get round to interviewing Rav. The passage of time hadn't done much to improve his mood, and the same appeared to be true of the cheap suit-clad detective who ended up interviewing him. He motioned Rav to sit on the opposite side of the interview table, and then loaded a pair of old style cassette tapes into a device mounted on the wall that looked old enough to qualify as an antique. Another man was sitting beside him. He was dressed not in uniform, nor suit, but instead wore a casual jumper and jeans.

The policeman started speaking. "I am Detective Sergeant Wayne Trencher. Also present are Mr Dennis Conner from Manchester Social Services department," – the duty social worker, Rav realised – "and the interviewee, Mr Ravinder Shah. Mr Shah has been cautioned. He is aware that he has a right to legal representation, but had not exercised this right. Interview is starting at–"

He examined his watch.

"Five-oh-three."

In other circumstances, Rav would have most definitely exercised his right to legal representation. Hell, he wouldn't even have had to worry about a bill, given that he probably had a half dozen uncles and cousins who were solicitors of some sort. But since this was Manchester, and not Hounslow, he'd be reduced to picking random names from the phone book or relying on whichever legal firm was next on the legal aid rota, and either way – especially given the way his luck was currently running – it was probably near inevitable that he'd end up with a member of the Rotarians representing him. Which left him on his own. He sat up straight and tried to look as much like a respectable professional as one can when one is clad in a harlequin gimp suit.

Trencher resumed talking. "Mr Conner is here purely in an advisory capacity. He would normally have been called only if an arrested person appeared to have possible mental health problems. However, given that it has been suggested that Mr Shah is a social worker who was accompanying a patient of his, we felt it best to have Mr Conner here as an expert." He looked at Rav. "Are you happy for Mr Conner to be present?"

Rav shrugged. Either way this was going to be an awkward conversation. He'd had several hours now to come up with a plausible reason as to why a social worker from Hounslow might be taking a client of his to a costumed flash mob in a Manchester nightclub, three days after he checked said client out for an overnight excursion via a somewhat rules-circumventing phone call, and had thus far come up blank.

And then a thought began to occur to him, something that might actually get him out of this. Of course, he'd still have the minor problem of being hunted by a bunch of vampires and Rotarians who wanted to kill him, but that was for later. Right now, he needed to concentrate on getting out of his current predicament. He paused for a moment, put a calm look onto his face that entirely failed to accurately represent his current state of mind, and then asked a simple question. "Have you talked to my client yet?"

Trencher didn't look particularly happy to have Rav seize control of the interview. He wasn't particularly old, but he had the look of an old-style cop, for whom an interview should consist of him making a monologue of the "I put it to you" variety, following which the suspect would ideally confess. Actual dialogue wasn't apparently in his desired manner of working. Nonetheless, Rav had asked him a direct question, to which he had no real option but to respond. "What client?"

"Professor Quentin Richardson. The older man I was arrested with. He was wearing a highwayman's costume."

"Oh, him. We were going to talk to you first and get the story."

"But we were arrested about eight hours ago. According to Department of Heath guidelines and performance metrics, as a potentially vulnerable person, he should have been seen by a duty social worker within three hours of being arrested."

Trencher smirked. "I know the rules, Mr Shah. And if I had a pound for every lawyer who's claimed that his client is a potentially vulnerable person I'd be sunning myself on a beach right now, not here. Those guidelines you cite also lay down the factors by which we might judge a person to be potentially vulnerable." The detective began to check points off on his fingers. "Has Mr Richardson been behaving in an overly agitated fashion? No. Has he displayed an unusual level of anxiety? No. Has anything he's said or anything he's done indicated that he might be suffering from some kind of mental illness or learning disability? No. During the entire period of his arrest, your client has behaved in an entirely sane and reasonable manner. We've had no reason to think that he might be a vulnerable person."

"Except for the fact that he named me as being his social worker. To one of your police officers. In front of several witnesses. Something that you've just acknowledged in this interview. On tape."

From the sour look on Trencher face it was clear the one-word phrase "Bugger" was bouncing about his brain. He gave the social worker, Conner, a hard look, and got a helpless shrug in return. "Fine. Whatever. Mr Conner here can go and visit him once we're done."

"It's too late. First clock started ticking when he was arrested. Second clock started ticking when you made the phone call to my colleague here. When was that, by the way?"

From the look on his face, the detective's mood looked to be somewhere between anger, suspicion and curiosity. "About two hours after you were arrested. Why?"

"Because if you mentioned that the reason you wanted Mr Conner to come in was because you'd arrested a social worker with his client, then Mr Conner should have realised that there was a vulnerable person involved, meaning that it was his department's performance metric the clock was now ticking on, not yours."

Trencher took a few seconds to consider that, before apparently coming to the conclusion that his best course of action was to go with what Rav appeared to be saying. He wagged an appreciative finger at Rav. "Good point."

"Hang on a minute!" the social worker shouted. "You said there was no hurry. You didn't mention anything about me needing to come in to see this Richardson bloke."

"Didn't matter," the detective told him. "I said he was with his client, which means that you'd been officially informed."

From the look on the social worker's face, he was clearly considering the merits of launching a violent assault on Trencher, and was being deterred only by the facts that: a) Trencher was a policeman, b) they were currently sitting in a police station, and c) the entire encounter was being recorded on two cassette tapes by legally admissible devices. The social worker instead spent several long seconds staring at the detective, before turning his attention back to Rav.

"Fine. Whatever. It's not a problem. That metric only applies to someone who's being arrested. We'll just take Mr Richardson in as a patient instead."

Rav pursed his lips. "You could. But then you'd have to do a new statement of needs for him. That'll take a few days. Meanwhile, that will all be coming out of Manchester social services' budget. And once you've taken responsibility for him, you'd need Hounslow's cooperation to transfer him back again. Given that he's been under our care for more than twenty years now, you might find that a bit tricky. You know how it is. Paperwork has a knack of getting lost in cases such as these."

Conner gave Rav a smug smile. "We don't have to do a new statement of needs for him. We just have to send a request to Hounslow to allow us to use his existing statement of needs on a temporary basis."

"Yeah, but that request needs to be put in within twelve hours of any change of responsibility and it needs to be countersigned by representatives of both the receiving and the relinquishing authorities. It's supposed to be used for managed changeover. So you need to get someone from Hounslow here within about four hours, or the request is invalid. Good luck."

"But under the emergency provisions of the guidelines we can provisionally write a temporary statement of needs and make allowance for it to be replaced by the existing one later."

Rav shook his head. "That's for when you find someone wandering in the street and you have no idea where they came from. But you know where he's come from because I've just told you." Rav had him now. This was like that point in a chess match when you realise the game is yours, that your next move will be followed the words "check" and "mate". He gave himself a second to savour the moment, then delivered his coup de grâce. "Or, alternatively, if you had a validated representative of Hounslow social services here now, in possession of an official ID, and prepared to sign to say that Professor Richardson is currently under the care of Hounslow social services, we could just fill in a nice simple form to say that Hounslow would take full responsibility for him, and Richardson could walk straight out of here. Neither of your departments would take any hit on their budgets. Neither of your departments would fail any performance metrics. And neither of you would have to have any sort of conversation with your bosses." Rav shrugged. "I'd happily sign that form, but I'm not in a position to do so, given that I'm currently under arrest."

Conner and Trencher exchanged glances, then got up and retreated to the doorway, where they proceed to have an urgently whispered conversation, in which recrimination and attempted blame-shifting appeared to be the main themes. Eventually, they returned, and sat back down in front of Rav. It was Trencher who delivered the verdict. "Mr Conner and I have agreed that the most sensible course of action would appear to be for us to release both you and Mr Richardson, and have Mr Richardson signed over to you. I'd suggest you take more care in the future when it comes to planning activities and excursions to take your client on."

Rav got out of his chair and held out a hand to the detective, which the detective reluctantly shook. "Thank you." He turned to Conner, who wore the face of the man currently sucking on a lemon laced with chilli. "You couldn't see your way to lending me a pool car, could you, so I can get my client to a place of safety?"

Conner's pool Ford Fiesta looked to be well-maintained, if a trifle scruffy inside. Rav drove it slowly through the rear gates that guarded the police station's car park, waited a few moments for a break in the passing traffic, then turned into the road and accelerated away. He wasn't quite sure how Conner was planning on making it back to the office, but in the words of Rhett Butler, he didn't particularly give a damn.

Rav liked to think of himself as a strong individual, but events were now piling in on him at a pace and rapidity that exceeded his ability to cope – like a man on a shore who, having been knocked over by one wave, climbs to his feet just in time to be knocked over by the next. In the past couple of days he'd been shot at, tortured, arrested, wandered cold and lost in a wilderness, and been captured and threatened with death twice. He knew that this most recent escape was only temporary; sooner or later Manchester Social Services' record of events would find his way to his boss's desk, and then events would truly begin to spin out of his control.

Beside him, the Professor stirred. "Are you okay, Ravinder?"

Rav was not okay. Rav was far from okay. He felt like he was inside a vice, with fate gleefully spinning the tightening lever every few hours or so. Something, somewhere had to give. There comes a time in a man's life when the most sensible course of action is to snap, and this was that time. Like a model aircraft whose elastic band motor has been wound up to buggery and back, it was time to either soar high into the heavens, or explode in a hail of shattered balsa wood and angry recriminations. It was time to completely lose it, to go biblical on someone's rear end before they went medieval on yours. It was time to start getting nasty.

"Do we have a plan?" the Professor asked.

Rav nodded. He did indeed have a plan. A plan that had occurred to him in the several hours he'd spent in a cell in the company of a couple of drunk Mancunians whose command of the English language was so pitiful they'd made Liam Gallagher look like Oscar bloody Wilde.

"And that plan is?"

"We're going to pick Jess up and get changed. And then we're going to have a chat with Judith."

Chapter Twenty Six

Rav had been the Professor's designated social worker for some years now, long enough that the Professor felt he knew the younger man as much as one can know any man under the type of circumstances by which they'd been bought together. But something quite fundamental appeared to have changed in him over the course of the last several days. There was a grimness to his general demeanour now, a harsh edge to the few words he spoke, and a look of cold fury in his eyes.

He was also driving like a lunatic.

The Professor had more than once considered the possibility of asking Rav to stop and let him out, but had decided that ethics, morality, and common decency compelled him to remain in the car. Rav was more than his social worker, and more than his colleague in the agency. Rav was his friend. A true friend. Friendship is not optional; not something to be discarded when inconvenient or awkward. To call someone a friend means to accept them in all circumstances, be those good, or bad. Or, as in this case, absolutely bloody awful. A friendship must endure when it is frankly not worth having or it was never anything more than a convenient arrangement between acquaintances. And so the Professor had remained in the car, praying to a maker he'd never previously believed in, and clinging tightly to the door's side pocket.

A half hour or so after leaving Manchester they exited the M62, with Rav still driving like a man not merely possessed, but possessed by a spirit with severe anger management issues. He tore down Ecktonshaw's main strip at a good twenty miles an hour above the speed limit, swearing frequently, and overtaking in a manner so dangerous that it would not only cause one to fail a driving test, but would give the examiner good cause to sue his employers for failing to provide a safe working environment. He drove through a couple of ambers some seconds after they'd turned red, cut a right-hand corner so tightly that it could only have been legal had they been driving on the Continent, and finally skidded to a halt a little way short of Judith's house. The Professor took a few moments to breathe, then asked the question he'd been carefully avoiding asking for the last forty minutes or so. "What exactly was it you were planning on saying?"

"Well, let's just say it'll involve a few home truths. Do you think Tabitha's in?"

The Professor pointed down the street. "Her car keys had a Fiat key fob. When we were here last a small yellow Fiat was parked outside the house. It's not here now."

Rav didn't reply, but instead got out of the car and began walking along the pavement towards Judith's front gate. The Professor was not without experience of angry men. Both university politics and academic debate can get quite heated, and when that had been the realm in which he'd dwelt it had not been unknown for discussions to devolve into fist-fights, albeit typically of the flappy slaps, handbags at dawn variety. But he'd never seen a rage as cold as this, and it scared him. He got out of the car and headed after Rav, pausing only to tell Jess they wouldn't be long.

He caught up with the younger man at the far end of the front garden path. Rav was already leaning on the doorbell, ringing it in short but insistent bursts. After a few seconds, the door opened a fraction. Whether through carelessness, complacency, or simply by being flustered by an unexpected early morning call, Judith was still in the process of hooking her chain onto its little catch when she opened the door. It would only have taken her a moment to get it attached, but that was a moment too long, because as soon as she'd opened the door a crack, Rav had pushed it open and forced his way into the house.

Rav was advancing upon her as she backed away, jabbing his finger at her as he spoke in a low whisper. "We're going to have another talk, Judith, and this time you're going to tell me the truth. Because if you don't, so help me God you'll regret it."

After they'd arrived, the Professor had suggested that he and Judith go off and make cups of tea all round, while Rav took a moment to compose himself. Rav had initially disagreed; he was still in the grip of a righteous fury. But deep down he knew the older man was right. He needed a clear head now, not a rage that was only a notch more than panic. The two of them returned a few minutes later. Judith looked like she'd been crying, and she let out a strangled half-sob as she placed a cup and saucer in front of Rav. Calmer now, he felt a small pang of guilt and sympathy, but pushed it away. It wasn't a time for sentiment or pity; not if he wanted to get out of this situation with his nuts intact. He waited for her to sit down opposite him, then fixed her with a very stern gaze. "Okay. No bullshit. We know you've been pretending to be Tabitha online. She gave up her goth lifestyle six months ago and you stole the online identity she'd built up. You going to try and deny that?"

For a long moment she held herself, then she let out another half sob, and shook her head.

"Okay. You've been communicating online with a guy called Alan, who's a twenty-year-old goth student from Leeds, studying philosophy. He thinks you're Tabitha, yeah?"

She nodded, then spoke, the words coming out in a rush. "I didn't mean to do it, it just happened. I was lonely, and I only went to the laptop to get a book from Amazon, but when I started typing I hit Z instead of A and that auto thing happened where it tries to guess what you want and it came up with the Zone and I let it. I don't know why."

"And Tabitha had left it logged into her account, had she?"

Judith couldn't even look at Rav now, but was instead staring hard at the carpet. "Yes. When I got onto the page there was a bit that said 'Welcome TabbyCat27', and I don't know why but I suddenly realised that this was a whole life. Tabitha didn't want it anymore, so what harm could I do by using it instead? I knew it was wrong. I've been trying to stop."

She broke off, sobbing. Rav could fill in the rest of her actions himself: change password, change the email address the Zone account pointed at, perhaps even get a different laptop or tablet. Then getting guilty, the guilt and shame culminating with her stopping talking to Alan a few weeks ago. But he didn't care about details. "Okay, Judith, here's how it's going to be. You're going to show us the laptop or tablet or whatever the hell it is you use to contact Alan. We're going to do something on it, and then we're going to take it away."

"You can't."

"We can. Because if you don't, we'll just sit here and wait until Tabitha gets home and tell her all about what her lonely, middle-aged mother's been getting up to behind her back. I'm sure she'll be very understanding."

Judith broke into sobs, but Rav kept his heart hard.

"And, of course, we'd have to tell Alan all about who you really are. But if you cooperate with us..."

"Yes?"

"You can have the laptop back when we've finished and we won't tell anyone – Tabitha, Alan – no one needs to know. Deal?"

She nodded.

There was a sound in the hall, and Tabitha appeared in the doorway. She was wearing her blue coat, a set of car keys in her hand. She looked at Rav and the Professor in confusion. "Mum? You okay? What's up? Who are these guys?"

Rav gave her a smile. "We're friends of your mum's. Met her through work. We were passing through and decided to drop by and say hi. Isn't that right, Judith?"

Judith nodded, and made a reasonable attempt at a smile.

Rav got out his phone. "Tell you what, let's get a selfie of us all, yeah? One for Facebook."

Chapter Twenty Seven

Alan's Tuesday night shift had been unusually busy, and he'd had no opportunities to retreat to his cubbyhole and look at his tablet. He got home a little before sunset, intending to defrost a bag of frozen pigs' blood for supper before turning in. It wasn't until the bag of blood was in the microwave, defrosting, that he had a chance to switch his tablet on and fire up his email.

What he found caused his dead heart to skip the beat it would never have taken: a notification from the Zone that a message was waiting for him. He clicked through to the Zone and found two unread messages. One was from the vampire hunter, Shah.

The other was from Tabitha.

For several seconds he paused, frozen, before finally mustering enough courage, resolve, and hope to click on the link to Tabitha's message.

Hi Alan i met a friend of yours 2day, he said u were really nice. he seemed nice 2, he said there was something u cud help him with. i hope u can, it would b really nice & i no u r nice. Maybe then we shoud think about meeting up. What do u think.

Could it be true? Had the vampire hunter really found his love? Talked to her? He clicked through to the second message. It had a picture embedded within it, showing the vampire hunter, an older woman, and a young girl, blonde, but strangely familiar. He looked closer, pinching at his screen to zoom in on the picture. It was Tabitha, but looking very different. And slightly confused. A cold sort of fear began to spread through him. He zoomed back out and started to read.

Alan, hi! Ravinder Shah here. The good news is that I've managed to find Tabitha. Here's a photograph of me with her and her mother. (She's not dressed as a goth because she's at home, and just got back from work, and besides, her mother isn't too keen on that sort of thing).

Alan paused for a moment to think on what Shah had said. So Tabitha didn't always dress and look as she had in her profile picture. Did that matter to him? Of course not. It was the real her he'd fallen in love with, not her appearance. He zoomed back in on the picture, close enough that he could crop out Shah and her uncaring mother. Blonde or brunette, goth or not, his Tabitha was still beautiful. That was what mattered. He spent several seconds admiring her image, before zooming back out to read the rest of the message.

The bad news is that I think she might still need a bit of "expectation management" before she's ready to meet you. You know that I'm currently investigating the flying pigs and the people behind it. I figure you probably know some stuff about that which could help me. Tabitha seems to like me, so perhaps if you help me out that might show her how caring you are? Of course, some might say that I ought to be honest with her about who you really are. I could just tell her. Anyhow, call me.

At the bottom of the message was a mobile phone number. Alan's English wasn't too good, and some of the words Shah had used were unfamiliar to him, but he wasn't stupid. He could work out by context what those words meant, and he knew precisely which English word summed up the overall theme of the vampire hunter's message.

Blackmail.

Shah had met Tabitha, talked to her, and knew where she was. He had it in his power to introduce her to Alan having first paved the way. If Alan wanted Shah to now help him, he had to help Shah first. But what Shah wanted was the Project itself. All Alan's hopes and dreams for the future were tied up in that endeavour. Could he sacrifice that for what might only be a chance of a future with Tabitha, for what might be no more than a possibility? He went to reply, got as far as clicking on the reply button and bringing up a new message screen; but that was as far as he got. How can you type a reply when you have no idea what to say? After minutes spent staring, paralysed, at his tablet's display, Alan shut it down and crawled into his coffin. The pigs' blood was still in the microwave but he had no stomach for feeding now.

Sleep often didn't come easily for Alan, but today, it didn't come at all. Eventually, he gave up, channel surfed a bit, and found Jeremy Kyle USA, which turned out to be just like Jeremy Kyle in the UK except that it somehow managed to be even worse. He tried some of the pigs' blood, but it tasted warm and insipid. He found his gaze wandering, first to his tablet, and then to his phone. Should he message Tabitha back? What would he say? Should he call Shah?

And then his phone rang.

Nicolae. If Alan had been asked to write a list of the people he didn't want to speak to right now, he'd have written Nicolae's name down straight away and only then started sucking on his pen. He let it ring several times, but he knew that some people demand attention, and Nicolae was invariably one of them. He answered. "Yes?"

Occasionally, Nicolae would begin a conversation with pleasantries, as though the relationship between them was that of old friends and colleagues, rather than what it effectively was, an abusive father and his perpetually disappointing son. This was apparently not one of those occasions. "Don't you 'yes' me, you retarded son of a Carpathian whore!"

160

Nicolae sounded very, very angry. "Is there a problem?"

"Of course there's a fucking problem! That bastard vampire hunter, the one you didn't kill, that's what."

The fog that had already been clouding Alan's thought processes thickened further. All the vampire hunter had done was contact a girl. Why would that have so enraged Nicolae? "Why?" Alan asked cautiously. "What's he done?"

"He's made me look like a fucking Hungarian, that's what! The bastard turned up at Everidge's place. No one's got a clue how he found out about that. Anyhow, Everidge tried to capture him on his own, but the stupid son of a bitch managed to fuck it up and the vampire hunter escaped."

"And that's the problem?"

"No, that's just the beginning of the problem. Everidge managed to track him down to where he was hiding and went in with a bunch of Harry Jack's guys to try and capture him. He was still trying to handle it on his own, but he screwed up again. Then Shah turned up at Harry Jack's joint in Manchester. Jack had him, but something went wrong. Shah got away, and Jack's place got totally trashed. The Rotarians are mad as shit; they're out for blood, and the only reason I haven't told them that this entire balls-up is down to you is because it would make me look bad."

"Oh."

"Is that all you can come up with, you stupid shit? 'Oh'?"

Alan was still trying to process the magnitude of the disaster that appeared to have happened. Shah might have found Tabitha, but he'd clearly been pursuing his original investigation all the while. Then Nicolae resumed speaking.

"Anyway. Damage is done. I have work for you tonight."

"Tonight? I've got a shift at my hotel. I have four shifts in a row."

"Tell them you're sick. This is important, Alan. It concerns the Project. Get this right and I might actually forget this fuck-up."

The Project. Whatever Alan's feelings, the Project had to come first. "What's the job?"

"It's for the Rotarians. Their head's coming over from Chicago tonight to give them a good arse-kicking over the Project running late. After last night, they're all shitting themselves about Shah, so they've asked me to provide a little extra security when he's taken to the meeting. Everidge is renting a blacked out van. He'll pick you up in half an hour and bring you over here. Try not to get too sunburned getting in and out."

He hung up.

On the TV, dysfunctional families continued to self-destruct for the amusement of the watching audience. The mist-cast shadows clouding Alan's thoughts swirled, then cleared, momentarily allowing a fresh thought free passage. Shah was wanting information about the people behind the flying pigs. And it was the Rotarians he'd been bothering. Perhaps Alan could, as the English were fond of saying, have it both ways. Maybe there was a way he could give Shah something that would satisfy the vampire hunter, while still leaving the Project intact.

He could give Shah the head.

Alan picked up his tablet and turned it on. The vampire hunter's message was still on the screen, the number at the bottom. He grabbed his phone and began to dial.

After leaving Judith's place, Rav and the Professor had holed up in a Wi-Fi-equipped Starbucks (from now on, independent, owner-occupied businesses were strictly off Rav's menu). Their task: to craft a couple of messages. The first one was relatively simple, being a message from his account to Alan. The second, from Judith's Tabitha account, was harder.

They'd crafted the message carefully, agonising over each and every wrongly spelt word, misplaced comma and missing apostrophe. After all, they weren't simply attempting to emulate Judith's writing style; instead, they were attempting to emulate the writing style Judith used when attempting to emulate her daughter's writing style. Given that they couldn't give Alan what he wanted, and given that they also had the Rotarians after them, their only hope now was to lever something, anything, out of Alan that they could then use to get both parties off their backs.

As ghost-writing went, this was pretty hard core.

Then, finished, they settled down to wait. Hours ticked by, with the passing of each hour marked by another trip to the counter to buy a further set of beverages and the occasional trip outside for Jess to stretch her legs and have a wee.

Then Rav's phone rang, with a call whose number it didn't recognise. He answered, and found himself talking to Alan. The vampire's message was short and to the point. "There is meeting tonight. People who make pigs fly. Big shot boss from United States will be there. The Head, they call him. I am on security team protecting him on journey. I phone you later with more details."

Rav tried not to give anything away in his reply. "Okay, that's good."

"And if I help you, you give me Tabitha, yes?"

"Yeah. Course."

"You not screwing with me?"

"No way. Honestly."

The vampire hung up.

The Professor listened while Rav filled him in on the salient details of the conversation he'd just had, thought for a moment, and then spoke. "I see. Do we have a plan?"

Rav shook his head. He'd been thinking on a particular decision for a while now, and he knew in his heart, deep down, that now was the time to take it. "No. We, you and I that is, don't have anything. I'm putting you on a train back to London. I'll call the Hounslow office and get someone to pick you up, then return the car to Manchester's people."

"But why?"

"Because in the last few days, you've been arrested, captured, and threatened twice; shot at once; and come bloody close to a death by hypothermia. I'm supposed to be your social worker. I'm supposed to be taking care of you. It was totally wrong for me to drag you into all of this."

The Professor shook his head. "No."

"What do mean, no?"

Twenty years seemed to drop off the Professor's face as he gave Rav an almost fatherly smile. "I mean no. You might have been thinking about this, but so have I, and my decision is that I'm not going back. Not just because you're my friend. Not just because I don't want to abandon you in your hour of need. And not just because, frankly, I've rather enjoyed our recent adventures. And it's not even that this is my fight too, that I myself might have scores to settle with the Rotarians. These are bad people, doing a bad thing. It's about more than simply you or I now. I've lived the last twenty something years feeling worthless and useless, feeling that my life, such as it might have been, was effectively over. But not now. There's a task that needs doing and I believe I can help you do it." He stuck out his hand. "If you'll have me."

Rav considered this for a moment, then took the older man's hand and shook it. "Okay. And thank you. I appreciate it."

"Expressions of gratitude are unnecessary, but are gratefully accepted nonetheless. So what now?"

Rav took a few seconds to mentally reconfigure his plans. "Well, I think if I make a phone call to Manchester's people saying I need the car for another day due to unforeseen circumstances, that might keep them off my back for a day or two. Course, shit will still hit the fan back in Hounslow by tomorrow at the latest, but I guess we can worry about that then."

"Quite."

Rav took a few more moments to consider the situation. All the sane options – walk away, negotiate, inform the police, go to the papers – had either never existed or had long since departed Possibility Station. There are times in life's Great Game of Poker when you just have to go for it. Times when, no matter what face-down cards Destiny may have originally dealt you – and no matter what face-up cards Fate may subsequently have added on the flop, the turn, and the river – you just have to take a deep breath and push every chip you have into the centre of the table, knowing that one of the people at the table will be the proverbial fool and hoping to hell it isn't you. This was just such a moment.

He looked the Professor square in the eye. "We're going to kidnap the Head."

Chapter Twenty Eight

A little before noon Alan phoned again, to give Rav an outline of the Head's itinerary. Flight from Chicago to Leeds Bradford Airport via Heathrow, accompanied by a bodyguard; followed by a short limousine trip to the private conference centre where the meeting was taking place. The bodyguard would likely be packing some kind of firearm. Alan, Nicolae, and Everidge would be meeting the Head at the airport and then driving escort to the limousine in Nicolae's Skoda. In addition, one of Harry Jack's tooled-up bouncers would be in the limousine alongside the driver.

At first, the problem at hand – the extracting of the Head from an armed bodyguard, a tooled-up bouncer, and a couple of Warsaw Pact trained vampires – seemed pretty insurmountable, even with one of those vampires actually being on your side. But as he sucked hard on his pencil – HB, bought with a pad from a WHSmith's during a lunchtime excursion for supplies – a plan began to occur to Rav.

If was simple, of necessity – they were, after all, Ravinder Shah's two and a half, and not Danny Ocean's eleven. But as Rav checked out all the angles and ran through each possible cock-up opportunity he started to feel a spark of anticipation. This might actually work. He sketched out the plan in a graphical form and took the Professor through it. When he'd finished, the Professor nodded approvingly. "Well thought out, Ravinder, well thought out."

"You think it will work?"

The older man tipped his head, and spread his hands. "It has the potential to. With a fair-wind and a well-set sail it has every chance, and I think that's as much as we can hope for at this stage of the game."

"Cool. Okay, let's get to work."

If this had been a gritty 1970s movie or an episode from a 1980s action TV series, this would have been the point, midway through the third act, where three minutes of the pumping theme tune would have played over a montage of shots of Rav and the Professor running up steps, punching frozen slabs of beef, welding large amounts of metal tubing onto what had once been a Manchester City Council pool car, and shaking hands with a succession of extras to seal what was presumably a series of deals.

Of course, this wasn't a gritty 1970s movie or a 1980s action TV series. No frozen slabs of beef were punched, and any flights of steps ascended were done so cautiously, given that it was winter and such surfaces can often be slippery. The reality of Rav and the Professor's afternoon was, in fact, the making of phone calls, the conducting of research on the web, the attending of a select number of discreet appointments, and finally the arranging of a short-term loan from Wonga.com at an APR so high that the authors of Leviticus would have recommended a good stoning as the only reasonable response. And then, finally, just a few hours before the Head's plane was due to land, they were ready. "You good?" Rav asked the Professor.

The Professor nodded, an almost impish smile playing across his lips. "I am, Ravinder. I am."

"Okay. Let's go."

The longer they waited for the Head, the more nervous Alan got. Everidge was pacing up and down, muttering. Nicolae was being, well, Nicolae. Meanwhile, beyond the glass frontage of Leeds Bradford's sole arrivals area, the stretched limousine the Head's American people had requested stood in the early evening darkness, waiting.

It wasn't actually a stretched limousine, of course. No Briton of any class would choose to travel in a conveyance so tacky as a stretched limousine. As a result, the entire British stretched limousine industry actually exists to serve a single market, that market being young working-class women on drunken hen-parties. It was for this reason that the black, stretched Lincoln Continental the Head's American people had requested was actually a stretched Hummer painted a shocking shade of pink.

But it wasn't the pink Hummer that was making Alan nervous. In fact, Everidge's hysterical reaction upon seeing it, and the blazing row he and Nicolae had then proceeded to have, had thus far been the one bright spot in an otherwise tiresome day. No, what was making Alan's neurones twitchy was the knowledge that Shah was out there somewhere preparing to make his move, combined with the fear that the vampire hunter might not merely screw it all up, but might do so in a manner that would implicate Alan as the traitor who'd squealed. He whispered a silent prayer to the God his mother had believed in.

Everidge was consulting first his watch, and then the information screen that hung from the ceiling. "Look sharp," he told Alan and Nicolae. "The Head's flight landed a few minutes ago. He should be with us pretty soon."

A little while later, two men walked through the opening from the flight-side area. They were suited, booted and groomed, with smoothly tanned skin and perfect teeth, and they walked in the manner of men who

166

wear power and wealth with a languid ease. The two men glanced across the arrivals hall, taking in Everidge in his suit and Alan and Nicolae hidden beneath their shapeless hoodies, and nodded, knowingly. They walked over, one of them holding a hand out to Everidge.

"I'm Jonathan," he said in a smooth, mid-Western accent. "I'm guessing you'd be Peter Everidge?"

Everidge nodded. "Yes. Yes, I am." He indicated the man's companion. "And this would be-"

"This would be the Head. Shall we go?"

"Of course, yes." Everidge turned and pointed at the waiting Hummer. "We did have a little issue with the transport, I'm afraid."

From their vantage point at the other end of the terminal, wearing the new suits they'd purchased that afternoon, Rav and the Professor watched the five figures exit: Everidge and his two guests to the Hummer, Alan and Nicolae to Nicolae's Skoda, which had been parked behind it. After a few seconds delay, the two vehicles glided smoothly away, heading for the adjacent A658. Rav took a final sip of his coffee, then looked over at the Professor. "You ready?"

"As I ever will be, Ravinder."

"Cool. Let's roll."

There was no direct route to the combined hotel, conference centre, and health spa the Rotarians had selected for the meeting, with the result being that their two-vehicle convoy was forced to follow a cross-country, zig-zagging path, along largely unlit roads. With each first-exit turn off a roundabout, or right-turn across traffic, Alan's nervousness increased. He had no idea what move the vampire hunter was going to make; Shah had not seen fit to take Alan into his confidence. But it was going to happen.

Ahead of them, the Hummer was indicating right, slowing to a halt on the crest of a hill before drawing into the dinky right-turn lane painted upon the road in white markings. Nicolae drew up behind it as it waited, indicator blinking, for a gap in the oncoming traffic. A little way down the hill, a man sat on a bench by a bus-stop, illuminated by its sole light. As Alan watched, the man scratched his nose. Was this one of Shah's people, signalling somehow?

A tractor was already chugging slowly away from them along the side-road they wished to turn into, towing a small trailer almost comically overloaded with straw bales. Did the bales conceal something? Was the tractor part of Shah's plan? Then the Hummer began to glide forward, awkwardly crabbing across the junction and into the side-road, taking so long over the manoeuvre that by the time it was clear, the gap through which it had driven was already gone, replaced again by a solid stream of traffic. The Hummer headed down the lane, overtook the tractor, and disappeared around a bend.

Nicolae let out a stream of Romanian curses and thumped the steering wheel. He was obviously feeling as nervous as Alan, even if it was for a slightly different set of reasons. Thirty seconds later, a small gap appeared in the oncoming traffic, just big enough for Nicolae to wheel-spin into the side-road and set off in pursuit of the Hummer. The lane was narrow and winding with high banked sides, lit only by the dim moonlight, and in possession of a slowly moving tractor lurking somewhere along its length. Only a madman with a casual contempt for the lives of those he shared existence with would have attempted to traverse the road at any speed greater than twenty-five or perhaps thirty miles per hour. Luckily, Nicolae possessed a compassion for the wellbeing of others so pitifully small that set against it even Jeremy Clarkson would appear positively Gandhiesque, which enabled him and Alan to catch up with the Hummer within forty-five seconds by the simple expedient of driving like Lewis Hamilton might were he a) on drugs, and b) not Lewis Hamilton.

It wasn't the worst forty-five seconds of Alan's life. Frankly, Alan had lived a pretty shit life, and had he been assembling a top ten shortlist of its worst moments, he'd have had a considerable amount of material to choose from. But it was easily the worst forty-five seconds of Alan's week so far, and if there was any consolation he could draw from it, it would be that the car which had received three separate, crunching blows – two with dry stone walls and one with a tractor – belonged to Nicolae, and not him. By contrast, the Hummer – when they caught up with it – looked unscathed. But that wasn't enough to stop Alan's paranoia tingling. "Do you think it's the same Hummer?" he asked Nicolae.

"Of course it's the same fucking Hummer. You think there are two of them in the same fucking one-lane road?"

Alan said nothing.

Five minutes of comparatively uneventful driving later, they pulled up into the driveway of the hotel. It had a plush appearance, with a posh gravel drive and manicured lawns. A hotel manager accompanied by a phalanx of suit-clad porters emerged and, after a brief exchange of words with Everidge, ushered them through the entrance lobby and into a meeting room. A number of Rotarians were waiting for them. Most of them were unfamiliar to Alan, but he recognised one: Harry Jack, the man whose nightclub had apparently been smashed up the previous night. Jack stood up, and extended a deferential hand, clearly unsure which of the two men who'd arrived was the Head. "Good evening. I'm Harry Jack?"

Alan found himself a seat at the side of the room. Shah hadn't made his move on the journey. Was he going to make it here, instead, with the Rotarian's entire Northern leadership present? The two American Rotarians made no move, leaving Harry Jack hanging, his unshook hand outstretched. Finally, the one who'd introduced himself as Jonathan broke the excruciatingly awkward silence.

"The exercise is over now, right?"

Harry Jack slowly withdrew his hand. "Exercise?"

"You've got some visitors coming in tomorrow, yeah? Some bloke called the Head, and his aide. We were hired to act as them for this, the practise run?"

"Hired?"

The bloke who apparently wasn't actually Jonathan was starting to look a little worried now. He clearly didn't know who Harry Jack was – if he had, he probably would now be initiating a process that would conclude with his bowels prolapsing. But even as an unrecognised figure, the old man was managing to exude an air of raw menace so terrifying that the room felt as though the air conditioning had been whacked up to maximum.

"Yeah," not-Jonathan stuttered. "We're actors who run a training agency on the side. You know, role plays and stuff. A bloke called this afternoon and requested that we take the afternoon flight from Gatwick to Leeds Bradford, wait flight-side until the eighteen forty-five flight from Heathrow was just about to land, and then come out and play the role of your Head, and his aide. So you could do a dry run." He looked around the room, his body-language suggesting that he was in the process of realising the enormity of the mistake he'd made in accepting the job. "That's what you wanted, right?"

Chapter Twenty Nine

The plan had run like quality, Swiss-produced clockwork. Everidge, Nicolae, and Alan had walked out of the terminal with the fake Head and aide and driven away. Then, five minutes later, two men came walking out through the flight-side doors. One of them was slim, with saturnine features and steely eyes and a wardrobe clearly purchased from the better side of town. His companion, who was pushing a luggage-laden trolley with one-handed ease, was squat and muscular and looked like a brick outhouse might if you'd asked a team of top-quality tailors to clad it in woollen pinstripe.

They hadn't been the only ones walking through the flight-side doors. The Heathrow plane on which they'd landed had no doubt discharged a good hundred or so passengers. But where the other passengers had given forth an air of ordinary Yorkshireness, these two had not. They alone possessed auras of power and wealth and of being from another place and another culture. Rav had risked it, walking up to them and declaring, "Everidge sent us. Welcome to Yorkshire."

Now, a half hour later, their rented BMW was gliding smoothly down the driveway of the country hotel Rav had booked them into. In the passenger seat beside him sat the Professor; behind them were sat the Head, his bodyguard, and the hatbox the bodyguard had refused to put into the boot. Neither the beamer nor the hotel had been cheap, but this wasn't a time to skimp on details. They drew up in front of the hotel to find the manager, primed by Rav, already waiting for them, greeting them in a manner so oily they could practically have slid straight through into the lobby like small boys sliding on ice.

"Welcome, welcome," he told them, launching into a high-octane stream of structure-free bullshit. "It is both an honour and a privilege. Please accept our quality, comfort, style, and heritage." He wrung his hands, and smiled, then gestured at the porter standing uselessly by with a golden trolley of the sort that people with taste know to be tacky, but people without taste think is class. "Now. Quickly. Not all day!"

The porter wheeled the luggage straight through the lobby to the lifts, and from there to the top-of-the-range suite that Wonga's wonga had paid for. The Head gave the porter a tip so large that it produced an exaggerated, cartoon-like double-take, waited until the man had scuttled away, then fixed his attention on Rav, the Professor having disappeared on a final errand when they'd entered the lobby. "Okay, the Head's pretty keen to get down to business. Where are Jack and Everidge?"

For more than thirty minutes the plan had gripped the road tightly through every bend Rav had hurled it into, but now, suddenly, something wasn't quite right, as though his formally rock-solid scheme was aquaplaning, its steering wheel loose in Rav's hands. "Aren't you the Head?"

"What? No, Mr–" The man stopped, dead, the brain between his steely eyes no doubt calculating away. The charm was gone now, the smooth bonhomie stripped away to leave a cold hardness that made it very clear that this was the sort of man who, if crossed by you, would have only one question in mind, that question being whether to go with new-style concrete boots or the old classic of chains and an anvil when throwing you off a bridge. "Who exactly are you?"

The Professor chose that moment to re-enter both the literal room and the metaphorical story, accompanied by a grumpy looking Jess. The dog sniffed the air once then hurled herself forward, jumping onto the bed and attacking the hatbox which, up until this moment, had been sitting quietly on the bedspread, minding its own business. The box rocked back onto its side, rolled across the bed, and fell to the floor with a thud. "Jesus H Christ!" it shouted in an accent more usually associated with Robert De Niro than hatboxes.

Jess was already at the edge of the bed, poised to leap forward in a second attack. But the second man, the bodyguard, who'd moved at a speed normally associated with the contents of a brick outhouse rather than the outhouse itself, was already there, blocking her way, an impressively large pistol held in his huge hands. The dog looked up at the man mountain before her and began to back quickly away, whining in fear. She made it a few feet like that, then spun round, jumped off the far side of the bed, and crawled underneath a rather plush armchair.

"What fucked up kind of operation are you limey bastards running here?" shouted the man who apparently wasn't the Head. He let the question linger long enough for Rav's sphincter to get in a good two to three second workout, then turned and strode over to the hatbox, which was still producing a torrent of New York accented cursing. "Sorry, Chief," he told it. "Had a bit of an accident." He picked it up and placed it on the bed, then began to undo the heavy straps that secured it shut.

The second man meanwhile was advancing upon Rav and the Professor. He pointed with his gun at the two easy chairs, beneath one of which Jess was currently cowering. "Perhaps you gentlemen might like to sit down there. I suspect the Head will want to speak to you."

They sat down. The bodyguard gave them each a nail-gun strength glare, then backed away, returning the pistol that he absolutely should not have had, having just come through airport security, to the holster beneath his jacket. Eventually, the last strap was loosened and the box's lid removed and placed carefully to one side. From where Rav was sat he couldn't see into the box itself, but he could see that its interior looked to be richly lined with a deep red, padded velvet, with the box itself being constructed not of thin cardboard, but of some kind of wood. Almost as though, he realised, it had been built in the manner of a coffin, but in the size and shape of a hatbox.

The first man reached into the box and lifted out an old, and rather wizened head, whose neck ended in a blunt-ended stump. He placed it carefully upon the now upturned lid, then took a step back. The head's two eyes – which were blue and faded and set into a pair of sunken sockets – examined Rav and the Professor. As they did so, an unimpressed sneer settled upon the head's thin lips. "Which one of you two bastards is Harry Jack?"

If there was one overriding emotion at play in the Rotarian's summit meeting in the immediate, fifteen-minute aftermath of their apparently fraudulent guests' stunning revelation, it was panic. Phone calls were made to associates at the airport, searches ordered. Within minutes the results came back, confirming everyone's fears: wherever the Head now was, he wasn't anywhere in the arrivals lobby of Leeds Bradford Airport. Only Harry Jack seemed immune to the panic, choosing instead to bollock Everidge in a voice whose calm tone served only to increase its menace, with said bollocking interspersed with the occasional aside that back in "the old days", he and Jimmy would have given a "fucking good kicking" to everyone and anyone with any connection whatsoever to the "mother of all fuck-ups" now unfolding.

Eventually, the two actors were dispatched on their way in a hastily ordered minicab, under the terms of a compromise negotiated by Everidge under which they agreed not to tell anyone about the job they'd just done, and, in return, Harry Jack agreed to not have them shot. That immediate issue resolved, conversation then turned to the more pressing matter at hand, that being the task of first establishing the whereabouts of the Head, and of then retrieving him from wherever that might be. With Harry Jack temporarily quietened by a rather old example of his favourite single malt and a rather young example of his favourite type of prostitute, both of whom had apparently been ordered in advance by Everidge, the rest of those assembled got their heads together and began to plan.

"This will be that bastard, Shah," Everidge snarled. "It's got his bloody finger prints all over it."

Suggestions bounced around the table.

"We need to check the CCTV logs from the airport. Who have we got who works there?"

"How did they get away from the airport? Car? If so, can we get the number plate?"

"Can we track Shah's bank account? How about his phone?"

More phone calls were made. Emails were sent. Within half an hour the data was starting to trickle in. The CCTV showed a young Asian man and an older white man walking into the arrivals area just as Everidge, Nicolae, Alan, and the actors were leaving. It showed them meeting two individuals coming off the flight and taking them to a dark blue BMW parked in the car park. "Number plate?" Everidge asked the Rotarian who was relaying the report.

The other man shook his head. "Not enough resolution. It's a basic system. Operator would have had to zoom in to check it and there was no reason to."

Alan didn't need to look at Everidge's face to know that the Rotarian wasn't happy. "So we've confirmed that Shah collected the Head and his aide, and drove them off somewhere, but after that we've lost them." He looked around the room, glancing at each one of them in turn, with Alan's paranoia spiking when it was his turn to be stared at. "What else have we got?"

Minutes ticked by. More phone calls. More emails. More tapping away on laptops. And then a clearing of a throat from a Rotarian at the far end of the room, followed by his quiet voice. "Pete. I might have something."

Chapter Thirty

Obvious physical freakishness and brusque manner aside, Rav couldn't help but see something of a mythical, noble quality about the Head. To be in his presence was to experience something of life as it had been eons ago, in the primeval world of myth and magic that had existed before men of learning uncovered the clockwork that lay behind reality's turning. In that primeval world men had valued respect over money and tradition over efficiency. It had been an age when men would treat captured enemies with respect and hospitality, treating them to food, wine and conversation before slaughtering them with their bare hands. The Head seemed to come from that other age, and while there was no suggestion that he himself would be doing any killing that night, he certainly appeared to be in the mood to talk, and he did get his aide to order food and a round of drinks from room service.

Some hours later, the Head was still telling his story, stopping now and again to nibble at a chicken drumstick his aide was holding for him. (Scared shitless as he was, Rav was still, nonetheless, fascinated by the question of just where the food would go, but felt that to ask would qualify as stratospherically rude on multiple levels). Having made it through his birth in Italy and subsequent emigration to the United States, followed by his later conversion into a vampire in New Orleans at some point in the middle years of the nineteenth century, the Head was now deep into an anecdote that involved a gypsy girl, her mother, and an assignation that had gone horribly wrong. Rav was getting the feeling that he didn't get out much.

"And then that gypsy bitch cursed me, even more than I was already cursed. She said something so that when she had her sons cut off my head, instead of dying, I still lived. Like this."

"That must have been awkward," said the Professor.

The Head didn't even bother to look at him. "Shut the fuck up. I'm talking."

"I'm terribly sorry."

The Head then paused for several seconds, in the manner of a man about to get to the point he's long been working towards, before resuming. "I spent twenty years in a drawer in a San Francisco junk shop. I spent ten years in a travelling freak show, with a bearded lady, a dwarf, and a guy who could suck his own cock. I spent fifteen years working for a bent ventriloquist. And those were the good years. But along the way I learned how to tell when someone was full of bullshit and you two bastards are so full of it that it's practically slopping over the sides."

"Well-" Rav began. "I can expl-"

"I thought I told you two to shut the fuck up. I came here to meet that useless cocksucker Jack and that fucking optometrist who was supposed to be running my project. I'm here to talk with the organ grinder and his monkey, not you two useless bastards. I didn't fly four thousand fucking miles as hand luggage in an overhead locker just to have Jack jerk me around like I was a two-bit whore with syphilis and he was my fucking client. Do you understand?"

"Erm, yes," said Rav, who in truth was currently understanding only one thing, that thing being that the Head was not a being to whom you would ever say "no".

"Well, fuck off out there, and tell Jack and Everidge that if I don't see them in here within a half hour I'll have my men here turn their dicks into cigars and their hands into ashtrays."

The Head resumed nibbling at the drumstick, leaving Rav, Jess, and the Professor to edge backwards out of the room, the two men crouched and bowing like a pair of supplicants leaving the court of a tyrannical and capricious emperor. In the corridor outside, they turned to each other. The Professor gave Rav a desperate querying shrug that managed to summarise their predicament more efficiently than mere words ever could.

It occurred to Rav now that so taken had he been with the idea of kidnapping the Head, he'd never actually considered what he would then do. The end point of his plan had been merely a vague assumption that he could somehow leverage the resulting position to figure out what was going on and how to stop it. Clearly, with hindsight, that had been a highly flawed and incomplete assumption. From somewhere within his mind a video clip began to play, as though looping on a six second gif. Hudson from Aliens, after watching the drop-ship crash and explode: "That's just fucking great, man. Now what the fuck are we supposed to do?"

"We could just leave," suggested the Professor. "Just run, now."

They could, Rav knew that. But to walk away with nothing having just played their one and only joker, Alan, would be one hell of a turd sandwich to munch down on. He shook his head. "There must something we can do."

It was at this precise moment that Harry Jack and Everidge arrived, accompanied by Nicolae and Alan, a fistful of tuxedo-clad bouncers, and a couple of middle-aged men in suits whose pale faces betrayed their nervousness. Jack reintroduced himself with a hard punch to Rav's face, and then motioned Nicolae and Alan to grab the two of them. Nicolae's hand closed around Rav's neck and he felt himself being lifted high before being rammed against the wall, his feet dangling helplessly beneath him.

"What have you done with our guests?" asked Jack.

Rav nodded at the door beside them as best he could, given that his entire body-weight was currently being suspended from the claw around his neck. "In, room. There."

Jack nodded, already turning away towards the door. "Excellent."

It's sometimes said that nothing spurs creativity and inspiration more than greed. But if that's so then raw, bowel-trembling terror must come a close second, because Rav now found a fully formed idea materialising deep inside his brain as though it had been beamed straight in by Mr Scott or Chief O'Brien. He swivelled his eyes as far in Jack's direction as they would go, and coughed, something which was actually rather easy given the way Nicolae's fingers were clamped around his jugular. "They're. Guarded. I've. Got. People. In. There."

Jack laughed, and waved a hand at his bouncers. "Am I supposed to be scared?"

"They've. Got. Guns."

Jack laughed again, and then reached into his jacket to pull out a quite seriously large pistol. "So have we." He nodded to his bouncers, who were pulling out their own shooters, counted silently with his fingers – one, two, three – then pointed at the door. The biggest of the bouncers kicked it hard, causing its flimsy lock to shatter and the door itself to fly open. A second bouncer dived through the door with his pistol held high, followed by a third.

"Hands up!" one of them shouted. "Don't mov–"

There was a very, very loud crack from inside the room. It's a cliché oft-repeated that when Americans hear a distant car backfiring they assume it's a gunshot, while when British people hear a distant gunshot they assume it's a car backfiring. In this case, either someone had installed a one thousand, five hundred horsepower, twenty-seven litre, World War II era, Merlin aero engine in the hotel room in the few seconds since Rav had left and then screwed up an attempt to start it – or someone had decided to set off his oversized hand-cannon.

The remaining bouncers dived into the room, followed by Harry Jack. A cacophony of noise erupted from beyond the door, a base-line of gunshots played under a melody of shouts, cries, and screams. For several seconds more the demonic symphony played, with those who'd remained outside in the corridor – Rav, the Professor, Alan, Nicolae, and the two middle-management types – left to deduce what might be happening from the sounds alone, as though they were listening to a particularly bad radio play. Finally, the stream of gunshots dribbled to a halt, leaving only a background accompaniment of moans and whimpering.

Nicolae released his hold on Rav, allowing him to crumple to the floor and take a deep, shuddering breath into his burning lungs. Then he found himself being hauled to his feet by the vampire and shoved through the door. Inside the suite they found a scene of Tarantinoesque bloodshed. The Head's aide and bodyguard were both either dead or dying, as was one of the bouncers. Harry Jack was slumped against the wall with blood pumping from his leg while two of his men tried fruitlessly to staunch the flow. A fourth bouncer was propped up in a chair, his blood-covered arm being tended to by the fifth bouncer. And, to complete the scene, Everidge was standing in the centre of the room waving his gun wildly in the air and shouting like a lunatic at no one in particular. "Where is he, you bastards? Where've you put him?"

On the bed, apparently stunned into silence and seemingly overlooked and ignored by all present, was the Head, still placed upon his padded and upturned lid. For a moment, Nicolae's grip upon Rav's shoulder loosened. This was it. This was the time.

Rav dived.

Chapter Thirty One

When he'd been younger, Rav had enjoyed a brief flirtation with the sport of American Football (or as an elder cousin had put it, "Rugby with padding for ponces"). Despite, or perhaps because of, his cousin's derision, Rav had got as far as playing in the under sixteens team of the local amateur side, the Heathrow Jets. The coaches at the Jets had quickly marked him down as a running back, more in recognition that he was too scrawny to do anything else than through any genuine belief that he might possess either speed or agility. But in the few months it had taken for the glamour of playing this All-American sport to be quite literally beaten, bashed and shoulder-charged out of him, Rav did acquire a certain skill in the art of running very fast along a weaving path while holding an approximately ovoid object under your arm.

Which, somewhat fortuitously, proved to be exactly the skills needed to scoop the Head up from his vantage point and somehow make it out of the door without being captured, detained, tripped, or just plain shot. The Professor was still in the corridor, guarded by Alan. Rav tipped Alan a wink, grabbed the Professor with his spare arm, and set off down the corridor, with Jess – who'd appeared from somewhere – running alongside them. There was no plan. If there had been, Rav would have turned right upon leaving the suite to head towards the main staircase that was located at the centre of the hotel. He had, however, turned left, with the result that the three of them were now running away from the main staircase. As mistakes go, this one could very well have been terminal. But whether it be due to fate, luck, or a foresighted implementation of strict building codes by politicians and planners who'd lived before Rav had even been born, escape was in fact at hand, in the form of the ubiquitous sign of the running man. Rav didn't need to have gone on any kind of safety course to know that the running man indicated an escape route, be it from fire, flood, or a bunch of tooled up nutters.

At the corridor's far end was a ninety-degree bend that led straight into a wood-panelled fire door. The three of them crashed round the bend, crashed through the door, and then proceeded to crash down the bare, lino-covered stairs at a speed considerably in excess of what might be considered socially acceptable. After four floors of breakneck descent they reached the ground floor and found a fire exit leading to the lawns outside. Rav hurled himself into its unlocking bar, and bounced off. It was locked. From the stairs above came a sound of skidding footsteps.

The Professor grabbed him by the arm and pointed at a second, wood-panelled fire door. "That way."

Rav shoved his way through the door and found himself tumbling into the far end of the hotel's lounge, his feet sliding on polished tiles. The Head was slipping from under his left arm. He reached across with his right arm and rammed it back into place, but in the process managed to move it such that a mouth that had previously been firmly rammed into his armpit was now unmuffled, and free to verbally express its displeasure.

"You're a dead man, you fucker! I'm gonna have you fucking maimed!"

There were people in the lounge. Older, cultured people, with the shocked expressions on faces you'd expect to see if you've just skidded into view with a decapitated, but very much alive and angry head stuffed under your arm.

"Hey! You stiffs over there. First man to take this piece of shit down gets a hundred thousand big ones in cash."

Rav gave the lounge's inhabitants a desperate grin. "It's a theatrical prop. Short circuit." Then he grabbed the Professor by the arm and dragged him forward. "Come on!"

The lounge looked to be a nice sort of place. It might not quite have contained the great and the good; this was, after all, rural Yorkshire, not Mayfair. But those individuals scattered across the easy chairs and elegant sofas were at least the quietly accomplished and the rather nice, and they certainly didn't deserve to have their post-dinner drinks disturbed in such a crude and unpleasant fashion.

"Goddammit, you useless Limey bastards! These two fuckers are kidnapping me!"

Somewhere behind the lounge's centrally located bar, a cocktail shaker spun by a barman who'd clearly been operating under the delusion that this was a movie and he was Tom Cruise, fell, uncaught, to the floor. The barman stared open-mouthed at Rav and the Professor as they sprinted past, Rav weaving between two clusters of chairs and behind a potted palm as he worked his way down the lounge's right-hand side.

The Head was still shouting. "Okay, what do you fuckers want? Coke? Blowjobs? Money?"

The Professor was somewhere to Rav's left. For a moment, Rav dared hope that they might be home and free. But that moment ended with the emergence into the lounge's far end of Nicolae, Alan, and a bunch of Rotarians, who'd presumably taken the short cut down the main staircase. Given the smallness of the lounge and the combined closing speed of the two parties, it took only seconds for them to collide. Rav hurdled an upturned set of golf clubs, ducked underneath someone's outstretched arm, and then attempted to dive past Nicolae. Another inch and he'd have made it, but life's victories and defeats both are often measured in inches alone and this was just one such defeat; Nicolae had managed to grab a good inch's worth of Rav's suit and that was enough. Rav felt his momentum being checked, his feet sliding out from under him. He was falling, and as he fell he felt the Head beginning to slip from his hold. He reached over, and managed to scoop it into his right hand, but he was still falling, still crashing to the ground, still trapped by Nicolae's vice-like grip.

Instinct took over, where planning had failed. As he impacted hard with the wooden floor, he swung and threw.

Unlike Rav, the Professor had not, in his early years, engaged in the pastime the Americans term "football". He had, however, been forced to participate in the somewhat similar sport of rugby union, that sport being, along with beatings and buggery, the leading leisure pastime at a British public school. He wouldn't claim to have been particularly good at the sport, and he'd certainly never troubled the First XV, or even the Second. But he had acquired a certain proficiency in the positions of outside centre and full-back, and now, some fifty years or so later, he suddenly felt those near-forgotten skills returning.

During the headlong dash down the lounge, with Rav heading down its right-hand side, and the Professor finding himself going down its left, the younger man had, not surprisingly, managed to draw just a little ahead, enough that his tackling by Nicolae was just about visible to the Professor out of the corner of his eye, as was the desperate one-handed throw he made as he tumbled to the floor.

It was a near-perfect pass; a little forward, perhaps, but with no line-judge poised to raise a flag, frankly, who cared? The Head arched high over a couple of Rotarians, seeming almost to hang in the air at the top of its arc. The Professor planted his right foot, feeling his momentum turn into a stress that vibrated up his right leg, letting that leg flex and then rebound, turning his momentum into a jump. He stretched high, as high as he could, and somehow found himself rising higher than the Rotarian who'd jumped beside him. His outstretched hand reached up, caught the Head, and knocked it down; he pawed again as he fell back to the ground, batting it once more, and then somehow he was down, crouched, with the Head held firmly against his chest.

He ducked to the left, avoiding a set of outstretched arms, and pushed off into a sprint, weaving, ducking, bobbing, one arm holding the Head firmly against him, the other a counter-balance, waving first this way and then that. He made it past a second Rotarian and then a third, but then he found his way blocked by a solid phalanx of Alan and at least four other Rotarians. As it had for Rav just moments ago, instinct and long-forgotten skills took over. He tossed the Head in front of him, dropping it onto his hard kicking shoe and chipping it up and over Alan and the Rotarians.

The Head let out a long scream as it sailed over the vampire and his comrades. They, in turn, tracked it with their gazes, transfixed, allowing the Professor to crash through them and catch it as it came back down. And then he was skidding through the wide archway into the lobby. Outside was a dark night, the car park, and the car. There was just one problem.

Rav had the keys.

Rav had impacted the floor with enough force to blast the air from his lungs and damn near crack his ribs. But throwing the Head to the side had triggered Nicolae into releasing his grip, with the result that when Rav rolled back upright and bounced onto his knees he was granted an uninterrupted view of the Professor chip-kicking his way out of the lounge, with Jess following a second or so behind him. This was a good thing. Rav didn't begrudge the older man his escape. He just wished he'd been with him to share it, rather than where he now found himself: trapped in a dead-end section of middle-class hotel architecture with a very angry Romanian ex-secret police vampire blocking his only line of escape.

The vampire paused for a moment and looked back over its shoulder to where Alan and the Rotarians were milling in confusion. "Get after the old man, you idiots." It turned back to Rav. "This one's mine."

Chapter Thirty Two

With the car locked and unavailable, the Professor's only obvious option was to keep running, so he proceeded to do just that. He sped across the gravel car park and over a small and twee hump-backed bridge that spanned a small gurgling brook; an action that triggered a small gasp of pain from the head. Vampire, the Professor realised. Running water. Sited just beyond the bridge was a circular area of closely mown grass, with the dim outline of a flag-topped pole set somewhere in its middle. The Professor wove past the flag, bore left to avoid a bunker, and then set off down what was presumably the fairway of the hotel golf course's eighteenth hole. From somewhere behind him came the sound of a screamed Romanian curse. The Professor risked a quick look behind. Alan, a grimace of pain on his face, had made it over the footbridge and was now heading across the green, accompanied by a phalanx of Rotarians.

The Professor put his head down and resumed sprinting. The Head had given up outright shouting now, preferring instead to mutter under its breath about the many and terrible things it would be doing to the Professor's person at the first opportunity, the general gist of which was that death, when it eventually came, would be a relief and a release rather than a disappointment. The Professor ignored it, and carried on running down the fairway, choosing to stay on smooth terrain rather than risk the rough that flanked the hole to either side.

Some way down, a ghostly grey shadow loomed up out of the darkness. As the Professor drew nearer, its true identity was revealed – an American-style golf kart that had been parked, abandoned even, midway down the fairway. The Professor would have stolen the kart even if his lungs hadn't now been on fire. He jumped in, tossing the Head into the luggage compartment at the back. Jess jumped onto the seat beside him and looked expectantly up. He'd never driven one of these things before, but how hard could it be? The answer, it turned out, was not very. One pedal go, one pedal stop. The Professor hit hard on the pedal that meant go, spun the kart round through a tight one eighty, and headed off, away from his pursuers.

He didn't intend to press the pedal that meant stop.

In hindsight, Rav should have had the foresight to arrange some kind of secret signal to give Alan at an appropriate time. He hadn't had that foresight, giving him no option save to curse hindsight as he'd watched

Alan depart, leaving him entirely alone. Alone save, of course, for the Romanian vampire who was going to kill him, and the shocked inhabitants of the hotel's lounge who, like middle-class bloody sheep, were just going to sit there and watch the tragedy unfold. Nicolae was advancing remorselessly towards him, cracking his knuckles, smiling, laughing. "I kill you slowly, vampire hunter."

Rav stood his ground, not through courage, or even bravado, but because he was standing against a wall which apparently wasn't going anywhere. "You can't do this!"

"Yes, I can."

"But all these people are watching?"

"Let them. Who do you think owns this hotel?" The vampire paused for a moment, before launching a right hook so huge that from the vantage point of its target it seemed almost cartoon-like, as though lifted from a crudely rendered video game. Rav had little doubt that had he left his head in the punch's path it would surely have killed him. He hadn't, of course; all things considered ducking had seemed like the best option. The punch screamed over his descending head and smashed into the wall behind him. Dozens of tiny plaster shards fell down, upon and round Rav. He twisted round, skipped a step sideways, and straightened up into his best fighting stance, ready to face the inevitable follow up blow from Nicolae. It transpired, though, that his fate might not be as terminal as he'd feared, for having smashed his fist into the partition wall, the vampire appeared quite unable to withdraw it. He was, in fact, trapped.

Rav didn't waste any time on witty taunts or a well-deserved kick to the nuts, but simply turned and ran, out of the lounge, through the lobby, down the stairs, and onto the crunchy gravel of the car park. Of the Professor, Jess, Alan, and the Rotarians, there was no sign. They were gone, enveloped by the darkness. The keys of the Manchester pool car were still in his pocket, from when they'd parked it here several hours ago. He grabbed them and headed for it. Not much he could do now but take a spin around the hotel and then up the drive and see if he could spot them.

With its accelerator pedal mashed hard to the floor, the golf kart had swiftly accelerated to its maximum speed of a little more than walking pace, enough to lose the Rotarians, but not enough to shake off the doggedly shambling figure of Alan. The Professor took a straight line up the eighteenth fairway, slid past the night-shrouded tee, and then headed up the slightly sloped path that led through two sets of woodland to the seventeenth hole. He was driving on intuition more than vision now, weaving a path between two sets of merely shadowy outlines. He somehow made it through a switchback sequence of curves, then reached what appeared to be a short, straight section. He risked a quick glance behind him. Alan was gaining.

The path bent slightly round to the left, and then emerged over the crest to reveal the bowled depression that held the seventeenth green. The Professor gunned the kart down the slope. It picked up speed, bouncing over the ruts in a manner that triggered a renewed bout of outraged swearing from the luggage hollow behind him. Then he was at the bottom and speeding across the green. He wove around the flag and headed onto the fairway. This appeared to be a long hole, perhaps a par five, with a dogleg to the right midway down. The woodland thinned, being replaced by a strip of rough bordered by a road he recognised as the driveway leading to the hotel, which from the golfing point of view was presumably out of bounds.

A car was driving along the road, slowing down to stay level with him. A figure was leaning out of the window, shouting at him. It was Rav, he realised. The car lurched to a halt, and Rav got out, waving. The Professor waved back, then wrenched the wheel sharply to the left, sending the kart careering off into the rough. This action, while sending him in Rav's direction, did have the unfortunate side-effect of slowing his speed quite considerably, given how rough the rough turned out to be. He eventually drew up a little way away from the car, the two vehicles separated by several feet of extreme rough and a low, wooden barrier. The Professor clambered out only to find Alan already trotting up alongside him.

The vampire looked tired, and slightly out of breath, but very, very dangerous. He walked past the Professor and instead advanced on Rav, eventually pinning him against the car's bonnet. Jess took a few paces forward, then apparently thought better of it, tucking herself in behind the Professor instead. "We had deal," the vampire growled in a low whisper.

For the second time in the space of a few minutes Rav found himself backed up against an immovable object with a very angry vampire in front of him. At least this particular one wasn't trying to kill him. Yet. "Yes, we did have a deal. That's true."

"So. You give me Tabitha?"

"That's exactly what I'm going to do. But you do have to understand that it is all a bit delicate."

"Delicate?"

"Yeah, yeah. Delicate."

The vampire stared hard at Rav, the eyes in his ruined face the only signs of the human being he'd once been. They flickered this way and that, and then an understanding seemed to come into them. "You is bullshitting."

"No, no, honestly. I'm not bullshitting."

"Can you get me Tabitha? Now?"

"Well, erm. No."

For an instant Rav thought Alan was going to kill him there and then, rip him to pieces, perhaps, or maybe just smash him through the car's metal bonnet. Then the vampire released his hold on him, and took a step back. "Next time I see you, I kill you." He turned, hopped back over the low wooden barrier, brushed past the Professor, and walked over to the golf kart. The vampire leaned over the rear luggage area, peering in. "It okay, Mr Head. I here to rescue you." Then he climbed in behind the steering wheel, pushed down upon the accelerator, and spun away.

Rav and the Professor watched him go. It was the Professor who finally broke the silence. "Dare I ask what the plan is now?"

Rav had no idea. He'd played every card he'd had, gone all-in with all the chips in his pile. This had been his final roll of the dice, and with it made he had nothing left. He was a man without a plan and without hope, his reserves of resolve gone, his tank of resolution dry. He shook his head. "There isn't one. Except get the hell away from this place as fast as we can."

Chapter Thirty Three

Two hours and a hundred or so miles later, as they were heading past a night-shrouded Northampton in a most decidedly southern direction, Rav's phone rang, its X-Files theme-tune ringtone now merely mocking his shat-upon dreams. He considered not answering, but after letting it play for a few seconds he fished it out of his jacket pocket and hit the answer button, resolving to simply throw it out of the window if it turned out to be anyone connected with either vampires or Rotarians. "Yeah?"

"Ravinder?" It was his mother. "Oh my gods – it's horrible – it's..." Her voice was so broken with terror and sadness that he could barely make out her words.

"Mum, what's wrong? What's happened?"

"It's Mindy! She's been kidnapped!"

"What?"

"She was at home, asleep – with your Uncle Tony and your Auntie Pooja – some men – they burst in – took her away."

"What?"

"The police are there now..." Her voice trailed away, leaving only the sound of her crying.

"Mum, I'm on my way home. I'll be there in an hour. Okay?"

"Okay. You be safe." She hung up.

Rav still hadn't quite taken it in.

"What's wrong?" asked the Professor.

"It's Mindy. Some blokes have just kidnapped her."

"Kidnapped her? Your cousin Mindy? The girl I met at the wedding?"

"Yeah. They just broke into her mum and dad's home and took her away."

"Why?"

Rav didn't answer. He knew why, knew exactly whose fault it was. His. His cousin, and her family, were going through hell right now because of him and his stupid dreams to be someone special with a life less ordinary. He slammed a fist into the steering wheel. "Shit! Shit! Shit!"

"You think this is the work of the Rotarians?" the Professor asked.

"Of course it's the sodding Rotarians! Who else?"

"Quite." The Professor paused for a moment, thinking, then clicked his fingers. "We left her car at Mr Partridge's smallholding."

Rav gave the steering wheel another pound. "Of course. All they had to do was contact someone they've got who works for the DVLA and give them the number plate, and that would give them the name and address of the car's registered keeper."

"Mindy."

"Yeah. Mindy."

Rav pushed the accelerator even harder. The motorway flashed past. Slowly. Too slowly.

The next several hours slid by with an agonising lack of pace. Rav had headed straight for his Uncle Tony's place in Hounslow West and found it in uproar and chaos, full to the brim with crying and weeping friends and family, all bewildered, all struggling to understand the tragedy that had befallen them. Rav had said nothing. What could he say? The police were there, of course: a couple of family liaison officers who managed to keep up a constant flow of platitudes while not actually saying anything at all. And then there were the questions, delivered with concerned smiles that had strong hints of suspicion riding shotgun. Had there been a row? Did Mindy have a boyfriend, someone who the family might not have approved of? Did the family fear she'd grown up too Westernised?

Still Rav said nothing, sitting silently to one side as his Uncle Tony answered the questions again and again, insisting there'd been no rows, and asking, pleading with the police to stop asking him questions and actually do something to find his daughter. "Shouldn't there be something on the TV?" cried his Auntie Pooja at them. "Some sort of appeal?" Again the blank, patronising smiles, the meaningless words about it being too early for publicity, about things needing to run their course. On any other such occasion, Rav would have ascribed this to plain, simple, good old-fashioned institutionalised racism, lubricated with a bit of equally old-fashioned laziness.

They wanted an arranged marriage, she went out and got herself a boyfriend, so her dad and her brothers topped her. She's probably in a bin liner out back.

That's what the police would think. That's what they'd say to themselves when they were huddled out of earshot, sipping away on their polystyrene mugs full of instant coffee. But deep down, in a heart that felt as though it had been chilled to absolute zero, Rav knew there was a deeper truth here. Men with the power and influence to have people kidnapped from their own houses have the power and influence to make investigations die. A word here. A suggestion there. The police weren't going to find Mindy. They weren't even going to try.

Sometime around midday Rav was awoken from a depressed trance by his mother tugging on his sleeve, a look of worry upon her face. "Ravinder? You look as though you haven't slept for days. And when did you last change your clothes? Why don't you go home and try to get some sleep." Rav shook his head. Sleep was about the last thing he felt able to do. "I'd rather stay here, Mum. Just in case. You know?"

She nodded. "You're a good boy. Why don't you have a look on the Internet to see if there is any news about Mindy?"

This, at least, was something he could do. So he pushed himself painfully to his feet and went out to his car to retrieve his laptop. On the way back he bumped into the Professor, who'd been busying himself in the kitchen making an endless supply of tea for the apparently endless stream of concerned visitors. The older man, too, looked worried. "How are you bearing up, Ravinder?"

Rav shrugged, but said nothing. Right now he just needed to be away from people. The conservatory turned out to be icy cold, but empty, so he sat down there and flipped open his laptop. As he'd feared, outside of friends and family on Facebook and Twitter there was nothing. BBC News, the Guardian – Christ, he even tried Mail Online and still drew a blank. The Professor appeared beside him, holding a mug of tea. "I thought you might need this."

Rav nodded thanks, then took it, noticing as he did so the small icon at the bottom of the screen that indicated he had new mail. Acting on autopilot now, he clicked on it. Presented before him was the usual list of spam and automatic notifications, but one subject title not so much caught his eye as ripped it out.

We have Mindy!!!

The sender name was garbage, and would no doubt lead to an impossible to follow trail of virtual accounts and dodgy servers. But he knew damn well who it was from. The Professor must have noticed his double-take. "Ravinder? What's wrong?"

Rav pointed at the screen.

"Ah."

Rav opened the mail. It was empty save for a single link, a link which he then found himself unable to click, so badly was his hand shaking. Finally he mustered up the resolve, and clicked. A window appeared, with the image of a distraught, but very familiar face set within it.

Mindy.

She was sobbing, softly, but holding it together in a way that made Rav very, very proud of her. She looked away, presumably being given some kind of off-camera instructions, then looked back to the camera and began to speak.

"Rav. I don't know if you're listening to this. They say they're going to send it to you. They haven't done anything to me. I'm okay, just a bit shaken up. But they've told me what they'll do to me if you don't do what they say, and, it's really horrible."

She broke down a bit then, and Rav found himself touching the laptop's screen, desperate to offer her some comfort, but absolutely unable to do so.

"They say you need to be somewhere."

She looked away, her eyes flickering as she read something off-camera.

"You've got to wait at the taxi rank at Leeds train station at ten o'clock tonight. They'll phone you and give you instructions. They say to make sure you've got plenty of cash on you. And, and – you have to do everything they say, or–"

She stopped and took a deep breath. A hand extended into view from behind the camera, waving her to continue.

"If you don't, they'll courier me to you. In pieces."

The image froze, then disappeared. A crawl of white, sans-serif text began to climb up the now black screen.

*If you tell the police, she will
die and we will hunt you
down and kill you. If you tell
anyone, she will die and we
will hunt you down and kill
you. We cannot be bargained
with. We cannot be reasoned
with. We don't feel pity, or
remorse, or fear. We absolutely
will not stop, ever, until you
are dead.*

The window went black, and this time it stayed black. Rav closed it.

"What are you going to do?" the Professor asked.

"Hand myself in. What else can I do?"

"But they'll kill you."

"Probably. But they might let Mindy go." In a strange kind of way, Rav was relieved. At least now there was something he could do, some way he could pay for the misery he'd caused. The Professor had been right, he realised. He was the tethered goat. He'd always been the tethered goat. He felt a calmness settling upon him, then looked back up at the Professor. "Let's go. We may as well hole up somewhere near Leeds."

Chapter Thirty Four

They made it most of the way up the M1 before pulling off into a service station. It had been a long time since Rav had eaten, and it wasn't until he'd headed into the station's gaudy interior for a slash that he realised how hungry he was. So while the Professor took Jess for a walk round the car park, Rav headed into the station's cheap, tacky, own-brand eatery to refuel, eventually plumping for the all-day full English. It wasn't the sort of thing he would ever have freely chosen, but for now it would do. He was a sausage and a half into the meal when his phone rang. The screen showed an unknown number. He picked it up and answered. "Yeah?"

"Mr Shah."

He recognised the voice immediately. Reece. A succession of feelings crashed in on him, like successive waves falling upon a shingle shore. Hope came first, a thought that perhaps she could help him. But following hard upon that was a strong desire to tell her, quite sincerely, to piss off. He couldn't quite claim that what was happening to Mindy now was entirely Reece's fault, but her interventions thus far sure as hell hadn't made things any better. In fact, the situation he was in right now was probably exactly what she'd hoped for, and that was a realisation that stung like hell. But smug, annoying, and superior as she was, she was the enemy of his enemy, which for now made her a grudging friend. "Look," he said firmly into his phone's mic. "Before you start the puppet master act, I'm not in the mood. If you can help, I'm open to offers, because right now I'm a dead man walking. But it's got to be straight, open, and honest from now on. Or you can sod off right now and let me finish my last meal in peace."

"Fair enough. Are you northbound or southbound?"

"What?"

"Northbound or southbound? I presume you are at Woolley Edge services?"

"Erm, yes."

"So?"

"Northbound."

"Excellent. I'll see you shortly."

The line clicked dead.

Rav thought for a moment, then returned to his full English. He still didn't feel like eating, but fuel was fuel. One and a half sausages down, half a sausage to go.

Reece arrived within ten minutes of hanging up, which was pretty impressive given that Rav could quite literally have been anywhere when she'd called. She slid onto the bench opposite him, dropping a plain black backpack onto the stretch of seating beside her, and gave him a smile. "You look like crap."

"Thanks."

"Well, you said you wanted me to be honest."

"Not that honest."

"Noted." She nodded at his empty mug. "Another one?"

"Black, two sugars."

"Coming right up."

She returned a few minutes later with two mugs, and took her place opposite him. She said nothing, but just sat with her hands wrapped around her mug. Rav said nothing in turn, but instead merely took a few sips from his own coffee. In the end, it was Reece who broke the game of verbal chicken by speaking. "Isn't there something you ought to be asking me?"

"How'd you know where I was?"

"I'm tracking your mobile phone. Your provider can always tell your approximate location by looking at which cell on their network the phone's connected to. That information isn't available to everyone, but they will divulge it to certain parties, of which I'm one. The rest was a lucky guess. I knew you were in the vicinity of Junctions 38 and 39 of the M1 and I figured you might be looking for somewhere anonymous to pass some time in. And since there was a service station within that area it seemed the obvious place for you to be. Is that honest, open, and truthful enough?"

"Erm, yeah. Does that mean the Rotarians can track me too?"

"They most certainly can, and they almost certainly are. But that's not the question you're supposed to be asking me."

Rav fought down the urge to mutter a few curses under his breath. She might have been managing to be open, honest, and truthful, but for her to also avoid being smug and superior would clearly require a further step. "What should I be asking you?"

"It's not how I found you that matters, but why I found you. Why I want to speak to you."

"Because the lion's about to pounce on this tethered goat?"

She smiled. "Well, that's honestly not the way I would have put it, but yes, you do appear to have stirred up something of a hornet's nest within the Rotarians – and well done for learning about them, by the way."

"Thanks. You going to give me a gold star?"

"I'm not your enemy, Mr Shah. But the Rotarians most certainly are. Their traffic, or at least the portion of it I can see, is buzzing with your name, and I don't know why. I think you're in a lot of trouble, and I want to help you. Why don't you tell me what you know, and then we'll see if we can figure a way out of this?"

His coffee had gone cold by the time Rav got to the end of the story, but he drank it down in one go, anyway, while Reece was pondering on what he'd said. When she did finally speak, it was with a new tone in her voice. "I'm impressed, genuinely. You've made more progress in three weeks than I've made in two months."

Rav wasn't quite sure how seriously he should take this admission. "Really?"

"Yes. How about we agree to work together from here on in?" She held out a hand, inviting him to shake it. " Partners?"

He thought for a moment, then took her hand and shook it. "Deal. So what now?"

She took a sip of her own coffee, grimacing as she realised it, too, had gone cold. "Could I watch the ransom video?"

Rav shrugged. "Sure." He pulled out his laptop and was about to connect to the station's wifi when he felt Reece's hand on his arm.

"Better not. Aside from the fact that they might trace you here, if they see you watching the video again they might start getting ideas. It might still be somewhere in your cache." She grabbed the laptop, tapped away for thirty seconds or so, then swivelled it back so that they could both see its screen. The image of Mindy appeared, relaying the Rotarian's demands. Reece watched intently, eyes flicking from side to side as though computing, calculating, and recording. And then the final text of the video was scrolling up the screen.

We cannot be bargained
with. We cannot be reasoned
with. We don't feel pity, or
remorse, or fear. We absolutely
will not stop, ever, until you
are dead.

"Terminator quote," muttered Reece. "Classy. Time was you'd get a better class of bastard, one who might throw in some Latin, perhaps a bit of Greek."

Something in Rav snapped. "Well, seeing as how these are the bastards we're stuck with, is there anything in there that might help me dodge my impending death?"

She held up an apologetic hand. "Sorry. But the answer's no, I'm afraid."

I was hoping there might be something in the video that gave something away, but there isn't. If you're looking for a plan that doesn't involve you handing yourself into them, I haven't got one."

"So that's it? I hand myself in, let them take me off to what passes for a Bond-villain lair when it's been built by small, independent, Yorkshire businessmen, and just hope that I can figure something out really clever when I get there?"

Reece was tapping her fingers on the table's formica top. "I didn't say there wasn't anything we could do, just nothing that might avoid you handing yourself in."

"You've got a plan?"

"I might have." She pulled a pad and a pen out of her pocket, then scribbled a Leeds address on it. "That's a safe place. Turn off your phone now, go there, and tell the woman who answers the door that Reece sent you. Don't talk to her, just wait for me."

"Wait for you?"

"Yes, Mr Shah. Wait." Reece placed her hand over his. "I will do everything in my power to help both you and Mindy walk away from this alive. That's a promise you can take to the grave; yours or mine."

Alan had been in his coffin, catching up on some sleep, when his phone rang. It was Nicolae, a fact that would make anyone want to climb into their coffin, dead or not.

"Alin? Are you awake?"

"I am now."

"Good. I just heard from Everidge."

"Oh. How is he?"

"Sounding like a man who's just had his balls cut off, deep fried, and then served back to him as lunch."

"He's not happy?"

"No. He tried to have a go at me, but I reminded him it was you and me who got the Head back from the vampire hunter, not him."

Alan didn't actually recall Nicolae being involved in the retrieval of the Head, but he figured that was a point best avoided, given that it was he who'd been responsible for losing said decapitated entity in the first place. Nicolae was still speaking. "Anyway, that's not why I called you."

"It's not?"

"Of course it's not, you stupid bastard. You think I haven't got better things to do than phone you in the middle of the day just to trade pleasantries? You don't think I'd rather be sleeping?"

"No. So what's happening?"

"Well, I don't know how big an ass-kicking the Head gave the local Rotarians, but they've gone nuclear. Everidge had some of his people track down the girl who owned the car the vampire hunter was driving. She'll be friend, or family. They kidnapped her. You called in sick at your hotel, right?"

"I called in sick for last night."

"So call in sick again, you dumb shit. I've got a job for you."

A stronger man would have argued, but Alan had spent the last three hundred years under Nicolae's spell, and if anything is calculated to give a man the strength and courage to break such a spell, working as a night porter in a dive of a hotel for addicts, whores, and assorted deadbeats isn't it. (York doesn't really have a dodgy area as such, but nonetheless, Alan had managed to find it).

"Okay. I call in sick. Where do you need me?"

"Leeds. Tonight. I'll meet you there." Nicolae paused, apparently for effect, because when he resumed speaking it was in a tone of occasion and command. "The project is going operational."

"But I thought we needed a test subject? Someone who has previously been enraptured by one of us. Someone who believes in vampires."

Even through the phone line, Alan could sense the smirk that Nicolae's face was wearing right then. "We'll have our subject. He's going to come walking right up to us tomorrow night."

Chapter Thirty Five

Reece's safe house turned out to be a nice middle-class home in an apparently prosperous neighbourhood, presided over by a grandmotherly lady who'd simply nodded when Rav said Reece had sent them and shown them into a spare room equipped with a small TV and a stack of fresh towels. Rav and the Professor watched the TV for a couple of hours, fuelled by the endless supply of tea, biscuits, and cakes their hostess apparently had at her disposal, until the Professor decided that Jess really needed to be taken for a walk. Sleep had been a tempting option at that point, but Rav resisted that urge and instead dragged himself into the spare-room's small en suite bathroom where he let the power shower blast several days' worth of dirt, grime, and tiredness away.

It felt good.

Reece turned up an hour or so later, by which point he was lying on the bed wrapped in a towel watching the TV. She didn't knock; she simply came straight in and dumped several shopping bags' worth of stuff onto the bed beside Rav. He quickly checked the towel to make sure it was covering everything that mattered, then spluttered out a protest. "Do you not knock?"

She gave him a grin that might almost have been cheeky, then started pulling things out of the bags. "Okay, I've got you a set of replacement clothes. I've gone with a look that's smart casual, but still practical. If you go in there dressed like a ninja action man they might get suspicious. Equipment wise, there's nothing you can really take that wouldn't arouse suspicion, but I've got you a couple of Mars bars to snack on if you need a temporary sugar hit. Then there's three watches, already set and synchronised. Oh, and three pay-as-you-go phones, one each for each of us."

"What's the point of giving me a phone? It's the first thing they'll take away from me."

"Which is why-" She rooted around in the pile of crap and pulled out a small something, which she threw across at Rav, "-you'll need this."

He looked at the something, and found it to be a tube of lube. A worrying thought began to take shape somewhere in the fear centre of his brain. "Would I be being overly optimistic if I thought you were planning on giving me a romantic encounter of a speciality nature as some kind of good luck treat for the condemned man?"

"You would indeed, Mr Shah. One of us will shortly be taking something up the back passage, but it isn't going to be me."

"Now, look. Hang on–"

"Would you rather we let them take you away with no means for you to contact us, nor for us to track you?"

Rav didn't like the sound of this. He wasn't wild about being trapped in a lair of vampires with no way of calling for help. But equally, he wasn't wild about the idea of forcing a pay-as-you-go Nokia up his rectum, either. That he would soon be going into battle against vampires and an evil world-spanning conspiracy was an abstract threat. By contrast, as threats went, having a mobile phone inserted into a location that receives less sunlight than Lapland in December was very, very real. "Couldn't you have got some spy stuff or something? Something I could just, like, hide on me? Like a wire, like the police use?"

"A wire would get you discovered, and that would get you killed. Best keep it simple."

"James Bond never had to have a phone shoved up his arse!"

"You're not James Bond."

"Right."

Rav grabbed the clothes and headed into the small en suite bathroom to get changed, emerging five minutes later to find Reece just finishing packing two backpacks with the supplies. The TV behind her was still playing the twenty-four hour news channel Rav had left on, the sound now turned down to a low murmur. It was showing footage of some war somewhere, but then the image on its screen changed to show a picture of a now familiar looking Harry Jack. Rav grabbed the TV remote and thumbed the volume up.

"...died peacefully in his sleep at his Manchester home last night. A legendary figure in the Northern club scene, Sir Harold Jack began his career as a DJ in the early 1960s but made his fortune from managing a string of nightclubs and bingo halls. He was a noted philanthropist and fund-raiser whom friends and colleagues say will be sadly missed. Returning to domestic news–" Rav muted the sound, then looked at Reece. "The Rotarians really can just make things go away, can't they?"

"Yes. They can. And now they've got an extra reason to be pissed off at you, given that you've dispatched one of their main men."

Rav felt his already depressed spirits sliding down one more notch. "Well, that's just fucking brilliant."

Reece grabbed a can of Diet Coke, opened it, and then sat down in the room's only chair. "This doesn't change anything. We've got an hour or so. I know it's easy for me to say, but there's nothing you can do now but wait and try to relax."

Rav grabbed himself a can of Diet Coke, then gave her a grim smile. "You're absolutely right. It is easy for you to say."

Reece and the Professor dropped Rav off in a quiet street, a little way short of the city centre. As he watched Rav work through his mental checklist with calm precision the Professor felt a surge of almost fatherly pride for the younger man. This was truly the best of times and he was with the best of men.

"Are you ready?" Reece was asking.

Rav shrugged. "I guess so. But seeing as how you're supposed to be the cavalry, shouldn't it be me asking you if you're ready?"

"We're ready. We'll be there."

The younger man nodded. "That's nice to hear. Guess I ought to be heading on over to the train station then."

"Good luck," Reece told him. "It's a brave thing you're doing."

"Thanks." Rav looked across to the Professor. "Look after yourself, Prof."

"You too, Ravinder," the Professor replied. "You too."

Rav found the cab rank in front of the station, and waited, as he'd been instructed. Cabs came, cabs went. People queued, people departed. A constant stream of humanity. Some heading home at the end of their day; some party animals only just heading out. Girls in mini-dresses; men in suits or gaudy shirts. Ten o'clock ticked slowly into view, only to then tick slowly by. Minutes passed. Rav had his phone - his real phone, not the cheap pay-as-you-go that had earlier bought tears to his eyes - in his hand; this was one call he definitely didn't want to miss. The minute hand of his watch ticked to five past, and then to ten. Fifteen minutes past came and went. Still the phone didn't ring. It had signal. It had power. Sixteen minutes past. Seventeen. It rang. He answered on the first ring. "Yes?"

"Rav?"

It was her. "Mindy! You okay?"

"Yeah. But you have to do what I tell you. Everything. And you can't speak to anyone. At all. They say if you don't do exactly what they want, they'll, they'll–"

He hated hearing the fear in her voice, but he was so proud of her for the way she was holding it together. He wanted more than anything to reach out and hug her, but he couldn't. She was still alive, though, and still with the Rotarians. There was no guarantee they were holding her anywhere near where they were going to take him, of course, but there were many details in the plan where he, Reece, and the Professor would have to play things by ear, and this was just one of them. He tried to put as much reassurance into his voice as he could. "It's okay. I'll do it. Whatever they want. What do I need to do?"

"They want you to get a cab. But not just yet. They'll say when." A train must have just arrived, because a whole bunch of cab-seeking, suitcase-pulling people chose that moment to pile into the queue. The waiting cabs began to edge forward, each filling up, before pulling away. Mindy's voice re-emerged from the phone's speaker. "The third cab back. The big Renault people carrier."

So the Rotarians were watching, Rav realised. Either someone right there, on the ground, or via the CCTV cameras that the city centre was undoubtedly plastered with. He ignored the paranoid desire to turn and look and stare and instead concentrated on barging past the Asian couple who were just about to board the big people carrier. "Sorry," he told them as he shouldered his way between the man and his hijab-wearing wife and climbed into the cab's interior.

"What the hell are you doing?" screamed the man, in a broad Yorkshire accent.

"Sorry mate, but I really need this cab," Rav told him. He tried to slide the big central door shut but found this task rendered considerably non-trivial by the presence of the Asian guy's hand holding it shut.

"So do we!" screamed the woman.

Up front, the cabbie was looking, and sounding, worried. "Come on guys, I don't want any trouble."

Time to play the racial solidarity card, Rav thought. He held up a hand. "Hey brother, let's all stay peaceful, yeah?"

"Don't you fucking brother me, you southern twat!" the guy shouted.

So much for the racial solidarity card. Rav was still holding the phone to the side of his head. "What's happening?" asked Mindy.

"I'm having a bit of trouble with the cab."

"What do you mean, you're having a bit of trouble with the cab?" She didn't sound very happy.

"Hang on a minute." He smashed his elbow into the Asian guy's fingers, waited a moment for them to be withdrawn – an action accompanied by a considerable amount of Yorkshire accented cursing, blended with some choice Urdu – then rammed the door shut.

"Fucking drive!" he screamed at the cabbie.

"Where?" the cabbie screamed back, clearly, genuinely, scared.

"Anywhere!"

The cabbie floored it, spinning the cab out of the parking rank, its tyres squealing. There was the sound of a fist banging on the side of the cab as it fishtailed away along with more shouts and swearing. "I'm charging extra for this, mate," the cabbie shouted. "I don't have to put up with this shit!"

"Yeah, yeah, whatever." Rav took out a twenty pound note and shoved it through the gap in the screen. "Take this for starters, just keep driving." He bought the phone back up. "Where now?"

"They want you to get onto the inner ring road and head west. They'll give you further instructions."

After seeing Rav off, Reece, the Professor, and Jess had driven to the outskirts of the city centre and parked up in a layby that was empty save for a currently closed burger stand. Reece opened a laptop up on the car's bonnet and began to fill its screen with an assortment of things that looked rather complicated, all scrolling text, numbers, dials, and sliders. There seemed to be quite a lot of typing and concentration involved, so the Professor left her to it and instead contented himself with walking Jess up and down the layby so she could have a good sniff.

Three wees, one of which had been by the Professor himself, one poo, and about forty-five minutes later, Reece called over. "Okay, he's moving."

The Professor quickly hurried back, persuaded a not entirely enthusiastic Jess to get into the back of the car, then slid into the front passenger seat alongside Reece. She handed the still open laptop to him, then started the engine.

"I've got a location monitor linked to Rav's phone, and I've slaved that to a modified satnav app so, every thirty seconds, his location gets fed in as our destination." She pointed at the screen. "We're the red arrow, he's the blue dot."

The Professor looked at the screen. The blue dot was located a little way from the station; as he watched, it jumped a little to the north.

"Turn around where possible," the laptop announced.

Chapter Thirty Six

Rav's journey so far had been an erratic and confusing one; intentionally so, he guessed. The phone calls came every five minutes or so, always with Mindy speaking, always accurate enough to make it clear he was under continuous observation. He'd switched to another cab, and then another, then taken a walk along a winding path through a forest, beside a stream. From there he was instructed to take another cab to Leeds Bradford Airport, where he was to head into the terminal, buy a Yorkshire Evening Post, then await further instructions. He bought the paper, sat down on one of the terminal's hard plastic benches, and waited, not bothering to read. After a few minutes the phone rang. Mindy. "They want you to get the next 757 bus to Leeds."

The call went dead.

He found the sign for buses, followed it, and found a mostly empty number 757 bus due to depart in a few minutes. He paid his fare to the driver, in cash, and found a seat, clutching the paper ticket, running it through his hands as though he were a Catholic and the ticket were his rosary beads. Why a bus? Harder for any allies of his to follow him by car, he realised, not if they didn't want to make it really obvious. But how were the Rotarians tracking him? Did they have someone else on the bus?

He found himself checking out his fellow passengers. Was it the young guy in the hoodie with no luggage who was probably just an airport worker, heading home? Or the brash young family, with the kiss-me-quick hats and stuffed toys, who he guessed weren't just back from a cultural visit to Copenhagen? Perhaps the businessman-type-bloke with the small travel suitcase and a folded copy of the Times? He tried giving the businessman a long look of pure, utter hatred. The businessman looked awkwardly away, which proved, Rav realised, absolutely nothing.

The bus eventually departed, winding its way across the countryside until it reached the outskirts of Leeds, where a further call from Mindy instructed him to get off. As he left the bus he noticed that the businessman was on his phone. He would have liked to have lingered, eavesdrop perhaps, but he couldn't; Mindy's relayed instructions had been for him to sprint – not run, sprint – back down the road the bus had come up, and to continue sprinting until he received further instructions.

He couldn't help but feel self-conscious. After all, to be a member of an ethnic minority sprinting at night through a largely white suburb is an activity that many consider "suspicious". Still, he thought, as he got into a rhythm, it could be worse. He could have been in one of those Deep South, US states where to be a member of an ethnic minority merely walking through a mainly white suburb at night is an activity that might be considered "reasonable grounds" for a member of the public to perform a "citizen's execution".

He sprinted past a group of slightly surprised teenaged youths. He sprinted past a clearly scared old geezer taking his whippet out for what was presumably its end-of-day piss. He sprinted past two pubs, a chippy, and a Chinese, by which time his lungs were burning, his legs were two pillars of raw pain, and he was considerably past both tiredness and exhaustion and into that physiological state that doctors would describe as "lactic acidosis", but which everyone else would describe as "completely fucked".

He continued sprinting, past a rugby club, a working man's club, and a couple more pubs. Then, finally – just as he was about to lie down on the pavement, vomit, and quite possibly die – a bashed up Skoda drove past him, hand-brake span through more than one hundred and eighty degrees, and slid backwards into the gap between two parked cars. It was a frankly flashy and impressive manoeuvre, marred only slightly by the fact that the driver had slightly overcooked it, resulting in his slamming into the furthest of the two parked cars.

The Skoda's passenger-side doors burst open, and two men tumbled out. They wore identical rubber Silvio Berlusconi masks, but their clothing gave them away – the shambling figure wearing a hoodie and trainers looked awfully like Alan, and Rav would have bet good money on the slim man in the suit being Everidge. They picked Rav up and bundled him into the back of the car. Exhausted to the point where death was more than a merely metaphorical prospect, Rav was unable to resist, although he did manage to vomit onto the suit-wearer's crotch.

Deep in his not altogether conscious brain, Rav was quite proud of himself for such well-targeted vomiting. The suit-wearer clearly felt differently, something Rav was able to deduce not merely from the anguished cry of, "Bastard! This is a three hundred pound suit!", but also from the several angry blows the man leaned in to deliver to Rav's face after they'd dragged him into the car.

A good few blows in, the driver – who was also wearing a Silvio Berlusconi mask – hissed at the suit-wearer in a guttural, Eastern European accent. "We must go! People will notice."

From the sound of front doors opening, and the shouts of "Margery, call the police!", people were indeed noticing. The suit-wearer finished punching Rav, slammed the door shut, climbed into the front passenger seat beside the driver, and in a voice that was clearly Everidge's, shouted, "Well, fucking drive then! And try to not bloody crash this time."

The car lurched and slithered first this way and then that, accompanied by a squeal of tires and an acceleration that forced Rav back into the seat. A hood was pulled roughly over his head, and he felt a hand pressing him down. Something that felt so like a rough, woollen blanket that it probably was a rough, woollen blanket was draped over his prone form. "Don't move!" said a voice he recognised as Alan's. "Stay quiet."

Rav didn't move.

After the first few minutes of trailing the blue dot that apparently represented Rav, it became clear that the Rotarian's plan was to have him spend his immediate future going round and round in circles. "No point wasting petrol, even if I am on expenses," Reece had announced when this became apparent. She'd turned off into a convenient layby, and for the next couple of hours this had become their modus operandi: drive a bit, park, watch the dot, drive a bit more.

But then, having slowed almost to a halt in a west Leeds suburb, the dot suddenly resumed its movement, heading north this time on a route that was straight, if not necessarily true. Reece started the car and pulled out. The Professor felt his heart starting to race. It seemed the prologue was over. The story proper was about to start.

Rav wasn't quite sure how much time had elapsed since the kidnap. Time becomes highly subjective when you're unable to see and can judge progress by only the lurches to and fro of the vehicle in which you're travelling. It felt like an eternity, but had probably been more like twenty to thirty minutes. The three men with whom he was sharing the journey said little, save for the occasional argument over directions. The car would frequently glide to a halt, only to then pull away. But then another such halt was accompanied by the blanket being removed, and the face of an angry Alan staring straight at him. "You are going to come with us," the vampire announced.

As each word was slowly spoken, Rav could feel Alan's gaze ripping through to his soul, just as it had done in Whitby. He tried to resist, fighting to keep some sense of sentience intact. Not because it was the plan; the plan, after all, was to be captured and taken to Mindy. But because to submit willingly to this power was to surrender something of one's soul. Even as he fought, though, he felt all awareness of his very existence crumbling and dissolving.

And then he was gone.

As a driver, Reece was proving to the Professor to be everything Rav wasn't: calm, skilful, quite possibly in possession of an advanced driving certificate, and quite likely the holder of a clean driving license. Carefully and methodically, following the Professor's directions with neither error nor hesitation and with her hands always in the approved "ten to two" position, she'd reeled the kidnapper's car in, eventually settling a mile or so behind to reduce any chance of being spotted. Then the blue dot came to a halt.

"They seem to have stopped," the Professor told her.

"Where?"

He peered at the map displayed upon the laptop's screen. "It says... Full Sutton airfield."

"I'm not liking the sound of that."

The Professor nodded agreement. They drove on for a few minutes, then stopped in a layby from where they could see the dim lights of an airstrip. Reece reached behind the seats for her backpack, eliciting a confused whine of protest from the sleeping dog that had previously been using it as a pillow. "Sorry Jess."

She rooted around inside and pulled out a pair of binoculars that, to the Professor's 1950s born eyes, looked like something ripped straight from the pages of Dan Dare. Her slim fingers fiddled with a few switches and dials. Then she returned her binoculars to her eyes, peering straight out into the inky blackness. "Okay, I can see what I'm guessing is the car. It's pulled up next to a helicopter." She pulled the binoculars away for a moment to change the settings then put them back up to her face. "The 'copter's hot. Looks like it's been warming up for a while." She paused to change the settings back. "Okay, I've got four figures walking from the car to the helicopter. One of them's being led. They're getting in."

"That doesn't sound good."

"Not particularly, no."

She continued observing, saying nothing for what must have been approaching a minute. Then a couple of the lights that were scattered across the airfield began to lift. The helicopter, the Professor realised. "They're taking off?"

"Yes."

The lights began to move forward, slowly at first, but gathering pace as they headed to the south-east. On the screen, the blue dot began to move in the same direction. The Professor pointed the moving blue dot out to Reece. "What do we do now?"

She thought for a moment. "Well, we can probably still track the phone while they're aloft, even if we can't keep up with them. And even if we lose them, they'll have to land somewhere, and I don't think it's likely they'll be heading across the North Sea to Denmark."

The Professor looked back at the laptop screen. "Then I suggest we begin heading south-east."

Reece and the Professor hadn't bothered to track the helicopter directly. The blue dot representing Rav's position had been moving too fast and too intermittently for that. Instead, as it jumped, jerked, and occasionally disappeared, they'd headed south-east down the A1079, some way behind the dot on a roughly parallel track. Ahead of them, the helicopter crossed over the Humber just to the east of Hull and then turned to fly over Grimsby and out into the North Sea. The Professor cleared his throat. "They've crossed the coast."

Reece swore under her breath. "Where the hell are they going?"

The blue dot jumped forward, further out to sea, paused a good thirty seconds, jumped forward again, and then paused once more. With each of those jumped moves the Professor had felt the sadness within him building, a sadness that was not yet grief, but was accompanied by a sense of foreboding that it soon might be. Reece guided the car past a convoy of lorries in the slow lane, then sailed smoothly past an elderly BMW. Still the dot remained stationary. The Professor continued to stare intently at the screen, saying nothing as Reece took the car around a long sweeping bend. Thirty seconds passed, a minute, ninety seconds. "Anything?" Reece asked.

The Professor shook his head. "They appear to have stopped."

"What do you mean, stopped? Have they gone back over land and landed?"

The Professor pointed at the laptop. "No. It's just stopped a few miles off Grimsby. Perhaps we lost the signal from his phone when they flew too far from the coast?"

Reece took a quick glance at the screen and shook her head. "No. The dot's still there. Which means the network's still receiving a signal."

"So what do you suggest we do?"

She shrugged, helplessly. "I don't know. Drive to Grimsby, I guess."

As it had in Whitby, consciousness returned to Rav as though a power switch had been flicked to the on position. Regaining awareness in this way was a strange and unpleasant sensation; confused and disorientated without being in any way groggy or sleepy. There was a face in front of him. Everidge. "Are you with us, Mr Shah?"

Rav tried to take in his surroundings as discreetly as he could. He appeared to be tied to a chair, and was naked except for the pair of boxer shorts Reece had bought him earlier. Behind Everidge was a table, around which sat Nicolae, Alan, and another individual who Rav had never before seen, but who had the rotting features of a presumably long-lived vampire. Unlike Everidge, who looked pretty wired, Nicolae appeared merely bored, amusing himself by alternately balancing a ten pence piece on its edge, then flicking it over.

The room itself was tatty and cheap, like a large-sized version of the Portakabins that sprout on building sites, except that it was round, instead of square, with patches of bare concrete showing through the gaps in the cheap plasterboard screens. A metal spiral staircase led up through a hole in the ceiling and down through a hole in the floor. A smell came from below; an incongruous whiff of the countryside.

"Sorry about the smell, Mr Shah," Everidge told him, in a tone that made it abundantly clear that he wasn't sorry at all. "But we've got a pig down below and he's not too keen on personal hygiene." The optician turned his attention briefly to the three vampires sitting at the table. "Alan. Why don't you go and feed him? And try not to let this one escape." Alan left, giving Rav a hate-filled look of anger and betrayal. Everidge turned his attention back to his captive. "So, Mr Shah. Let's have a chat, shall we? Let's start with how you came to be in my shop."

Thirty-five minutes after the helicopter had crossed the coast, the Professor and Reece reached Grimsby, parking up on a quayside that looked out onto a sea jet black and velvety save for the dim, scattered lights of boats and buoys. Reece leaned over to examine the laptop's screen, presumably made a few mental calculations, then brought the binoculars up to her face and began to slowly scan the horizon, fingers carefully twiddling at various controls. "Got it," she announced after a while.

"What exactly is it?" the Professor asked her.

She handed the binoculars to him, then pointed out to sea. "Do you see the light just over there?"

The Professor lifted the binoculars to his eyes and found himself looking at a strange and ghostly landscape of dark, mottled-green swirls and the occasional bright green light. He dropped the binoculars momentarily to allow himself to note the direction of her still pointing finger, then looked back through them. Yes. There was the light she'd been indicating. He peered closer. There were other smaller lights around the main light, and a shadow around them. Two thick and stubby pillars, topped by a platform, with what – he peered harder now – might have been a helicopter atop it. As he watched, the dark blob of the helicopter began to lift. "I think the helicopter is leaving," he told Reece.

She grabbed the binoculars from him. "Yeah, there it goes. The question is, will the dot go with it?" A minute ticked by, followed by a second, and then a third. Still the dot remained stationary. "It appears," said Reece, "that having delivered our Mr Shah to that destination, the chopper's now departed, leaving him, and presumably his captors, there."

This was not a conclusion that made the Professor feel any less desperate. "But what is that... thing? And how in God's name are we supposed to help Ravinder when we're here, and he's out there?"

Reece, as ever, was calm to the point of being icy. "I'm guessing it's some kind of abandoned World War II anti-aircraft platform, built to protect the Humber estuary against planes dropping sea-mines. As to how we're going to get out there, let me worry about that. But there is one thing I need you to do."

That she had some kind of plan was, in itself, enough to lift the Professor's spirits. "Of course. What is it?"

She grabbed the laptop, tapped away at it for several seconds, then returned it to the Professor. A list of names and numbers were displayed upon its screen. The Professor squinted at the topmost name.

"Happy Paws Dog Grooming Services?"

"That's a list of the dog grooming services in Grimsby, Hull, and the surrounding area. Start phoning them. We want one that's prepared to work right now, in the middle of the night, in exchange for a cash payment considerably higher than their usual fee."

"What exactly would this work consist of?"

"Grooming a dog. Call me when you've found someone and I'll give you the details. In the meantime, I'm going foraging for supplies." She got out of the car and headed away down the quayside.

"Oh, right," said the Professor to no one in particular. "Okay. Let's try using this phone then, shall we?" He fished the phone Reece had earlier given him out of his pocket and peered at its interface. "Right!" he told himself. "You can do this, Quentin. Perhaps the green button?"

He pushed the green button. The phone's display changed. The Professor muttered to himself in satisfaction. Excellent. This was getting somewhere. Now to try pressing another button. He hunted around and pressed.

Chapter Thirty Seven

It might have been minutes since he'd found himself in the room, or it might have been hours. Time had blurred, and Rav was no longer experiencing events as a chronological narrative. Instead, events appeared to be occurring around him, chaotic and disconnected from both cause and effect.

A cut would appear upon his arm.

A razor blade would appear in Nicolae's hand.

Everidge would ask him a question, his face so full of arrogance that even a nun would want to punch it, his voice oily enough to fuel a thirty-eight ton truck to Moscow and back. They hadn't gagged him; they didn't seem to care how loudly he might shout or cry or scream. Question. Pain. Pain. Question. Truth. Lies. Question. Pain.

Time.

More questions. More pain. Someone was screaming. Rav knew the cries were his own, but his fragmented mind was failing to connect the noise to the pain surging through his body, and it was somehow comforting to not challenge that mistake. Then his bowels exploded with a tingling, vibrating sensation that in another context might actually have been pleasurable, but in this one most certainly was not, and which was accompanied a moment later by a faint sound, distant, muffled, but clearly audible. He gasped, involuntarily. Everidge paused in the act of drawing back his fist, and rocked his head back and forth slightly, searching for the noise. "What the fuck's that?"

"What the fuck's what?" asked Nicolae. The sound continued, barely audible, barely there. The vampire paused, looking up as though sniffing the air. "It sounds like music." He walked away and around Rav, head spinning as he tried to locate the source of the tune.

Rav's body was already screaming from a dozen or so cuts, some shallow and some deep, not to mention the bruises forming from the few dozen punches Everidge had landed. Now it had this new sensation to contend with. He gritted his teeth and focussed on the far wall. Everidge took a step back, blinking. "It sounds like – the William Tell Overture?"

Nicolae stopped beside him. "No. No. Is theme from Lone Ranger."

"Look, I'm telling you, it's the William Tell Overture!"

Nicolae waved a hand. "Whatever. But from where is coming?" The vampire spun round, stopped, and gave Rav a look of considerable suspicion. Rav said nothing, and instead simply stared blankly back, partly because he didn't want to give Nicolae anything to go on, but mainly because resisting the effects of a mobile phone vibrating against his prostate was currently taking every ounce of his concentration. Then the vibrations stopped, the music ceasing also. Rav very slowly and carefully ungritted his teeth, scared he might spasm and bite off his own tongue were he to simply relax. In front of him Nicolae shook his head. "Was probably loud radio miles away. You know what is like at night out here."

Everidge nodded. "So Mr Shah, where were we? That's right. I was punching you in the face."

Pain.

All things considered, Jess was not having the best of weeks. Being a dog, as she was, she had but four simple requirements from life: food, toilet breaks, walks, and sleep. But the humans currently in charge of her had somehow been managing to fail to provide all four of these on anything like a regular basis, and tonight was no exception. Darkness was supposed to be for sleeping, but some while ago she'd been quite rudely prodded awake and dragged into a place of buzzing noises, cold tingling metal, and strange scents, and a person who grabbed her and twisted her first this way and then that. Jess had tried to struggle, but some sharp words and a sure touch had convinced her that compliance was her only option.

She'd emerged back into the darkness outside with a strange smell attached to her and feeling strangely lighter. And cold. As the wind had blown across her, it had chilled her in a manner that was both strange and unfamiliar. Now, sometime later, she was still cold, but had yet another thing to be unhappy about. Having managed to get back to sleep in the car, she'd been awakened yet again and dragged onto a different place, one that rocked and creaked as though it were alive.

She found a comfortable corner and curled up. But this time sleep didn't come. The two humans were tense, now, even tenser than they'd previously been. Something was about to happen. Something bad.

Some men are born to endure and triumph. To such men, pain, suffering, and torment are nought but a challenge against which they might measure themselves. They have no need of hope, nor of courage, either, for they live their lives in a state of confident expectation, assured of their ability to sail through any storms they may face, returning unscathed to collect the fame, fortune, and ghost-written book contract that awaits them. Rav had not begun this day as any such type of man, and several hours of being tortured had done little to change this.

Alan had returned some while ago from feeding the pigs. He sat now on a chair placed against the wall, hunched, sneaking only the occasional glance at Rav, anger and betrayal still showing in his eyes. A weasel-faced man had brought a tray of sandwiches: neat triangles with the crusts cut off. Everidge and Nicolae had paused their torture while they ate, and then resumed. Everidge was back before him, goading, again. "This isn't real torture, you know. I'm just an enthusiastic amateur. Nicolae's the real professional. He'd have had you singing like a girl within an hour, quite possibly permanently." The optician looked across at the vampire. "Isn't that right, Nicolae?"

The vampire, apparently bored with the torture, was now reading an old magazine. (If reading is the correct term to describe an activity in which it is frequently necessary to turn the magazine sideways in order to look at the double-spread portraits that each "feature" ends with). The vampire looked away from the magazine for just a moment, and shrugged.

Everidge turned his attention back to Rav. "But why let him have all the fun? And besides, we don't want you *too* damaged, do we?"

There was something in the way he'd stressed the word "too" that stirred a thought in Rav's now drastically misfiring brain. Why didn't they want him too damaged? What difference did it make to them? Everidge smirked, then did a stupid little dance in front of Rav, for reasons that Rav couldn't even begin to fathom, save that Everidge was a stupid little man, and stupid little things were what stupid little men did. Along with stupid big things, of course, like conspiring with vampires and trying to take over the world – or at least that portion of it called "Yorkshire".

Rav's plan, such as it was, had been to wait until an opportunity arose, and then seize the moment, with Reece and the Professor as the cavalry, perhaps darting in to create that opportunity, perhaps charging in to apply the coup de grâce. It hadn't been much of a plan, but once Reece had come on board he'd figured his odds of walking out alive were evens at least, and if that gave Mindy any chance whatsoever of walking away, it was a chance he was always going to take.

But Reece and the Professor hadn't come.

He realised that now. If they'd been here watching, if they knew where he was, they'd have stepped in to end his torture. They hadn't, so they weren't. And with that realisation came a surprising calm. He didn't have to wait any longer, didn't have to endure any more pain. If there was an opportunity to be seized, a time for action, that opportunity was here and that time was now. He forced words through his dry, splitting lips.

"Where's Mindy?"

Everidge stopped dancing. "Mindy?" He clicked his fingers. "Oh, you're talking about your car-loaning friend, Ms Patel. You want to know where she is? How sweet."

Rav put everything he had into lifting his lolling head and staring hard at Everidge. "You want something from me, right? I've answered every question you've asked me. So cut the crap. If you want me to be cooperative, I want to see Mindy first."

"How do you know she's here?"

"I don't. But I'm not naïve enough to believe you'd have released her when I gave myself up. Wherever this place is, it's probably as good a place as any to keep her, and you'll probably want her around in case you need leverage against me." It wasn't much of a speech, as speeches go, but, weakened as he was, it had taken every bit of strength Rav had and then some to make. He could only watch now, as Everidge considered what he'd said.

Finally, the other man spoke. "How perceptive, Mr Shah. I'm almost impressed. You're almost there. It's not so much that we want something from you, as that we want you. Or perhaps her." He shrugged. "Our good Slavic doctor says that the odds of success for the first attempt are probably less than fifty per cent. But he says they would be better if the subject submits willingly." He clicked his fingers. "I'll give you a deal, Mr Shah. Submit willingly, and if the procedure works, you can have Mindy for yourself. Keep her, let her go, we don't care. Fail, and we make the second attempt on her. So you'd better be as good a patient as you can."

"How do I know you're not lying?"

"You don't. But this is deal or no deal time, Mr Shah. Do we have a deal?"

The sea wasn't particularly rough, but it was still managing to set the small fishing boat rocking. The Professor hung on tight as it ploughed up and over a white-flecked swell, then turned back to Reece, who sat hunched beside the outboard motor, her slim hand gripping its tiller. "I still don't understand how you managed to purchase all this equipment in the middle of the night?" He paused, taking the risk of letting go with one hand in order to use it to indicate first the boat, and then the thick woollen sweater and captain's cap he now wore. "The boat? The clothes?"

"I didn't say I purchased it. I said I acquired it."

"Ah. I see." The Professor looked back through the small half-cabin's front windscreen. In the distance, the platform's bulk was coming into view: a dark grey smudge against the jet-black sky, highlighted by the various warning lights scattered across it. "What do we do when we get there?"

"Scream for help and start lighting distress flares. It's hard to ignore people when they're sinking right in front of you, especially if you want them to stop attracting attention."

"But– we're not sinking?"

She nodded at the toolbox that lay at the bottom of the boat, amid the scattered fishing equipment. "There should be a hammer or something in there. Grab something and wait for my word."

After several hours spent tied to a chair, being released was almost agonising. Each staggering step on his numb, frozen legs sent new chords of pain shooting through Rav's nerves to accompany the Wagnerian epic his various wounds were already playing. Only Alan's encircling, vice-like arm was preventing him from crashing to the floor. The two of them limped across to the staircase, with Everidge leading the way and Nicolae bringing up a casual rear. Then down they went.

The room at the base of the staircase was the same size as the one above it, but where the venue of Rav's torture had been largely empty, this room was full of equipment. Computers. Sophisticated instruments. Glass vials. Bottles. It was some sort of lab, Rav realised. To one side of the room a pig lay down on a bed of dirty straw behind a barrier of stout metal mesh. It looked up as they approached, a look of quiet desperation in its eyes, eyes that, having locked onto Rav's gaze, no doubt saw the same look of quiet desperation reflected back. The animal's head dropped back down to the straw, broken, defeated.

In the centre of the room was a bed of the sort Rav had encountered in various mental institutions, equipped with restraints strong enough to hold firm those individuals convinced they were Jesus, Elvis, or that bloke who did that thing on Big Brother. (And which, after one particularly negligent misdiagnosis, had proved easily strong enough to hold the bloke who it turned out actually had been that bloke who did that thing on Big Brother). Rav gave the bed a quick, professional glance. Yeah, this was a top of the range model. You could probably be the genuine, actual Jesus H Christ himself and still have difficulty getting out of it. A man was standing at the rear of the room, adjusting the controls of something that was spinning very rapidly. He turned, revealing himself to be an academic, middle-aged man wearing a crisp, white lab coat.

"Ah, Dr Ivanov," Everidge said. "How are things progressing?"

"A few minutes more," the doctor replied, his slightly guttural Eastern European accent overlain with an inappropriate American twang. "And then we will be ready. Long enough for a smoke, if you want."

"We can wait," Everidge told him.

Nicolae physically interjected himself into their conversation, a horribly eager expression on his face. "Would it help if I partially drained him of blood first?"

Ivanov shook his head. "No. I have told you many times. It is not necessary."

"But it's how we do it, when we do it the old way."

Everidge glared hard at the vampire. "This isn't the old way." He kept on glaring until Nicolae retreated, muttering, and then turned his attention back to Rav, motioning at the bed. "Mr Shah, if you would?"

"Where's Mindy?"

"Ah, yes. The delightful Ms Patel." He nodded at Alan. The vampire walked over to a marked square on the floor, lifted it up, and then disappeared down the flight of stairs it revealed, returning thirty seconds later with a scared, but intact, Mindy. She rushed over to Rav, briefly hugging him only to recoil in horror as she realised how much pain the contact had caused him.

"Jesus, Rav, what the fuck have they done to you?"

He managed a smile. "I'm okay. Are you okay?"

"Well, better than you."

This was it, Rav realised. If ever he was going to make his move, it had to be now. He looked around the room, trying to formulate a plan, but then the third vampire came crashing down the spiral staircase and spat a rapid-fire stream of syllables at Nicolae.

"What the fuck's he jabbering about?" Everidge shouted.

Nicholae turned and whispered an explanation to Everidge. "Get up there and sort it out," the Rotarian replied. "Take Alan and Grigore. I'll stay here with Ivanov and babysit our soon to be erstwhile vampire hunter." He produced a pistol from somewhere inside his jacket and waved it at Rav.

"Just in case you were getting any ideas. If you could take a seat on the bed please, Mr Shah. Ms Patel, if you could sit beside him."

Nicolae paused for a moment, then nodded reluctantly, turned, and disappeared. A bat flapped up the spiral staircase, followed a second later by a further two bats as first Alan, and then the other vampire, Grigore, vanished. Mindy let out a gasp – amazement blended with fear, topped with absolute, utter incomprehension. The moment, such as it was, Rav realised, had passed. He sat down on the bed and gestured to Mindy to sit beside him.

As with art, the Professor's view of the sea had long been tinged by a pungent blend of romance and nostalgia. He'd dreamed of gentle swells flecked with white, set against a fire-red sunset, and of a boat that rode smoothly through one towards the other. At no point had his romantic notions involved sinking.

Sinking was not romantic, and nor – it turned out – were "gentle" swells flecked with white. A few feet away from them, one of the platform's two huge concrete pillars stood against the waves like a cliff, unyielding and unmoving. The platform itself was perhaps twenty feet or more above them, utterly out of reach. There was no dock around the pillar and no ladders scaled its sheer face. Meanwhile, the water inside the boat was already a good six inches deep and rising at a rate fast enough that the craft's life could be measured in minutes only, and mere ones at that. Reece, as always, appeared calm, standing on the still exposed rail and methodically firing flare after flare. Jess, meanwhile, had managed to scramble onto the boat's bow, from where she was letting out periodic whines of fear.

"One doesn't wish to be defeatist," the Professor whispered to Reece, after waiting for her to fire the latest flare. "But what exactly is the plan if they don't decide to help us on board?"

Reece loaded another flare into the flare gun, then grinned. "Swim."

As he emerged, wings flapping, onto the platform's open upper deck, Alan felt the force of the wind hit him. The weather here was always fierce, as you'd expect for a structure located eight metres above the surface of the sea, five or so kilometres off the coast. But a wind that was merely fierce to an adult-sized man hit with the force of a hurricane when it blasted into a small, frantically flapping, bat. Had the winds been blowing onshore Alan might have been tempted to let them blow him off the platform and back towards home; but they were offshore, and besides, this was about the Project, and any future he might have with Tabitha. He snapped back into human form and crashed awkwardly to the deck, landing in a heap besides Nicolae, who had – unlike Alan – landed like a jaguar and now stood poised like a lion.

A human, one of a large group of Rotarians huddled near the loading platform, waved at them. Alan, Nicolae, and Gregore walked over to the man, and then leaned over the rail to see just what it was his outstretched hand was pointing at. Below them was a small boat, half sunk already, its stern fully underwater with the rest about to follow. Three figures sat on the bow: an old man who wore a rough jacket over a thick woollen pullover and a captain's cap perched upon his white mane; a youngish boy who wore a bulky jacket and a woolly cap; and a mangy looking dog, with short, mottled brown fur. As Alan and Nicolae watched, the boy lifted a flare gun and fired a flare. It burned close by them, its fiery trail bright enough to leave Alan blinking away the blobs that now filled his vision. Nicolae let out a loud string of Romanian curses.

"You have gun?" he asked the middle-aged Rotarian. "Kill them!"

The Rotarian took a step backward, holding his hands out. "Woah! Hang on lad."

Alan didn't have much experience with the Rotarians, but the man's nervousness was plain. He'd no doubt signed on for a bit of networking, with perhaps some low-level corruption and a few semi-exciting adventures. Killing people in cold blood hadn't been part of the deal. Alan grabbed at Nicolae's sleeve. "People will have seen flares. They will come. If we've killed them, they will search for bodies. Dive for boat. Ask questions. Better we just bring them on board, call coastguard, have them picked up. No?"

Nicolae was still rubbing his eyes. "Fine!" he spat. "Whatever." He turned to the Rotarian. "Lower the cargo lift."

The Rotarian nodded, clearly relieved, then tugged on the lever set into the control panel beside him. An electric motor began to whine and a section of the platform's deck began to drop towards the sea below.

Chapter Thirty Eight

A couple of minutes had passed since Everidge had ordered them onto the bed, time that the Rotarian had spent spewing forth a rambling monologue that was one part arrogance, one part ambition, and two parts plans for revenge against all those who'd ever crossed him – starting with the boy who'd not shared the tricycle at playschool and moving right on up to whichever bastard had blackballed him when he'd tried to join the Masons. Somewhere along the way, he managed to outline the grand plan. "Army of genetically modified vampires" ... "superior strength" ... "extraordinary senses" ... "looking like normal human beings and able to withstand sunlight".

He paused his monologue for a moment, and nodded at the pig. "Young Hamlet over there's the proof of the pudding. A vampiric pig able to sunbathe without turning into bacon, and entirely normal looking – for a pig, that is." He glanced over at the cage. "Aren't you, Hamlet?" The pig gave him a look of pure hatred. Everidge laughed. "Hamlet's not the most even-tempered of research subjects. I am rather hoping that our next subject will be more co-operative." He looked at Rav. "Are you going to be cooperative, Mr Shah?"

Mindy grabbed hold of Rav's arm. "What the hell's he talking about, Rav?"

"Of course, Ms Patel, you don't know, do you? Your cousin here has volunteered to be our first human research subject, in exchange for your life."

She turned away from Everidge to look straight into Rav's eyes. "Rav, you can't. You can't let him turn you into one of those – things!"

Ivanov chose that moment to reappear from wherever in the room he'd been hiding himself. In his hand he held a large syringe filled with a thick fluid coloured an unearthly shade of green. "The serum is ready," he announced. He smiled at Rav. "Is good shit. Specifically tailored to your genome."

Everidge frowned at the scientist. "Can it not wait until Nicolae and Alan are back?"

"No. It's ready to go now. Wait, and it will start to separate."

The Rotarian sighed. "Fine. Okay." He waved the gun at Rav and Mindy. "Ms Patel, if you could stand to one side and try not to get in the way. Mr Shah, if you would be so kind as to get onto the bed and place your legs in the shackles?"

Rav's eyes met Mindy's. This was it, decision time. If he saw in her eyes a desire only to live, then he would submit to this, submit to whatever his life might then become. But if he saw a desire to fight, to resist, then he would know that this was the moment. He looked into her eyes. A look of cold, steely courage looked back. He nodded, imperceptibly, to her, and got an equally imperceptible nod back.

He started to slowly work his way onto the bed.

Alan watched as the descending cargo lift reached the sinking boat with barely seconds to spare, the craft's three occupants scrambling aboard moments before its bow sank beneath the waves. The Rotarian who stood beside Alan at the control panel rammed the control lever to its up position and the lift began to rise out of the swelling sea, foam pouring off its rough surface. Nicolae grabbed Alan and hauled him back into the shadows, whispering a curse-filled warning about being seen. Grigore, obedient in a way that Alan had never been able to stomach, followed. The lift rose into view and locked into place at the edge of the deck. The boat's elderly captain extended a hand to the Rotarian at the controls as he walked carefully aboard. "Thank you. We're most grateful."

His voice was a cultured one, somewhat at odds with his workmanlike appearance. The boy stood behind him, wearing a thick padded jacket beneath a woolly hat that was pulled well down. "Yeah, we was well fucked." Unlike the man, the boy spoke with a local, working man's accent, albeit somewhat high pitched.

Between them stood the dog, a skinny runt of a thing with short, brown hair. It sniffed at the Rotarian, looked across at Alan, Nicolae, and Grigore, and growled. It wasn't a loud growl, but it had menace and purpose, and carried more weight than a less subtle frenzied outbreak of barking would have. Alan looked into the dog's eyes. The beast stared back.

It knew. And in that instant, Alan knew too. He saw beneath the shorn hair and the brown dye and saw the dog that had attacked him in York. He saw beneath the seaman's jersey and captain's cap and saw the old man who'd stood beside the vampire hunter that day. And he saw beneath the woolly hat and saw, a woman? This was it, he realised. The vampire hunter's last, desperate roll of the dice, his final attempt to smash the project and take Alan's dreams of the future away. These people had come here to threaten the project. They had to be stopped. Then for just one, frozen moment Alan thought of Tabitha. Whatever lies Shah might have told, he had met her, Alan was sure of that. What would she think now, of this? What would she want Alan to do, if she were with him, now? Shah had failed to deliver Tabitha, but she'd never been his to give nor Alan's to take. And in that instant, Alan knew what his love would want him to do. She'd want him to do what was right. Nicolae and the Rotarians were on the side of the darkness. Whatever good Alan might want to come from the project, they meant to use it for evil.

For more than three hundred years Nicolae had forced Alan to eschew the path of a righteous man. No more. This was for Tabitha, even if she were never to know it. He turned to his sire. "Nicolae!"

The older vampire sighed. "What? What is it now, Alin?" Nicolae turned his head to receive Alan's answer, just in time for Alan's clenched fist to hit him square in the face. The fist had been thrown with every bit of vampiric strength Alan could muster, backed up by a fury pent up and nurtured through three centuries of being at the beck and call of someone he despised. It was a fist that would have made Bruce Lee cry with joy. It was a fist that, had it been deployed in a gay porn film of a certain speciality nature, could not only have single-handedly carried an entire ninety minute Fistings of Fury, but could have easily carried on through Fistings of Fury II, III, IV, the unnumbered sequel, the differently cast prequel, the inevitable reboot, the 3D version, and the twenty-fifth anniversary director's cut edition. Nicolae was harder than granite and tougher than God, but the fist with which Alan hit him was thrown with such force that it sent the vampire flying through the air and over the side of the platform.

For an instant there was a stunned silence. Then the fight started.

Jess wasn't quite sure what was going on. Three beasts had stood before her, but then one had struck another and now only two remained. They were beasts, she knew that, tainted hard with a scent of evil and wrongness and of something that simply should not be allowed to exist. They thus occupied exactly the same category as cats, but where cats were small and stood on four legs, these beasts were the size of a man and stood upright. She'd tangled before with the nearer of them, and could still remember the ease with which she'd been overpowered.

Jess's brain might have been small, crammed as it was into a not particularly large skull that was already half-filled by jaw muscles strong enough to crunch through bone. But it was a well-formed brain, and right now it was crunching the numbers and the numbers were urging caution. Something was happening, she knew that. She knew that she had to act, had to do something. But what? There was a human standing beside the Professor. Jess had never met him, had no reason to distrust him, and he'd made no overt move against her. But she was having a very bad day, and he was there, so after a short period of consideration, she bit him.

When it came to violence, the Professor was very much an amateur, and an ungifted one at that. Luckily, however, it seemed that the dozen or so Rotarians were in a similar position. In fact, the combat that had now begun resembled nothing so much as a semi-successful, middle-class, wine-bar brawl, with only Reece, Jess, Alan, and the other vampire appearing to have any idea of how to conduct themselves. Jess was snapping at the leg of the Rotarian who'd been at the platform controls, with the man making ineffectual attempts to deflect her head away. He looked to be as good a place to start as any. The Professor tapped him on the shoulder. "Excuse me?"

The Rotarian looked up, at which point the Professor punched him in the face. The man's lower lip quivered and he burst into tears, which was a considerable relief to the Professor as his hand was now throbbing with enough pain that he really didn't care to hit him again. He turned away from the blubbing Rotarian to survey the scene. Reece was carving through the Rotarians as though she were Moses leading an away-day across the Red Sea. Whirring, kicking, punching; weaving patterns of cold beauty and efficient elegance. Some of the Rotarians had guns, but they either watched those guns be kicked out of their hands or found themselves unable to find a target amid the maelstrom. Alan, meanwhile, was grappling with the third vampire, the two of them locked in a hold from which each could only half pummel the other. The Professor took a step forward, and considered his next action. And then a bat flapped back onto the platform and in a flash of otherness transformed into a wet, snarling, and very, very angry vampire. It turned to the Professor with hate in its eyes.

"Enjoy your death, human."

Everidge's first mistake, excepting of course his overall mistake of being a small and petty man with misplaced ambitions to be an evil, criminal mastermind, was to attempt to affix the bed's shackles around Rav's legs with one hand, whilst still holding his gun with the other. His second mistake was to look away for just an instant when the muffled sounds of a brawl came echoing down from above. His third mistake was to not spot Rav's foot heading for his head. And his fourth mistake was to turn his attention back to Rav just in time to present his face to Rav's incoming kick.

The kick hadn't been made with anything like as much force as Rav would have wanted. Had its force been in anyway representative of Rav's feelings towards his torturer, the Rotarian's head would now be arcing across the North Sea on a track that would take it into a low-Earth orbit. But, alas, while several hours of torture is an excellent way of feeding a man's desire to give someone a serious mullering, it isn't the best conditioning regime to put him in the right physical shape to deliver said mullering.

In short, Rav was broken, and the kick he'd just delivered to Everidge's face represented the last of his reserves. Had he been a character in an old-style fantasy arcade game, his little energy bar would be down to a small red stub and on-screen messages would be urgently requesting the insertion of additional coinage. The kick was, however, sufficient to not only send Everidge rocking back on his heels, but also to cause the gun to go flying from his grasp. It skittered across the floor and down the open trapdoor. Rav let the kick's momentum carry him off the bed and into a somewhat awkward, crashing, crouching heap on the floor.

As Rav had launched his kick, he'd snatched a corner-of-the-eye glimpse of Mindy launching herself at Ivanov. The Russian was screaming, now, and the large syringe he'd previously been holding was sticking out of his leg. Its plunger was most of the way down, and its chamber was nearly empty. "You bitch!" he screamed at Mindy. "That's tailored for his genome. It'll kill me."

Rav launched himself at the stumbling Everidge, sending the Rotarian crashing into some expensive looking lab machinery. Rav staggered after him and gave him a couple of kicks in the ribs, then held out his hand to Mindy. "Let's get the fuck out of here."

Ivanov took a few shambling steps after them, still staring numbly at the syringe sticking out of his leg. "But what about me? I'm going to die!"

Rav shrugged. "Works for me."

219

Chapter Thirty Nine

The Professor reached inside his open jacket and pulled out the plastic water pistol that had been sitting in its inside pocket. "I think perhaps not," he told Nicolae, before gently squeezing the trigger. The gun's electric pump whirred, sending a thin jet of fundamentalist holy water arcing across the space between them. It hit the surface of Nicolae's leather jacket and splashed, some spots shooting onto the vampire's hands, others across his face.

The vampire screamed a scream of pure agony. Even in the near darkness, lit as it was by only the few dim lamps set across the platform's upper surface, the Professor could see the steam rising as the holy water literally burned into Nicolae's skin. He fired again, aiming for the head this time, the jet spraying across the vampire's scalp, causing an eruption of blood-tinged vapour. The Professor kept firing, restricting himself to short, sharp bursts just as Reece had shown him during their practice session earlier that evening.

Then the gun whined onto empty.

Nicolae was still standing. The vampire let out a long cry of pain, took a staggering step forward out of the cloud of steam that still enveloped him, and gave the Professor a snarl of grim defiance. "I still alive, human. Your holy water old, no? Your God has forgotten he blessed it, just like he has forgotten you. It stings, but it does not burn."

Given the still-steaming blisters now scattered across Nicolae's face, the Professor wasn't completely sure of the correctness of Nicolae's assertion that the holy water had merely stung; but, frankly, this seemed like neither the time nor place to argue such a point. He took a step back, and then another, retreating before the vampire's remorseless advance; but then found himself backing into the platform's encircling guard-rail. Nicolae halted before him and began to slowly wind his fist back for a punch that would likely be terminal. Then a small, brown furry object launched itself upwards, fastening its jaws around the vampire's outstretched arm. Nicolae shouted in fury, shook the limb hard to dislodge Jess free, then threw her over the railing. She flew across the night sky and disappeared from view.

The vampire turned back to the Professor. "Time to die."

Rav ran up the spiral staircase as fast as his battered legs would carry him with Mindy close behind. They went up through the room where he'd been tortured and onto the floor above, where they found themselves in a window-lined control room. There was some kind of commotion going on beyond one set of the control room's windows, so Rav headed the other way, through a door set into the opposite wall. "Come on!" he told Mindy.

He shoved the door open and took a step forward. The cold air hit him like a sledgehammer, in the way that cold air is wont to do when it's a winter night and one is clad in only a pair of boxer shorts. Above them the sky was velvet-black, the stars hidden behind clouds. They appeared to be on some kind of flat roof, its edge lined by railings, an undefined drop beyond. Rav took hold of Mindy's hand again and dragged her forward, looking for an exit, steps down, perhaps, or a ladder maybe. They jumped over ropes and wove past boxes, and then they were at the railings. Rav looked over and found himself looking at a rolling sea. "What the fuck?"

He looked forward, trying to focus on whatever lay beyond. Sea. He looked to the left. Sea. He looked to the right and saw the dim outline of a coast at least a few miles distant, lit by the lights of the town that sat upon it. The sea below was rising and falling with the swell, but the thing they were currently standing on stood resolutely firm in the way that boats simply don't, ever. Mindy was shaking her head. "Where the hell are we? What the hell is this?"

Then came a sound from behind them, as the door was thrown open once more. They spun round and found Everidge approaching. Blood was dripping from a deep cut on his face, and his stagger was that of a weakened man, but he was holding the gun in his hand and pointing it like he knew what he wanted to do with it. "You think we'd make it that easy to escape, Mr Shah?"

As imminent death – personally delivered by an ex-Securitate, ex-human being, but very much not ex-vampire – approached, the Professor had found the significant events of his life playing before him. It had started off like some kind of 1960s tale of middle-class urban life written by a very angry young playwright; morphed into a slightly glossy and semi-decadent Ken Russell directed depiction of 1970s academic life; turned rather gritty around about the time the braces and shoulder-pad 80s boom was morphing into the downturn of the 90s and the initial phase of his eventual breakdown had arrived; and had then come to a grinding halt when Reece landed a rather impressive kick on Nicolae that sent the vampire flying off to one side and bought the Professor back, if perhaps only temporarily, into the land of the not yet about to die.

Reece followed up the kick with some kind of forearm chop, a punch and then a spinning kick, before launching a straight kick to Nicolae's groin so vicious that even the most ardent, man-hating, dungaree wearing, fundamentalist feminist would have felt some sympathy for the being whose goolies had previously been attached to that groin. A normal man would have been felled by such a blow, left in a state where he wouldn't be capable of anything save whimpering and vomiting for at least several minutes. Hell, a male grizzly bear so hit would right now be limping back off to the forest, weeping, and in dire need of a comfort shit.

Nicolae was not any kind of man, normal or otherwise. He roared in both pain and anger, took a couple of staggering steps back, halted, then launched himself forward at Reece, throwing a blizzard of punches from a platform of dancing steps in a manner that implied significant skills in the art of combat. Reece dodged back behind one set of blows, edged in to deliver a sharp jab to the ribs, then fell back just in time to avoid a blow that would surely have killed her.

For twenty seconds, perhaps thirty, the two of them engaged in a combat of such speed and intricacy that everyone else on the platform – Alan, Grigore, the Professor, those Rotarians still upright – found themselves standing and staring. Gradually, the two of them shifted backwards, towards the control cabin that stood at the platform's centre. Nicolae was the stronger and the tougher, unafraid to take blows from Reece if it meant he could focus his attacks on her. In turn, she was forced on the defensive, and slowly but surely and bit by bit, the vice he was trapping her in tightened. Eventually, she found herself backed against the wall and taking blows, glancing and partial at first, but then solid and full. She went down, crumpled, blood flowing down her face and onto her padded jacket. Nicolae barked an order at the surviving Rotarians. "Kill the old man. The woman's mine." He turned to Alan and Grigore. "Alin! Submit now, or we kill you too."

Alan turned to the Professor, despair written across his pathetic, rotting face, a despair mirrored in the Professor's own thoughts. They had rolled the dice, admirably so, but when the dice had ceased tumbling and their verdict was revealed, it showed a merciless judgement: death. And then a plan occurred to the Professor. It was sketchy in outline, desperate in nature, and long in odds. But anything will look attractive when set against an alternative of oblivion, and this plan was no exception. The Professor held up his hand and fixed his attention on Nicolae. "What exactly is all this for? Why are you working with these people." He indicated the Rotarians. "Look at them. Middle managers. Accountants. Small businessmen. And you are taking orders from them?"

Nicolae laughed. "I give them orders. In case you not notice, old man, I just told them to shoot you."

"Yes, you're giving them orders. But their boss gives you orders, correct? Everidge, the optician?" The Professor took care to put particular emphasis on the syllables making up that last word. "You think he gives a damn about what you want?"

"You not know what we want."

"I can guess. And you won't get it from Everidge. You think he wants you people around? Everidge wants power, for himself." The Professor was guessing, now, but it was a guess he was willing to stake his life on. "His plan's obvious. To give himself and the other Rotarians the good aspects of your vampiric powers, but without the bad. They'll walk away with the superior strength and senses. You'll walk away with nothing."

"No! You lie!"

"Think about the experiments. Think about the pigs. They weren't starting with already-vampiric pigs, were they? They started with normal pigs and tried to give them just the powers that they desired, yes?"

"Is not true."

Thus far, the entire conversation had been conducted in shouts, set as it was against the background noise of the sea - the crashing of waves against the concrete pillars and the whistling of the wind across the deck. But now a new sound appeared: a rhythmic thwopping noise that cut through the night sky and which was joined, moments later, by the amplified sound of a man's voice. "This is the police. You are all under arrest. Drop your weapons and put your hands up."

A searchlight swept across the platform, its harsh white light dazzling to eyes grown accustomed to the night time gloom. The remaining Rotarians paused for a moment, then dropped their guns. The Professor walked cautiously over to Reece, making sure to keep his arms held high, pointing at the fallen figure to let those hovering above know his purpose. The thwop-thwop noise came nearer, deafening now, the helicopter hovering close enough for its downdraft to whip up a tornado of dust and discarded crisp packets. The Professor knelt down beside her. "Ms Reece," he said, shouting to be heard over the noise of the rotor. "Are you all right?"

She sat up, painfully, a hand held against her side. "I'll live. Where's Nicolae?"

The Professor looked around, but the vampire was nowhere to be seen. "I don't know. He appears to have left us."

"You know what I find so frustrating?" Everidge asked, keeping the gun pointing straight at Rav and Mindy.

Rav reached for Mindy's hand. "No. But I suppose you're going to tell me."

"You had a chance to become something great. The first of a new breed of human. Homo Superior. All the superior strength and enhanced abilities of the vampire, with none of the disadvantages."

"Yeah. Because it would be a bit hard to take over the world when you look like a corpse and tan like a Buddhist monk."

Everidge chuckled. "Enjoy your little jokes, Mr Shah. It's always good to die happy."

Then Rav's ears picked up a noise. A rhythmic beating that within seconds sprouted a dazzling search-light and an amplified voice that proclaimed it to be the police. The searchlight lit up the other end of the deck.

"It's over!" Rav shouted at Everidge.

"That's such a cliché, Mr Shah. I'm afraid it's only over for you. I'll kill you now, explain everything to the police, and then start again. It's a shame you've dispatched our poor Mr Ivanov, but scientists can also be replaced."

"Like vampires?"

"Exactly. To think the idiots thought we gave a damn about them. We couldn't help them, even if we wanted to. As if we could make three hundred years of rot and decay magically reverse itself."

A hand reached round from behind Everidge and pulled the gun from his grasp. "You said you could make us sparkle in sunlight," Nicolae screamed. "You said you could make us look beautiful, like in books, like films. You said we could have our lives back!"

The Rotarian tried to reply, but Nicolae's hand was already around his throat, lifting him off the ground and squeezing the life out of him. There was a rather horrid crunching sound as Nicolae tightened his grip around the optician's neck. The vampire paused for a moment, holding the now lifeless body of Everidge aloft like some kind of trophy. Then he tossed the corpse over the side of the platform and into the waters below. He turned back to Rav and Mindy. "I could kill you, vampire hunter."

"I'm not actually a vampire hunter."

"I could still kill you."

"I know."

The vampire lifted the gun, spun round, fired an entire magazine full of bullets at the shadowy shape of the police helicopter, then dropped the gun on the deck and disappeared.

A small bat flapped away into the night.

Chapter Forty

The park's lines showed soft in the dim twilight. A little way distant, Alan and Judith sat beneath a tree, the dark ribbon of the river behind them. They were talking, and neither had yet walked away, which, given the awkwardness both sides had bought to the introduction was something Rav was provisionally calling a result. He glanced across at Reece. Her left arm was in a sling, and he knew that beneath her baggy hoodie were a couple of broken ribs. "You okay?"

She shrugged, carefully. "I'll live. How about you?"

Right now, less than twenty-four hours since the events at the platform, pretty much all of Rav's body was hurting, with enough time having elapsed for the adrenaline to wear off, but not enough time having gone by for anything to start healing. But he'd walked away intact, and Mindy was waiting for him back at the car, and that was a result by anyone's standards.

Admittedly, they had all spent several hours in the cells, the police having followed their standard modus operandi of arresting everybody, dividing them into factions, and then releasing the faction that contained victims of assault, torture, and kidnap and which didn't have their fingerprints all over the recovered firearms. "About the same, I guess," he told Reece.

"It was a shame about what happened to Jess."

"Yeah." He looked down. Jess stopped sniffing, and looked back up at him, giving him a very suspicious look. "Still, I'm sure she'll be okay once she gets over the shock. And it was nice of that police launch to haul her out of the sea."

"Well, it is what they're paid for."

Rav kicked idly at a pebble. "I'm just glad the cops turned up when they did. We got lucky there."

Reece laughed. "Luck? You continue to disappoint me, Mr Shah."

"What?"

"They turned up at exactly the time I told them to turn up. A couple of minutes early, actually. I've got a contact very close to the top of the Humberside police."

"What, like a Deputy Chief Constable, or something?"

She smiled. "The Chief Constable's wife, actually."

Rav mentally filed that away. "Right."

Over by the tree, Alan and Judith stood up. They waved at Rav and

225

Reece, then turned and walked away, hand in hand. Reece nodded at them. "Well, it looks like something good might have come out of this."

"Yeah." Rav thought for a moment. "Are we going to have more trouble with the Rotarians? I know Everidge and Ivanov are dead, but the Head's still out there. Nicolae too."

"I wouldn't worry about the Head."

"Why not?"

"Because a little while ago, two Yorkshire businessmen were stopped by Heathrow security while trying to smuggle something onto a flight bound for Chicago. Apparently, they'd been tipped off to look for male business travellers carrying an elaborate hatbox as hand-luggage."

"Really? I wonder who might have tipped them off?"

"I have no idea. But it was all handled at what could be termed a special level of security. You know, D Notices and Official Secrets Act all round. I understand the Head is now being transported to a government laboratory somewhere, where he will no doubt spend the next several years being experimented on before being put into some sort of secure storage."

"Like that bit at the end of Raiders of the Lost Ark?"

Reece smiled. "Something like that."

"What about Nicolae and the rest of the Rotarians?"

"Well, I suspect the Rotarians will lie low for a little while. They don't like embarrassing screw-ups and right now anyone in their hierarchy who had anything to do with this will be doing everything they can to put distance between it and themselves. And sick evil psychopath that he is, Nicolae does operate according to a code of honour, albeit one that's straight out of the Middle Ages. If he didn't kill you last night it's because he figures you and he are even."

"That's fine by me. I've got enough trouble as it is, seeing as how I'm going to be unemployed pretty soon, and probably struck off too."

"Leave that with me. I know people who can have a word with your boss and get it sorted away."

"Really? You can do that?"

She nodded.

Rav thought for a moment. "So what's next for you? More going after Rotarians and vampires?"

"Perhaps. Perhaps not. There's an awful lot of weirdness in this world, Mr Shah, and not all of it involves Rotarians and vampires. I'll turn in my report, take some leave, and then get working on whatever case I'm tasked for next."

"Tasked for?" Rav took a couple of quick steps in front of her then turned to block her way. "Just who exactly do you work for? The government?"

She shook her head. "No, Mr Shah. Governments prefer not to have to admit the existence of the sort of things I hunt, to either their people, themselves, or the thirty year rule."

"So who?"

"Does it matter?"

"Yeah. It matters to me. One day, those Rotarians might decide to come back after me, and I want to understand the world in which they're operating."

She sighed. "I belong to a private organisation that is in many ways a mirror of the Rotarians. Like them, we're an international organisation with branches in many countries. We were founded at around the same time, and, as with they, most of our members have no idea of the true purpose for which we were created. But where they serve greed and ambition, we serve a higher cause."

"But who are you?"

She turned and began walking away from him. "I'm afraid that's not something I can tell you, Mr Shah."

"Do you not think I have a right to know?"

She halted and turned. "Perhaps." She paused for a moment, and then a rueful smile appeared on her face. "Let's just say that we're not all jam and Jerusalem." Then she spun back, and walked swiftly away, towards the city walls beyond.

Rav watched her go. Jam and Jerusalem? Jam and sodding Jerusalem? Was this elite, kick-ass secret agent seriously trying to tell him that she worked for... The Women's Institute? His thoughts whirred – until they were interrupted by the ringing of his phone. He pulled the slim device out of his pocket and answered it.

"Hi Brian. Yeah, sorry, I've been busy and kept on missing your calls. Yeah, I know, I know. You've had to turn down work. I'm really sorry and I'll make it up to you. What's that? Is Jess okay?" He looked down at the dog, who'd resumed her sniffing. "She's fine, mate. Absolutely fine. Although I should warn you... she does look a little bit different. But no, I won't be needing her again." He looked across the night-shrouded city and thought again on the words Reece had spoken. "There's an awful lot of weirdness in this world, Mr Shah."

Then he lifted the phone back up to his face.

"Well, not until we get our next case, that is."

THE END

227

Dear Reader,

Thank you for purchasing and reading *If Pigs Could Fly*. All of us at Wild Jester Press hugely appreciate it. We hope you enjoyed the read and, if you did, we would ask one small favour of you: that you take some time to write a short review in the online location of your choice.

Online reviews are hugely important for independent and small-press publishers like us. We don't have marketing budgets. We can't pay to be prominently displayed in bookshops. We sell by "digital word of mouth", and reader-produced online reviews are the means by which that happens.

Thank you!

21140789R00139

Printed in Great Britain
by Amazon